KU-474-847

SPECIAL MESSAGE TO READERS

This book is published under the auspices of

THE ULVERSCROFT FOUNDATION

(registered charity No. 264873 UK)

Established in 1972 to provide funds for research, diagnosis and treatment of eye diseases. Examples of contributions made are: —

A Children's Assessment Unit at Moorfield's Hospital, London.

•

Twin operating theatres at the Western Ophthalmic Hospital, London.

•

A Chair of Ophthalmology at the Royal Australian College of Ophthalmologists.

•

The Ulverscroft Children's Eye Unit at the Great Ormond Street Hospital For Sick Children, London.

You can help further the work of the Foundation by making a donation or leaving a legacy. Every contribution, no matter how small, is received with gratitude. Please write for details to:

THE ULVERSCROFT FOUNDATION,
The Green, Bradgate Road, Anstey,
Leicester LE7 7FU, England.
Telephone: (0116) 236 4325

In Australia write to:
THE ULVERSCROFT FOUNDATION,
c/o The Royal Australian and New Zealand College of Ophthalmologists,
94-98 Chalmers Street, Surry Hills,
N.S.W. 2010, Australia

NEVER LOVE A STRANGER

Whilst investigating Paul Martin, the estranged husband of a missing Richmond architect, undercover detective Julie Taylor finds murder, mayhem and the love of her life. Why does Paul's mother-in-law insist he's done away with his soon-to-be ex-wife? Is he an innocent victim, framed for someone else's crime? Or is Paul a clever monster in disguise?

Books by Nancy Madison
Published by The House of Ulverscroft:

CLUES TO LOVE

NANCY MADISON

NEVER LOVE A STRANGER

Complete and Unabridged

ULVERSCROFT
Leicester

First published in 2001

First Large Print Edition
published 2004

This book is a work of fiction. Names, characters, places, and incidents are either the product of the author's imagination or are used fictitiously, and any resemblance to actual persons, living or dead, events or locales is entirely coincidental.

British Library CIP Data

Madison, Nancy
Never love a stranger.—Large print ed.—
Ulverscroft large print series: mystery
1. Women detectives—Fiction
2. Detective and mystery stories 3. Large type books
I. Title
813.6 [F]

ISBN 1–84395–292–0

Published by
F. A. Thorpe (Publishing)
Anstey, Leicestershire

Set by Words & Graphics Ltd.
Anstey, Leicestershire
Printed and bound in Great Britain by
T. J. International Ltd., Padstow, Cornwall

This book is printed on acid-free paper

1

Thunder rumbled and lightning streaked across the late winter skies that morning while rain poured down on Pollard Park, an older suburb of Richmond, Virginia.

Julie Taylor opened the front door and stepped out on the porch. Taking a deep breath, she raised her collapsible umbrella and ventured into the storm. The small umbrella provided little protection, and soon her jeans stuck to her body like a wet, uncomfortable second skin. Her soggy Reeboks swished with every step she took.

'Misty! Misty!' Tired and frustrated, Julie called her elderly Schnauzer until she was hoarse. The dog had wandered away before the storm hit, while Julie was unloading her car.

The last straw came in the form of a strong gust of wind that turned her umbrella inside out. In less than a minute, the rain had plastered her hair to her head and soaked her shoulders. Despite all of her efforts, Misty didn't appear. 'You should have paid more attention to her,' Julie scolded herself. 'You know how she likes to roam.'

Soaked to the skin, Julie gave up, temporarily. With sinking spirits, she turned around and headed back the way she'd come. Maybe the dog had found shelter from the storm or returned home.

Julie reentered the rental house, dropped the damaged umbrella in the foyer then kicked off her soggy shoes. Watching where she stepped, she climbed the stairs. Like the rest of the older frame house, the tired burgundy carpet with its ragged edges had seen better days. The last thing she wanted to do was catch her foot in the carpet and take a tumble.

In the spacious if dated bathroom, the white tiled walls and old-fashioned footed tub seemed to invite her to take a long, leisurely soak. Relieved to take off her soggy jeans and sweater, she heaped them in a corner then turned on the hot water faucet and waited. Nothing! She frowned and twisted the cold water faucet. That worked fine.

'Damn. I don't know what's wrong with this stupid plumbing but the realtor is going to hear from me.

'Oh, well. Pretend you're back at Girl Scout camp. Cold showers never bothered you then.' With a shrug, Julie stepped into the tub and turned on the shower. The icy fingers of cold water didn't encourage her to linger.

Moments later, she got out, dried herself, and slipped on her flannel robe. She hugged the robe to her cold body and walked into the bedroom she'd claimed to get dressed.

A lump formed in her throat at the mental image that had haunted her since Misty slipped away — a lost, frightened, little dog out in the rain. Maybe a kindhearted neighbor had found her pet. As soon as the storm passed, she'd go out again and conduct a more thorough search.

While Julie stood in front of a wall mirror in the bedroom, trying to unsnarl her wet, tangled hair, the doorbell chimed.

Who could that be? Experience had taught her to be cautious so she didn't rush to the door. The bell chimed again and again until she ran barefoot downstairs.

At the front door, she paused. Just two people in Richmond knew she'd arrive that day and neither of them would visit her at home. She peered through the peephole on the door but couldn't see anything. At last, curiosity got the better of her and she pulled the heavy door open. Startled by what she saw, she sucked in her breath and stepped back.

A tall, blue-eyed man stood on her front porch with Misty in his arms. His dark auburn hair sparkled with raindrops.

‘Hello.’ She recognized him right away but gave no sign.

‘I’m Paul Martin from next door. Are you the new tenant?’

‘Why, yes. I’m Julie Taylor.’ The good looking guy whose photograph she had studied more than once was the last person she’d expected to find on her doorstep. Later, she would’ve made an excuse to go next door and meet him.

‘I found this dog on my front porch. Is she yours?’ He patted Julie’s pet and Misty licked his hand.

‘She sure is! Thanks for bringing her home.’ Julie reached for her soggy canine.

Paul clutched the bedraggled dog against his chest and wagged his finger at her. ‘You ought to be more careful. Your pooch could’ve strayed into traffic and been hit by a car. This’s a busy street.’ As if to prove his point, a ramshackle vehicle raced up the hill, splashing water to the sides of the street.

‘Look, I don’t need a lecture.’ Who does this jerk think he is? ‘She slipped out while I was unloading my car. She must have wandered off, then the storm hit and I couldn’t find her.’ Julie again reached for her pet and this time he surrendered the Schnauzer.

‘Are you okay?’ Julie checked her beloved

pet's body for signs of injury and found none.

She must be more tired than she'd realized. She'd just been rude to the person who rescued Misty. Besides, Paul Martin was the last person she wanted to antagonize. He was the reason she'd moved to Richmond. 'Sorry. I didn't mean to be impolite. Thanks for bringing her home.'

'It's all right.' His voice warmed, became friendlier. 'I shouldn't have scolded you. I can see you care for her. It's just that so many people neglect their pets.

'Well, if you've just arrived, you must have a million things to do. Keep an eye on her, okay?' Brushing wet dog hair from his navy sweater, he patted Misty's head then stepped off the porch. Before Julie could reply, he'd slushed across the soggy lawns and entered the neighboring house.

Closing the door, Julie addressed the wet bundle in her arms. 'Well, he sure isn't what I expected. After I get unpacked, I'll go over and thank him again. The sooner I get to know him, the better.'

Julie rubbed her pet with a towel and laid her in the dog bed she'd brought from her condo outside Washington, D.C. The one-bedroom unit had been her home for four years since she'd graduated from college.

'Now stay there and you'll be dry soon.' A

few minutes later, she returned to the den with several dog biscuits and enticed Misty to eat them. With a sigh, the Schnauzer curled up in her bed. The fragrance of wet fur filled the air.

Perched on the brick hearth, her shoulders soaked up the warmth of the fire while Julie studied the room. The worn carpet and the armchair near the television indicated the deceased owner of the house had spent a lot of time here. Of course, it didn't matter what kind of place it was. She was here to do a job. Still, she was grateful to be somewhere warm, dry, and relatively comfortable on a rainy cold night.

The old man's son, a State Department employee, had been delighted to lease the house, furnished. Eager to return to his overseas assignment, he'd removed his father's personal effects then turned the house over to her.

Impatient to make a fresh start, she'd still use all of her expertise in the days ahead. 'Always do your best.' That was one ethic her father had instilled in her, and one she strived to uphold. Thinking of him brought an ache to her heart. Six weeks ago today he'd died of a massive heart attack. She missed the man who'd been both father and best friend.

With a sigh, she pushed back the ripple of

loneliness that slid into the room and threatened to overcome her. Better get settled in now. This is home until you're finished here.

She lugged her suitcase upstairs to the bedroom she'd claimed and hoisted them onto the four-poster bed. While catching her breath, Julie gazed at the room. A glass case of dolls and the pastel draperies and comforter soothed her, reminded her of her bedroom when she was a child. Misty wandered into the room and begged until Julie picked her up and placed her on the foot of the bed.

Worn out by her adventure, the old dog wasted no time in falling asleep. Soon, her soft snores broke the silence.

While she unpacked, Julie thought of Paul Martin next door. She had to admit he was the best looking man she'd met in a long time. Get a grip on yourself. He's a good-looking hunk, but you've seen handsome men before this. Finding a suspect attractive is just another sign you need to get out of law enforcement. But as she hung her clothes in the large double closet, she remembered her neighbor's light blue eyes, reserved smile, and the cleft in his chin.

That afternoon, the sun reappeared. Through the breakfast room window, Julie watched faint, wispy clouds chasing each other across the sky. A quick call to the realtor eased her mind. They'd send out a plumber right away.

She pulled on a heavy ski sweater and jeans. Resolved to get settled as fast as possible so she could tackle her latest and last case, she opened the front door and marched outside to unload her car. Out of the corner of her eye, she caught a glimpse of Paul Martin raking debris the storm had dumped in his yard.

Beside the yellow Honda her father had given her as a graduation gift, she moaned. The left front tire was flat like the cakes she'd cooked in her junior high home economics class. Even now, cooking was an unsolved mystery.

Julie located a jack in the trunk of the car and knelt to examine the wounded tire, the spare beside her on the driveway. While she fumbled to unscrew the flat tire, a fingernail broke. 'Dammit.' She swore softly.

The crunch of footsteps on the driveway and a whiff of a woodsy aftershave cologne alerted her.

'Need some help?'

Her gaze traveled up long legs to narrow hips encased in tight, faded jeans. Paul Martin gazed at her, even more attractive in the sunshine. His auburn hair curled over the turtleneck of his blue sweater. Julie looked past thick, dark eyelashes into eyes as pale as the March sky.

Nodding, she accepted his offer. She could change the tire herself, had done it a dozen times, but this was too good an opportunity to observe him.

'Stand aside.' He pushed up the sleeves of his sweater, displaying muscular forearms, and got to work.

Slouched against the side of the car, she watched the tall, wiry man, just a guy helping a neighbor in distress. But that could be a clever façade.

Unexpectedly, he glanced her way and smiled, his eyes glinting silver in the sunlight.

A flush crept up her face to her hairline. He'd caught her giving him the once-over.

'Thanks a lot. Looks like you've helped me again. First you rescued Misty and now you've fixed my tire.'

'Your pooch's a charmer. We had a dog once, but she ran away.' A wistful tone crept into Paul's words. He circled the Honda and examined the other tires. 'You need to think about replacements. All of your tires are slick.'

'I hadn't noticed.' For the second time, she was struck by his thoughtfulness. Or was it an act? She'd met too many con artists in her career not to be skeptical of the man she'd come to investigate. 'Have you lived here long?'

'A few weeks.'

'Does your wife like the neighborhood?' Julie waited for him to explain his situation.

'I'm not married.' He looked away.

'Really?' His dishonesty alerted her. 'Did you move locally?'

'No, I didn't.' His lips clamped shut and a wary expression appeared on his face.

'Lucky for me you chose this neighborhood too.' Careful. Don't appear too interested and make him suspicious. Let him accept you as his neighbor first. 'Well, thanks for your help.'

'You're welcome,' Paul responded. He stored the flat and the jack in the trunk of her car before wiping his dirty hands on his handkerchief. 'Guess I better get back to work. Those wet leaves in my gutters won't go away by themselves. See you.' In a few seconds, his long stride took him back to his own yard.

* * *

Later, Paul paced his den, annoyed with himself. Maybe he should've left his new neighbor alone, but she appeared so helpless with that flat tire, he felt he should help her. Then she started asking questions and he'd lied. Frustrated, he raked his fingers through his hair. The problem was he didn't feel married, though legally he still was, at least for the next few days until his divorce was finalized. As soon as Sheila and he married, she'd turned into a control freak and made his life hell. His love for her gradually changing to a strong dislike, Paul filed for divorce. The day she moved out, he'd breathed a sigh of relief. Next time he saw Julie, he'd explain his situation.

Julie hadn't meant any harm. She was his neighbor, that's all. With that blonde hair, brown eyes and warm smile, she was a real beauty. Not that he was interested. He had enough problems already. Getting involved was the last thing he'd do.

Considering his current situation, Paul grimaced. Thank God Marcus Turner, his father-in-law, was more rational than Dorothy, his troublesome second wife. Dorothy insisted Paul was responsible for her stepdaughter's disappearance. His jaw clenched and he swore under his breath. What did Dorothy think, that he'd axed his estranged wife Sheila, and kept her in the cellar in a trunk?

Anger gave way to sorrow when Paul's gaze

strayed to a small picture on his desk. Jay and himself in their Boy Scout uniforms. It had been fifteen years since Paul had seen his brother. So far, his efforts to find Jay had failed. Maybe he should stop searching. His twin could be gone for good.

Seated at his desk, Paul turned on the computer and began a letter to Jon Phillips, a longtime family friend. Although Jay had admired and looked up to the psychiatrist, Paul always found the older man smug and self-important. Nevertheless, the doctor doted on Jay, so there was a chance Jay might contact him.

'Dear Jon,

Haven't heard from you for awhile, so I expect your practice is keeping you busy.

I'm sure you're tired of this question, but you never did hear from Jay, did you? Even if he was angry when he ran away from Portland, it's been a long time. That one postcard he mailed me on his arrival in New York City is all I've ever received from him.

You've advised me to forget him, and maybe I should, but part of me just won't let go. No matter what happened, he's still my brother.

If Jay ever gets in touch with you, please call me right away. He and I need to talk things out.

Remember, since I changed my name, he can't reach me except through you.'

Paul read the letter then hit Delete. It would be better if he spoke to the psychiatrist in person. He dialed Phillips' office number and listened while the phone rang again and again in Portland. At last Paul slammed down the receiver in frustration.

⋆ ⋆ ⋆

That evening Julie sat at her kitchen table, sipping her third cup of coffee. She frowned and shook her head. Twice that day she'd knocked on Paul's back door and borrowed household items, a cup of sugar, some bread. Each time he gave her what she requested but didn't invite her in. When she saw him outside, she waved. He nodded and walked in the opposite direction. She tapped her fingers on the table. Everyone who knew her told her she was too impatient. Maybe so, but she still had to find a way to jump start this investigation.

Stepping into her back yard for a breath of fresh air, her nostrils twitched at the acrid scent of smoke in the cold night. Through the wrought iron fence between the two yards, she spotted her neighbor. Paul was feeding a fire in a tin garbage can. What was he up to?

'Got a good fire there,' Julie called.

The sound of her voice must have startled him since his head jerked. 'What?' Glancing around, Paul acted like he'd been caught doing something wrong. Then he saw her at the fence. 'Oh, hello. I'm just burning some junk.'

'GoodWill and the Salvation Army pick up donated items. Why don't you call them?' She stretched her neck to see what he'd just shoved into the fire.

'This is junk,' he repeated, stubbornly.

'They take almost everything . . . clothing, shoes, books, household items.' As she watched, a shiny object fell beside the garbage can.

'Charities don't want this stuff,' he insisted and tossed two cardboard boxes into the blaze.

Julie tried twice more to continue their conversation until Paul's lack of response showed her he'd tired of her chatter. Enough. Don't antagonize the man.

'Good night. It was nice talking to you.' Yeah, thanks for nothing. His indifference irked Julie. She'd just wait until he went to bed then have a closer look at the remains of that fire.

At eleven o'clock, all of the houses on the block, Paul's included, were dark. Armed with a small flashlight, Julie crept outside. The gate to his back yard rattled a little as she eased it open, and she paused to listen. No lights came on inside Paul's house so she continued.

The ashes from the fire were still hot. With a stick she poked in the garbage can but didn't find anything. It was too dark. She'd come back in the daylight.

Next morning, she maintained surveillance through her half-closed front venetian blinds. Her wristwatch indicated it was almost eight o'clock. By this time of day, she'd have finished her second cup of coffee at work. Paul must not be in a hurry to go to his law firm.

At last, when she'd begun to think he was home for the day, he stepped out his front door dressed in a business suit, a briefcase in his hand. His cursory glance in her direction caused her to draw back from the window, though she knew he couldn't see her. Paul stepped into a dark green BMW and drove down the street.

While she waited to make sure he didn't return, Julie slipped a warm jacket over her sweater and jeans, then she opened the front door and scanned the quiet street. The block appeared deserted. Her neighbors had either gone to work or stayed inside this late winter morning. The brisk breeze and a wind chill of thirty degrees didn't encourage anyone to linger outside.

If anything had survived the blaze Paul set last night, she'd find it. A few quick steps carried her across her front yard to his side gate.

In his back yard, Julie leaned over and dug through the ashes in the garbage can. The realization that the investigation was underway at last energized her, and she dug with vigor through the ashes until a cloud of dust made her cough.

As she paced around the receptacle, her boot hit metal. Julie knelt to pick up a sooty rectangular object that had escaped the fire.

Carrying it indoors, she held it under her kitchen sink faucet before she wiped it clean. Now she could make out a small metal belt buckle, like one from a woman's dress or skirt.

Excitement coursed through her veins. He'd burned women's clothing.

One possible explanation came to mind. He had burned his wife's clothes because he knew she wouldn't need them. Julie shivered and her mouth turned desert dry.

2

Julie laid the buckle on the table and called Corbeille.

'Yeah?' Her partner's voice sounded tired, like he could've used a few more hours sleep.

A quick glance at the kitchen clock told her it was almost nine o'clock. 'It's Taylor. I may have found something.'

'Go ahead.' From his tone, she got the impression the senior detective didn't expect much from her.

'Martin burned a bunch of stuff last night. This morning I found a metal belt buckle that survived the fire. The size of the buckle indicates he was burning women's clothing.'

'Mmmm — what else?' Corbeille didn't appear impressed. Did he resent being teamed with her? Maybe he'd prefer to handle the investigation on his own.

Irritated, Julie demanded, 'What did you expect? A body? Give me a break.'

'Take it easy,' Corbeille replied, a trace of amusement in his voice. 'Go back and see what else you can find. We'll need a lot more than a belt buckle to nail this guy.'

'You don't have to tell me that.' He had a

lot of nerve, talking to her like she was a rooky. 'I'll be in touch.' She hung up and shook her head. That was all she needed — a know-it-all cop telling her what to do. They hadn't even met and already she disliked Corbeille.

In Paul's backyard again, she turned up her jacket collar and focused on her task, trying to ignore the low temperature. The cold wind knifed through her clothes while she probed the contents of the garbage can and found nothing but ashes. Next, she bent over to examine the earth around the container.

A tap on her shoulder made her suck in her breath and jerk her head sideways. Her heart stopped then thumped hard and fast against her rib carriage.

'What the hell are you doing?' Six-two and angry, Martin scowled down at her.

Aware how ridiculous she must appear, she straightened, pushed the hair off her face, and wiped her sooty hands on her jeans. 'I was just . . . ' Pausing, Julie searched for a logical explanation.

Unfortunately, none came to mind. Her cheeks flushed and her stomach lurched. Out of the blue, an idea appeared and she jumped on it.

While she was growing up, her father had often teased her about something. 'I'm so embarrassed. Dad always said I've got too much curiosity for my own good.' Julie tried to look ashamed.

Paul's pale eyes pierced her, pinned her to the spot for what seemed an eternity before he spoke. 'You've got to be on the level.' The corners of his mouth twitched. 'That's the most asinine excuse I've heard in years.'

Relieved, she let her tense muscles relax. Good. He'd bought her story, just thought she was a nosy female.

'Did you find anything of interest?'

'No, but I sure got dirty.' With a grimace, she pointed to her jeans and jacket. At a sudden move of his hand, she flinched.

'Hold on. Just let me wipe the soot off your face.' The puzzled expression on his features seemed to question her reaction as his fingers opened to display an immaculate handkerchief. 'May I?'

Nodding, she let him dab at her forehead. His warm breath on her cheek made her heart beat faster. Steady. This guy could be a criminal.

'That's better,' Paul murmured, surveying his work.

'Thanks.' With a shiver, Julie drew her jacket closer to her body then took a step back. More than the weather shook her. He was standing too close for comfort. 'Guess I better go home.'

Uncertainty crossed his face then he announced, 'I came home to get some papers for a case.' He hesitated then added, 'I'm having beef stew tonight. Do you like stew?'

'Sure.' Was he going to ask her over for a meal? 'Your supper beats mine, hands down. My specialty is TV dinners.'

'Would you like to share the stew?'

'Why, yes, I would,' she answered fast before he could change his mind.

'Well . . . all right.' He looked a little surprised, either at himself or at her quick response. She couldn't tell which. 'Why don't you come over around seven?'

'All right. See you then.' Julie spun on her heel and left before he reconsidered. She could've turned a somersault. At last, she was making progress. He'd been angry when he found her in his backyard but seemed to have accepted her lame explanation. Elated over this breakthrough in her investigation, Julie welcomed the chance to get to know Paul. Once she gained his confidence, he might slip up and reveal what he knew, if anything, about his estranged wife's disappearance.

The plumber called to her as he climbed into his pickup truck. She'd been too occupied next door to realize he'd arrived earlier. 'I cleaned out the hot water heater valve, Miss, so you shouldn't have any more problems.'

Thank goodness. She really needed a bath now. Julie entered her kitchen through the back door, kicked off her dirty shoes, then stopped long enough to make a cup of coffee. With her chilled fingers wrapped around the warm mug, she continued upstairs. In the bathroom, she stripped off her grimy clothes, added them to a growing heap of laundry on the tile floor, and turned on the hot water. While the tub filled, she made a quick call.

'It's Taylor again,' she informed Corbeille. 'Martin's invited me to dinner tonight. I'll call you later.'

'Be careful,' Corbeille's deep voice warned her. 'The man could be dangerous.' As if she didn't know.

* * *

On the drive back to work, Paul's thoughts lingered on his new neighbor. Why in the world did he invite Julie over for dinner? It hadn't been his intention. The words just slipped out of his mouth. Her explanation for being in his backyard didn't make sense. How often did your neighbors go through your trash, burned or not? But if she'd been up to no good, she would've come up with a much better story.

The expression on her face had been priceless, like that of a naughty little girl caught with her hand in the cookie jar. Paul smiled as he recalled how she'd looked from the rear, bent over to examine the area around his garbage can. Such a firm, well-rounded derriere. Julie wasn't a child by any stretch of the imagination.

Without warning, his usual companions, wariness and skepticism, surfaced. 'Dammit.' Paul slapped his forehead. His brain must have turned to mush. Dorothy could have hired Julie to spy on him. He had found her snooping in his backyard.

Halted by a traffic light, he scowled. The light turned green and he continued on his way. He wouldn't put it past Dorothy. For some unknown reason, she insisted he'd done away with Sheila.

As for Julie . . . On the surface, she appeared open and friendly. But that might be a clever façade.

He'd watch her. Having her over for a meal was a good start.

⋆ ⋆ ⋆

That evening, Julie crossed the lawn to the house next door, eager for the evening to begin. Tonight was a golden opportunity to get to know Paul. She'd make the most of it.

Paul answered the door, a butcher's apron over his maroon sweater and slacks.

'You're right on time. I hope you have a good appetite.'

Delicious fragrances of herbs, broth and wine teased her nostrils and her empty stomach rumbled while she followed her host back to the spacious, modernized kitchen. Two places had been set on a small, linen-clad drop-leaf table placed near the warmth of logs crackling in the stone fireplace.

With the skill of a magician extracting a rabbit from his top hat, Paul lifted two small loaves of hot bread from an oven. He gracefully deposited one on each earthenware bread-and-butter plate on the table.

'I'm impressed. You didn't say you were a gourmet cook.'

'It's a hobby,' he murmured modestly, taking her jacket and seating her in one of the armchairs pulled up to the dinner table.

Julie accepted the glass of red wine he offered and sipped it while he ladled out two bowls of steaming beef stew. Carrying both dishes to the table, Paul sat down across from her and poured himself a glass of wine.

'Hope you like Beef Burgundy. Dig in.' He began to eat with gusto.

A spoonful almost made it to her drooling mouth before she paused to slant a glance at Paul. He was the subject of her investigation, not a Saturday night date. This pleasant setting, the flickering fire, Sinatra singing a Gershwin medley in the background. She'd been on numerous undercover assignments, but never with such an appealing suspect.

Paul smiled across the table at her, the firelight playing on his dark hair. Their fingers touched as he passed her the butter plate. Julie's nerves tensed and the room seemed warmer.

Concentrate. You may be having dinner with a wife-killer. That thought brought her back to cold reality, and she shifted her attention to the food in front of her. She'd seen him eat the stew so it must be all right. Hungry, she wolfed down her dinner.

'Where did you learn to cook like this?' She inquired between mouthfuls. The fork-tender beef was complimented by tiny new potatoes and sweet baby carrots. The red wine lent a tangy taste to the other ingredients.

'It comes from being on my own for a long time.' Gazing at her, Paul explained, 'My parents died when I was fifteen. The aunt who took me in wasn't much of a cook, so I learned.'

'I'm sorry about your parents. Was it an accident?'

Pain flashed across his face then was gone. 'I'd rather not talk about that tonight, if you don't mind,' he said. Pushing his chair back, Paul stood by the table. 'Can I get you another serving?'

'Oh, no thanks, but it was wonderful.' He'd lost his parents? It was hard not to sympathize with a man who grieved for lost loved ones, though it could be a clever ploy to win her over. Maybe he wanted her to feel sorry for him. In her four years as a police officer, she'd met several criminals who appeared honest at first then turned out rotten to the core.

She dabbed at her mouth with a napkin and examined her empty bowl. 'As a rule, I don't eat so much.' She couldn't tell him that the late hours and tension of her work killed her appetite.

Paul helped himself to more stew then returned to his chair. 'Tell me about yourself, Julie,' he said. 'What brings you to Richmond and how long will you be here?'

It was natural he'd be curious about her. Pasting a bright smile on her face, she tried to sound convincing. 'The Washington D.C.

agency, where I worked as an administrative aide, downsized and eliminated my position. That same week, Dad died in a Richmond nursing home so I decided to come home. Soon I'll find another job.'

'I'm sorry about your father,' Paul responded.

'Thanks.' Julie blinked away an unexpected tear.

'I hope this doesn't spoil the evening, but I didn't tell you the whole truth the other day,' he told her.

'I don't understand.' She watched him closely.

'I'm married but just until my divorce is finalized.'

'But you said . . . ' Julie frowned as if confused.

'When you asked me, I should have said I was separated. I don't feel married. My wife agreed to give me a divorce right after we moved here.'

'Do you see her often?'

'No, the last time we spoke was a few weeks ago. Sheila called, wanted to come by and pick up some personal items.'

'The last time? Do you mean she didn't come?' Julie waited for his explanation. It was satisfying to get so close, so fast. She'd absorbed every word he said and watched him closely. On the surface, Paul appeared sincere. Had his sincerity and charm lured another woman to her death?

Paul nodded and a muscle twitched in his cheek. When he spoke, the words seemed to drag out of his mouth. 'She never showed up. I guess I better tell you what happened before you hear it from one of the neighbors. Sheila's vanished and I may have been the last person to hear from her. But I swear I don't have any idea where she's gone. Dorothy, my mother-in-law, suspects the worst.' His expression was dead serious.

'The worst?' Julie wrinkled her brow.

'Dorothy thinks I killed her stepdaughter Sheila.'

'And did you?' Though her lips curved in a slight smile to show she wasn't serious, Julie's nerves tensed. In her four years with Alexandria Police Department, she'd never experienced a conversation like this.

Paul reached across the table to touch her hand. His blue eyes glistened as he asked in a quiet voice, 'What do you think?'

3

The hair prickled on the back of Julie's neck. Was Paul playing cat-and-mouse with her? Her muscles tensed, ready to move fast if necessary. He removed his hand from hers and sat back in his chair, so she relaxed a bit.

In an attempt to sound sincere, she smiled. 'Of course I don't suspect you. It's understandable your mother-in-law would be upset if she's fond of your wife. What I don't understand is why she blames you.'

'I don't know.'

'Do you mind if I ask how long you were married?'

'A year, but it seemed longer.' His chin set in a stubborn line.

It was obvious Paul's failed marriage wasn't his favorite topic of conversation so she didn't persist. At least she'd made a start. She'd find a way to return to the subject again.

Paul rose to stoke the fire that had died down while they talked. 'Did you save room for dessert?'

'There's dessert, too?' Out of nowhere, an irrelevant thought struck. Was he as good in bed as he was in the kitchen? Her cheeks burned as he left the table.

'Just chocolate souffles. I'll get them out of the refrigerator.' In less than a minute he placed the two desserts on the table.

The smooth, sweet chocolate slid down Julie's throat and she sighed, sated by the food and lulled by the soft music. Their desserts finished, Paul led the way into the living room and served Bailys liqueur in Waterford crystal.

That evening he'd become more attractive though his appearance didn't make any difference. She was on an assignment.

After an hour of easy conversation, Julie rose. 'This has been a lovely evening, but it's late and you have to go to work in the morning.' She placed her liqueur glass on the coffee table.

'I'll walk you home.' Paul escorted her to the front door and opened it for her. 'Just one thing, Julie.' His voice turned hard and flat.

Already on the front porch, she turned to glance his way. The light was behind him so his face was in the shadows. 'Yes?'

'Tell Dorothy Turner I'll let her know if I hear from her stepdaughter. She didn't have to hire a private detective.'

'What? What are you talking about?' Julie sputtered. 'I've never even met this Dorothy.

How could I work for her? Never mind seeing me home.'

She stalked across the yard, her head held high, like she was deeply offended. Inside, anxiety churned her stomach. Paul's guesses were too close to the truth.

Slamming her own front door, Julie sank onto a chair in the foyer. What had she done to give herself away? She walked into the kitchen to call Corbeille.

Her partner wasn't home so she left a brief message to let Corbeille know it was possible Paul was suspicious. Climbing the stairs, she undressed and went to bed. Too troubled to sleep, she lay in the darkened room and reviewed her conversation with Paul. If she'd blown her cover, the investigation was over. At last she drifted off.

A loud chiming woke Julie. Her bleary eyes squinted at the clock on the nightstand. One a.m. Good Lord, who'd come to see her at this ungodly hour? Tying a robe around herself, she staggered downstairs, followed by a yawning Misty who let out a sleepy bark then curled up on the stairs.

Julie looked through the peephole on her door. A tall man in a maroon sweater and slacks stood on her front porch. Paul? She opened the door a little but left the chain on.

'From your appearance, I'd say you were

asleep. I'm sorry to wake you but I just couldn't rest until I apologized.' He wrapped his arms around himself and shivered. 'Can I come in? It's freezing out here.'

'Well, all right. Just for a minute.' Julie unfastened the chain and let him step into the foyer.

I'm sorry if I misjudged you.' Looking upset, he wandered into her living room. 'Talk about paranoia. Since my wife disappeared, her stepmother has done her best to convince the police I'm responsible. Dorothy would like to turn my firm against me too. You seemed so curious when we met that I began to wonder if there could be a connection between Dorothy and you. That's absurd, I admit. We don't know each other well, but it's clear you wouldn't associate with a woman like her.'

'Of course not.' If he discovers the truth, the investigation goes down the drain.

'Can we shake hands and start over?' He stuck out his hand.

'Sure.' Julie swallowed hard and tried to look forgiving as he took her hand and held it for a moment. She liked the way her small hand nestled in his larger one. The urge to move closer welled in her. She resisted the impulse and tugged on her hand until he released it. 'It's late.'

Paul took the hint and walked to the door. 'Thanks for being so understanding. Good-night.'

Julie shut the door, turned the dead bolt, and fastened the chain. Relieved that the investigation was still intact, she returned to bed. Sleep didn't come right away.

⋆ ⋆ ⋆

Paul entered the corporate headquarters of Turner and Borman the next morning, his footsteps echoing on the marble floor. As he strode down the hall, a light seeped through the half-closed office door of John Meenan, the Managing Director. What's he doing here so early?

When Paul walked by, Meenan appeared at the door. 'Would you come in for a minute? There's something we need to discuss.' Meenan's brisk manner gave no clue what he wanted.

Moments later, Paul sat in the spacious office, expensively decorated for the executive. Gas logs inside an imported marble fireplace warmed the room. While he watched, Meenan's well-manicured fingers flicked tiny morsels of food to his collection of exotic tropical fish. Once that task was completed, Meenan perched on the corner of his desk, his cool gaze fixed on Paul until he felt like a specimen under a microscope.

The executive cleared his throat. 'You've become a valuable player since you joined our firm. We're all impressed.'

'Thank you,' Paul responded, bowing his head in acknowledgement while a cold knot formed in his stomach.

'However . . . ' Meenan sighed and laced his fingers together. 'There is a problem.'

'Sir?'

'Not only have the police questioned me about you, but Dorothy Turner's convinced some of our partners you're involved in her stepdaughter's disappearance.' Meenan put up his hand when Paul started to protest. 'Our senior partner, Marcus Turner, dotes on his wife and gives her free rein so what Dorothy says throws a lot of weight around here. Do I make myself clear?'

'Yes.' Paul gripped the arms of his chair so hard his fingers grew numb. 'Dorothy holds me responsible for whatever's happened to Sheila. That's unfair since I'm as much in the dark as everyone else as to where she's gone.'

The older man's flint-grey gaze narrowed on Paul's face. 'I believe you. Still, we think it best that you take a leave of absence until this business is resolved.'

Paul felt his anger flare and this time he

gave it free rein. 'I can't believe this is happening. You tell me how impressed the partners are with my abilities. And in the next breath, you send me away, all because of a malicious woman's overactive imagination.' He directed a heated glare in Meenan's direction and had the satisfaction of seeing the other man shift uneasily in his chair.

Drawing a deep breath, the executive continued. 'Of course, you'll draw your salary. So if you'll hand your cases over to John Riffer, you can be on your way.' Meenan stood, adroitly steered Paul to the door, then shook his hand. 'Good luck.'

Paul found himself alone in the hall, the door closed behind him. At the thought of how Meenan had sent him packing like a truant school boy, indignation took hold. Moments later, his common sense told him there was no sense in being upset with Meenan. The man had just followed orders. Dorothy was the reason he was in this predicament. Paul silently cursed the woman. She'd turned his firm against him.

Shaken and apprehensive as to what would happen next, Paul parked his car in his driveway an hour later. The sight of Julie and Misty strolling down the block in his direction lightened his morose state of mind. In spite of the unpleasantness at work that morning, he had to smile. After all, how many dogs walked with their leash handles in their mouths and the other end clipped to their collars? Slamming the car door, he waited for his neighbor.

Julie cocked her head at his box of books and quipped, 'That looks like a lot of heavy reading.'

'I won't be going to the office for awhile.' He hefted the box down on his porch steps. 'The senior partners at my firm are nervous about having me around right now.'

'They said that?' She appeared concerned.

'Not in so many words, but I got the message.' With a shrug, he forced a smile to his face. It hurt to be misjudged. 'I'll hang out here at home until Sheila turns up. The more I think about it, the more I think she's gone off on a lark.' He attempted to banter but a deep sigh escaped his lips.

'I hope you're right.' Julie hesitated then asked, 'Do you think you'd like to get back with her?'

'Not on your life.' Paul's gaze slid over the slender blonde before him. Being on his own had never bothered him in the past, but for some reason he'd felt lonely the last few days. Spending a little time with Julie won't hurt. That's as far as it would go, no involvement, no pain. 'How about having supper with me tonight?

If you like shrimp, I have a great recipe.'

'Wonderful. Can I bring anything?'

'Do you know how to cook?'

'Not unless you count TV dinners.' She grinned. 'Maybe some of your culinary genius will rub off on me before I gain too much weight eating dishes like your chocolate souffles.'

'I think it's safe to say you don't need Weight Watchers yet.' Smiling, he admired Julie's slim figure. The line of her breasts moved against her baggy red sweatshirt with each breath. It was pleasant to have a friend with a sympathetic ear. The fact that she was an attractive brown-eyed blonde didn't hurt, either. He knew better than to get involved, yet his heart beat faster standing close to her.

'Hello.' Waving her hand before his face, she tried to get his attention. 'Are you in there?'

Paul flushed. 'Sorry. Why don't you bring the wine? White or rosé would go well with the seafood.' Lifting the box of books into his arms, he reminded her, 'See you at seven?'

In his den, he arranged his textbooks on a shelf and promised himself he'd take advantage of his free time. It would end the day Sheila turned up and his firm called him back. Stretched out on the sofa, arms under his head, Paul reviewed an old dream. He'd won a few prizes in high school and college for his short stories and had an almost finished novel tucked away in his desk drawer. He'd written it before his friends convinced him it was a waste of time.

His job paid well but bored him. An idea formed in his mind. Why not use this time to finish the book begun in college?

* * *

Julie's mind was on Paul while she surveyed rows of Chardonnay in the liquor store. Not being a connoisseur of wines, the many choices made it hard for her to decide which to buy. She needed to call Corbeille and let him know Paul had invited her to dinner again. The last day or two, her fellow officer had begun pressuring her to find out the truth. Her hand picked up a bottle of wine. She read the label before returning the bottle to the shelf.

A frown crossed her face. If Paul had done away with his wife, they needed evidence. So far, all she'd found was one singed belt buckle. Undecided, she chewed her bottom lip. She should have asked Paul to tell her his favorite wine.

She wouldn't be on this assignment if her

boss weren't an old classmate of the Richmond police chief. Chief Hood had called Lieutenant Edwards and asked to borrow an undercover detective after Richmond PD hit a dead end. The Chief wanted to appease the Turners, especially Dorothy, who insisted Paul was involved. Julie grimaced. It was election year after all, and the Turners were quite influential in Richmond.

Once the case was closed, where did that leave her? At that moment, she made up her mind to stay in Richmond. The slower-paced Southern city was a pleasant change after the rush of the Washington metroplex. Also, the idea of graduate school became more attractive every day. She noticed another brand of wine, stretched to reach it from a higher shelf. Too expensive. She put it back.

Though it didn't matter, would Paul stay in town? Sheila had been the reason he'd moved to Richmond in the first place.

One of the lessons she'd learned in the police academy was keep your objectivity. Keep things in perspective. Paul was the suspect in this case, nothing more. Whether he was innocent or guilty, she'd never lay eyes on him again once the investigation concluded.

So why did she feel drawn to a virtual

stranger? Maybe she was more vulnerable right now while she mourned her father. That must be it. Why else would her fingers tingle when Paul took her hand?

Julie shook her head to clear it. Selecting a random bottle of Chardonnay from the rack, she strode to the checkout aisle.

* * *

That same morning, Jay Arnold scrutinized his surroundings at La Sorrento, a fashionable Italian restaurant on New York City's West Side.

Tables were arranged around the large circular room, the walls covered with murals of ancient Rome. In the center of the room, a large stone fountain bubbled surrounded by marble statues and ferns. Overhead, the ceiling resembled a night sky complete with twinkling lights. The total effect was that of dining in a Roman piazza under the stars.

The hostess, stylish in a knee-length black dress, stood at the front desk and talked in a low voice to a waiter.

Antonio, the owner, beckoned to him from the hallway.

'Jay, can I see you a second?'

His inspection completed, he hurried to join the older man. 'We open for lunch in ten minutes,' he reminded his boss.

'I just wanted to tell you I'm retiring this year.'

'We'll miss you,' Jay replied. That was the truth. The short, stocky Italian and he had become good friends, almost like father and son, since he'd applied for a busboy position.

'Oh, don't worry. I'll come by and check on you,' the older man grinned, then added, 'you'll be a great manager.' Antonio punched Jay on the arm.

'Thanks.' He smiled, pleased with his boss's praise. 'Well, we'd better get ready.'

Three hours later, the last luncheon guests strolled out of the restaurant many considered one of New York's finest Italian eateries, and La Sorrento closed to prepare for the evening.

A short time later, Jay walked into his apartment, conveniently located a few blocks from work. Removing a couple of the travel books that fueled his dreams, he sprawled on the shabby but comfortable sofa he'd found at a thrift shop and napped in preparation for a busy evening at the restaurant.

Feeling refreshed after he'd rested, he stretched then gave in to the sudden impulse to call Aunt Louisa. The kind-hearted spinster, his deceased mother's aunt, had taken Paul and him in after the family tragedy. The old lady seemed delighted to hear from him. She asked when he could come to visit her.

'I don't know, dear. One of these days.'

They chatted about Louisa's kitties, her health, and her new neighbors who didn't speak a word of English but had nice smiles.

'Well, I'd better go, Auntie. I have to work this evening, but I promise I'll come to see you soon. I have a few days of vacation coming, and I'd love to spend them with you.'

Following his call to Louisa, Jay thought of his brother. It had been a long time. He wondered about Paul and what kind of life he'd made for himself. Would he ever see Paul again?

* * *

Paul leaned both elbows on his kitchen counter while the phone rang in Portland.

At last the psychiatrist answered. Today Phillips seemed a little shaky, unlike his usual confident, masterful self. As always, he had no news of Jay. The doctor closed their conversation with his customary warning.

'Be careful, Paul, if you ever do find Jay. Although we'll never know for sure, there's no doubt in my mind that he had something to do with your parents' deaths.'

Phillips, their next door neighbor, had been his mother and father's closest friend. Without proof, he insisted Jay could have set the fire that killed their parents. Even so, Phillips had been kind to Jay and him after the tragedy.

Sometimes Paul let his mind drift back to the days before his twin turned rebellious. They'd been good friends then. Jay and he had shared everything, their room, clothes, a love of fishing, even a budding interest in girls.

That was before their father clamped down on Jay. Dad had been easier on Paul since he kept his curfew, brought home good grades, and didn't aggravate his parents. It was sad that the more Dad pressured Jay, the more difficult he became. Their father and Jay had terrible fights, even that last day.

Paul straightened up. Enough reminiscing. The past was gone and he must deal with the present and the future. The bleak light of late winter filtering through the kitchen windows was no more somber than his mood.

What future did he have while Sheila's disappearance hung over him like a dark cloud that wouldn't blow away?

4

Later, Julie knelt to weed a flower bed in the back yard. She sighed with pleasure at the tiny blooms on a forsythia bush. Had Spring come at last?

It was too beautiful a day to worry about the investigation. Still, it weighed heavy on her shoulders. Either Paul was innocent or a darn good liar.

A cough interrupted her thoughts. Startled, she turned around and found Paul.

She hadn't heard him open the side gate. 'I was just daydreaming about spring.' Her laugh sounded hollow to her own ears.

'The wind's been playing with your hair,' he said. He leaned down and smoothed a lock off her face. In spite of the brisk temperature, her skin warmed with his touch. Recalling the reason they'd met, she took a small step back. If he noticed, he gave no sign.

'Since we're dining together tonight, how about a picnic? There're some tables and brick ovens in that park down the road.'

She played her part and managed a light response. 'Ah, that brings back memories. You might tempt me if you mentioned marshmallows and chocolate cookies. Ever tried Smores?'

'No, can't say I have.'

'My Girl Scout Troop gorged on them at camp.'

'That lets me out. I'm afraid I flunked the test for Girl Scouts.' A boyish grin lit up his face. It tugged at her heart.

'Just get the goodies and I'll initiate you.'

'I just bet you could.'

Her mouth curved into a smile. Paul strolled away and she went inside to tackle chores she'd neglected the past few days. Housecleaning was no more her forte than cooking and this older two-story frame house with its large rooms and high ceilings was like a cavern after her small but comfortable condo.

Julie turned on the vacuum cleaner and concentrated on the worn carpet on the staircase. She ignored Misty vying for her attention with a soggy tennis ball.

Paul drifted into her mind again. He was more at ease with her now. For some reason, her conscience twinged. She wasn't supposed to like him . . . but she did. Frowning, she focused on the investigation. As of that moment, she hadn't discovered anything other than his strong dislike for his mother-in-law, Dorothy. If he was innocent, he had good reason.

Julie's mind jolted back to his invitation. He had been joking, hadn't he? It was too early in the year for a picnic.

Having completed her chores, she rested at the kitchen table with a cup of tea late that afternoon. The doorbell chimed. Paul stood on the porch with a picnic basket on his arm.

'I didn't think you were serious. It's March.' Julie gazed anxiously at the skies, now leaden gray.

'According to the weather forecast in this morning's paper, no rain's expected, just cool, pleasant temperatures like we've had today,' he informed her. 'Come on, Julie. We both need an outing.'

'I guess so.' She took off her apron. A quick glance at the freshly vacuumed carpets and polished furniture helped her make up her mind. 'Well, I've done just about everything I intended to do today. Just let me get my coat.'

In the hall closet, she found a red wool hooded jacket to wear over her jeans and sweater. 'Shall I bring an umbrella?' She liked teasing Paul, he was too serious, needed to relax more.

'No.' His arm on her elbow, he escorted her to his car. Along the way, he confided, 'I even got your marshmallows and chocolate cookies.'

They found the park deserted. By the time he built a fire in one of the barbeque ovens, dusk had fallen and a strong wind blew through the deserted picnic grounds. One gust hit an empty soda can and sent it rattling under the wooden tables.

'Brrr. Maybe we should go home.' Julie surveyed the bleak winter sky then turned up her collar and huddled by the fire.

'Kiljoy,' Paul muttered and shoved a burned marshmallow-cookie mess at her on a bent coat-hanger. 'Eat your s'mores.'

A few tentative raindrops hit her cheek and she jumped up, glad for an excuse to leave.

Paul shook his head in disbelief. Then the rain poured down hard and convinced him it was time to go.

They tossed the remains of the picnic in the hamper then dashed to shelter in Paul's car. As he turned on the ignition, he sighed. 'Oh, well. At least we got some fresh air.'

'Fresh air?' Julie chuckled and rolled her eyes. 'If I catch pneumonia, I'll send you my doctor's bill.' Her laugh turned into a shiver and she hugged her jacket to her.

'Let's go to my place and I'll build a fire then ply you with hot rum toddies.'

'That's the best offer I've had all day.' Or

was it? She'd have to stay on alert. Suspect or not, he was getting to her.

★ ★ ★

Thirty minutes later, Paul sat beside Julie on the hearth of the fireplace in his kitchen, their backs to the fire, and sipped the hot rum he'd prepared.

'Isn't this better?' She glanced his way.

'Yeah.' Puzzled, he shook his head. 'My mind must have turned into marshmallows. I could've sworn today's forecast was for mild weather.' He wandered over to the kitchen counter and rummaged through several newspapers until he found what he wanted. With a section of the Times Dispatch before him, he read aloud, 'Here, it says no precipitation's expected until next week.'

Raising an eyebrow, she asked, 'What's the date on that paper?'

'Why, it's March 23rd. Whoops.' He hung his head, embarrassed. 'I'm sorry, Julie. Today's the 30th.'

'It's all right. Your intentions were good.'

'Thanks. You're one nice lady.' He poured them each another cup of hot buttered rum. It was pleasant to be inside this warm, cozy room with a friend while rain fell outside. For the first time in years, he wished he could confide in someone, someone like Julie. He'd come across information that day that he'd like to share.

While he hesitated, the phone's ring broke into his reverie. Paul frowned. 'I wasn't expecting any calls.' Crossing the kitchen, he picked up the phone, annoyed at the intrusion. His jaw tightened while he listened to his caller.

'You know what you can do, Dorothy,' he replied at last and slammed the receiver down hard.

'Problems?' Julie looked concerned.

'Yeah,' he replied, too angry to say more. His hands clenched into fists. It was good Dorothy wasn't in the room. He wasn't sure what he would have done.

When he continued to stand there, Julie spoke. 'I couldn't help but hear your side of the conversation. You said 'Dorothy.' She hesitated as if she didn't want to intrude on his privacy. At last she asked, 'Was that Dorothy, your mother-in-law?'

It took a real effort but he managed to relax his taut muscles. He stared at Julie.

'Yes, it was.' His glance locked on her face. 'I need to talk to somebody.' He needed to talk to her. What was there about Julie that made him feel he could trust her?

'I'm here, Paul.' Her sympathetic smile

drew him back to his seat on the hearth. 'What's wrong?'

He took a deep breath. How much should he tell her?

'Now,' she paused to sip her drink then glanced in his direction as if to say, 'Go ahead.'

'Dorothy called to gloat. She said she'd heard about my leave of absence from her husband.' He shrugged. 'That's a joke. According to our Managing Director, Dorothy encouraged the firm to dump me.'

'Why does she think you had anything to do with your wife's disappearance?'

'Search me.' Paul shrugged.

'What about your father-in-law? What does he think?'

'Dorothy may have convinced him I'm guilty. The last time I saw him, Marcus seemed cooler.' Paul was relieved when Julie didn't ask any more questions.

'This is a bad time for you, but your wife may turn up yet.'

'Thanks.' Setting down his mug, he gazed at the pretty brown-eyed blonde beside him. The urge to kiss her had been growing all evening, but he'd been unsure how she'd respond. Julie's manner was friendly, companionable, yet she didn't flirt with him. Maybe she just wanted a friend. Well, he'd never know if he didn't try.

Paul cupped her face with his hands and kissed her forehead. He'd guessed right. Her skin was soft like rose petals. Julie didn't object, so he put his lips on hers. His heart skipped a beat or two, inhaling her light fragrance. But when he tried to deepen the kiss, she pulled away. Had he moved too fast? He'd sensed she liked him. Maybe he'd been wrong.

⋆ ⋆ ⋆

Julie yearned to wrap her arms around Paul and prolong the kiss, but she was a police officer so she resisted the temptation. That wouldn't be a good idea. She'd been assigned to watch Paul, not to kiss him. A shaky breath escaped her then she stood and checked the time.

Staring at her watch, she blinked in amazement. 'I had no idea it was so late. This has been a lot of fun, but it's time I went home.' While she talked, she eased into her jacket.

Paul got to his feet and followed her. Did he sense her ambivalence? Perhaps he'd try to convince her to stay.

With a wave, she slipped out of his front door fast before he could object. The cozy room, his presence, and the cold rain tapping on the roof, it'd be so easy to stay, slip into his arms and return his kisses. But the timing was all wrong. This was her job, not a date. And this man she found so attractive could be a hardened criminal.

Next door, the key stuck in the lock then gave way when she pushed against the heavy door. Julie stepped into her foyer. That kiss had caught her off guard. Maybe she'd over-reacted, but her emotions were on overtime where Paul was concerned.

Reaching for the phone, she called Corbeille.

As usual, the other detective got right to the point. 'I've been expecting your call. How was your evening?'

'Our plans changed. Instead of dinner at Martin's place, we went on a picnic then ended up at his house after the storm hit. I just walked in the door.' There was no reason to tell Corbeille that Paul had kissed her, or that she'd enjoyed it. She'd promised to get close to Paul, but her fellow officer didn't need a blow-by-blow description.

'You must have learned something. What the heck did Martin and you talk about?' Her partner inquired about the evening.

'Not much. We had some drinks, listened

to his stereo. While I was there, he got a call from his mother-in-law, Mrs. Turner. According to Paul, she called to gloat over his firm's forcing him to take a leave of absence. He got red in the face then swore at her and slammed down the receiver so hard, it's a wonder he didn't break the telephone. It's the first time I've seen him explode like that.'

'That's interesting,' Corbeille said. 'Is it possible Martin lost his temper with his estranged wife?'

'Maybe.' She had to admit she'd been surprised by Paul's sudden outburst. He'd seemed so in control.

'Martin hasn't let anything slip, has he?'

'No.' Corbeille's attitide bothered Julie. 'You sound like you've already decided he's guilty. Shouldn't we be impartial, just find out what really happened?'

'Of course. Just do your job, Taylor.'

After the call, she sat on the side of her bed. Frowning, she picked at the fuzz on the worn comforter. It disturbed her that Corbeille had already made up his mind about Paul. He knew as well as she did, their job was to find the truth.

* * *

That night, Jay Arnold's phone rang as he trudged up the last flight of stairs to his floor. He unlocked his door then dashed into the apartment to grab the telephone. His hand gripped the receiver hard at the sound of a voice from his past.

'Jay? It's Paul. I'm relieved to find you at last.'

'I've been right here in New York City.' And his brother could have found him if he wanted. Resentment stirred inside.

'Yeah? Well, I tried. I even hired a private detective to look for you, but he gave up. He said New York is one of the worse places to find anybody. Thank God a friend from work had dinner at your restaurant last weekend then called to tease me about my look-alike at Le Sorrento. I contacted the restaurant and convinced your manager I was on the level so he'd give me your home phone number.' He paused as if unsure Jay would want to talk to him.

Trying to forget how much Paul had hurt him, Jay admitted he was glad to hear from his brother. 'It's been a long time, Bro. I've thought about you a lot.'

'How are things there?'

'Fine. I'm Assistant Manager at Le Sorrento. You're lucky to reach me at home this week. One of our waiters had an emergency appendectomy so I've had to work extra, filling in for him' Jay glanced out the window. In the street light, he could see fluffy flakes of snow falling. 'Looks like I got home at a good time. It's starting to snow here.'

'It's raining in Richmond.' Paul's voice was sad.

'You sound down in the dumps. What's the matter?'

'The past month or so, I'd had my share of problems, but that's nothing for you to worry about. We haven't seen each other for so long.' Paul hesitated. 'I've missed you.'

'Same here, chum.' Jay cleared his throat, embarrassed by his feelings. 'Uncle Jon said you graduated from law school.'

'You know Phillips isn't any relation to us.' Paul snapped at him. 'Besides, if you talk to him, why the heck haven't you called me? I've been worried sick about you.'

'I would have if I'd known where you were. Uncle Jon told me he'd lost touch with you years ago.'

'That's an outright lie. I talk to him now and then, hoping he's heard from you, but he always says he hasn't.' He paused. 'Something's not right here. He's never told me the two of you stayed in touch.'

'Same here. Anyway, we're talking now,' Jay replied. 'You're a lawyer in Richmond?'

'Yeah.'

'You don't sound too enthusiastic about your work.'

'It's okay. Corporate law can be dull. You know how I used to want to be a writer when I grew up?'

'Yeah, and I wanted to be an astronaut. Guess we didn't make it, did we?' Jay said.

'No, but I won some prizes for writing in college, and I've decided to take a chance and see if I can write.'

'Great. Let me know when you sell your first book.'

'Don't hold your breath. I probably don't have a snowball's chance in hell,' Paul admitted ruefully, 'but there's a novel I started in school — it's almost complete and, I'm going to finish it and try to get it published.'

'Good for you. I don't intend to stay in restaurants forever, either. I'd like to be a tour guide and see the world.'

'Sounds like we both have our dreams, don't we?'

'Yeah. Well, where would we be without them?'

'You're right about that.' Paul hesitated. 'Let's get together soon.'

'That sounds good to me.' Did Paul mean it? Jay struggled with his doubts, hoping his twin was sincere. Uncle Jon had almost convinced him Paul didn't care if he lived or died.

'I mean it.' Paul sounded sincere. 'We're brothers and we ought to see each other. I'd like to meet your family, too.'

'I'm not married, Paul. Are you?'

'I was, but I'm separated. It won't be long until my divorce is finalized, at least it will be when my wife turns up. You may find this hard to believe, but she's vanished and the police suspect foul play.'

'Wow. Has anybody asked for a ransom?'

'No. She just disappeared, and it looks like I was the last person she contacted.'

'That's too bad. I hope she turns up.'

'Me too. The police may think I was involved. They've come to see me twice.'

'They'll find her. It just takes time,' Jay suggested.

'Right. Well, I'll let you go. I meant what I said about our getting together, if you'd like to.' Paul seemed unsure.

'I'll look forward to it. Give me your address and telephone number. We'll plan something soon.' He wrote down Paul's information. 'It was good to talk to you, Bro. Good night.'

Jay leaned against the wall in his Pullman kitchen and sipped a mug of decaf. His brother sounded worried. It was no wonder if his wife was missing. For a moment, he wished he could help.

At bedtime, he stepped out of a hot shower where he'd scrubbed away the odors of the Italian restaurant. Putting on his pajamas, he slipped between the sheets of his twin bed and turned off the light. For a few minutes he lay there, his arms under his head. Something bothered him. He got up, turned on the lamp and dug through the contents of a dresser drawer. There it was, a small framed picture. He placed it on top of the nightstand then got back in bed.

During the night, Jay woke and looked out the window. The snow had stopped, and the moon shone into the room. A quick glance at his nightstand brought a smile to his face. A few pearly moonbeams illuminated the picture he'd placed there earlier, two small boys in baseball outfits smiling snaggle-toothed grins, their arms around each other. Filled with a deep contentment, he closed his eyes and slept.

* * *

Next morning, Doctor Jon Phillips received a call from Jay. They'd stayed in touch after Jay ran away to New York.

'If I ask you something, will you tell me the truth?' Jay's tone was brusque, not like him at all.

'Of course I will.' Phillips' stomach muscles clenched.

'I talked to Paul last night.'

'But how did . . . ' Phillips stopped in mid-sentence. This shouldn't have happened. He'd kept in touch with both of the brothers, yet denied to each he knew the other's location. 'That's great news, Jay. Tell me all about it.' The possibility that they'd find each other had worried him over the years. But the odds were so slim, he'd begun to relax recently.

'Paul heard about me from a friend then got my telephone number.' Jay paused then asked, 'Why did you keep us apart?'

'For your own good.' That's it. Make the best of a bad situation. You're smarter than they are. 'Remember, you were furious with Paul the day you left town. I was afraid you'd do something foolish.' He'd bought Jay's plane ticket and put him on a plane.

Trying to sound sincere, Phillips gave Jay what he considered to be a reasonable explanation. Give people what they'll believe, that was his policy.

'Like what?'

'Oh, I don't know, maybe hurt Paul.'

'That's the dumbest thing I've ever heard.' Jay's usually mild voice shook with emotion. 'He's all that's left of my family, except Aunt Louisa.'

'All right, Jay. Perhaps I used poor judgment, but I had your best interests at heart.' So they'd talked. But one phone conversation didn't mean they trusted each other again. He decided it was time to change the subject. 'Tell me about yourself. How's the job?'

'It's okay, but I still want to be a tour guide.'

'So you've said. Have you had any dizziness or headaches since we talked last time?' Jay had received a harsh blow to the head the night of the fire, and as a doctor, Phillips knew, in such a situation, years could pass before problems appeared.

'Nope. I feel great.'

'Do you have trouble sleeping?'

'No, yet . . . ' Jay hesitated then continued. 'I dream about the night Mom and Dad died.'

'You've done that for years.' Phillips' muscles tensed while he waited, afraid of what else Jay would tell him.

'Yeah, I have. I've relived that evening, up to where I leave my room to go and apologize to Dad for fighting with him. That's where I always wake up. The other night, it was a little different. In my dream, I heard yelling downstairs.'

'Was it your parents?'

'Yeah, but there was a third voice. It seemed familiar, yet I can't place it.'

Phillips squeezed the pencil in his hands so hard it snapped in two. Jay's memory was returning, after all of those years, just when he felt safe. 'You're just imagining things. As I've told you before, you probably caused the fire by leaving a lit cigarette in the den. The week before, your mother told me you'd gone to sleep on the sofa, dropped your cigarette on a cushion, and burned it.'

'That's impossible,' Jay protested. 'I'd run out of cigarettes, so I couldn't have started that fire. But if it takes the rest of my life, I'll find out what really happened.'

'Don't waste your time. And don't get your hopes up about Paul. The two of you live in different worlds now. Face the facts, Jay. Your brother went on with his life and left you behind. Just think, you could have become a professional like Paul. Lawyers don't scrounge for tips in restaurants.'

His criticism of Jay's occupation hit a sore spot. 'It's not like that at all,' Jay replied in his own defense. 'I'm Assistant Manager of a well known restaurant, and when my boss retires,

I'll be the Manager.'

Though Jay protested, Phillips smiled at the uncertainty in his words. 'Of course you will,' he said. 'My next patient's here so I'd better go. Call me soon. I enjoy our talks.'

Hanging up the phone, Phillips remained seated at his desk while his thoughts whirled.

A trained psychiatrist, he knew there was no way to predict how much Jay would remember or when. But if what happened that night so long ago became public knowledge, Phillips would lose his practice and his luxurious life style.

The idea of prison horrified him, and it was possible that could be his future. Frightened, he called on an inner strength and managed to rally. He'd come too far to give up now. Whatever it took, he'd protect himself. It was too bad about Jay, but if the young man became a threat, there was a solution.

The wheels were already in motion. Once Paul was out of the way, Jay would be no problem.

Phillips eyed a picture of his sister on his desk. When he offered her a way to get what she wanted, his little sister had agreed to his scheme. She'd always obeyed him.

'To you, Sis,' he toasted her with his coffee mug. 'We're two of a kind, practical to the core.' After all, the end did justify the means.

He'd always liked that old adage.

What Sis would never comprehend, and he wouldn't bother to explain it to her, was he stood to gain far more than she. All she could see was dollar signs. He would win the assurance that he could continue his life in peace, never be discovered.

Once the brothers were gone, he'd be the only one who knew what happened that night. And he could live with the knowledge.

5

Bemused with Julie and that kiss last night, Paul arranged the canned goods he'd just bought in neat stacks on his pantry shelves. The sharp ring of the telephone shattered his daydream, jolting him back to reality with a thud.

Damn. He had to stop thinking about her. No matter how much he liked her, he couldn't get involved. It was too risky to love someone, it made you vulnerable. Shaking his head to clear it, he reached for the telephone.

'Paul?'

His brother's voice surprised Paul. Though he'd looked forward to seeing Jay, he hadn't expected to hear from him today.

'Are you all right?' Jay sounded concerned when he didn't respond right away.

'Sure. Are you calling from New York?' As unpredictable as Jay was, he might be in a local phone booth.

'Yeah. I just got some sad news. Auntie died yesterday. Now I wish I'd flown out there to visit her. Anyway, her lawyer's making the arrangements, but can you come to Portland for the funeral? It would have meant a lot to her.'

'Of course. I'll be there.' Memories of their childhood and Aunt Louisa filled Paul's mind. The kindhearted old lady had baked their favorite cookies and always had time for a chat when Jay and he stopped by her house for a visit. She'd taken them in the day their parents died.

'I'm sorry to hear that she's gone. If you'll give me a few minutes to get a reservation, I'll call you back with my flight information.' They reminesced about their great-aunt for a few minutes before hanging up.

Alone in the kitchen, Paul felt depressed as he realized that no one remained of their family now except Jay and himself. Needing company, he finished putting away the groceries, then he walked across the lawn to the house next door.

Julie opened the door and greeted him with a bright smile.

'There's been a death in my family, and I've got to go to Portland,' he said. 'My favorite aunt just died.'

'I'm so sorry,' Julie responded. 'How can I help?'

The sympathy in her voice and her kind expression touched him. All at once his grief became more bearable, his loneliness lessened.

‘Would you take in my newspapers and mail?’ For some reason, Paul hated to leave town though she’d cut their kiss short the other night. Julie probably wasn’t interested. It was just as well. Still, down deep inside he wondered how she really felt about him.

‘Why don’t you give me your aunt’s name.’

She must have noticed his raised eyebrows since she explained. ‘I’d like to send flowers.’

‘That’s very kind of you.’ On an impulse, he picked up her hand and kissed the palm. This time Julie didn’t pull away and a thoughtful expression crossed her face. An unexpected warm feeling engulfed him, though it didn’t matter if she liked him.

⋆ ⋆ ⋆

Paul’s plane taxied to a halt at a Portland Airport gate. An unexpected wave of shyness struck, and he hung back while the other passengers swarmed from the plane. How ridiculous. There was no reason to feel shy around his twin.

To make up for his indecision, Paul hurried into the terminal. Spotting Jay, he strode toward his brother, not sure what to say or how to act. At the sight of a broad grin on Jay’s face, he blinked in surprise and stuck out his hand. Jay moved forward and gave him a quick hug then stepped back, his face flushed.

What Paul saw before him could have been his own reflection in a mirror — same lanky frame, same cool blue eyes and auburn hair. But Jay was thinner, his hair longer. He wore a 'I Love New York City' tee-shirt, ragged jeans and Nikes. Fifteen years since they'd seen each other, it seemed a lifetime. Paul was close to tears.

'Why did you do that?' Touched by Jay's gesture, he coughed to clear up an unexpected huskiness in his voice.

'Why not? I'm damn glad to see you.' Jay picked up his overnight bag, led him outside to a waiting cab, and gave the driver their great-aunt's address.

'I thought I'd stay in a hotel,' Paul said. That way he wouldn't inconvenience Jay. Also, he felt awkward with his brother after so long. His last recollection of Jay was of an angry fifteen-year-old boy. Today a smiling man who resembled his twin looked at him through Jay's eyes.

'Not on your life.' Jay shook his head. 'We'll both stay at Auntie's. It's just the two of us. There's plenty of room.'

'Okay.' Paul eased back in his seat, watching the Portland scenery flash past his window. Each familiar landmark brought back bittersweet memories. Admit it, he told himself. He'd stayed away from Portland because of the memories.

'Besides, I need to talk to you about something,' Jay said.

'Wait until we get there,' Paul suggested. This wasn't the time or place to discuss personal matters. His brother's remark somehow reassured him the man seated beside him in the cab was Jay. His twin always had something to tell him when they were boys. More often than not, it was a scheme that would get them both in trouble. Paul stared out the window until the taxi stopped in front of Auntie's house.

As Jay led him into the shabby yet comfortable home, Paul felt he'd entered a time warp. Heavy dark furniture, yellowed framed pictures on the tables, worn Oriential carpets. An old house mustiness prevailed, mixed with the scent of a pitcher of fresh flowers on a table.

His brother led him back to the kitchen. Someone, maybe a neighbor, had left a package of cinnamon rolls on the the oil-clothed table. It reminded Paul of the sticky-sweet bakery goodies his brother and he'd shared as boys. Did Jay remember, too?

'It hasn't changed since last time I was here.' A wave of guilt rushed through Paul.

He should have come to see her more often. But things just kept getting in the way, law school, Sheila, his job. He set down his bag at the foot of the stairs, half-expecting to see their great-aunt come into the room to greet them.

While they lounged on the sitting room sofa with mugs of instant coffee, Paul glanced in his brother's direction, curious as to what Jay wanted to discuss. They'd been in the house for awhile, yet Jay still hadn't told him what he wanted. That was another characteristic of the teen-aged Jay, get his attention then act reluctant to tell him what he wanted.

'Okay. What's on your mind, Bro?' Their boyhood nickname for each other slid off Paul's tongue as if they'd seen each other the previous day. He had to smile.

Jay studied his shoe for a moment then replied in a low voice. 'I need to clear the air about something. Uncle Jon said you blame me for Mom and Dad's deaths.'

'That's not true,' Paul protested. 'I admit I was upset and angry at first. You couldn't remember what happened and Phillips kept insisting the fire was your fault. To tell the truth, I didn't know what to think. Then you had a nervous breakdown and had to go in that psychiatric facility. Phillips treated you himself and refused to charge us anything.'

'I was angry with you for a long time, Paul. Two years ago, I found a therapist who's helped me a lot. He reminded me that we were just kids. Looking back, it appears Doctor Phillips didn't do either of us any good.'

Paul rubbed tired eyes. It had been a long day and their conversation about the past had opened old wounds that still hurt. 'Since we're being candid with each other, Phillips said you resent me. He warned me to be on guard if I ever saw you again,' he said then gazed at his twin, wishing he could gauge his reaction. Unable to read Jay's bland expression, Paul's stomach knotted with nerves. He better shut up. Today of all days, he didn't want to fight with his brother.

'You're safe. Unless you're afraid of my cooking.' Jay quipped then became serious again, his voice sounded strained. 'Uncle Jon means well, though I don't always agree with him. For instance, he advised me to forget what happened, so I tried to bottle up all of my emotions. My therapist in New York has encouraged me to talk things out, and it's helped a lot.'

Paul tried to reassure his twin. 'It was a tremendous shock to come home and find

Mom and Dad gone, and you with no memory of what happened.' For a moment, he catapulted back to that grim morning. A police officer had held him in his arms so he wouldn't enter the smouldering ruins of their home to search for their parents. His vision blurred and he walked to the window and stared without seeing at the street outside. Some pain never went away.

'The police couldn't tell what caused the fire and you'd lost your memory,' Paul explained. 'Later, Doctor Phillips and I came to the hospital to pick you up, but you'd run away. That hurt me a lot.'

'For what it's worth, I never would have hurt Mom and Dad,' Jay responded. Paul turned and they faced each other.

'I know that now and it eases my mind to be able to talk to you.' Paul finished his coffee. 'Let's take this one day at a time.' He checked his watch. 'Can I use the phone?'

'Help yourself. I'll put your bag in one of the bedrooms.'

While Jay went upstairs, Paul called Julie.

* * *

The phone rang. Julie glanced at the kitchen clock. It was about time for Paul. Eager to hear from Paul, she rationalized it was because he was the man she was investigating. It was important that she keep in touch with him.

At the sound of his voice, she asked, 'How was your flight?'

'Uneventful. I'll be home in a couple of days. The funeral's tomorrow afternoon.'

'You're not alone out there, are you?' He hadn't mentioned any family or friends in Portland.

'No, I'm with a relative.'

Oh? That's convenient.' Julie was curious about his living arrangements but didn't press him for details. Paul liked his privacy, so she'd proceed with care. In fact, he struck her as a loner. Her instincts told her he'd be long gone if any woman pressured him to make a commitment, not that it was any concern of hers.

'Well, I'd better go,' he said. Would you meet my plane?'

'Of course. Call me with your flight information.'

'Thanks.'

Once he'd hung up, Julie sat in her chair thinking about Paul. But it was the wrong time, the wrong place, and he sure wasn't the man for her.

With Paul's door key in hand, she stepped outside. The postal truck had just driven down the street, so this was a perfect occasion to search his house. If Paul's elderly next-door neighbor noticed, she'd assume Julie was just taking in his mail.

She stepped into Paul's quiet foyer and locked the door then stacked the mail and paper on a table.

Where to start? She'd better go upstairs and work her way down. Corbeille had been eager for her to search Paul's home, but this was her first real opportunity. Since the day Paul discovered her nosing through the ashes of his fire, she'd been reluctant to do anything else that might raise his suspicions.

She wouldn't disturb anything so he wouldn't have a clue his house had been searched.

His bedroom was neat and gave away little about its occupant. It didn't appear to be a room he used much. No pictures or magazines. A heavy dark striped comforter covered his king-size bed. In the double closet located in his bathroom, she found a row of expensive-looking suits, a cedar rack of shoes and dress shirts still in their plastic cleaners bags.

Julie fingered a sports jacket and laid her cheek against the rough tweed, inhaled a trace of his woodsy cologne. Out of the blue, a tiny twinge of guilt struck but she pushed it away. She was just doing her job. The other side of the closet had an abandoned look with a collection of empty coat hangers.

Back to the master bedroom. This time she pulled open drawers and found neat stacks of men's pajamas, underwear, handkerchiefs. An ornate armoire held heavy sweaters. Everywhere, order prevailed. Her eye was drawn to the night stands. A book on investing and a few men's handkerchiefs indicated which was his. The other nightstand drawer held a few fashion magazines.

Julie sighed. This was turning into a waste of time. As she replaced the magazines, her fingers touched something in the back of the drawer. She pulled out a small leather address book. Ah. Her heart beat a little faster.

Seated on the Berber carpet by the king-size bed, she leafed through the book. The handwriting was small and feminine. From the notes in the margins, most names appeared to be business contacts. Under the letter 'F,' she found one entry which interested her — just the first name Francoise and a phone number. Julie wrote down the name and telephone number on the small loose-leaf pad she'd brought with her.

One of the other bedrooms was empty. Paul had said Sheila and he broke up soon after they moved into the house. Either he hadn't furnished that room or his wife had taken furniture with her. The third and fourth bedrooms were furnished with heavy oak furniture that resembled something a single man might buy.

Downstairs again, Julie was drawn to a small study lined with bookshelves. A large desk dominated the room. It looked like he spent time here. A computer and word processor perched on one corner of the desk. Paul had mentioned he was working on a novel. Based on the masses of crumpled computer paper in the wastebasket, he'd experienced writer's block.

Where did he keep his valuables? She slid a cautious finger along the shelves of books. No hollow books that people without safes sometimes used to hide valuables. With care, she removed the two pictures from the wall. There was no hint of a safe.

An oriental throw rug covered the area in front of the desk. Julie nudged it aside and bent to examine the hardwood surface. A small panel set in the floor alerted her. Paul had a safe. That could be useful information. The Richmond PD had questioned him, but had no grounds to search his home.

The kitchen revealed nothing more personal than a bookcase full of cookbooks. That made sense since he enjoyed cooking.

Enough for now. The name she'd found in the address book might help. Julie stepped out of Paul's house, locked the door behind her. Who was this Francoise? She'd better find out.

* * *

'Why do I get the feeling Auntie's funeral wasn't the only reason you wanted me to come?' Paul encouraged his brother to talk to him while they lunched on pizza from a nearby restaurant.

'You always could read me like a book.' Jay smiled. 'First, I agree with you about Uncle Jon. His behavior has been odd.'

Paul nodded. 'That's the understatement of the year. I was shocked to hear he'd kept in touch with you. Sometimes you think you know somebody. Then they act out of character, and you wonder if you know them at all.' A flicker of memory stirred in the recesses of his mind. It involved their mother and Doctor Phillips one wintry Sunday afternoon years ago. Paul struggled to recall more, but the image had already faded away.

'I've never believed I caused the fire, Paul.'

'Not even by accident? Like the lit cigarette you forgot?'

Jay shook his head. 'That night I went

downstairs to see what was going on. Then, lights out. When I came to, I was stretched out on the front lawn, an oxygen mask over my face.'

Paul stared at his brother. 'Go on.'

'The truth could be locked in my file in Uncle Jon's office.'

'You have the right to see your records. Did you ask him?'

'Several times, and he always makes excuses, like he doesn't think I'm ready.' Jay's chin raised defiantly and he added, 'But I'm going to take a look.'

Paul shook his head. He'd seen that determined expression on his twin's face in the past right before Jay got into trouble.

'I need to know.' Jay's voice shook. 'As my brother, you gotta understand.'

'I won't let you break into his office . . . '

'Try and stop me.' Jay glared at him.

'You didn't let me finish. I won't let you break into his office alone. I'm going with you.' He needed to know the truth, too. Uncertainty had gnawed at his insides for years.

'You'd do that for me?' Jay's eyes shone.

'You bet.' Numb with grief, he'd walked away, let Doctor Phillips take care of his brother years ago. This time he resolved to stand by Jay and damn the consequences.

His twin offered a cold, clammy hand and Paul grabbed it. He'd come to pay his last respects to the great-aunt who raised him. Now he was about to break the law. Yet Jay was his brother, and if he went along, maybe he could keep things under control.

⋆ ⋆ ⋆

At the close of the funeral service, they took a cab. Making one stop at a local business along the way, they ended up at Phillips' medical building. Paul stood with Jay while office workers swarmed from the building at the end of the day.

His heart pounded and he sent up a silent prayer. Please don't let us get caught.

Well, it was too late to back out. Determined to see this through, Paul drew a deep breath and squared his shoulders.

'Let's go. Just walk like you know where you're headed and have a right to be there,' Jay directed, distinguished in his grey wig and beard from the local costume shop they'd visited. Paul had selected a hooded jacket, heavy glasses, and a moustache. No one would recognize them in a million years. His lips twitched at the absurdity of the situation.

'What about security guards?' Paul hissed.

'There're just two,' Jay said. 'They patrol

alternate floors on the hour every night.'

'How do you know?' Paul hoped his twin knew what he was doing.

'I called Building Management and pretended to be a prospective tenant,' Jay said. There's a lot of unleased space in the building, so they were happy to brag about their security.'

They walked through the revolving doors, then Jay led him to a bay of elevators and punched the number for Phillips' floor.

'Now what? Do we break in?' The gravity of their situation hit Paul. He could get disbarred for this. A chill slid down his spine.

'You'll see,' his twin said. At the twenty-sixth floor, Jay touched his coat sleeve. 'This is where we get off.'

The hall was deserted. They walked a few doors to the doctor's suite. Jay glanced around then slipped a small tool from his pocket, inserted it into the lock, and opened the door.

'My brother the burglar,' Paul muttered.

'I got us in, didn't I?' Jay grinned.

'You sure did. I'm impressed.'

'We can't turn on the lights. Take this.' Jay handed him a small flashlight and kept the other. 'If we hear anyone walking this way, we turn the flashlights off fast.' His brother led the way down a corridor to Phillips' darkened office then pointed to a tier of file cabinets recessed in a wall.

'Don't tell me you can open these cabinets too.' What in the world had he been thinking — breaking into a doctor's office? His firm would be thrilled to see that story on page one.

Sure.' Jay fished a smaller pick out of his suit coat pocket then walked over to the cabinets. 'Here we are, A to F.' A moment or so later, he slid the drawer open. The light of his flashlight aimed at the letter-headings helped him locate the 'A's.' Pulling his own file out of the drawer, he gestured to two leather chairs arranged on one side of the massive oak desk.

'Do I dare ask where you learned these skills?' Paul relaxed a little. Maybe they'd get out of this alive after all.

'You don't wanna know.'

Jay opened his file and handed half of its contents to him. 'Don't get it mixed up. If we see anything suspicious, we'll make copies.'

'Where's the copy machine?' Paul shone his flashlight around the room.

'Over here, I guess.' Jay stepped across the room and opened a closet door. A copier had been installed inside the small space. 'Last month, Phillips told me he'd bought new office equipment. We can use this machine and no one will hear or see our lights.'

For a few minutes, the only sound was the slight rustle of pages turning while they both scanned the material.

'Paul, I don't see anything except a lot of medical gobbly-gook. Do you?'

'Not really,' Paul responded. As he shuffled some more pages, a piece of stiff paper fell to the floor. Paul picked it up, turned the paper over. In the dim light, they saw a faded picture of an attractive young woman. Younger than they remembered her, their mother smiled into the camera. The photograph had been torn in half then taped back together.

'Why would Phillips keep Mom's picture?' Paul's finger touched the photograph, the last thing he'd expected to find in Jay's file.

'Who knows? Mom and Dad were good friends with Uncle Jon,' Jay said.

'You don't suppose he had a yen for Mother?' In the dim light, Paul glanced in Jay's direction. Out of the blue, he remembered what had eluded him earlier. He'd come home from a friend's house. As he walked into the den, Mother and Philips moved apart. Her face was flushed, and the doctor appeared annoyed. Paul puzzled about that for days, but didn't dare ask his mother for an explanation. He was just a kid and kids didn't question their elders.

'Of course not. They were just friends,' Jay said. 'Hey, look at this — a cassette. It's not marked.' It went into his coat pocket.

The elevator doors clanked open and they threw themselves to the floor. Paul's flashlight fell under the desk. His heart pounding, he rolled on the flashlight and blocked the light just in time. The door opened. A bright beam swept the suite's corridor. He held his breath until the door closed.

'Who was that?' Paul gasped.

'Got me.' Jay sounded as breathless as he was. 'According to the building management office, the guards just patrol the halls. Maybe Uncle Jon asked for a check of his office after hours. Lots of doctors' offices are broken into by junkies. Let's get the hell out of here.'

'How about this?' Paul held up the picture.

'Stick it back in the folder.'

Back at their aunt's home, they removed their disguises, then sank onto the sofa. Jay looked disappointed.

'He kept a picture of our mother.' Paul thought that strange. 'Her hairstyle and clothes seemed dated, so it must have been taken years ago when Mom, Dad and Phillips were young.'

'I wanna hear this tape,' Jay said. 'Stay there. I think I saw a cassette player upstairs in Auntie's bedroom.' He ran upstairs then returned with a battery-run cassette player. 'Here goes.' It turned out to be Doctor Phillips's interview with Jay the day after the fire. The psychiatrist introduced himself then questioned Jay.

'Jay, can you tell me what happened last night?'

'I don't know, sir.' Jay sounded sad, confused.

'You must remember something,' the psychiatrist urged.

'I remember going downstairs last night. Dad and I'd fought and I — '

'Your father and you fought a lot, didn't you?' The doctor interrupted Jay mid-sentence.

'Yeah, but — '

'You were angry with your father.'

'Yeah, but that doesn't mean I'd do anything to hurt him or Mom,' Jay insisted. His voice broke.

'What else do you remember?' Phillips persisted.

'Not much. I woke up with an oxygen mask over my face. A fireman was leaning over me.'

'The fire was your fault, wasn't it?'

'No, sir.'

'How can you say that? You don't remember anything.'

'That's true but I wouldn't have hurt them.'

'I certainly hope not. That's all, Jay.'

The tape stopped.

'That sure didn't sound like Uncle Jon, did it?' Jay wrinkled his brow.

'It was fifteen years ago. Voices can change,' Paul reminded his brother. He stood and rubbed his eyes. It had been a long day. 'Let's get some sleep. I don't know about you, but I'm exhausted. We could have been caught.'

'I know, but we weren't.' Jay tapped him on the shoulder. 'I won't forget you helped me tonight.'

'Go to bed. I'll see you in the morning.' Paul climbed the stairs and found his way down the dim upstairs hall to the room he'd claimed. With a yawn, he undressed and got in bed. His fist beat the tired goosedown pillow into shape, then he lay his head down and drifted off to sleep.

A cry pierced the night. Paul jolted upright then leapt from his bed. Barefoot, he ran down the hall to investigate.

Outside Jay's room, he switched on the hall light. The room was dark and he could just make out his brother's figure under his bed covers. No one else was in sight. A moan escaped Jay's lips as he turned and twisted in the bed. Paul let out a sigh of relief. There was no intruder. Jay was having a nightmare.

Paul strode over to the bed, put his hand on his brother's shoulder and shook him. 'Wake up. You're dreaming.'

Jay moaned then rolled over on his side. His eyes opened.

'What? What time is it?' He seemed surprised to see Paul.

'Time you stopped having bad dreams, Bro. You cried out and I thought a burglar had you by the throat.'

'Sorry,' Jay muttered.

'What the hell got you so upset?'

'It's the same old dream. I'm asleep then I hear Mom and Dad's angry voices, so I run downstairs to see what's wrong. Something hits me on the head and I fall. At that point, I always wake up.'

'Angry voices? Mom and Dad were fighting?'

'Yeah. I've had that dream for years. The last few days, I've heard three voices — theirs and someone else's. The third voice sounds so familiar. But for the life of me, I can't identify it.'

6

Next day, Jay played the cassette over and over. Unable to stand any more, Paul raised a hand in protest. 'Enough. What's so fascinating about that darn tape? It's just Phillips and you.'

'That's what's so weird.' Jay pushed the hair out of his eyes. 'Uncle Jon's voice sure has changed. It doesn't sound like him on this tape, yet I know it is. Let's run it one more time.'

'Be my guest. If you don't mind, I'm going for a walk.' Paul pulled on his jacket then stepped out of the house and strolled down the street to a strip shopping center to kill a few minutes.

In the pharmacy he leafed through the newest edition of a magazine then waited in line to buy it. Leaving the store, he retraced his steps to the old house Louisa had called home for over sixty years.

While he strolled his thoughts were of his brother. On the recording Jay's voice sounded so young and defenseless. His twin had been alone that day except for Phillips. Remorse hit Paul like an old wound that aches when least expected. If he'd been more supportive, Jay might not have disappeared for fifteen years.

The house was silent as he walked into the front hall. 'Hello?'

'I'm up here.' A voice called from upstairs then Jay leaned over the banister, lather on his face. 'Thought I'd shave and get cleaned up so we can go out to supper. If you like Italian, I've found a good restaurant.'

'Great.'

'I worked a double shift the week before Aunt Louise died. On the phone yesterday, my boss said I could take off a few more days. Antonio thought you and I might want to spend some time together.' Jay hesitated then added, 'would you like some company when you go home?'

'Sure, if you have the time.' Paul didn't want to sound unenthusiastic, but the idea of more than a couple of days with Jay made him nervous. They'd lived apart for so long. Except for brief flashes of recognition, his brother could be a stranger.

'I'd like to see where you live.'

Paul confided, 'In case I didn't mention it, I'm trying to write a novel.'

'Wow!' Jay's eyebrows went up. 'My brother the author. What's the story? Is it an adventure, a whodunit or what?'

'It's still a little rough. The basic plot is the story of two brothers whose lives take different paths.'

'I see.' A cloud passed over Jay's features. 'Like us?'

'This is just a story, something I made up.' Paul could have kicked himself for his stupidity, mentioning his book to his brother. It was inevitable Jay would think of their own lives. Annoyed with himself, he frowned.

'Maybe they'll work out their differences?'

'It's possible. I haven't decided yet.'

Jay cleared his throat and changed the subject. 'Tell me about your neighbors in Richmond. Have you met them?'

'Yes, I have, at least the nearest neighbors.'

'Anyone our age?'

'One neighbor's elderly and the other's a little younger than we are. Julie will meet our plane. We've become friends since she moved back to Richmond from Washington, D.C.'

'Do you like her?'

'She's okay,' Paul replied and shrugged in an attempt to appear disinterested. To avoid further discussion of Julie, he reminded Jay, 'you need to take that tape back.'

'I will right after supper.' A hopeful expression appeared on Jay's face. 'Want to tag along?'

'No, thanks. My heart can't stand many

experiences like last night.' Feeling like a mother hen, Paul added, 'Be careful.'

'I'll make a copy first.'

'All right, and while you put the tape back, I'll see about our plane reservations for tomorrow.'

That evening they enjoyed an early supper of spaghetti and meatballs at a small Italian restaurant in a red brick house a few blocks away. Auntie's older neighborhood was in transition and several restaurants and shops had opened in what had been previously private residences.

After supper they parted. Paul strolled back to the house and called the airline, arranged to pick up two tickets on the noon flight to Richmond the next day.

Once his business was finished, he strolled into the sitting room and tried to relax. He'd be on edge until Jay got back. Maybe he should have gone with him.

Slouched on their aunt's lumpy sofa, Paul tried to avoid its loose springs while turning on her television. He channel-surfed then settled down to watch a few thirty-something situation comedies. It was strange how each bright young actress on the shows reminded him of Julie.

Out of nowhere, the urge to go home hit him. He would've jumped on a plane that night if possible. Tomorrow, he'd see Julie tomorrow. His resolution to avoid commitments wavered as he recalled her soft curves, her braid of blonde hair, and her warm brown eyes. He wanted to see her with her hair loose on her shoulders.

Paul's muscles tightened as lust took hold. All right, he admitted to himself — he wanted her. Julie was a knockout, even in her jeans and baggy shirts. He wanted to strip off her clothes, carry her to bed and make love to her. Arousal heated his blood until the room became close and stuffy. He stepped to a window, opened it and leaned out, inhaling the cold air. What he needed right now was a cold shower, a very cold shower.

The time crept by. One hour, two. Where was his brother? Anxiety gnawed at him.

To ease his mind, he again concentrated on Julie. Maybe tomorrow night they could go out. Then he remembered. Jay would be with him on the flight to Richmond, and he wasn't a child they could give cookies and milk and put to bed early. Never mind. He'd figure out a way Julie and he could be alone together. But what to do with his house guest? Sight-seeing. That was it. Julie had grown up in Richmond and would be able to give him a list of tourist attractions.

The clock in the hall stuck ten then eleven

o'clock. Jay's key clicked in the lock and Paul sighed with relief. 'Did you have any problems?'

Jay collapsed in an armchair across the room, closed his eyes. A few moments later, he raised his head. 'If you really want to know, I almost got caught. They've added extra guards. I closed Uncle Jon's office door, then a guard strolled down the hall. If I'd been a minute later, I would have run right into him.' His stomach rumbled and he asked, 'are you hungry? There's some fudge ripple ice cream and orange sherbert in the freezer. They're great together.'

'No thanks.' Paul's stomach lurched. Besides missing Julie, he had another reason for wanting to go home. His brother and he didn't share the same tastes in food. Jay liked to put ketchup on everything and singed every dish he cooked. 'I'm fine until breakfast.'

Removing a piece of paper from his shirt pocket, Paul examined it then announced, 'We have seats on an early flight tomorrow. The plane's pretty full so we can't sit together. You're in 3D and I'm 36C.' As the wall clock chimed midnight, he stood. 'It's late. Don't you need to pack?'

'That won't take long. I travel light.' Jay slid a cassette out of his jacket pocket. 'Here's a copy we can take with us. I'll pick up an inexpensive cassette player so we can listen to the tape a few more times. I still can't understand why Uncle Jon's voice sounds so different.'

Paul yawned. 'Who knows? Maybe he had a cold.'

'I don't think so.' Jay's expression brightened as if something had just occured to him. 'He told me the other day that he smokes too much and his doctor's after him to quit.'

'I never saw Phillips light up a cigarette when we were kids, did you?' Paul was eager to help Jay find an explanation.

'No. Would being a chain smoker change his voice?'

'I wouldn't be surprised.' Maybe now Jay would at least stop fretting about that topic.

Paul admitted the psychiatrist's attitude was peculiar. Why did he want to keep them apart? He didn't like to think the man they'd considered their friend was a liar. The hour was late, however, and no time for another lengthy discussion of Phillips. Once he got home, he'd contact the psychiatrist and demand an explanation. He hadn't told Jay, but he'd called Phillips and left a message the day he arrived in Portland. The psychiatrist hadn't returned his call.

Jay and he'd have a pleasant, brief visit in

Richmond then his brother would return to New York, and they'd both get on with their lives.

* * *

Julie parked in the lot by the terminal that served Richmond and the surrounding area and walked inside, stepping around a harried woman who tried in vain to soothe her fretful twins in their double stroller.

The arrivals board informed her that Paul's flight was thirty minutes late so she had enough time to finish the mystery novel she'd started last night.

Seated across from the terminal windows, she opened the mystery and tried in vain to concentrate on the twisted plot of murder and mistaken identities. Closing the book, she rested her head on the back of her seat.

Paul drifted into her thoughts, as he did so often. Nothing had appeared to link him to his wife's disappearance. With no leads, it was just a matter of time until the Richmond police called off her investigation and looked elsewhere for an explanation as to what had happened to Sheila Turner.

His trip to Portland seemed valid. A Portland PD sergeant had checked the local paper and faxed her a copy of the old lady's obituary. The woman's survivors consisted of two great-nephews, Paul Martin and Jay Arnold. Paul hadn't mentioned any siblings, but the other man could be his cousin. Perhaps that was where he'd stayed in Portland.

She remembered her reluctance to take this last assignment. But if she hadn't, Paul and she would never have met. One event followed another — his separation, Sheila's disappearance, then her investigation.

What an appealing man. Given different circumstances, who knew what would have happened. As things stood, she could only do her job. She found that difficult when he was around. Thank goodness he was a lawyer, not a mind reader. All it took was one of his slow, easy smiles, and her cool professionalism flew right out the window.

Before long, an airline employee announced Paul's plane had parked at the gate, then passengers streamed into the terminal. Most hurried to meet family or friends or to catch another flight. A few strolled like they had all the time in the world. Maybe they didn't have a reason to rush or anyone waiting for them. Julie's heart beat faster.

In a moment, Paul came into view, ambling along behind the other deplaned passengers. There was something different about his appearance. As she recalled, his hair just hit his collar. Today it seemed longer. And where on earth did he get that scruffy 'I love New York' tee-shirt and those tired jeans?

'Paul.'

The way he strolled by her, she could have been invisible. 'Paul.' This time she raised her voice and waved.

Turning around, he glanced her way.

'I get it. The FBI's on your trail, and you don't want to reveal we know each other. Right?' She smiled conspiratorially and winked.

He stared at her but didn't respond.

'All right. That's enough. You've had your fun.' She walked over to him. 'You could at least say you're glad to see me.'

'I am. You're a real doll.' A shy smile crossed his face, and he stuck out his hand for her to shake.

A deep voice sounded in her ear. 'Julie.'

She whirled around. Another Paul stood before her. A flush covered her face and she moaned. 'You didn't tell me there were two of you!'

* * *

Jay trailed Paul and Julie from the terminal. Her stiff posture and the way she never looked back to include him in their conversation made it obvious she was upset. Although he'd known who she was when she addressed him by his brother's name, he hadn't known how to handle the situation. With his smooth manners, Paul would have managed. Jay found himself tongue-tied and shy around women, especially attractive women. At thirty, he doubted he'd ever change. Seeing Julie turn to his twin and smile, Jay felt a pang of envy.

Jay hoped his visit wouldn't cause problems for Paul. The last thing he wanted was for his brother to regret his coming. What was Paul and Julie's relationship, anyway? Paul said he'd met her several weeks ago.

For some reason, Jay recalled how angry he'd been the day fifteen-year-old Paul stole a girl he liked. That seemed a lifetime ago, yet he still felt a tiny twinge of resentment. Pushing aside the past, he increased his gait until they all walked side by side. 'Julie.'

She glanced in his direction.

'What do you do besides pick up neighbors at the airport? Are you a lawyer, too?' She piqued his curiosity.

'Don't I wish.' Her eyes slid past his. 'I was employed as an administrative aide at a government agency in Washington until the agency down-sized and eliminated my position. Before long, I'll need to find another job. Since I moved back to Richmond, I've begun to think I'd like to stay. It's my home-town.'

Paul opened the airport door and they walked through a light drizzle to the car.

'You don't have to go back to work yet, do you?' His expression was serious as he glanced at Julie. 'It's nice to have you next door.'

So that's how it is. Bro likes her, but he's in no big hurry to get involved. He better not take too long. As pretty as she is, Julie just might find someone else. Jay smiled.

As Julie drove out of the airport parking lot, Jay leaned forward and asked, 'Has my brother told you he's the author of the next great American novel?' He joked to mask his jealousy.

She frowned at him in the rear view mirror. Did his teasing Paul annoy her? In any case, she sprang to his twin's defense. 'Yes, and I'm sure he'll do just fine.' She sounded irritated. 'What's your profession? Let me guess. Are you a lawyer or maybe a brain surgeon?'

'Nothing so grandiose, I'm afraid.' Jay barked a humorless laugh, for the first time ashamed to admit what he did for a living. 'I'm Assistant Manager of Sorrento, an

Italian restaurant in New York City.'

'I'm sorry.' Julie's tone became contrite. 'That was rude of me. Sorrento? I've read about your restaurant. Hasn't it won awards for its cuisine?'

'Yes, a few.'

'Jay, you have a perfectly respectable occupation.' Paul scolded him. 'There's no need to apologize.'

'Sorry. It's just that I can't begin to compete with what you do for a living.' In the rear-view mirror, he saw Julie frown and heard her sigh.

During the drive home, Julie had little to contribute while Paul and he chatted. They stepped out of the car in her driveway and she addressed him. 'It's been nice to meet you. I hope you have a good visit.' She held out her hand.

Jay took her hand in his. 'Thanks, Julie. It was swell of you to come and meet us at the airport.' Her fingers were icy cold. She must be upset to discover Paul had a twin. Why hadn't his brother told her about him? The poor girl must have a million questions to ask Paul. He watched her go into her house and shut the door.

'She didn't know about us, did she?'

'There wasn't any reason.' Paul said.

'Probably not. You didn't expect me to

come home with you. In fact, I bet you didn't think you'd ever see me again until a few days ago. That must have been a shocker.'

'I admit I was surprised. That doesn't mean I'm not glad to see you. It was just good luck my friend had dinner at your restaurant. Come in and I'll show you your room.'

Jay glanced around the first floor of the spacious, older brick home. The living room's polished hardwood floors reflected a handsome upholstered sofa and chairs and a large mahognany secretary. Neat stacks of boxes in the corners of the living room and dining room reminded him that Paul hadn't lived there long.

'You've done okay. This's a palace.' What a contrast between Paul's home and his own small apartment furnished with thrift shop furniture.

Paul smiled as if he appreciated his praise then he led Jay upstairs to a guest bedroom.

Jay laid his suitcase on the bed. 'I'll unpack. See you downstairs later.'

'I really am glad you came.' Paul said then went back downstairs.

As soon as he'd put away his clothes, Jay stood at the back window. This unexpected vacation would be fun. He hoped Paul didn't mind his tagging along with him to Richmond.

In the next yard, Julie in a bright blue sweater and jeans strolled into view, followed by a small fuzzy dog. She bent to inspect a bed of blooming daffodils. As she wandered around the yard, the dog yapped and ran in giddy circles around her. Unseen, Jay stood at the window and admired her.

'We need to go to the grocery store if I'm going to cook dinner.' Paul called to him from the foot of the stairs.

'Food. My favorite subject. Let's go.' He followed Paul outside to his dark green car. 'Wow! This's a beauty. What is it?'

'A BMW.' Paul laughed. 'Don't you have cars in New York?'

'Yeah, but my friends ride buses or take the subway.'

Paul backed the car out of the driveway. 'What do you think of Julie?'

'She's a real doll. You like her, don't you?' His brother had all the luck. And what did he have?

* * *

Glad to be home, Paul sat at his computer and scanned the page he'd just typed. Since they'd flown in from Portland that morning, he'd made real progress on his story. The characters in his novel became more real each time he wrote about them.

Jay had been a good sport. Julie had located some brochures on the local attractions and Jay attacked sight-seeing with gusto. This afternoon, he'd visited the White House of the Confederacy and the Virginia Museum of Art.

His twin appeared to like Richmond, even hinted that he might like to stay in the area. Paul had mixed emotions about that, though he liked to be with Jay.

As he straightened up his desk, Paul noticed the books on one bookshelf were slightly out of order. When did that happen? It couldn't have been Jay since there was no reason for him to visit the study. Besides, he preferred the large screen television in the living room. And Julie had left his mail and papers in the foyer, so she wouldn't have come in this room. He tried to think if someone else had been in here and came up with a blank.

His watch told him it was time to stop. Had he worked on the novel all afternoon? He stretched then peeled off his clothes and headed for the shower.

While he dressed, he wondered if he should've asked Jay to go out to dinner with them. When he mentioned their plans, Jay seemed content to stay home.

Downstairs, he found his guest sprawled on the sofa, absorbed in the sports news. The litter Jay'd dropped, empty soda cans, papers, and his shoes, reminded Paul that his twin was still a big messy kid. One he was fond of, he had to admit.

'There's a chicken-and-wild rice casserole in the refrigerator. Just pop it in a 350 degree oven for thirty minutes.' Feeling a little guilty, he asked, 'Are you sure you don't want to come with us?'

'Nope, and take your time. I can entertain myself.' Jay grinned and turned back to his program. He seemed to have bonded with the wide-screen television set.

The doorbell alerted Paul to Julie's arrival. She stepped inside, and he noticed she'd discarded her usual jeans and sweater in favor of a becoming short purple dress. The soft silk material clung to her body, accentuated her firm breasts and sleek torso.

His soft whistle of appreciation brought a blush to her cheeks. Glancing in Jay's direction, Paul noticed a peculiar expression slide across his brother's face. Then his twin smiled, waved goodbye, and turned back to his program.

On the drive to the restaurant, Paul asked her about Jay. 'What do you think of my brother?'

'He seems a nice person . . . ' Julie paused and looked embarrassed, like she was trying to be tactful.

'Well, go on.'

'I was just about to say he's almost like your kid brother. He seems a little immature for thirty,' she admitted.

'Jay's never taken life too seriously.' With an eye on the evening traffic, Paul pulled over to the side of the road and parked the car. 'Let's stop here for a minute.'

Turning off the engine, he unfastened his seat belt and turned to Julie.

'My brother never measured up to our parents' expectations, but I . . . never dreamed things would turn out the way they did.' He stopped and reconsidered what he'd just said. He hadn't meant to badmouth his twin. 'That's not fair to Jay. There was no proof it was his fault. To this day, I still don't know what really happened.'

'You'd better explain.' Julie frowned. 'I don't understand a word you've said.'

For some reason he found himself wanting to tell Julie things he'd never discussed with anyone but Phillips. 'One Saturday morning fifteen years ago, I returned home from a friend's home. As I walked down the block to our house, I had no idea our lives were about to change. Nothing was left of our home except a mass of ashes. There'd been a fire during the night and the house was gone.' He stopped, remembering his shock and fear that morning.

'That's too bad,' Julie responded.

'Wait, that's not all.' Feeling the old pain sweep over him, Paul held up his hand. 'Our parents died in that fire.'

Another car pulled up beside them and the driver gestured at Paul to see if they needed help. Paul shook his head and the other car sped away.

'That's terrible. I'm so sorry,' Julie patted his arm.

Grateful for her sympathy, he put his hand over hers and gave it a squeeze. 'Jay was in the house yet he escaped. A few days later, he ran away. For years, I've searched for him. It was just good luck that I found him again.'

'It's so sad. You lost your entire family at almost the same time.' Julie sighed.

From the tremble in her words, Paul sensed she was on the brink of tears. He hadn't meant to tell her. He'd just wanted to explain about his brother. Reaching across the car, he put his hand on hers. 'No more gloomy topics tonight, I promise.' Then, words he hadn't planned slid out of his mouth. 'Why don't we talk about the two of us?'

'Everything's so unsettled.' Julie sounded unsure, edgy. 'You have to wait for the police to find Sheila so you can go back to work, and there's your book. Also, I may not be around much longer. If I can't find a job in Richmond, I'm going back to Washington.'

His heart sank at the idea she might leave. 'I'm sure you can find something in Richmond,' he suggested. As bright and personable as Julie was, he was sure some company would want to hire her. In an attempt to encourage her, he asked, 'Have you tried a personnel agency?'

'No, but I probably should.'

'Let me say just one more thing.'

'Go ahead.'

'I think you're a special lady.' Paul leaned toward her, he slanted his mouth over hers and kissed her. Julie returned the kiss. Her lips opened and enticed him. He inhaled the fragrance of jasmine and roses and wished they weren't in the front seat of his BMW. He wanted to hold her in his arms. With reluctance, he ended the kiss.

'Let's hope we resolve our problems soon. Then, we'll continue this conversation. All right?' One way or another, he'd keep Julie in town. That would give him time to sort out his feelings. He knew he wanted her yet it was more than sexual attraction. He wanted to protect her, care for her.

'I'll look forward to it. Her voice was husky with emotion.'

Paul started the car and they continued on their way.

* * *

Julie watched Paul's strong profile during the drive to the restaurant. By his matter-of-fact expression, you'd think nothing had happened between them a few moments ago.

Maybe their kiss hadn't shaken him, but she'd felt the impact down to her toes.

In her brain, alarms sounded, warned her not to get in over her head. What would she have done if he wanted to continue their love-making in a more private place?

Take it easy, an inner voice warned her. You need to keep your mind on the case. You're a police detective on an assignment.

Then, Paul turned his head, his mouth curved into a smile. 'You're so quiet. Deep thoughts?'

Smiling back at him, she replied. 'Not really.'

Julie again reviewed the case. There was no evidence so far linking Paul to his wife's disappearance, just one singed belt buckle. She'd overreacted the day she'd found the buckle. It wasn't what you'd call evidence.

What she couldn't understand was why Paul's mother-in-law wanted to hurt him. Julie wished she could interview Dorothy Turner. That was out of the question since it would blow her cover.

Her next move would be to talk to Francoise, the woman whose name was listed in Paul's wife's address book. She'd found Francoise had been Sheila's hairdresser at a small, exclusive saloon on River Road in the fashionable West End of the city.

Paul opened her car door outside the restaurant and Julie studied his features. He was either the innocent victim of a deranged woman's fantasies or a clever monster in disguise. Her job was to find out which.

7

Jay finished his supper an hour after Julie and Paul departed for the restaurant. At home in NYC, he would've left his dishes on the table until he felt like washing them. But things were different here. If he messed up Paul's neat, spotless house, his brother would be annoyed, so he stacked his dishes in the dishwasher, then wandered into the living room and turned on the television. The phone rang.

'Damn it.' He stomped back into the kitchen and picked up the receiver. 'Yeah?'

'We haven't talked for awhile but I've been thinking about you,' an unidentified woman's harsh voice told him. 'Here's a word of advice. Enjoy life while you can. You'll be in prison before you know it.'

'What? You've got the wrong number, lady.' You just never knew what fruitcake would call nowadays with all of the crazies running around loose.

'Idiot,' the woman muttered. 'It's Dorothy.'

'Dorothy Turner?' Now Jay began to understand. He was talking to Paul's mother-in-law. His brother had told him she'd called to harrass him since Sheila disappeared. Each time she accused Paul of doing away with her step-daughter.

'As if you didn't know.'

'I see. Well, you've reached the right number, but this's Jay Arnold, Paul's brother. We've never met, but Paul has mentioned you.' That was the truth. Paul despised the old witch.

'He does?' As if in response to Jay's friendly manner, her tone became more pleasant and she asked, 'What does he say about me?'

'Just that you're a horse-faced old bitch who ought to be put away somewhere and forgotten.'

'You . . . you . . . you creep.' Her throaty voice shook with rage. 'You're the one who should be put away. And this time, don't expect your dear brother to visit you because he'll be in prison for life.' She slammed the phone down so hard, Jay's ear hurt.

Pleased to have told off the woman who'd caused Paul so much grief, Jay sauntered back to the living room and hit the sound button on the remote control. In the movie, Cary Grant was charming the beautiful Grace Kelly. Slouched on the sofa, Jay lost himself in the love story.

Two hours later, a car stopped outside. Through the half-open front blinds, Jay caught a glimpse of Paul escorting Julie to her door. A few minutes later, a key turned in the front lock and his brother stepped inside. Did Paul kiss Julie? All of a sudden, he wished he had someone special himself. Once he had, he thought. Sophia, Tonio's raven-haired daughter had encouraged him then broken his heart.

Not wanting to appear too interested, Jay kept his gaze glued to the television screen. 'Did ya have a good time?'

'We certainly did. I hope you weren't bored.' Paul strode into the kitchen and opened the refrigerator door. A bottle cap popped. 'Want a beer?'

'No, thanks.' Jay remembered his news. 'Well, the Dragon Lady won't bother you again.'

'What? What did you say?' Irritation crept into Paul's words as he stood in the doorway.

'Dorothy Turner called to let you know you'll be in prison before long.' Jay chuckled. 'She thought she was talking to you. I explained who I was and told her what you'd said about her.'

'What did you tell her?' Paul frowned.

'That you think she's a horse-faced old bitch.'

'Sure you did.' Paul smiled uneasily.

'I also mentioned she should be put away

somewhere no one will have to bother with her.'

'Is this a joke? You're kidding, aren't you?' A skeptical expression crossed Paul's face.

'Would I kid you about something like that? Take my word for it, Bro. That's one dame who won't bother you anymore.' What was the matter with his twin? Jay'd expected Paul to roar with laughter at his news and thump him on the back.

'The hell she won't.' Paul growled. 'Now she'll want to crucify me. Before, she just wanted to put me in jail for life. Why don't you mind your own business?'

'You can't be serious.' Here he'd thought Paul would be pleased he'd gotten rid of Dorothy. Disappointment flooded him as Jay stood and stared at his brother. 'What can she do except make nasty phone calls?'

'I don't know, but you can be sure she'll come up with something. This could cost me my job.' Paul plowed his fingers through his hair then glared at him. 'Just don't try to help me anymore. All right? I've got enough problems without your interference.'

'Sorry, Bro. All I wanted was to get the old broad off your back.'

'Yeah.' Paul turned and marched upstairs.

Jay turned off the television and slumped into the sofa. Hurt by Paul's angry words, he punched a sofa cushion. He'd sure messed up this time. Paul must wish he'd never laid eyes on him.

* * *

Next morning, Julie stepped outside for the morning paper and found Jay huddled on her front steps. His pained expression and hunched shoulders startled her. 'You look terrible. What's wrong?'

'Paul's furious because of something I did. I apologized last night, but he stormed out of the room.'

'What did you do?'

'Nothing much, I just told off someone who bothered him,' Jay said.

Julie creased her brow. 'Who are you referring to?'

'Paul's mother-in-law Dorothy.'

'Is he concerned about the repercussions?' Paul had told her about Dorothy and her vicious attacks. Julie began to see the picture. She could understand why Paul might be upset.

'Yeah. I told him he worries too much and all he said was 'You don't know Dorothy.''

Julie smiled, sympathetically, but said nothing. According to Paul, Dorothy Turner was a formidable foe and not one you should underestimate. 'Let's get some coffee and go out in my backyard. The garden will cheer you up.'

'Okay.' He shrugged and followed her to the kitchen. She poured them each a mug of coffee then led him out the back door.

Julie gave Jay time to unwind. The lovely view of flowers swaying in the breeze and a mourning dove's soft call from a nearby tree soothed her. Perhaps it'd help Jay.

A few minutes later she caught him staring overhead. 'Why are you looking at the sky?'

'I just wanted to make sure Dorothy's not flying over us on her broom.' His mouth turned up in an impish smile.

Julie grinned, pleased to see him more his old quirky self.

Julie and Jay strolled together down the back yard, surveying the rows of daffodils and tulips along the wrought iron fence. She laughed at one of his silly jokes.

Paul's kitchen door opened. He stepped out onto the back porch and called, 'Hello.'

They both turned in his direction and Julie waved. 'Come over and have breakfast. I'm heating an apple streusel and it'll be ready in ten minutes.'

'That's the best offer I've had today. Make that fifteen minutes and I'll be there.'

He must have taken the world's fastest

shower since in less than fifteen minutes, he reappeared in Julie's back yard, wearing jeans and a sweatshirt, his hair wet and slicked back.

Paul held out his hand to Jay. 'I'm sorry. It wasn't wise for you to insult Dorothy, but I overreacted. You don't want to confront her. She's treacheous.'

Beaming with relief, Jay shook his hand. 'Sorry. I didn't mean to interfere, but when she talked about you in prison, I just saw red.'

Let's go inside,' Julie said. This was more like it. It troubled her to see them at odds. They both appeared to be nice guys, though she found Paul much more appealing. Jay reminded her of a big kid compared to his brother. Julie herded them into the kitchen then gestured toward the kitchen table.

'Sit down.' As she opened her oven, a whiff of apple-cinnamon fragrance escaped. She carried the streusel to the table then poured them each a glass of orange juice. 'Coffee?'

'Yes, please.' Paul eased into one of the chairs and Jay took a seat across the table.

While she glided about the room, she felt Paul's gaze on her. Memories of the previous night came to mind. Those kisses . . . She recalled how tender he'd been and how good it felt to be in his arms. At that moment, she wished they could be alone together. Maybe he'd kiss her again. Glancing his way, her gaze locked with his. Paul smiled as if he had read her mind then took a sip of juice.

Jay laid down his fork and frowned.

'What now?' Paul cocked an eyebrow.

'I keep thinking about that telephone conversation last night.' Jay fidgeted with his napkin, folded and unfolded it.

'Don't brood,' Paul ordered his brother. From his tone, it was apparent he'd grown weary of the topic. Paul passed the coffee cake to Julie. 'She's just a crazy, malicious woman.'

'You're right about that. But I just remembered something. Dorothy said I should be put away, and this time you won't be able to visit me since you'll be in prison. How did she know about me?' Worry covered Jay's face.

'You must have misunderstood what she said,' Paul replied.

Jay shook his head. 'No, I don't think so.'

'No one knows about that except the two of us and Doctor Phillips.' Paul frowned. In an aside to Julie, he commented, 'I don't guess I've mentioned the doctor to you, but he's an old family friend.' Paul redirected his attention to Jay. 'Do you mind if I tell Julie?'

'No, go ahead.' Jay nodded in agreement.

Paul elaborated on what he'd told her the previous evening. 'Jay had a nervous breakdown and spent a few weeks in a psychiatric facility in Portland after our parents died in the fire that destroyed our home.'

'I see.' What a terrible ordeal. Her heart went out to them both. 'If you don't mind my asking, what caused the fire?'

'The police were never able to determine the exact cause, maybe a lit cigarette left in the living room,' Paul said. 'Both Dad and Jay smoked.'

'I try hard to remember that night yet all I can recall is going upstairs to bed.' Jay responded, a worried expression on his features. 'What I can't figure out is how Dorothy could know about it.'

'You must have misunderstood what she said.' Paul reassured his brother. 'That's the only logical explanation.'

'I guess so.' Jay agreed. He leaned over and fed Misty a piece of coffee cake. Julie's Schnauzer had stationed herself by Jay's chair since he slipped her treats.

Paul shrugged. 'Let's find another topic of conversation. Anything would be more pleasant.'

⋆ ⋆ ⋆

Jon Phillips yawned into the phone. Squinting, he eyed the clock radio on his nightstand.

'It's working, just like you said it would,'

his younger sister's elated voice prattled into his ear.

'What? Of course. Did you have any doubt?' Sis sure had a lousy sense of timing. He'd drank his share of champagne at a recepion following a performance of the Portland Symphony the previous night and it'd been late when he crawled into bed.

'No. And soon you and I will both have what we want.' She paused then added, 'What would I ever do without you?'

'That's a good question.' He yawned again. What indeed? Without him, she'd still be trying to figure how to get her sticky fingers on Sheila's estate. 'If that's all you wanted, let me go back to sleep. It's just six a.m. here.'

'Oh, all right.' Her voice drooped as if she'd expected to have a long chat. 'By the way, I called Paul last night.'

Phillips' senses went on alert. 'Really? And how is he?'

'He wasn't home so I talked to his brother, Jay. Did you know he's staying with Paul now?'

'No, I didn't.' Phillips' nerves tensed. So Paul and Jay had found each other. He'd tried his damnest to keep them apart. But had they healed the rift that separated them?

'Did you enjoy talking to Jay?'

'Don't be absurd.' She sniffed. 'The little

punk was downright nasty to me.'

'What did you expect? You want the police to arrest Paul.'

'I told John Meenan that Paul insulted me on the phone last night. He would have if he'd had the chance,' she rationalized. 'Meenan's calling an emergency meeting so the partners can decide what to do about Paul's horrible behavior.'

'Oh, I see. Poor Paul gets blamed for everything, does he?' Phillips chuckled. Why not? The sooner Paul is out of the picture, the better. 'The wheels are in motion now, Sis. Sit back and enjoy the ride. I'll talk to you later.'

So the brothers were together. And what had Jay told Paul about his memories of that night? Better still, had Jay remembered anything else? He better find out.

Dialing Paul's number, Phillips was pleased when Paul answered. 'Well, hello. Sorry I missed you in Portland, Paul. Please let me express my condolences on your aunt's death. She was a fine woman.'

'Thanks.'

Paul was cool, too cool. Some things never changed. Even as a child, the boy had made him feel uneasy. 'What's the matter?'

'Jay says you've always known how to get in touch with him. How could you lie to me all of his time, Phillips?'

'It wasn't easy since I knew how much you wanted to find your brother. But before you pass judgement, let me explain. For years, Jay was angry with you, so angry in fact that I was afraid to bring the two of you together. He might have harmed you.' He sighed, waited for his words to sink in.

'You believed he'd get violent?' Paul sounded unsure.

'Yes, though he appears to have mellowed in the last few months. At least, I hope he has. His new therapist seems to have helped him. In fact, if you hadn't found each other on your own, I would have brought you together soon,' Phillips said.

'Is that the truth?' Paul's tone turned a little warmer.

'I swear it.' He did his best to sound sincere.

'All right, I guess I believe you.'

'Great. Now for the other reason I called. In a couple of days, I'll be in Washington D.C. for a consultation. Afterwards, I'd like to fly down to see you before I return to Portland.' The lies slid smooth as silk off his lips. He could cancel a couple of appointments and be in Richmond the next day, long before Paul expected him. Maybe he'd rent a car at the Richmond airport and watch Paul and Jay without their knowledge before they expected him. It was fascinating to catch others unawares.

'Jay came back with me from Portland so you'll be able to see both of us.' Paul volunteered but didn't sound enthusiastic.

'That's wonderful,' he said. 'Would you mind making me a hotel reservation somewhere near your house? With my busy schedule, this will have to be a short visit, and I hate to waste time driving back and forth.'

'This place's is still full of boxes, but if you don't mind camping out in one of the spare bedrooms . . . '

'That'll be fine. Thanks for the offer.' Phillips pounced on the reluctant invitation. See you soon.' He hung up fast before Paul could reconsider. Now he could observe how things were between the two brothers and how much Jay had remembered. A new scheme began to form in his brain.

* * *

Right before noon, Julie drove across town to the beauty salon Sheila had frequented. With its canvas awning and ornate sign, the place looked too pricey for a police detective. Good thing she'd withdrawn extra funds from the bank. If the BMWs, Mercedes, and Jaguars outside the sylish glass and chrome shop were any indication, the clientelle was well-heeled. With extreme care, Julie nosed her old car into a slot between a metallic green BMW and a sleek black Mercedes. Smoothing the cotton knit top over her faded jeans, she entered the salon.

The receptionist, a pencil thin redhead in a silver smock and black tights, escorted her to a stall larger than the others at the rear of the salon.

'Bon Jour.' A tiny brunette of indeterminate age sent Julie a speculative glance. The hairdresser's melodic accent evoked memories of Julie's college vacation in Paris.

'Ah, good morning.' So this was Sheila's hairdresser.

Francoise motioned Julie to a chair. As soon as she was draped, the hairdresser touched Julie's braid. 'May I?'

Julie nodded her consent. The Frenchwoman untied Julie's braid and ran her fingers through her hair, fluffing it, pulling it away from her face. She rotated the chair and studied Julie's head at various angles.

The older woman's keen gaze was unnerving. It was almost as if she could see right through Julie's hair, even her skull, to the real reason she'd come to the shop.

'How did you hear about me, mademoiselle?' Francoise asked.

'As a matter of fact, from a lady ahead of me in the checkout line at the grocery store.' Julie tried to sound convincing. Then inspiration took hold. The Parisian appeared haughty. A little flattery wouldn't hurt. 'I heard the woman tell her friend you're the best,' Julie added, 'and I hoped you could do something with my hair.'

The eagle sharp eyes blinked. In the mirror, Julie saw a less guarded expression flitter across Francoise's features.

'Of course. You do have lots of hair. That's good, but that braid's too severe.' She played with Julie's hair. 'You must think of your hair as your crowning glory.'

Julie nodded, as if absorbing all of the Parisian's words of wisdom.

'Young women don't realize how much long, flowing hair appeals to men.' The Parisian eyed Julie. 'You do not want to cut off all of this,' she ran her fingers through Julie's hair then let it cascade to her shoulders.

'Oh, no.' Julie was ready to agree to anything to keep in Francoise's good graces.

'All right, then. I will shape it and give you a new look.' Francoise cocked her head like a wise old owl. 'The color could be a little improved, nothing drastic, just a slight change.'

By the time Julie left the shop, she was two hundred dollars poorer, but it was money well spent. Her appointment with Francoise had paid off in more than a new hairdo.

'Does your family live in Richmond?' Francoise inquired while she combed out Julie's hair.

'Not anymore.' Tears welled in Julie's eyes. 'My father died a few weeks ago so I'm all alone.' She bit her lip. That wasn't quite true since there was Paul. His kisses and words last night had made her feel he cared. It wouldn't be hard to fall for him, if circumstances were different.

'It's not good to live on your own.' The Frenchwoman patted her on the the shoulder and offered a box of tissues. Pointing her finger at her own chest, Francoise declared, 'I share my home with Cosette, Madeleine, and Therese, so I'm never alone.'

'It must be wonderful to have three sisters. I'm an only child,' Julie replied.

'Mais non, child.' The woman's light laugh pealed like a bell. 'Cosette, Madeleine and Therese are my Siamese cats.'

Julie chuckled at her faux pas. 'Living on my own bothers me. Even with security locks on the doors, I still feel a little uneasy. There's so much crime everywhere, it's frightening. Every day, the paper's full of reports of robberies, rape, even murder.' She frowned as if something had just occurred to her. 'By the way, did they ever find the woman architect who disappeared?'

'Sheila Turner? No, they never found her. Such a charming young woman. And a client of mine.' Francoise's face hardened. 'That man, that horrible man. He's still loose. God only knows what he did with poor Sheila.'

'Horrible man?' Julie hoped she wasn't referring to Paul.

'Oui, Paul Martin. A relative of hers told me Sheila and her husband had terrible fights.' Francoise shuddered. 'The day she disappeared, Sheila came in, sat where you are now. I could tell she was frightened.'

The Parisian leaned over Julie. 'If Sheila's dead, he killed her,' she announced. Her voice was husky with emotion.

Julie sucked in her breath. Another person who believed Paul was guilty. How many people in Richmond felt the same way? A small shadow of doubt reappeared from the dark recesses of her mind. Her heart counterattacked and reassured her of Paul's innocence.

Gripping the arms of her chair, she stared at the hairdresser in the mirror, then asked in a cool tone, 'Do you have any proof of that? If so, you'd better call the police.'

'Proof? Mais non,' Francoise admitted. 'But the person who told me is certain he's guilty, and she's an important woman.'

'Be careful who you call guilty,' Julie advised the hairdresser. 'In the United States, a person can get sued for making false statements without proof.'

'Yes, yes.' The hairdresser looked nervous. 'I will take your advice and say no more.'

* * *

Paul stepped into his kitchen later that afternoon. As he walked across the room, the flashing light on the answering machine caught his attention. His finger punched replay and he heard the Managing Director's voice.

'This is John Meenan. Be in my office at four o'clock.' From Meenan's brusque tone, Paul surmised the Managing Director didn't have good news. His stomach muscles knotted.

Four o'clock that afternoon, Paul smoothed his tie and wiped his clammy hands on a pocket handkerchief. 'Well, here goes,' he muttered then locked his car and headed for the Managing Director's office. Tension rippled through him. The Roman gladiators must have felt this way entering the arena.

Meenan's secretary typed away at her desk. Without an upward glance, she nodded toward her boss's closed door. 'You're expected. Go in.'

What a change from the pleasant older woman who'd brought him home-baked cookies and shown him pictures of her grandbabies.

The Managing Director sat at his desk. Meenan's expression couldn't have been bleaker at a family member's funeral.

'Do you know why I wanted to see you?'

Trying to appear calm, Paul responded. 'I can't say that I do.' He smelled trouble.

Meenan waved him to a chair then got right to the point. 'You called Mrs. Turner last night and frightened her.'

So that was what this was all about. Jay's insults must have cut to the quick. Paul held up a hand. 'Wait a minute. It wasn't that way at all. She — '

'No, you wait a minute.' Meenan interrupted him mid-sentence. His voice rose an octave, something that just happened when he was stressed. 'Have you lost your mind? I expected better from you. To think that I've believed in you, even defended you against Mrs. Turner's accusations.'

Paul jumped up, towering over the other man and hit the desk with his fist.

Meenan flinched. A nervous muscle twitched in his cheek. 'Take it easy. Please sit down. We can discuss this man to man, can't we?' He tugged on his tie as if it were all of a sudden too tight.

Paul stared, unable to believe his eyes. Was Meenan afraid of him? Did Dorothy lie so well that even the Managing Director believed he was dangerous? Resuming his chair, he forced himself to speak in a calm manner, though his heart hammered against his chest. 'Sorry, I didn't mean to lose my temper.' He leaned forward. 'Dorothy didn't tell the truth. She called my home last night while I was away. My brother answered the phone.'

'Brother?' Meenan's mouth dropped open. 'You never mentioned having a brother.'

'There wasn't any reason to mention him. We've just reconciled after not seeing each other for years.'

'Yes, yes, go on.'

'Like I said before, my brother Jay answered the phone. Dorothy's called me several times since Sheila disappeared to accuse me of doing away with her step-daughter.' Paul sighed, 'Last night, she informed Jay that I'll be in prison soon. He lost his temper and told her off. That's why she's upset. I'll be happy to apologize if you think she'll speak to me.'

Meenan shook his head. 'It's not just about last night. Mrs. Turner wants you out of the firm. She's convinced our board members that the police consider you a suspect in Sheila's disappearance. As a well-respected law firm, we can't tolerate that kind of publicity. This morning we had an emergency meeting to discuss you.'

This was what he'd feared. Dorothy had retaliated. Paul took a deep breath and asked again, 'Do you think it would help for me to apologize to her?'

'That I can't say, though you should try to make amends.' Concern etched the wrinkles on Meenan's face and regret crept into his voice. 'There's no easy way to say this. I'm sorry, but you're terminated.'

Paul's shoulders sagged for a moment then he straightened. Too proud to reveal his pain, he spoke in a neutral tone. 'It will take me a few minutes to clear out my office.'

Once in his car, he sat behind the steering wheel, confused and unsure. What should he do? His instincts told him reconciliation was the last thing Dorothy wanted. It dawned on him that she'd always disliked him, though her animosity had skyrocketed since Sheila vanished.

Now Dorothy would hurt him any way she

could. A cold sweat broke out on his forehead. If her lies reached the right ears, he'd be blackballed at all of the law firms in the city.

Paul punched in her telephone number on his cell phone and found the line busy. The old witch must be on the phone, spreading her lies about him.

His mind awhirl, Paul turned on the ignition and started for home, then he clenched his jaw. It was time he struck back, put her on the defensive. At the first intersection, he made a u-turn and headed south.

On the other side of the James River, he drove past several developments. The houses became more impressive, the further south he drove in Chesterfield County.

Paul turned off the highway near Robius and followed a narrow, private road through a forest of pines. At the end of the road, an antebellum mansion stood alone in a clearing, surrounded by old magnolia trees.

A house maid he didn't recognize answered the door. Informing him that her mistress was on the terrace, she led him through the palatial residence.

A gaunt, weatherbeaten blonde in a hot pink and orange jumpsuit reclined on a chaise lounge and supervised a gardener who weeded the flower beds around the terrace. Purple, white and yellow iris bloomed around the terrace then marched down both sides of a stone walk to surround a lily pond. The flowers' pastel colors clashed with their owner's loud outfit.

'Dorothy.'

Startled by his unexpected appearance, she jumped. 'What the hell are you doing here?' Her throaty voice twanged. 'You're the last person I want to see.'

'I've come about last night,' he announced, unperturbed by her hostile behavior. 'My brother told me about your conversation. That's why I'm here.'

'I don't want an apology.' Her voice tightened and her facial expression became harder.

'Good, because you won't get one,' Paul said, still calm. 'What I want is for you to tell me how you found out about Jay's confinement after our parents were killed. Do you have a friend who knew my family?'

'You'd be surprised.' She smirked.

'I didn't really expect you to tell me, but I had to ask. That's all right. Based on everything you've done to hurt me, I can only conclude you were involved in Sheila's disappearance.' He didn't add he intended to prove it. Paul waited for her reaction.

Her face paled with rage and she denied his accusation. 'How dare you? Don't try to pin your crimes on me. You should have considered the consequences before you hurt Sheila.'

'We both know I didn't hurt her.' This conversation was a waste of time. Dorothy wouldn't tell him anything. Paul struggled to stay cool.

She placed her hand over her heart. 'Guilt's written all over your face. Don't try to deny what you've done.'

Then he did just what he'd vowed he wouldn't do — lose his temper. Standing over her, he shook a finger under her nose. 'You're the crazy one. Watch out who you accuse. One day you'll find yourself in deep trouble.'

Dorothy's long red sculptured nails grabbed her designer sunglasses and stuck them on her face. 'Don't you dare come into my home and threaten me. I should call the police this minute and have them arrest you.' She hissed at him.

'Go ahead,' he goaded her. 'Call the police. I need to talk to them about you anyway.'

Dorothy picked up a small cellular phone, punched in a number, then murmured something he couldn't hear. With a sigh, she lay back on the chaise lounge. Moments later, she seemed calmer.

Warning bells rang in his head.

Her voice was more pleasant moments later when she addressed him again. 'This is ridiculous. Why don't you sit down? I'll call for drinks.' Smiling, she patted the chair beside her.

Whoever she called, he bet it was trouble. He'd better get out of there. Fast. 'I don't know what you're up to, but I'm out of here.'

As Paul walked across the yard, a huge hand grabbed his shoulder then spun him around.

'What the hell?' Before he could say another word, he'd been picked up and dumped into the pond. The cold water chilled him, and he sunk like a stone to the bottom. Gasping for air, he surfaced through the roots of water lilies, Dorothy's spiteful cackling ringing in his ears.

8

Julie stood talking to Jay in front of her house, all the while she watched for Paul. According to Jay, Paul had left for an appointment with the managing director of his firm hours ago and hadn't returned.

Relief filled her, seeing Paul's BMW pull into his drive. He remained inside the vehicle for a few moments, and she became concerned. As he opened the car door and stepped out, she stared wide-eyed with shock.

'Were you in an accident?' His clothes were soiled and torn. His face was bruised and he avoided their eyes. Approaching Paul, Julie could see his bloody nose and the cut over his right eye. She winced when he turned to speak to them.

'What in the world happened to you?' Jay called out.

Paul drew a ragged breath and stared hard at his brother. 'They've terminated me.' His voice was shaky. 'Dorothy convinced the firm I've become a liability so they let me go. Meenan suggested it wouldn't do any harm to apologize. I had no intention of doing that.

I drove out to Robius to confront her.'

'I'm sorry,' Jay replied. 'I shouldn't have meddled.'

Paul dabbed at his bloody nose. 'Your insulting Dorothy didn't cause this. She's like a loaded gun with the trigger cocked. Anything would have set her off.'

Disturbed by his appearance, Julie spoke up. 'Do you want us to take you to the emergency room?'

'I don't need a doctor,' he groaned.

Paul looked embarrassed, like he wanted to crawl in a hole and die of shame.

'Okay. Can we do anything for you?'

'No, but thanks. What a day. Since I left home this afternoon, I've lost my job, had a run-in with Dorothy, and her oversized employee hurled me into her lily pond then beat me up.'

Seated on the front steps, Paul removed his shoes then peeled off the socks plastered to his feet. 'What I need is a double scotch, no, make that two, and a hot shower. And after I get cleaned up, I'm going to bed.' He stood and limped inside.

'I've never seen him so upset.' Jay looked worried.

'What a rotten person she must be. I've never laid eyes on the woman, but I hate Dorothy for what she's done to Paul.' Julie simmered with anger. Maybe Paul should press charges.

'Wanna get out of here for awhile?' Jay asked.

'Shouldn't we wait to see if he needs anything? I could get an ice pack for his eye.' She hated to leave Paul by himself.

'Take my word for it, he wants to be left alone, so let's do what he asks. I'll check on him later.' Jay consulted his watch. 'It's almost six o'clock. How about a pizza and the early show? There's an old Kirk Douglas film at the Bellevue.'

'Well, . . . all right. Go and tell Paul our plans so he'll know where we are if he needs us. I'll put Misty in the house and get my purse.' Maybe he'd feel better later.

Over supper at the noisy Italian restaurant, Julie leaned her elbows on the table, straining to hear what Jay said. He seemed pleased to have her to himself tonight. A baby cried in a nearby booth, and teenagers chattered at a table across the crowded room while Jay talked about being a tour guide.

'That's great. I've always wanted to travel, just never had the time.' She encouraged him, though her thoughts were on Paul. He'd insisted they take his car this evening.

Well, since Jay and she were alone, maybe she could use the situation to her advantage.

'Has he talked to you about his wife?' She was curious about Paul's marriage, and not just because of the investigation.

'Not much. From what he says, it was like the marriage from hell. Sheila tried to control Paul then things got worse last winter after her grandfather died and left her his estate. She dangled her inheritance over Paul's head until he filed for divorce.'

'I see.' The fortune hadn't mattered enough that he'd stay in a miserable marriage. He'd just wanted out. Julie was pleased.

Jay pushed himself away from the table. 'I'm full.'

'Same here. Shall we call and see if Paul's all right before the movie?' She felt a little guilty having fun with Paul at home hurt.

'No, he must be asleep by now. I'll look in on him when we get home.' Jay checked the clock on the wall. 'The show starts in fifteen minutes, but the theatre's just down the street.'

At the movie they shared a container of buttered popcorn and watched a young Kirk Douglas. During a romantic scene, Jay slid his arm around her shoulder.

Surprised, Julie sat erect. Why did he do that? Jay was Paul's brother and her friend, she hoped. She'd never encouraged him to think he could be more.

At that moment, she wished Paul, not Jay, sat beside her in the theatre. She would've loved the feel of his arm around her shoulders. Shifting in her seat, away from Jay's arm, Julie stood up.

'Be back in a minute,' she whispered. In the ladies room, she eyed her reflection in the mirror. There was no reason to make a big deal of this. It probably didn't mean anything. Back in the auditorium, she slid down in her seat. Absorbed in the story, Jay paid no attention to her.

The show ended and the movie goers straggled out of the theatre. Jay took her arm walking across the parking lot. No other cars were parked near theirs except a dark SUV with a raised hood. The driver leaned under the hood while he tried to determine what was wrong.

A silent alarm went off in Julie's head. As a police officer, with a sixth sense, a nose for trouble, she smelled a rat. Uneasy, she suggested, 'Let's take the expressway home.'

'Great.' Jay climbed into the passenger seat of the BMW Paul had insisted they take instead of Julie's old Honda which wasn't always reliable.

The BMW entered the expressway and Julie relaxed a bit until she glanced in her rearview mirror. A dark SUV pulled into the freeway behind them. Something clicked in her brain. Another dark SUV. There'd been the disabled one in the theatre parking lot, now this one. Or could it possibly be the same car? A couple of minutes later, the vehicle was still there, two cars behind them.

Frowning, she gripped the steering wheel tighter and glanced over at Jay.

'What's the matter?' He seemed to pick up on her concern.

'It's probably just my imagination, but I could swear that car's following us. Let's find out.' She changed lanes. The other vehicle did the same. A few minutes later, Julie exited the expressway. In the rearview mirror, the car followed, closer.

Speeding was out of the question in a residential neighborhood. Evasive action wasn't. 'I'll take a short cut.'

Julie made a sharp right turn, then a left at the next intersection. She breathed a sigh of relief when the car no longer appeared in her mirror. They reached their block. As they parked in the driveway, the SUV drove up and stopped in front of Paul's house. The car door opened and a tall, thin man got out.

'What on earth?' Julie wished she had her gun. 'Stay in the car. Let's see what that guy's up to.'

With a laugh, Jay threw open the passenger

door. 'It's all right, Julie. It's Uncle Jon.' He climbed out of the BMW and hurried across the lawn, calling to the man. The stranger hugged Jay and patted him on the back.

'Come and meet Uncle Jon, Julie.'

Trailing behind Jay, she couldn't help but hear the pleasure in his voice as he introduced her to Doctor Phillips, the old family friend and self-proclaimed 'uncle' Paul had mentioned.

Her first impression was of a charming, older man. Moments later, his cold smile revealed his jovality was just an act.

'Paul's probably asleep,' Jay informed the new arrival. He summarized what had happened. 'The poor guy's had a lousy day.'

'That's a shame.' The doctor oozed with sympathy.

Julie scolded herself for disliking someone Jay held in such high regard.

'Well, I guess I'd better go inside. Thanks for supper and the movie,' she said.

'Oh, don't let me interrupt your evening, you two.' Doctor Phillips turned to take an overnight bag out of the trunk. 'If you'll give me the key, I'll just let myself in. It's time for the news.'

'Wait a minute, Uncle Jon and I'll go with you.' Jay turned to Julie and gave her a peck on the cheek. 'I enjoyed our evening. See ya tomorrow.'

Jay led the doctor up the front walk. While he unlocked the front door, a comment of Phillips' drifted to Julie's ears.

' . . . a lovely young woman. You don't waste any time, do you?' At that point, the two men stepped inside and closed the door behind them.

Paul had told her Phillips kept Jay and him apart for years. She hoped he hadn't come to cause trouble.

Setting her alarm clock, Julie crawled into bed.

* * *

The alarm clock's shrill ring jolted her awake at eight the next morning. Julie yawned and picked up the phone on her nightstand then punched in a familiar number.

Moments later, her boss's gravelly voice rumbled on the line. 'Edwards.'

'You said to call if I needed to talk about the case,' she reminded him.

'And I meant it. What's happened?'

'I found out that Martin's brother was hospitalized for a nervous breakdown following a fire that killed their parents. According to Martin, just three people knew about it

— a Doctor Phillips, Jay and him, yet Dorothy Turner mentioned it during a telephone conversation with Jay night before last.'

'Maybe Martin told his wife then forgot.' Edwards suggested.

'He swears he hasn't mentioned Jay to anyone in Richmond. Either Jay misunderstood what Dorothy said, or she's got a contact who knew Martin's family,' Julie said.

'Before you go any further, let me remind you that the Turners are one of Richmond's most prominent couples.'

'Fine, but that doesn't explain her remark,' Julie insisted.

'You're right.'

'Could you run a background check on her?'

'Sure, though it's a waste of time. It doesn't make sense that a woman like Mrs. Turner would be involved in a crime.'

'You're probably right. It's just that I haven't found a shred of evidence against Martin so I've got to examine every possible clue. Paul and Jay didn't tell Dorothy. That just leaves this doctor friend of theirs, and there's no way it could have been Phillips. By the way, he turned up last night for a short visit.'

'Where does he live?'

'In Portland, but he was in Washington for a conference then stopped by for a visit with 'his boys.'

'Why do I get the impression you don't like the man?'

'There's no reason for me to dislike him.' But she didn't. The doctor pretended affection for Jay but his cold eyes betrayed him. Her instincts told her Phillips was trouble.

'And where does Mrs. Turner come from?'

'That's a good question. All Martin knows is somewhere out west. That covers a heck of a lot of territory.'

'What's her maiden name?'

'I don't know, sir.'

'I'll see what I can find and get back to you.'

'One more thing,' before he could disconnect, Julie spoke up. 'I could have sworn the doctor's SUV followed us home from the movie last night. That's not possible since he wouldn't have been coming in that direction from the airport. I went back outside after they'd gone in Paul's house and copied his license number. I'm going to call the airport and see if he really rented the car there.'

'Why? There's no reason this old family friend would be involved, is there?'

'Probably not. I just have a strange feeling

about him. Would you humor me, please?'

'Sure. As I recall, your hunches are usually right on target,' he said. 'You've been there over a week and haven't found any evidence against Martin?'

'Nothing. I did meet someone besides Dorothy Turner who thinks he's guilty.'

'Who?'

'Francoise, a hairdresser who does Sheila Turner's hair.'

'I see. Well, I'll have a background check run on Ms. Turner. One more thing, Julie?'

'Sir?' Her muscles tensed. Did he sense she'd gotten involved with Paul? If he did, he'd speak to Chief Hood and she'd be yanked off the case. Her stomach churned with uncertainty.

'Be careful and don't take any unnecessary risks.'

'I won't.' She sighed with relief. For a second, she'd thought he'd ask her personal opinion of Paul Martin.

Chances were good that Richmond Police Chief Hood would call off her investigation of Paul soon. No evidence had turned up, and she didn't anticipate any. However, if she found proof of Paul's guilt, she'd have to turn him in. Paul appeared to be a honest man. He couldn't be that good an actor. Could he? Julie looked up the telephone number for the car rental agency Phillips had used then called their office at the airport. Giving her name and badge number, she explained she wanted to check on a customer. The agency employee complained their computer had been down for days so he couldn't help her.

Julie concluded that she was probably imaging things. She didn't like the doctor, but that didn't mean he was dishonest. She walked downstairs for a cup of hot tea. As she let Misty out the back door, the tulips in her garden bobbed in the breeze and the fresh scent of lilac wafted to her nostrils from a neighbor's yard, luring her outside for a stroll.

'Did ya sleep well?'

She jumped. Glancing at the next yard, she didn't see him at first. 'Where are you?' Though he was Paul's brother, for a second, she wished Jay back in New York City.

'Up here.'

Looking up, she spotted him at an upstairs window.

'Stay there. I'll be right down.' He moved out of sight. A minute later, he stepped out on Paul's back porch.

'Are Paul and Doctor Phillips up yet?'

'Nope.' Jay walked down the porch steps to the yard. 'Uncle Jon was really taken with you, Julie. The funny thing was he thought you were my girlfriend, not Paul's.' From his expression, Julie could tell that pleased Jay.

'I hope you straightened him out.'

'Oh, sure. Paul saw you first. He has all the luck.' His shoulders slumped.

'There must be lots of girls who'd like you if you gave them a chance.' Was he kidding? With Jay, it was hard to say.

'There was one I liked when we were fifteen,' he said.

'What happened?'

'Paul took her away from me. If you don't believe me, you can ask Uncle Jon,' he replied.

'That must have been a long time ago,' Julie reminded him. Did Phillips just happen to remind Jay of an unfortunate episode?

'Yeah, but I haven't forgotten,' he responded, peevishly.

Where did all of this resentment come from? Phillips had just arrived last night and already Jay brooded over something Paul had done fifteen years ago. What was Doctor Phillips up to? Her conscience twinged a bit over spending last evening with Jay though that was ridiculous. Paul and she'd made no commitment to each other so he had no reason to be upset. Besides, he'd been in no condition for company last night.

'That drive home on the expressway was

scary, wasn't it?' Jay scratched his head. 'We both thought we were being followed and it was just Uncle Jon.'

Julie managed a faint smile, though she didn't see anything funny about Phillips. Her instincts warned her to stay alert.

An upstairs window screeched open then a sleepy voice called, 'I heard snoring then found Phillips asleep in the spare room. You should have woke me when he got here.' Paul sounded a little irritable.

He appeared at his window, squinting in the morning light. Seeing Julie, a half-smile drifted across his bruised face. 'You were out cold so we didn't bother you,' Jay replied.

'He told me he was coming, but I expected him today.' Paul frowned.

'Let me get dressed, and I'll come downstairs.'

A few minutes later, they all sat at the kitchen table. Julie winced again at the sight of Paul's bruises. She hoped it didn't hurt him too much. While she sipped a cup of tea, Jay passed around a bag of jelly doughnuts.

Jay went upstairs to check on their house guest. On his return, he spoke to Paul. 'Uncle Jon will be down in a few minutes. He's getting dressed. He forgot to bring his vitamins so he wants me to go with him and direct him to the nearest pharmacy,' Jay informed his brother.

Moments later, Phillips stuck his head into the kitchen. 'We won't be long, Paul. My, you sure got a beating, didn't you?' He smiled like he was pleased.

'It's good to see you too, Phillips,' Paul snapped. Irritation colored his voice.

Jay followed Phillips out of the house. From his excited manner, it was apparent he was delighted Phillips had come.

Paul shook his head. 'Jay's a big kid sometimes. Still, he's my brother and I love him.'

'I like him, too.'

A frown crossed his face. 'As much as you like me?'

'Unless you've lost your vision, that should be obvious.' Smiling, she winked at him.

Paul moved his chair closer to hers. 'I've missed you.'

His deep voice thrilled her, though she tried her best not to show it. 'I haven't been away.'

'No, but the other night seems a long time ago. So much has happened.' His gaze caressed her face. 'Our duenas are gone for awhile. Why don't we take advantage of the opportunity?'

'They just went to the pharmacy.' Her heart beat faster. She should have left when

Jay and Phillips did. Paul was too appealing and the two other men might take their time.

'We have a few minutes.' He turned in his chair, took her face between his hands, and planted a kiss on her lips.

Within moments, she'd pushed aside all thoughts of the case. Closing her eyes, she relaxed, her lips parted, and she submerged herself in the sheer pleasure of being kissed by this special man. His large, warm hands undid her braid and spread her hair loose on her shoulders. Soon, her cheeks were flushed and she felt dizzy. A nagging voice in her head scolded her for not being more resistant to his charms.

She played with his shirt collar then slid her arms around his neck, revelling in his touch. Paul bestowed light, teasing kisses on her ears, her forehead and her throat then his lips reclaimed hers. Her breath accelerated and her pulse shifted to high gear. So much for not getting involved.

Paul slipped his hands under her shirt and rubbed his thumbs over her breasts. Julie moaned with pleasure. Except for the possibility that the two other men might walk in at any time, she didn't think she'd still be dressed. The idea of Paul's stripping off her jeans and shirt excited her. Suspect or not, she wanted him.

Before things went too far, she forced herself to pull away. Paul got to his feet. His uneven breathing and the hungry look of desire in his eyes told her he was as aroused as she.

It was a good thing he had house guests. Paul was addictive, the more she saw him, the more she wanted him. Calming down, she scolded herself for losing control again. This had to stop. To take their minds off their mutual need, she changed the subject. 'How's the book coming?'

'Good, at least I think so. I sure could use a professional opinion.'

'Have you found an agent?'

'No. I guess I could look in the yellow pages. Do you have any ideas?'

'A woman I knew in college has a literary agency. I haven't seen her for years, but I could give her a call.'

'Sure. That'd be great.'

'In fact . . . ' She consulted her watch. 'Give me your telephone directory. I'll call Maxine and you can talk to her.'

'You're fantastic.' Paul's smile charmed her.

Julie had no difficulty locating her friend Maxine. Following a brief introduction, Julie listened while Paul sketched the plot of his story for the agent. At the end of the call, he signalled thumbs up. Maxine had asked for his synopsis and first three chapters.

'I can't thank you enough, Julie,' he said.

'If she sees potential, she'll help you.'

He leaned over and brushed his lips against hers.

'Well, I guess I'd better go.' Tempted to stay, she knew she better not. Julie headed for the door. 'See you later.'

In her kitchen, she sat quietly and thought about Paul. That was another close one. Sooner or later, her feelings for him would override her better judgment. She hoped she could hold out until he was cleared and she'd told him everything. Trying to think of something else, Julie took stock of her groceries. An almost empty Meaty Bone box sent her to Safeway.

On the way home, she drove past the postal service truck that wove its way down their block. Julie toted the bag of groceries to the kitchen to put away her purchases. Jay and the doctor must have come back since Jay sat on Paul's front steps.

A bloodcurdling scream outside startled her and Julie relaxed her grip on a glass jar of ketchup she'd been about to shelve on the refrigerator door. It slipped through her fingers and shattered on the kitchen floor, leaving a thick red puddle mingled with slivers of glass.

Julie darted down the hall and opened the front door, wishing for her police revolver.

A bright eyed Jay appeared on her front porch. He swept her into the foyer then placed his arm around her waist and whirled her in a mad jig across the living room until she broke away. 'What happened?'

9

'Come on, Julie,' Jay nagged and reached for her again.

'Stop.' She put up her hands in protest. Dizzy, she sank onto the sofa. In response, Jay picked up Misty and waltzed around the room with the yipping Schnauzer in his arms.

'That's enough. Why don't you sit down and tell me what's going on?' She stared at Paul's giddy brother. What set him off today?

At last he obeyed. 'I just received a letter from Aunt Louisa. Well, not from her exactly.' His impish expression turned serious. 'She's dead.'

'I know. I sent flowers to the funeral.'

'Her lawyers have contacted me.'

'Well, go on.' Julie waited, trying to be patient.

'The sweet little lady left me her home in Portland.'

'I can tell you're pleased.' Julie cleared her throat. 'This is probably none of my business but what about Paul?'

'I'm sure she remembered him too. There's a letter for Paul in today's mail from the same law firm. I wish you could have met her, Julie.

She was quite a gal.' Jay slanted a glance in her direction. 'I want to celebrate. How's this for starters?' He reached over and bent to kiss her. Julie turned her head and his kiss landed on her cheek instead of her mouth.

She sat still, not wanting to encourage him. Oh, boy. What did she do now? If he had any ideas about the two of them, she'll better straighten him out fast. If she had a choice, she'd pick Paul hands down over his immature brother.

As luck would have it, Paul chose that very moment to walk through the open front door. 'Well, excuse me.' Sarcasm dripped from his words. Turning on his heel, he left.

At first she thought he was kidding, he'd come back and they'd all have a good laugh. Reality sank in when he didn't.

'Now see what you've done.' She glared at Jay then ran to the door and called after Paul. 'Please don't jump to conclusions. Jay was just being a clown.'

'Three's a crowd.' Paul called over his shoulder as he strode across the lawns, went inside his house and closed the front door.

'This is ridiculous,' she exclaimed to no one in particular. Paul had no reason to be jealous of his brother. She'd have to explain what had happened so he'd understand.

Trailing Paul, she rang his doorbell. No

answer came so she opened the door and stepped inside. The sound of clattering dishes reached her ears.

Hurrying to the kitchen, she found Paul in the process of putting away clean dishes. He ignored her until she positioned herself between him and the dishwasher. 'Will you let me explain?'

'What's to explain?' He sputtered, slamming the dishwasher door. 'It's obvious. I walked in on my own brother kissing my girl.'

A brief flutter of joy passed through Julie like a butterfly fluttering from one flower to another. She reached over to touch his arm then asked gently, 'Am I your girl?'

He hesitated, a puzzled expression on his face. 'Well, yes, that is, if you want to be.'

She didn't answer directly, afraid to reveal how much his words pleased her. 'You know right here . . .' Her finger tapped his chest over his heart. 'You know that there was nothing to that kiss. Jay was excited, elated, over some good news. By the way, have you checked your mail?'

'What's my mail got to do with all of this?' Paul cocked an eyebrow as if baffled by the sudden change of topic.

'Why don't you check it and find out?' Julie took Paul by the arm and marched him to the mailbox.

He tore open an official-looking envelope, read in silence for a few minutes then beamed at her. 'I've inherited from Aunt Louisa.'

'What did she leave you?'

'Her antiques and personal effects.'

'That was thoughtful of her.'

'It sure was. I didn't expect anything.' He looked bewildered. 'She took us in after our parents died. But I never thought of an inheritance. This letter says I should call her lawyers in Portland. Where's Jay?' Paul marched across the lawn, headed for Julie's house. Jay stepped out on the porch.

Standing on the sidewalk, Paul looked up at his brother. 'Sorry I blew my stack but I thought . . . '

'That's O.K. I just got carried away for a minute,' Jay explained. 'Did Aunt Louisa leave you anything?'

'Yes, her antiques and personal belongings.'

'She left me her house, Paul. I hope you don't mind.'

'Of course not. It seems right that she'd remember both of us. She knew we loved her.'

'That's for sure,' Jay agreed. 'My letter says to call her lawyer in Portland.'

'So does mine. I'll call.' Paul strode ahead of Jay across the yard to Julie.

'Is everything all right now?' Julie was glad

to see his pleased expression.

'I'm going to get in touch with Aunt Louisa's lawyer. Come along.' He escorted Julie back into his house.

* * *

Paul reached the law firm and asked to be put through to their aunt's lawyer. As he waited, he realized he'd never thought of Aunt Louisa dying. She'd always been there when Jay and he were kids. How long had it been since he'd seen her? Two years at least. He'd meant to visit her more often, but things kept coming up. A few moments later, the lawyer picked up the phone in his office.

'Miss Louisa was quite concerned about your brother,' the lawyer told him. 'You have a profession while your brother's employed in a restaurant.'

'It's all right. You don't need to explain. I know she left him her home. Jay's right here with me,' Paul said. He appreciated Aunt Louisa leaving him anything. Without her comfort and support, he'd have been alone at fifteen, except for Phillips who he'd never liked.

'You both need to come to Portland and decide what you want to do about the house and furnishings,' the lawyer informed him.

'All right. Here, I'm sure you want to speak to Jay, too.' Handing the phone to his twin, Paul led Julie out of the room.

Julie spoke up. 'Do you have savings to carry you over until you get another position?' She sounded concerned.

For a brief moment, Paul revelled in the idea of someone worrying about him. His wife had cared for no one except herself. Soon after they were married, she'd shown her true colors, self-absorption and self-interest.

'Sure. There're some investments and a coin collection. So much has happened the last few weeks, I haven't even thought about the coins. I'll show them to you sometime. They ought to be worth quite a bit.'

'We could sell the house and split the proceeds.' Jay volunteered. He'd followed them to the kitchen.

Touched by his brother's generosity, Paul cleared his throat, momentarily at a loss for words. 'Thanks. I really appreciate your offer, but that won't be necessary. Besides, this's a golden opportunity. You've told me you want to work in the travel industry.'

Jay nodded. 'For years, I've dreamed of being a tour guide and leading groups to faraway, exotic places.' He gave Paul a lopsided grin.

'Then I'll tell you what I'd do,' Paul said. 'Take the required training and get your license to be a travel guide then find a job with an established firm for a few years. With enough experience, you might be able to start your own business.'

'You're right. I'll look into it. Now, about the house, why don't I fly out to Portland and have a realtor list it for sale? I can do an inventory and fax you a list. There might be a few pieces of furniture you'd like to keep. The rest can be sold. That way you can stay home and work on your book,' Jay reminded him.

'If you're sure you don't mind. I do need to prepare some chapters for Maxine.' Jay appeared so eager to help, Paul didn't have the heart to refuse. Besides, if his brother was assistant manager at a busy New York restaurant, he should be able to take care of this business.

Paul took a deep breath, relieved he wouldn't have to leave town again. Besides the book, he wanted to spend more time with Julie. And Sheila still hadn't been found. That worried him more than he let on. As time passed, he'd begun to feel something terrible had happened to her. She'd stayed away too long for this to be just the prank of a spiteful woman.

* * *

Next day Paul met with Maxine, the literary agent. She kept him in her office while she speed-read the first three chapters. She put down his manuscript and gazed over her horned-rim glasses at him.

'Have you had any training?'

'A course or two in high school and college. I wrote for the school literary magazine, had a few short stories published. This is a manuscript I started in college and almost finished. Friends convinced me it was a waste of time.'

'I'm glad you changed your mind. In my opinion, you have a natural talent. Go home and finish your book. How soon can you get me a rough draft?'

His heart leapt in his chest. More than he'd realized, he wanted his book to be a success. Maxine's words of encouragement thrilled him more than any court case he'd ever won. 'How soon do you want it?'

'The standard answer to that question is yesterday. Just get it to me as soon as possible. How about two weeks from today?'

'I'll do my best. Thanks for your confidence. I appreciate your taking the time to read my work.'

Maxine removed her glasses and sat on the

edge of her desk. Without the heavy frames, she was attractive. Not pretty like Julie. Different. Sharper features, shiny black hair worn short in a bob, and alert dark eyes that didn't seem to miss a trick.

'Here's my card. Call me if you hit a snag.' She shook his hand. As Paul left her office, she called after him. 'Tell Julie I'll be in touch. We'll do lunch one day soon.'

On the drive across town, Paul determined to give this book his best shot. Maybe it would attract a publisher. Stranger things had happened. His spirits soared. Dreams did come true sometimes.

Once home, he found Jay on the phone making a plane reservation to Portland. 'Sounds like you're raring to go,' he chuckled when his brother hung up the phone.

'Yeah. I got two seats on a late flight tonight,' Jay said. 'Uncle Jon's going home on the same plane.'

Words rushed out as Paul spoke from his heart. 'Have you considered relocating to Richmond? You can take the courses you need here, I'm sure, then qualify to work as a tour guide for a local travel agency.'

Phillips walked into the room. He must have heard them talking since he jumped right into the conversation. 'Are you sure you want to do that, Jay? Your job and friends are in New York. To pull up roots and move here might be too big an adjustment.'

Paul bit his tongue. Otherwise, he'd have told Phillips to mind his own business. 'But he'll be with his only brother, Phillips. We've missed each other too many years to want to be separated now.' He didn't add it was Phillips' fault they hadn't reconciled years ago. If he'd known where Jay was, he'd have jumped on the next plane to New York.

'Of course.' The psychiatrist said no more. Paul could have throttled him for interfering.

Jay looked at Paul long and hard. 'I didn't think I'd ever hear you say you liked having me around.'

'Yeah? Well, I do. It must be because you're so ugly.' Trying to hide his emotions, Paul joked with his brother. Happiness filled his heart. It would be all right. They were friends again.

'Watch it.' A happy grin spread across Jay's face. 'Who the heck are you calling ugly? Did you look in the mirror this morning? If I'm ugly, you are too, Bro.' Jay punched him in the stomach and they Indian wrestled on the living room rug.

A knock on the front door reminded Paul they were grown men, not kids. With a groan he disengaged himself from his brother.

On his way to the front door, Paul pushed

the hair out of his eyes then tucked in his shirttail. Julie walked in. Her apprehensive glance flickered from Jay to him. 'Who's murdering who? I can hear you two gorillas out in the street.' She laughed, obviously relieved.

'Bro and I were just wrestling.' Jay slapped a hand on Paul's shoulder then excused himself. Whistling, he ran upstairs to pack.

'Phillips and Jay are taking the same plane to Portland tonight,' Paul said. 'Would you like to ride with us to the airport?'

'Sure.' Julie straightened a lamp shade and picked up two throw pillows they'd knocked off the sofa while they roughhoused. 'I guess we won't see Jay again for awhile?'

'Are you kidding? He'll be back as soon as he gets Auntie's house listed and has an appraiser look things over.' Paul hesitated. What would Julie think about Jay's relocation to Richmond?

'Go on.' Julie raised both eyebrows.

'I've invited him to stay with me awhile longer.' He waited for her reaction.

'That's great.' She looked pleased.

⋆ ⋆ ⋆

That evening, Julie and Paul watched Jay's American Airlines Super 80 lift off the runway at Richmond International Airport. As they walked out of the terminal headed for Paul's car, her emotions were mixed. Though thrilled to have some time alone with Paul, she was also wary. How could she keep things from getting out of hand? 'Are you sorry to see the doctor go?'

'To be honest, no,' Paul said.

Julie didn't reply. She didn't know Phillips well. Maybe she'd been mistaken about him. And maybe not.

'I'm going to miss the kid.' Paul glanced her way.

'I'm glad you're more mature. Jay's a sweet guy though a little giddy.' A wave of affection almost overwhelmed her. Needing to touch Paul, she tucked her arm through his.

'That's good to hear.' Once in the car, he leaned over and gave her a light kiss. A shiver of wanting raced through her.

'Thanks, Julie.'

'For what?'

'For being there for me. The last few weeks have been tough. With everything that's happened, it sure helps to have you in my corner.'

Deep inside, she realized how much she wanted to believe in him. But his words made her want to cry. How would he react when he found out who she really was?

While Paul drove west on I-64, her thoughts wandered to her investigation. She'd been in town ten days now. Maybe she ought to pump Corbeille to see if the Richmond Police Chief had said anything about calling off her investigation.

'From what I've heard,' Paul jolted her out of her reverie, 'the job market for lawyers doesn't appear good right now.' Though his tone was casual, she sensed a worried undercurrent.

'Why don't you set up your own practice?'

'I don't think that would work. The local market's saturated with young lawyers who've hung up their shingles.'

'How about your book?'

'As much as I'd like to sell it, that's a long shot,' he said. 'It may be awhile before I have any new income. There's a coin dealer near my office. I think I'll call him and find out what my collection's worth. I might sell the coins if the price's right.' With those words, Paul eased the car into his driveway.

'Well, I've got some things to do around the house.' Julie stepped out of the car.

'This will just take a few minutes. Come in with me.'

Pleased that he wanted her company, she followed him into his small study and watched him kneel, turn back the Oriental carpet by his desk, and dial the safe's combination. Moments later, he lifted a metal box from the floor safe.

'Here they are,' he announced with a flourish. Paul placed the metal box on top of his desk and lifted the lid. A moment later, he swore under his breath. 'They're gone, all of them!'

Surprised, she peered into the container. 'Are you sure you left them in there?'

'Yes. Dead sure.'

'How long has it been since you looked at them?'

'It's been awhile. The last time I counted them was right before . . . ' His words died and a dark cloud of shock and disbelief distorted his features. 'Right before my wife moved out. That was the last time I saw them.'

'Do you think she took them?' From what he'd told her of Sheila, she was a self-centered woman who made her own rules. It was easy to think she could be responsible. Julie felt her temper rise.

'Look here,' Paul pointed to the safe, 'you can see the lock hasn't been forced, and only Sheila and I have the combination. Anyway, the coins are gone.'

'You need to report the theft.'

Paul picked up the phone and punched in

the number for the police. Following the brief call, he replaced the phone in its receiver. 'The officer I spoke to wasn't optimistic. He reminded me there's no way to identify the coins. Even if they're found, gold coins don't have serial numbers like paper money. One dealer gave me a certificate of ownership. That's gone, too. Why would anyone take that? My name's on it.' His troubled glance met hers.

'Was anything else taken?'

'There was nothing in the box except the coins and certificate. Sheila invested some of her own money in this house then we filed for divorce, and I bought out her interest. That used up most of my savings.' Paul managed a lop-sided grin. 'Now I really need to get my book published. Keep your fingers crossed. Who knows? Maybe it'll be a New York Times best-seller.'

Julie admired his spirit. Many people would have sunk into a deep depression in this situation. How much more would he have to endure before it all ended? Patting his arm, she tried to distract him from his troubles. 'Let's go out to dinner tonight, my treat.'

'Thanks, but I better work on the book.'

'All right. I'll talk to you tomorrow.' Their lips touched lightly, leaving her hungry for more, but he was preoccupied with what had happened and seemed to want to be alone. Perplexed, she let herself out the front door. It didn't make sense. Sheila was a wealthy woman. Why would she steal from Paul?

As a police officer, Julie tried to think of some way to help him. A quick call to Corbeille didn't raise her hopes.

'I'm sorry, Taylor, but as you say, the safe wasn't forced. Does Martin know when the coins might have been stolen?'

'Not really. He did remember looking at them before his wife moved out. That was the last time he recalls seeing them.

'Maybe he hid them somewhere else in the house and forgot where he stashed them,' Corbeille suggested.

'Would you, if they were your coins?' She shook her head then realized her partner couldn't see her and felt foolish. 'It's possible Sheila took them to get back at Paul for filing for divorce. Maybe she'll have some answers when we find her.' As she hung up the phone, a dark thought whispered in the back of Julie's mind, suggesting another answer. Paul could have staged the theft himself.

* * *

All night Paul plugged away on his story. At daybreak, he rubbed his burning eyes and saved his work. Turning off the word processor, he stumbled to bed.

Two hours later, a ringing jerked him into consciousness. He fumbled with the alarm clock before he realized it was the phone. 'Hello.'

'You sound terrible,' Julie replied. 'Did you sleep?'

'Not much, but the story's coming.'

'Great. Just don't kill yourself doing it. You've got thirty minutes. Get dressed and I'll treat you to brunch.'

He considered his situation while standing in the shower. Things could be worse. Julie had come into his life. He'd do his best on the book so she'd be proud of him. Who knows? Maybe the book would sell.

Emerging from the shower, he shaved then dressed in khakis and a sports shirt and walked out of his front door. Julie stood by her car, lovely as a picture in a short floral dress, pearls adorned her throat and ear lobes.

His muscles tightened with desire and he felt the old yearning. He'd like nothing better than to make love to her. Instinct told him to take it slow. Otherwise, he might scare her away.

Sauntering over to Julie, he kissed her on the lips. One kiss wasn't enough, so he kissed her again. 'Not every guy has a beautiful woman to take him to brunch.'

Her lips curved into a smile. 'You needed a break. Even aspiring world-class novelists have to eat once in a while. Let's go for a drive in the country after brunch. It's a beautiful day. Then you can get back to work.' Taking local streets, she drove them to Du Jour, a small French bakery-cafe in the West End.

Fluffy omelets, almond croissants fresh from the oven, and tangy orange juice revived Paul. 'At the rate I'm going, I'll have my rough draft ready for Maxine in a week. Bear with me. I'd much rather be with you.' Her optomism raised his spirits.

'Just come up for air once in a while.' Dabbing at her mouth with her napkin, she asked, 'Any news from Jay yet?'

Paul shook his head. 'I just don't buy into Phillips' theory that Jay would want to hurt me,' he told her. Not as close to Phillips as Jay was, he was still disappointed in their old family friend's behavior. He'd been polite to Phillips during his visit, but had no desire to see him again.

'Maybe I should keep my big mouth shut, but Doctor Phillips disturbs me, Paul.'

'I agree, but I can't forbid Jay to see his honorary uncle. My brother's a thirty-year-old man, not a child. Jay will do what he pleases and damn the consequences.' It'd be a relief to have Jay back in Richmond. The whole Phillips matter was a mystery, and he had enough problems already.

Julie turned to him as they left the restaurant. 'You know what? I'd like to see where Dorothy Turner lives. I hear it's a replica of Tara in **Gone With The Wind**.

'I'm not sure that's a good idea. Besides, it's quite a drive.' Paul winced, remembering his last visit to the Turner mansion. He'd avoid Dorothy like the plague.

'Oh, come on. At least let's drive in that direction. I'd like to see her neighborhood,' Julie coaxed him. 'Didn't you say she lives south of Bon Air?'

'Yeah, near a little town called Robius. The Turners bought a rundown antebellum mansion years ago and restored it.'

'Good. Just tell me where to turn.' They left the city and drove past open fields bordered by forests of oaks and pines with an occasional pink or white dogwood. 'It's hard to believe we're just a few miles from Richmond,' she murmured.

Paul pointed to a narrow lane that led off the highway. 'Her place is down that private road but you can't see the house from here because of the woods.'

'Let's just drive by. I've heard it's quite a

place.' Before he could disagree, she turned the steering wheel, aimed for Dorothy Turner's home.

Near the end of the private road, a large, navy blue sedan appeared out of nowhere. Julie grasped the steering wheel with both hands, swerved to avoid a direct hit. The Honda flew off the road and stopped in a field at the foot of a large maple.

10

Julie's pounding heartbeat slowed to normal, then she pried her clammy hands off the steering wheel. A quick glance across the car made her catch her breath. Paul's head lay back against the seat, and his eyes were closed. Dear God, was he hurt? Maybe he'd hit his head. Her heart plummeted. She unbuckled her seat belt and touched his arm. 'Are you all right?'

His eyes opened, and he shook his head before he responded. 'Yeah. How about you?'

'I can move my arms and legs. Guess nothing's broken. That big car came at us from nowhere, almost like the driver wanted to hit us.'

'Your lip's bleeding.' Pulling out his handkerchief, Paul dabbed at her mouth. 'For a minute I thought we were goners.' His worried expression gave away to relief, then his jaw tightened. 'The power of a car that size . . . if the driver wanted to ram us, he could have. That was just a warning.'

'Warning?'

'To stay away from Dorothy.'

'Oh, come on. You don't think that she was the driver.'

'At this point, I wouldn't be surprised. You don't know her. The old bitch is vicious.' Paul's voice seethed with anger. 'One time I saw her slap a servant just because the woman spilled a plate of soup on the dinner table.'

'I'll never understand how people can be so cruel.'

'Me either.' He unfastened his seat belt and opened his car door. 'Let's see if there's any damage.' He stepped out and walked around the car.

Julie got out and examined the Honda. 'Do you see any dents?'

'Nope.' Rising from where he'd knelt beside the car, he informed her, 'we're just lucky we didn't hit that.' He pointed to the large maple inches from where the car had stopped. 'Collision with a tree that size could be lethal. Let's get out of here. Would you like me to drive?'

'No, I'm all right.' Warmth slowly returned to her arms and legs. Julie climbed behind the steering wheel, put the car in reverse, and manuvered it back onto the narrow lane.

They drove home in silence. Glances in the rearview mirror reassured her that the large dark car hadn't found them again. She parked the car in her driveway then glanced at Paul.

With a heavy sigh, he informed her, 'Somehow, she's found out about you.' His gaze locked on her face so intently, she had to look away.

'Found out?' Her conscience twinged and alarm bells went off in her head. If he only knew. She raised both eyebrows. 'Found out what?'

His lips compressed into a narrow, grim line, and his voice grew rough with anxiety. 'Dorothy or someone in her hire must have seen us together. She may even know your license number and the make of your car.'

'But why would she want to hurt me?'

'Because we're friends.' Paul stepped out of the car then leaned inside. 'Better stay away from me,' he warned her, somberly. 'You'll just get hurt.'

Slamming the car door, he crossed the lawn to his house and went inside without a backward look.

Julie slumped in her car seat, feeling rejected. Was he really concerned about her safety or was it something else? Perhaps she was getting too close and it bothered him. Tears formed in her eyes until she remembered the look of dread on his face. No, he really was concerned about her safety.

Apprehension clutched at her. If it had been Dorothy in the dark sedan, she might just be trying to scare Paul. But running them off the road wasn't the act of a law abiding citizen or a rational mind. What would she do next?

Julie wanted to run after him. If Dorothy was as evil as Paul seemed to think, they should band together and prepare for her next move.

But he wanted her to stay away from him so she'd respect his wishes, for a day or so. Unlocking her front door, she went inside. A lot had happened that she didn't yet understand, but she couldn't let him shut her out of his life. The investigation demanded that she keep in regular contact with him. Also, she'd miss him.

All right, she'd leave him alone for a day or two. Maybe he'd miss her and come over. A frigid cold touched her deep inside and Julie shivered. There could be more involved here than a missing woman. What would come next?

* * *

The next morning, Julie eyed Paul's house while she took Misty for a walk. His front windows were dark and empty with no sign of life inside.

A knock resounded through her quiet rooms that afternoon. Opening the door, she found an unshaven, red-eyed Paul.

'I just gave my rough draft to Maxine. She skimmed it and asked for a finished draft. Based on the synopsis and first three chapters, she thinks an editor may be interested.' His hand held out a peace offering, a medley of spring flowers, Dutch iris, daisies, miniature tulips and sprigs of forsythia.

Julie nestled the flowers against her cheek, inhaled their sweet fragrance. She slanted a glance in Paul's direction. 'Thanks. They're lovely.' A small inner voice cautioned her not to build up her hopes. Paul was attracted to her, but he didn't seem to need anyone. The chances of her having a long-term relationship with a man like him were slim at best. He sure wasn't the 'forever' guy of her dreams, the man who'd love and cherish her the rest of their lives.

'Forgive me?' His glance melted her reserve. Warmth rushed through her when his hand reached out to smooth a lock of her hair. If only he were less appealing.

'It's all right. I appreciate your worrying about me, but I'll be fine.' Gazing into his blue eyes, she longed for a kiss. 'Would you like to come in?'

'I wish I could, but I'm on my way to the airport. Jay's flight arrives in an hour.'

'So soon? He's finished his business in Portland?'

'Yeah. Aunt Louisa's lawyer had an antique appraiser do an inventory and Jay faxed me a list. There're one or two pieces I'll keep since they remind me of our great-aunt. An antique dealer will take the rest. Also, the lawyer's located a realtor and arranged to have the house listed.' Checking his watch, Paul asked, 'Would you like to ride to the airport with me?'

With a shake of her head, she declined. Paul tilted up her chin. His finger touched her lips then he walked away.

He'd left without a kiss. Loneliness stood beside her while his green BMW disappeared down the street.

Several hours later, a light tap turned her from the TV dinner she'd just taken out of the microwave. Jay's face peered through the glass panel of her kitchen door, so she turned the security lock and let him in.

As he stood before her, she again noted how much Jay resembled Paul. They had the same build, tall and rangy, the same fair complexion, pale blue eyes and auburn hair.

There the similarity ended since Paul kept his hair shorter and well groomed. His clothes were neat and conservative, appropriate for a young lawyer. Jay wore his hair in a ponytail and preferred scruffy sweatshirts and shabby jeans. He was fun to be with but immature, with his constant barrage of jokes and his fascination with movie stars.

She caught him examining the aluminum package on her plate.

'Hey, don't eat that stuff. Paul sent me to invite you for supper.' Hitching his hands under his belt, he drawled, 'Now come along, little lady, or I'll have to throw ya over my saddle.'

Amazed at how he absorbed the persona of the old movies he watched on television, she ventured a guess, 'John Wayne?'

'How can you tell?' He responded in a normal voice.

It was almost like having a kid brother. 'As a matter of fact, I'd be delighted to have supper with you and Paul.' Picking up her purse, she left the TV dinner on the counter and led Jay out of the house. It would be pleasant to spend the evening with Paul, even if Jay was there.

Later, Jay offered to clean up the dishes. Julie stood to help but Paul shook his head. He cleared his throat and sent a warm glance her way. 'Would you look over my manuscript?'

Flattered that he wanted her comments, she nodded and followed him to his small, bookshelf-lined study. The minute the door was closed, Paul took her in his arms. Julie snuggled against him, the fragrance of his cologne tantalized her. He planted a light kiss on her forehead then tightened his embrace. Her legs turned rubbery as his lips descended and took hers.

She sank into his slow, deep kisses, his tongue explored her mouth, teasing her. Hungry for more, she pressed her body against his and wrapped her arms around his neck. His touch was magical, evoked a burning desire to submerge herself in him. She began to tremble and there was a mild roar in her ears.

At a tap on the door, Paul released her and put his finger over his lips.

'There's dessert on the kitchen table anytime you literary types want it,' Jay called through the closed door. 'I'm going to take a shower and go to bed. It's been a long day.' She heard him whistling a cowboy song as he went upstairs.

'How about that dessert?' Breathless, she slipped out of his embrace, annoyed with herself for succumbing to his charms again.

Paul opened the door and followed her back to the kitchen. Deliberately, Julie picked a chair across the table from where he usually sat. She had to calm down. Their session in his study had shaken her.

Paul served her a dessert plate of chocolate silk pie. As she raised her fork, he spoke.

'Let me feed you,' he offered. Moving his chair beside hers, he gave her a dainty bite of pie and watched her eat it. The rich chocolate and whipped cream melted in her mouth.

'Want some more?' He spoke in a low, husky tone.

'Sure.' She waited for him to give her another taste. Instead, he leaned over and kissed her on the lips.

'Ummmm. You taste good, sweet and chocolatey.' His intimate tone brought a flush to her cheeks.

'Why don't you eat your dessert and I'll eat mine,' she suggested. 'Otherwise, we may be here all evening.'

'That's a thought.' Paul smiled as if he liked the idea. 'We haven't spent a night together yet. Or better still, why don't we go away for the week-end?'

'Just the two of us?'

'Well, I didn't think we'd invite Jay and the neighbors.' He laughed.

The picture of a mass exodus of the block

headed for a romantic interlude brought a grin to her face. Then she became more serious. 'That's probably not a good idea, Paul. We haven't known each other very long.'

She had to draw the line somewhere. Though he aroused feelings she'd never experienced, he was the subject of her investigation.

As a compromise, she offered a suggestion of her own. 'Why don't we spend a day at the beach? It's past spring break but too early for crowds of people.'

'Well, all right,' he agreed without much enthusiasm. 'We could go first thing tomorrow morning.'

He raised her hand to his lips and kissed it. 'How long will it take to drive to the beach?'

'About three hours.' His touch made her nervous with excitement. For a heartbeat, she was tempted to change her mind about the weekend, but the investigation should be concluded before they became intimate.

Maybe by then, Paul would decide he was ready for a long-term relationship. If he wasn't, she'd be long gone. In her heart, she still clung to a girlhood dream of a 'forever guy' and would never settle for a casual affair.

It struck her like a bolt of lightning — she wanted him in her life forever. Stunned, she couldn't speak for a moment. Then she licked dry lips and cleared her throat. 'It's getting late. I better go.' As she stood to leave, the sound of an old western movie wafted downstairs, bringing Jay to mind. 'Will your brother be hurt if you leave almost as soon as he's returned?'

'Heck, no. In case you haven't noticed, he's the last of the romantics. He'll understand.'

* * *

Alone in the house the next morning, Jay entered the garage and located the old bike he'd bought at a sale in the neighborhood. He'd already put on new tires, but the ten-speeder still needed work. Maybe a fresh coat of paint would help. There was a hardware store in the shopping center a mile away.

For the first time in his life he needed a driver's license. Living in New York City since he was fifteen, he, like many of his neighbors, had never learned to drive. Now Paul was busy with his book, and Jay hadn't missed the expression of horror on Julie's face at his hint about driving lessons.

Maybe he'd find an ad in the newspaper. Seated at the kitchen table, he searched the classified section for driver instruction, circled two ads and called. A few minutes later he hung up the phone.

Disappointed, he slumped in his chair. Instructors were available, but he couldn't afford what they charged. The nest egg he'd accumulated at his job in New York City was limited, and his pride wouldn't let him ask his brother for funds. Paul had enough on his plate already.

From his brother's problems, Jay moved on to his own. For his peace of mind, he still must prove, to Paul and to himself, that he hadn't caused their parents' deaths. Jay plowed his hands through his hair. Some information had appeared at Auntie's which he'd wanted to discuss with his brother.

Old correspondence had turned up in a box in Aunt Louisa's attic. He'd recognized his mother's neat handwriting on one envelope addressed to Louisa, dated the year his parents died. As he read the letter, Jay recalled their parents' fights. But he was surprised to find their mother had considered leaving their father then changed her mind. If there was another man, his name was never mentioned. And if their great-aunt knew, she'd taken that secret with her to the grave.

A truck lumbering up the hill outside broke his reverie. Jay stepped outside and glanced down the block. Two doors down, a teenager washed his old jalopy with care.

An idea came to mind, and Jay walked, hands in pockets, down to the youth at work.

'How's it going?'

The boy's glance flickered over him. 'Okay, I guess.'

'This your first car?'

'Yeah, and it's cool. As soon as I get a few bucks, I'll fix it up.'

Even to his untrained eye, Jay could tell the car needed work. The windshield was cracked and there were large dents in the doors. 'I've never had a car.'

'No kidding?' The teen's eyebrows shot up in amazement. 'Man, where've you been? On the moon?'

'In New York City. People don't drive much there. They take cabs or ride the subway.'

'Well, you need wheels to get around Richmond. Unless you want to ride the city buses,' The boy curled his lip in scorn. 'And no cool chick will date you if you don't have your own transportation.'

'I can ace the written part of the driver's license test, but I need to find someone to teach me to drive. The problem is I can't pay a lot,' Jay said. He waited a moment for that information to sink in then asked, 'I don't suppose you'd have a buddy who'd like to pick up a few bucks? It wouldn't take long and I'd pay by the hour.'

A few minutes later, Jay walked back up the hill to Paul's house, mission accomplished. The teen had been more than willing to earn cash for a few lessons.

Jay glanced at the yellow bike that all but screamed for a new coat of paint. He'd fix it up and use it as transportation around the neighborhood until he could get a car of his own. Next, he'd get a temporary job and find out what classes he needed to become a tour guide.

Locking the front door behind him, he steered the bike to the street, hopped on and whizzed down the hill to a hardware store a few blocks away and a can of bright red paint.

An hour later, Jay pedaled back up the hill. Outside the store, his sweet tooth had nagged for chocolate, so he stopped by a drugstore for some peppermint patties. The creamy candy reminded him of his childhood.

Watching Paul with Julie the last few days, he'd resisted the impulse to tease his brother, though he could see Paul was crazy about her. Paul might not admit he needed anyone, yet he did.

Jay shook his head and admitted the closest he'd come to love was with his boss's daughter. One look at her long, black hair, dark, flashing eyes, and pouty red lips, and he'd fallen head over heels. She'd broken his heart the night she eloped with her employer, a wealthy dentist. So much for romance.

Without warning, a vehicle pulled up behind him. As he pedaled hard to get out of the way, a bone jarring blow bounced him through the air. The pavement came up fast.

11

Later that morning, Julie stood by the car while Paul opened the trunk and lifted out the picnic basket and cooler. He turned to her. 'Ready?'

'Sure.' His smile warmed her like a caress, and for a fleeting moment she was caught up in a lovely fantasy. How would it be, making love with him? She jolted back to reality when he slammed the trunk lid and handed her the large blanket he'd brought for the beach.

'It's this way, if my memory doesn't fail me,' she commented, leading him along a planked walkway. With the breeze ruffling her hair, she inhaled the salty fragrance of the Bay. Squinting in the sunshine, Julie could make out a couple of people far down the beach. One of them threw a stick and a large dog soared into the air, retrieving it gracefully. Patches of morning mist still lingered and there was a dream-like quality to the whole scene. She could have been watching a movie, the people and dog seemed so removed from the two of them.

Paul looked around, a pleased smile on his face. 'You said beach, so I imagined a crowd of thirtysomethings with noisy kids, yappy dogs, and a couple of teens with ghetto blasters,' he said.

'It's too early in the season for crowds. Besides, we're way south of the developed area. From here, the sands continue, off and on, all the way to the North Carolina border and the Outer Banks. Dad and I . . . ' Julie stopped, her memories of past times with her father bittersweet. It was still difficult to reminisce.

Drawing a deep breath, she went on. It was painful, but she could talk about him. 'Years ago, Dad and I visited friends down at Duck, North Carolina. Now, that area is developed, even has its own airport, but at that time, it was isolated with just a dirt road connecting Duck to Kitty Hawk. You could walk for miles and not see more than a few people.'

Paul found a sheltered spot by a ridge of sand and set down the picnic basket and cooler, then he helped her spread the blanket on the beach.

'I'm glad you suggested this,' he said, lying back on the blanket. With his eyes on the waves, he added, 'If I came on too strong the other night, I'm sorry.'

What an impossible situation. She yearned to tell him the truth. But she couldn't so she repeated what she'd said earlier. 'Let's take our time and get to know each other.'

Lulled by the warm rays of the sun, the call of the sea gulls, and the beat of the surf on the shore, Julie lay back and closed her eyes. It'd be wonderful if they could just relax and enjoy the day together, but she had a job to do. Raised up on one elbow, she asked, 'Would you tell me about Sheila . . . and Dorothy?'

'I thought we'd gotten away from all that today.' Paul sat up, a scowl crossed his face.

Reaching over, she touched his arm. 'If you don't want to talk about it . . . ' She mustn't push too hard. She didn't want him to feel she was interrogating him.

'It's all right.' Paul lay back down, apparently resigned to pacifying her. 'Shall I tell you how it all began?'

Trying not to look too eager, Julie nodded.

'Sheila and I met at my law school graduation. At the ceremony, Phillips just happened to sit next to Sheila who had attended for a friend in my class. At the end of the ceremonies, Phillips introduced us.'

'What was she like?'

'Unaffected, natural, and sweet was my first impression. We dated for a couple of years then lived together another year before marrying. Once I was her husband, she did a complete about-face. The change was so abrupt, I found it hard to believe. She always had to have her own way and didn't want me around except when she needed an escort or was lonely. And when we were together, she was a control freak.'

'That's too bad,' Julie said. 'I've read somewhere that people who try to control others are insecure themselves. For some reason, they're reassured, being able to control the people in their lives.'

'Maybe so,' Paul responded. 'All I know is things got even worse once she inherited from her grandfather last fall. For some reason, she insisted I be her primary heir. That wasn't my idea, it was hers. Then she held her wealth over my head. I filed for divorce and she moved out.' A pained expression flitted across his face. Paul scooped up sand then let the grains fall from his fingers to the beach.

'It must have been rough for you.' Julie's heart ached for Paul. An unhappy marriage could have made him reluctant to get involved again. 'But people aren't always what they seem, and sometimes it's not their fault.' Like her own situation. He had no idea she was a police officer.

In a way, they were alike, both victims of circumstance. Paul appeared to be caught up in something not of his own making. At the same time, her assignment forced her to lie, though she'd much prefer the truth. A gut feeling told her Dorothy could be the key to this case, so she persisted. 'How about Dorothy? Did you meet her at your graduation, too?'

'No, that came a few weeks later. Sheila invited me to a function at her father's firm at the Denver office. Dorothy was charming, witty and gracious, and it was obvious she liked me. Marcus was more reserved, but I sensed he'd go along with whatever his second wife wanted.'

Paul gazed out to sea for a moment before he went on. 'I heard later that Dorothy sang my praises and even told Sheila I was 'the one' for her. The woman literally danced at our wedding. It was only later that she turned against me. Why she wants to destroy me, I can't say.' He opened a soft drink can and offered it to her.

Julie shook her head. 'But why does she hate you?'

'Who knows?' He shrugged but the look of pain on his face showed his worry. 'That's enough on that topic, don't you think?'

'No more questions. I promise.' Handing him the sun block, she advised, 'better put some of this on your nose. You're getting red.' Windburned, she slipped a light jacket on over her sleeveless top and shorts.

The afternoon glided by. Stimulated by the fresh air, she cleaned her paper plate at lunch.

'Hey, slow down,' he teased. 'This isn't your last meal. Leave a couple of crumbs for the ants.'

With a grin, Julie eyed the picnic basket he'd packed. Her appetite was better recently. Maybe Paul's good cooking was to blame. He shuddered if she even mentioned fast food or TV dinners. 'Did I see homemade brownies in there?'

Paul shook his head and moved the hamper out of her reach. 'Not until we get some exercise. Can I interest you in a run down the beach?'

'Make that a fast walk and you're on. After all of that Smithfield ham and pasta salad, I'm too full to run.'

'All right, let's take a walk.' He pulled her up from the blanket and they strolled by the water, hand in hand. The steady beat of his pulse against hers was hypnotic. She'd heard of magical moments and this was one for her. If only it could last forever.

'How long do you intend to make me wait?' Raising her hand to his lips, Paul kissed the palm. In the sunlight, his pale eyes deepened to sapphire. She didn't reply right away so he continued in a lighter tone. 'Just picture us fifty years from now. I'll pursue you in my wheelchair and you'll fight me off with your cane.'

Her lips curved, but she didn't respond. What could she say, wait until the investigation's over? She hungered to tell him the truth. Soon, perhaps she could.

'When?' He persisted.

She could feel the intensity of his emotions. 'I don't know.' At that moment, she wanted him so much she ached.

'I've got it. This is a test.'

'It's no test. Hey, I thought we were going to have a fun day. Why don't we collect seashells?'

His eyes rolled in mock dismay. 'You want shells? I'll find you shells, lots of them.' He led her to the water's edge and eased her down on the sand. 'Now sit right there.'

Paul arranged shells in neat stacks. 'Here's one. Ah, here's another and another. And look at this nice slimy shell.'

'Stop,' she laughed at his foolishness. 'One or two shells are all I need for a memento.'

'Memento?'

'A souvenir of a lovely day.' Rising, she gave him a light kiss on the lips. He returned the kiss, deepened it, his hot hungry tongue teased hers.

'You won't make me wait forever, will you?'

'No,' she promised and meant what she said.

Alone on the sands, they kissed again and again. Dizzy with desire, she clung to Paul until the world around her vanished and only the two of them remained.

Windblown and sunburned, they drove back to Richmond and parked in Paul's driveway. A resigned sigh escaped her lips. It had been a day she'd never forget.

Paul must have felt the same way since he commented, 'It's too bad this has to end. It's been idylic.' He kissed her cheek. 'Let's go again, before the summer crowds hit the beach.'

With Paul standing beside her, Julie unlocked her front door. Their retired neighbor, Mrs. Lavere, strolled by with her miniature poodle.

'Paul? How's your brother?' The older lady called to him.

'Ma'am?' He frowned, unsure.

'This neighborhood used to be so quiet. Now cars race up and down our streets.' The old lady's poodle pulled on its leash until she picked him up. 'Have you been to the hospital?'

At his confused expression, she gasped. 'Oh, Paul, I thought you knew. Your brother was hit by a car this afternoon and they took him to St. Luke's Hospital.'

'Jay? Oh, no.' Anguish ripped through his voice then he ran toward his car.

'Wait for me,' Julie cried, not wanting to be left behind. He stopped long enough for her to jump in the passenger seat and slam the door.

* * *

Driving faster than the speed limit, Paul raced his motor at each red light.

As the speedometer hit eighty, Julie cried out, 'Slow down.'

The brakes squealed.

'We don't want to be stopped for speeding,' she reminded him.

Paul nodded and drove slower to the hospital.

Once there, he jumped from the car and hurried Julie inside. A nurse at the front desk guided them to the ER recovery room.

'You're Jay Arnold's next of kin?' A short, bald man in a white coat smiled at them. 'That's a dumb question, isn't it? It's obvious you're his twin brother.'

'He's going to be all right,' the doctor reassured Paul before he could ask. 'Let's sit over there and I'll tell you about Jay.' He pointed to a quiet corner.

'According to the police report, your brother was riding a bike in your neighborhood. There were no witnesses, but the car that hit him didn't stop. Another car came by and the driver spotted Jay lying in the road next to his smashed bike,' the doctor said.

He must have looked stunned since Julie took his hand and squeezed it. By the time the doctor walked away, his shock had turned to rage. 'There's no way this was an accident. Dorothy's out to get me and the people who matter to me. Jay was a convenient target.'

'You don't know that for sure.'

'I can feel it. Look at what she's done. She's cost me my job and encouraged the police to consider me a suspect. And don't forget the car that ran us off the road near her house. That could have been Dorothy or an employee of hers. Today, she hit Jay.' He took a deep breath. 'This has to stop before she kills all of us, Julie.'

'I don't blame you for being upset.' She looked worried.

'You agree with me, don't you?'

'Maybe. But couldn't it be coincidence?'

'Coincidence be damned. I've had enough. It's time I did something.'

'Like what?'

'Speak to the police. Then, if they won't do anything, I'll hire a private detective, the sharpest one I can find. Maybe the right kind of sleuth will be able to get the goods on her.'

Julie appeared alarmed. 'Are you sure you want to do that?'

'Damned right. I've put up with too much for too long. She needs to learn she can't get away with any more dirty tricks, not at my expense.'

'If Dorothy would run down Jay, where will she stop?' Julie bit her lip and blinked hard.

He slid his arm around her shoulders. Then Julie and he followed a nurse to his brother's cubicle.

They found Jay, pale and still, his right arm in a protective sling.

Leaning over his brother's bed, he tried to hide his worry. 'How're you doing, fellow?'

'It hurts like hell, but at least I didn't break my neck.' Jay's smile turned into a grimace.

'Can't you give him something for the pain?' Paul asked the nurse.

'He's had a shot and we'll give him a prescription for pain pills before he leaves the hospital.' The nurse hurried away to help someone else.

'How bad was he hurt?' Paul asked when the doctor darted into the cubicle.

'Your brother's a lucky man. The x-rays show no internal damage. His right arm broke on impact and will be uncomfortable for awhile, but his injuries could've been a lot worse.' The doctor scanned Jay's chart. 'He's complained of headaches so I'm keeping him overnight. We'll have a MRI run tomorrow morning. If all goes well, you can take him home after we get the results.'

* * *

Later that evening, Paul paced the floor of Julie's den. Misty followed on his heels until Julie picked her up and put her in her bed in the kitchen, closing the door.

'It was foolish of me to think we could get away from it all today. It's not possible to run away from your troubles. They find you, wherever you go.' He sounded tired but determined. 'I meant what I said at the hospital. I've had enough. From now on, I'm going to fight back.'

Julie wanted to applaud his brave words. 'I'll help you, anyway I can.'

'Thanks,' his glance turned tender and he took her hand. 'I don't want you to get hurt. If things get too bad, you'll have to leave for awhile.'

Not about to desert him, Julie didn't argue, just smiled. With her training, she could be a good backup, though she couldn't tell him that.

'Well, I'd better go home in case the hospital needs to reach me.' He kissed her cheek and left.

An hour later, Julie lay in bed, mulling over what had happened. Then the hair on the back of her neck prickled, and every nerve in her body went on alert. Though not a believer in the supernatural, she sensed an evil presence. In spite of her years of police training, the idea of an unseen menace hovering over them, ready to spring, chilled her to her bones. The shrill ring of the telephone made her stomach clench. She reached for the phone, thinking it was Paul. Her boss's voice startled her.

12

'Sorry to call you so late but — ' Lieutenant Edwards sounded tired and Julie's heart went out to the dedicated police officer she'd known since she was a child.

'That's all right,' she interrupted her boss. 'I wasn't asleep. Did you find anything?'

'We've traced Dorothy to Las Vegas. She worked as a dealer under the name Dotti Peters in the casinos before she married Marcus Turner.'

'That's interesting.'

'Right, but the trail ends there. It's almost like she didn't exist before Las Vegas.'

'Honest people don't try to conceal their pasts, do they?' Julie tried to curb the current of excitement that seared through her. She reminded herself that this new information might not have anything to do with her case.

'Well, not as a rule,' Edwards reluctantly agreed. 'Anything new down there?'

'Paul Martin's brother was in a hit-and-run accident today. He was lucky. His only injury was a broken arm.'

'Any idea who hit him?'

'No one saw the car or the driver.' As Julie

considered Jay's pain, anger flickered inside her.

'That's too bad. What have you found so far?'

'Nothing you'd call evidence, but this hit-and-run's the latest in a series of bad things that've happened to Paul Martin since his wife vanished. First he lost his job, then a dark car like Dorothy's ran us off the road. Also, he claims she's called several times to harrass him. He blames her for everything that's gone wrong in his life in the past few weeks.'

'Can he prove she's responsible?'

'No. He's also talked to me about his marriage. It sounds like his wife tried to keep him on a short leash. He rebelled and filed for divorce in spite of her naming him her heir.' That should speak in Paul's defense, he hadn't stayed for the money.

'That's interesting,' Edwards commented. 'Martin becomes his wife's heir, he files for divorce, then she vanishes. She did disappear before the divorce was finalized, didn't she?'

The way her boss put it all together got under Julie's skin. 'Yeah, but I don't think he's interested in her fortune.'

'Maybe not.'

Edwards' skeptical tone made Julie wish she could defend Paul. She had to admit the circumstances might look suspicious to anyone who didn't know Paul.

'What about his brother? Is he on the level?'

'When I first met him, I got the distinct impression that Jay was jealous of Paul,' Julie said. 'That's understandable since Paul's a lawyer and his brother's an assistant manager in a restaurant. But they've both inherited from their aunt recently and Jay's in better shape financially than he was earlier.'

'Has that changed him?'

'Even before he inherited, Jay's attitude began to mellow toward Paul. It's obvious they care for each other.' She couldn't imagine Jay trying to hurt Paul. Under the brothers' light banter was genuine affection. And tears had shone in Paul's eyes when he heard Jay was in the hospital.

'Her position in Richmond society doesn't rule Dorothy out as a possible suspect,' Julie reminded her boss. 'That would explain why she's tried to blame Paul for whatever's happened to Sheila.'

'I still think you're barking up the wrong tree,' Edwards responded. 'Keep me posted. Good night.' He hung up.

* * *

Next afternoon, Julie tidied up Jay's room while Paul went to pick him up at the hospital. She threw away old newspapers he'd dumped on the floor, smoothed his bed covers, and stacked his travel books on the nightstand. Even tidy, the sparsely furnished room needed a little color, so she drove over to Safeway and returned with red tulips in a pot. She put it on the top of the chest-of-drawers.

'Something tells me I should have accidents more often.' Jay quipped while his brother helped him onto his bed later. He winced with pain as he reached for a glass of water on his nightstand.

'Here, let me help you.' Julie inserted a straw in the glass and held it while Jay took a drink. 'You didn't get a glimpse of the vehicle that hit you, did you?'

'Nope. I was riding along, my head in the clouds. The car hit me so hard, I flew through the air and landed on the pavement. I think I heard a car accelerating down the street.'

'The police will search the area, I'm sure,' she said more for her own benefit than his. 'Let's hope the driver takes the car to a body shop for repair work and the shop owner notifies the police.'

Paul leaned over Jay. 'No more bikes for awhile, Bro.' His tone was light but Julie heard relief in his voice as he reassured himself that his brother was all right. It was obvious there was a strong bond of love between the two men, one that had survived the death of their parents and years of separation.

'In fact, let's all be more careful.' He turned to her. 'Julie, you stay on alert. Don't take any chances. Okay?'

'You think I'm in danger?' With all of his problems, he was so thoughtful to worry about her. She wished she could put his mind at ease, but how could she tell him she was a trained police officer and well-equipped to defend herself?

'Maybe.' His expression was grave.

Jay fell asleep and they returned to the living room where Paul slumped on the sofa, deep in thought.

'What is it?' The distant expression on his face made her feel alone, deserted. She hoped he wouldn't shut her out.

'The person who hit Jay could have mistaken him for me.'

'That makes sense. After all, he's your identical twin. But if the car came on him from behind, wouldn't the driver have noticed Jay's ponytail?'

'Maybe not. It all might have happened so fast, the driver didn't notice Jay's longer hair.'

Once at the airport, she'd mistaken Jay for Paul. Julie sighed. Since then, she'd come to know Paul, care for him. There was no way she'd confuse him with Jay now.

'You're convinced Dorothy's responsible?' She agreed with him. Too much had happened for it to be coincidence.

'Yeah, although I don't have any proof yet.' Anger crept into his words. 'But if I do find out she's responsible, Dorothy's in deep trouble.'

'Do you really think she's capable of violence?'

'I sure do. The woman's cruel and vindictive. She badgers Sheila to the point of tears. Also, she's mistreated her help on several occasions when we were in the house. During one dinner party, Dorothy slapped her maid and screamed at her in front of a room full of guests.'

'What did you do to turn her against you?'

'I wish I knew.'

'You must have some idea,' Julie persisted.

'Whose side are you on, anyway?' Paul glared at her.

He was so even dispositioned most of the time, she forgot he had a temper. Before she could speak, he apologized.

'I'm sorry. It's not your fault. I need to talk to the police about Dorothy.'

Her head began to throb. 'I'd better go home. We both need to get some rest.' She stood up and rubbed her forehead.

'You're welcome to stay over here, if you want.'

'Thanks, but I'll sleep better in my own bed.'

'That's fine. Just thought you might feel uneasy.' Paul stroked her cheek before walking her to the door.

* * *

Lying in the spare twin bed in his brother's room, Paul heard Jay moan that night. He found the pain pills the ER doctor had prescribed and gave them to his twin. They must have helped since Jay began to snore minutes later.

Unable to sleep, Paul stared into the darkness, weary but too keyed up to relax.

Propped up in bed, he clinched and unclinched his fists while he listened to the clock ticking in the hall. The minutes passed slowly, almost like his life. It slipped away while he did nothing but wait.

His thoughts turned to Sheila. At first, he'd been annoyed, then angry, thinking she'd vanished to spite him. Later, he began to worry. Something bad had happened to her.

His nerves stretched drum tight, and it was all he could do to lie still in bed. The last few days, a terrible idea had begun to form in his brain, something so monstrous he couldn't bring himself to speak of it, even to Julie. Dorothy had craved her stepdaughter's inheritance. Looking back in time, he realized that Dorothy had become hostile about the time Sheila announced she'd changed her will in his favor,

As things stood now, he'd inherit on Sheila's death, that is, he'd inherit unless he were found guilty and convicted for her murder. In that case, Dorothy would get what she'd wanted all along, the fortune. In Sheila's will, Marcus and Dorothy were second in line to inherit, if he couldn't. And convicted felons could not inherit. He'd learned that his first week of law school.

Dorothy had done everything she could to make the police suspicious of him. Paul shuddered. In the eyes of the law, he had the perfect motive for killing his wife. On her death, he'd inherit a sizable fortune. He had more to gain than anyone else in killing her.

What a scheme that would be. It was almost beyond his comprehension that Dorothy could have concocted such a plan. Unless she had help.

He told himself he was being foolish. The

whole idea was ridiculous. But he couldn't quite convince himself.

Jay sighed in his sleep and Paul shifted his attention to his brother. No matter what else happened, he'd keep watch over Jay . . . and Julie. She was the best thing that ever happened to him. Thinking of her had brought new feelings. He wanted her, but it was more than physical desire. She was so sweet and gentle, he wanted to protect her, cherish her.

Julie shouldn't be exposed to the violence and ugliness that filled his life. She was innocent, defenseless. His own innocence had been shattered the day he gazed at the ashes of his family home, and a policeman informed him his parents were dead.

The old grief stabbed him until he balled his fist and hit the pillow. Jay and he would never forget how their parents died. But they had to accept what happened and move on with their lives. Paul closed his eyes, willed himself to sleep.

* * *

Paul woke to the twitter of birds outside on the windowsill. A quick glance at the other twin bed reassured him that Jay was still sleeping. He tiptoed from the room, leaving the door half-open so he'd hear Jay if he called.

Alone at the kitchen table, he sipped a mug of coffee and made plans. As soon as his brother felt more his old self, he'd talk to the police about Dorothy. Getting off dead center energized Paul in spite of his lack of sleep.

A light tapping drew his attention. He opened the back door and greeted Julie holding a covered plate.

'I brought you some coffee cake.' She pulled out a chair and sat down. 'Did you have a bad night?'

'I've had better.' He stretched. 'Jay's arm bothered him. Then, after he drifted off, I couldn't go to sleep. I can't help but wonder what will happen next.'

'Like what?'

'Search me.' Paul wished he could tell her the whole truth. Something made him hold back.

Julie wrinkled her brow. 'So what're you going to do?'

'By tomorrow, Jay should feel a lot better. Then I'll call the Richmond detective who interrogated me and go in to see him. He may think I want to divert their attention from me, but at least I can tell them what's happened. Maybe they'll agree to investigate Dorothy.'

'Good for you.' Julie beamed at him.

'From the way the police questioned me, I get the impression they think I know more than I told them.' They'd been right.

'They need to find Sheila. That's their job.'

Taking her hand, he said, 'I'll be glad when this's over.'

'That makes two of us.' Her words were spoken with such intensity, he stared. Julie flashed him a nervous smile and pushed back her chair. 'Well, I have some errands to run so I'll be on my way.' She stood up.

'I'd better stay around here tonight. How does a quiet supper and a video sound?' He hoped she didn't mind.

'Good. I'll pick up a movie. See you.' Kissing his cheek, she let herself out the kitchen door.

* * *

'We have all of your favorite flavors of ice cream.' Julie addressed Jay at the end of their meal that night. 'What do you prefer, strawberry, fudge ripple, cookies n' cream or some of each?'

'I don't want any,' he responded.

From the scowl on his face, she figured his arm must really hurt. Jay never turned down dessert.

'That's a first.' Scooping ice cream, Paul grinned, obviously trying to tease his brother out of his bad mood.

'This damn arm's givin' me a fit,' Jay complained. 'I think I'll go to bed.' He pushed back his chair and walked out of the kitchen, moving like every joint hurt.

'Why don't you take a couple of your pain pills so you can sleep?' Julie called to him as he headed for the stairs.

'I will. Good night.'

Later, Paul and she settled down on the sofa in the den to watch a light romance she'd selected at the video store. Maybe it would take his mind off things.

Before he turned on the video, Paul turned to her, an uneasy expression crossed his face. 'Did I tell you the police questioned me twice about Sheila?'

She nodded, sensing his nervousness. Was he building up to something? His tone made her stomach clench, though as a police officer, she had to admit she was curious.

'You're the only person I can talk to about what happened.' His keen gaze fixed on her face. 'You see, the detectives were right. What I told them wasn't the full story.'

She stared at him in astonishment. 'What did you say?'

'Sheila did come over here that night.' Paul

rose and walked over to the mantel, leaned his arm on it.

'But you told me she didn't keep your appointment.' He'd lied, to the police and to her. Anger and disappointment washed over her. She'd believed she knew him. Had he deceived her?

'When I came in the front door from work, she was about to leave. Sheila seemed so upset, I asked if she was all right. She muttered something I couldn't make out then got in her car and drove off in a big hurry. I was worried about her. I went into the den and sat at my desk, wondered what I should do. 'At last, I left a message on her answering machine. If she was in trouble, I wanted to know what was wrong so I could help her,' he said.

'In your message, did you mention you'd just seen her?'

'No, I just asked her to call me. Later, I was afraid the police would link me to her disappearance if they knew she'd been here that night, so I did a really stupid thing. I told them she never kept our appointment, and I'd called to see what happened to her.'

Julie sighed with relief. She'd been afraid he'd say he'd hurt his wife. For a moment, she felt ashamed she'd doubted him. It was too bad the Richmond police weren't as trusting. They might come up with a different scenario — Sheila and Paul quarrelled, then he killed her.

'You should've told the truth, Paul. Lies can come back and cause you a lot of trouble.' Her spirits sank and she admitted that was her innermost fear, that her own lies might ruin her chances of a future with Paul. Or that she'd find he was guilty and have to turn him in.

'That's true, but I haven't told anyone but you, so I'm safe, aren't I?' His tense expression faded and he sent her a confident smile.

Paul wouldn't act so self-assured if he knew he'd just confided in a police officer. She ought to report what he'd said, but she'd wait and see what else he told her.

He took her in his arms and kissed her hard on the lips. For an instant, Julie stiffened, annoyed by his manner.

'What's the matter?' He seemed concerned.

'Nothing,' she replied, returning his kiss. As she clung to Paul, she realized nothing could change her feelings for him. Not even if he was as guilty as sin.

The telephone's ring jarred her. 'Don't you think you'd better answer that before it wakes Jay? It could be important.'

With reluctance, he let her go. 'You're right.' He walked into the kitchen and picked up the receiver.

Minutes passed. Growing impatient, she crossed the living room and peered into the kitchen. Paul stood motionless.

'Well, thanks for letting me know.' He spoke to the party on the other end of the line, hung up, and looked at her.

'What is it?' A tight band of fear bound her chest.

'That was the police calling me about Sheila!'

* * *

In the dim light from the television, Julie's mouth dropped open and she stared at him, speechless. She couldn't be more startled than he. Just a few minutes ago he'd confided in her, told her he'd lied. Now this.

He took a deep breath. 'Sheila's car has turned up in an abandoned quarry off Staples Mill Road.'

'I know the place,' Julie replied, quietly. 'It's always been a hangout for kids.'

Taking her hand, he led her back to the living room. They stood by the sofa, facing each other. 'Remember how uneasy I've been? I sensed something was about to happen, but didn't know what. It appears my instincts were right.'

She nodded. 'I guess so.'

Paul wanted to hold her but couldn't gauge her expression. She'd changed since they met and at times appeared almost inscrutable. Sometimes she wouldn't look him right in the eyes. Once or twice, he'd caught her watching him, a speculative expression on her face. An uneasy idea skittered across his mind. Could the Julie he thought he knew just be a clever façade hiding the real woman? He pushed that notion aside, but had no idea what she was thinking. Did she believe what he'd told her about Sheila?

'I've got this gut feeling Sheila's in real trouble. Otherwise, she'd have come back by now. The police don't seem to have any leads.'

'Give them a chance,' Julie advised him. 'Sooner or later, they'll find her.'

'I'd rather it were sooner.' Paul pulled her into his embrace. 'In the meanwhile . . . '

Kissing her, he tightened his arms around her waist when she clung to him. Her eager response delighted him and he deepened his kisses, holding her face with his hands. Blood pounded in his ears and his heart raced. While he still had a few shreds of self-control, he reined in his desire, held her at arms length, and smoothed a lock of hair off her face.

'What is it?' A little pucker appeared between her brows.

'If we don't stop, we'll end up in bed,' he warned her. 'Is that what you want?'

Her eyes locked on his and she whispered, 'Yes. Tonight I want us to be together.' She sank onto the sofa and tugged on his hand until he joined her.

He kissed her while he unbuttoned her blouse, his fingers clumsy with the small buttons until her hands came up to help his. A shiver racked her body when he pushed the blouse aside and his lips followed the curve of her throat down to her breasts. Her skin felt almost feverish. He continued his caresses for a few moments before a thought slipped through the heavy curtain of his desire. Suppose Jay woke up and came downstairs? They needed more privacy. 'We'd be more comfortable in my room.'

She smiled in agreement.

13

For days Julie had fought her desire for Paul. Why she succumbed on this particular occasion, she couldn't say. Perhaps the discovery of the car heightened her feeling that time was running out for them. Her investigation would end the day the real culprit was apprehended. Who knew what would happen then?

In silence she followed Paul upstairs and along the darkened hall past the room where Jay was sleeping.

Easing his bedroom door shut, Paul locked it as soon as she entered the room, then he pulled her into his arms. The slight tremble of his hands reassured her. She sensed this wasn't a casual affair for him either.

If he was nervous, she was scared to death. Paul would be her first. Though she was twenty-six, she'd never been with a man. Once or twice she'd met someone she thought was special. Later, she'd been disappointed and broken off the relationship before it reached intimacy. Tonight it seemed natural that they make love.

Kissing, they moved toward his king-size

bed, Paul lowered her to the bed then lay beside her, kissing her mouth, her shoulders, her breasts until her skin burned. His fingers caressed her body until she tingled everywhere he touched her.

'I want to feel your skin against mine. You don't know how long I've dreamed of our being like this,' he whispered in her ear. His hot breath tickled her ear, his cologne enticed her.

He slipped off her blouse and bra then eased off her slacks, his persuasive lips and knowing hands warmed her to a fever pitch. Naked except for her bikinis, she crossed her hands over her breasts, suddenly apprehensive. 'I've never . . . ' She stopped, embarrassed.

'I didn't think you had.' He kissed her lightly on the cheek. 'I'm glad I'm your first.

'Give me a hand, will you?' He raised his arms so she could pull off his sweater. Again he embraced her. At last, he sat on the side of the bed and slipped off his jeans and briefs. She could see he was fully aroused. Her eyes were glued to his handsome body, muscled yet wiry. A sprinkle of hair on his broad chest tapered down to his flat stomach.

Reaching out to Paul, Julie took his face in her hands and pulled his mouth down to hers. When a wave of passion hit her, she was swept away, locked in his arms.

Later, Julie curled up with her back to Paul and dozed, loving the feel of his warm, drowsy body against her.

When she woke, he was sleeping on his side with his arm around her. Her heart told her that he was the love she'd always wanted. Then she jolted fully awake with the realization of what she'd done. One of the cardinal rules of police officers was never get involved with your suspect.

Paul dozed peacefully. In the dim light, his features seemed relaxed, younger. She raised her hand then stopped in mid-air before she touched his cheek. Holding her hand over her lips, she stifled a sob. Torn in two by desire and duty, Julie struggled to find a way out of her dilemma.

If she stayed with Paul, her conscience would force her to tell him everything. He might not want her once he knew what she'd done. And if her superiors learned of her relationship with Paul, they'd remove her from the investigation right away, maybe even discharge her from the police force. She'd planned to leave law enforcement, but not in disgrace. Her father would never have forgiven her.

With silent tears cascading down her face, Julie slipped out of bed, dressed and left the house. She'd have to decide what to tell Paul in the morning. Not the truth. She couldn't tell him the truth. To preserve the investigation, she'd have to lie. She'd tell him she'd changed her mind. That she didn't want to get involved, that she regretted their lovemaking.

At home, she curled up on the sofa in her living room, reflecting on what she'd done. The hopeless situation bore down on her like a heavy weight on her chest. She'd wanted Paul, but not this way. Theirs was a relationship built on deceit. How could she convince him that the investigation was just the reason they met, how it began, that he meant more to her than she'd ever thought possible?

In the early morning light, Julie stood, stretched her stiff muscles, and dreaded having to lie to him again. He'd be at her door when he woke and found an empty bed. Unless . . . unless it had been just a one-night stand for him.

While she washed her face and combed her hair, her thoughts focused on Paul. Feeling chilled, she heated water for a much needed mug of hot tea. Right after she placed the kettle on the stove, a knock resounded through her quiet house. As if in response, her mouth turned dry and her heart beat seemed to slow. Misty barked and followed her.

'Why did you leave?' Paul looked puzzled when she opened the door. 'For a moment I thought last night was just a lovely dream.' He stepped into the kitchen and tried to embrace her. She evaded his arms, walked instead to the stove to remove the kettle of water. She couldn't meet his eyes.

'What's the matter? Are you sick?' Concern rang in his voice.

'No. It's just that . . . '

His grey-blue gaze scanned her face. 'Just what?' Paul shook his head. 'Last night was special . . . at least it was for me.' A brief pause then Paul asked, 'You aren't having second thoughts this morning, are you?'

Hating what she had to do, Julie sucked in her breath. 'If you really want to know, I am.' She looked at the top button on his shirt, not able to meet his earnest gaze. 'Last night was a mistake. You're quite attractive, and I guess I just got carried away.' She paused then continued. 'I'm sorry, but I can't get involved with you or anyone else right now.'

His face fell and pain flickered in his eyes.

'It's not you,' she said, grief stricken that she had to hurt him, especially him. In search of an explanation, she came up with what she hoped would be a convincing excuse. 'There was a man in my office in Washington. Our relationship didn't end well so I'm not ready to get involved with anyone else. I like you a lot but can't we go back to being friends?'

'What I feel for you goes beyond friendship. I want to be with you. I thought you felt the same way.' Bitterness tinged his words and he shook his head. 'If you just want a friend, find someone else.'

'I'm sorry. I didn't mean to hurt you. It's not a good time for me. If you'd let me explain — .'

'Don't bother.' Paul interrupted her. His mouth tightened into a thin line and his voice turned cold. 'I better go. Jay must be ready for his breakfast. See you around.' Three long strides took him out of the kitchen. The side gate slammed shut.

'You fool, you terrible fool,' she muttered while the tears she'd fought to hold back broke through. Slumped in her chair, she hugged herself and rocked back and forth, overcome by despair. All of those years of waiting and longing for the man who'd fill her arms, her life, and her heart, then she'd lost him almost as soon as she found him.

A few minutes later, she wiped her eyes and assessed the situation. At least he didn't know about the investigation. Maybe the car would lead the police to Sheila. Julie shivered.

Though she'd never met the woman, she felt she knew Paul's estranged wife. She'd seen her picture, spent time in what once had been Sheila's home, heard Paul talk of her. And she'd made love to Paul in the bed where Sheila and Paul . . . She flushed. Enough of that. They must find Sheila. Then Paul could get on with his life. And she could go on with hers, whatever that might be. A sigh of regret escaped her lips.

Picking up her phone, she punched in Corbeille's number.

Her fellow officer wheezed into the phone. 'I was about to call you.'

Listening to her partner's hoarse, scratchy voice, Julie couldn't help but comment. 'You sound terrible.'

'Thanks,' Corbeille croaked into the phone. 'The doc says this is just a twenty-four hour virus, but it's knocked me off my feet.'

'I won't keep you. I was just returning your call.'

'You weren't home last night when I called. Ms. Turner's car turned up.'

'I know. They called Martin while I was with him.'

'A team's examining every inch of the car and a diving team's ready to search the quarry,' he informed her. 'There may be another lead. An inmate at the State Prison insists he has information on Ms. Turner.'

Julie's ears perked up. 'That's good news. Will an officer from Richmond PD interview him?'

'That's the problem. The Chief asked me to see the convict but I'm sick in bed.' The older detective sounded disgusted with himself for getting sick.

She tried to hide her eagerness. 'I guess I could go and talk to the man, if you want.'

'That's gr . . . I mean, that might be a good idea, under the circumstances. But don't promise the con anything. Just talk to him and see what sort of deal he wants for his information then get back to me. Understand?'

'Of course.'

'Stay home this morning. I'll call you in an hour or so, as soon as I let the Chief and the Warden know you'll conduct the interrogation in my place.'

'I'll be here.' While Julie waited, she located a dark business suit and tailored blouse in her closet. Curiosity hammered into her. What did the convict know and what price would the police have to pay to unseal his lips?

14

'It's all arranged,' Corbeille informed Julie when she answered the phone. 'I've spoken to Warden Burke and he expects you at three p.m. Let me know what you find out.' His hoarse voice sounded anxious. Was he concerned she might bungle the interview?

'Don't worry. I've interrogated prisoners lots of times,' she reassured her fellow officer. 'And this con could lead us right to the killer.'

Following the call, her mind swam with unanswered questions. What was the convict's source of information? Was it valid or just speculation? Over a month had passed since Sheila disappeared on March 9th. What were the odds she was still alive? Having handled a few kidnap cases, Julie knew the chances were slim the police would find Sheila alive.

For a moment, sadness filled Julie for a woman she'd never met. Paul would grieve for Sheila. Whatever else she'd been, she'd been his wife.

Perplexed, Julie shook her head. Was anyone just what they appeared to be? Take Paul, for instance. Her heart told her she could trust him, but he'd lied about Sheila's last visit. That might not be the only lie he'd told.

Approaching the prison, Julie surveyed the grey brick walls while showing the guard her identification.

Directed to the visitors parking lot, she parked and locked her car before following the signs to the entrance. Inside the front doors, a trustee issued her a badge then led her down a quiet, empty hall to the warden's office.

Warden Burke, a short, bald man with broad shoulders and a barrel chest, hung up his desk telephone as she entered the room.

'Detective Taylor. Dick Corbeille just called to see if you'd made it yet. Have a seat and I'll fill you in on the man you're here to interrogate.' Burke motioned to a chair in front of his desk.

Steepling his fingers, he eyed her with open curiosity. 'Taylor. You wouldn't by any chance be related to Captain Phil Taylor?'

'He was my father.' Julie smiled, proud that law enforcement officers still remembered her Dad. He'd retired from police work years ago due to a heart condition. It had been his idea that she enter law enforcement upon her college graduation. Not sure what she wanted to do, she'd become a police officer.

'Your dad was a fine man. I went to the

academy with him.' Burke leaned back in his chair. 'So you've followed in his footsteps. He must have been proud of you.'

'I hope so. You were about to fill me in on the convict I'm here to see,' she reminded him, feeling vaguely guilty. How would this senior policeman react if she revealed she counted the days until she could resign from her position?

'Right. First, would you like a cup of coffee?' Now that he knew whose daughter she was, he became less business-like.

Eager to get on with her assignment, she shook her head.

'Well, I can see you're in a hurry, so here goes. This man's an habitual criminal, nothing major, but he just keeps coming back, like a song, you might say.' Burke chuckled at his own feeble joke.

'What's he in for this time, Warden?'

'Let me look at his record.' Burke flipped through several pages of a worn folder. 'Hmmm — he's served time for car theft, real estate scams, and petty larcency. This time it was burglary and he got ten years, of which he has three left to serve. He may want to trade information on Ms. Turner for a reduced sentence.'

Burke closed the folder and gazed across his cluttered desk at her. 'As you'll see,

Forsythe's not a young man. It's understandable that he wouldn't want to spend three more years behind bars.'

The Warden punched a button on his desk and summoned a trustee. The man entered his office and Burke directed him. 'Take Detective Taylor to the Visitors Room, will you? And get Tim Forsythe.' Burke reached across his desk and shook her hand. His hand was hardened. Under his pleasant visage, Julie had no doubt the man was the same.

'It's good to meet you. You resemble your father.' Burke called after her as the trustee led her down the corridor.

In the Visitors Room, she waited until a frail looking, white-haired man appeared on the other side of the glass wall. Forsythe took his seat and picked up the phone.

'It's not often a pretty young woman comes to see me.' His voice was mild, almost gentle.

Julie envisioned the old man by a fire telling grandchildren stories. Though she strived to appear official, she couldn't surpress a half-smile. 'Mr. Forsythe, I'm Detective Taylor.' She spoke briskly. 'You wanted to speak to someone about Sheila Turner?'

'Yes, I do.' Tobacco stained fingers touched the glass which separated them. 'I've got a tip for you.'

Her hands seemed all thumbs as she opened her shoulder bag and took out a pad and pen. 'Go ahead.'

'I know who killed the broad and where he dumped her.' She must have looked stricken since he paused and asked in a low voice, 'Did you know her?'

'No. Please continue.'

Forsythe scratched his head as if deep in thought. 'Let's see. I got three more years to serve in this dump.' He drew his prison issue sweater around him though the room was warm. As he continued, a quiet desperation crept into his voice. 'At thirty, forty, or even fifty, I could of done this sentence standing on my head. But I'm seventy. I wanna make a deal.'

Pity flickered then died in her heart. A police officer couldn't afford to feel sorry for criminals. This old man was a source of information, nothing more.

'I'll pass along what you tell me to my superiors. They'll have to decide whether they should speak to the Parole Board,' she advised him. 'Tell me what you've got.'

He chewed on his lower lip before speaking. 'A con in for passing bad checks was released last month. One day during our exercise time, he bragged about a job waiting outside that would pay him $10,000. That's a hell of a lotta money.'

'How would he earn this money?'

'In here, it's easy to get bored. Some guys make up stories to pass the time or to impress each other. Maybe this fellow was just pulling my leg, but he said he'd been hired to kill a Richmond architect.'

'Go on.' Julie managed to keep a bland expression on her face. Her stomach clenched with tension.

'I didn't think he was serious. Lots of cons shoot off their big mouths. Yesterday I read an article in the paper that said a Richmond woman architect, missing since early March, still hasn't turned up. So I thought maybe this guy was on the level.'

'Please continue.' She leaned forward.

'Not today. Tell your bosses it'll be a simple trade — my freedom for the killer's name and where he stashed the body.' His words contrasted so much with his gentle manner and soft voice, they chilled her.

'I'll see what I can do.' Julie rose from her chair.

A few minutes later, the trustee escorted her back to the front door and held out his hand for her badge.

* * *

At home again, Julie called Corbeille and summarized what she'd learned. 'If Forsythe's on the level, will your Chief speak to the Parole Board for him?'

'Maybe.' Corbeille still sounded like death warmed over. He coughed several times before continuing. 'I hate to keep dumping my job on you, but could you drive over to the quarry and see how the search team's doing?'

As she backed her car out of the driveway five minutes later, Julie caught a glimpse of Jay at a front window next door. He waved to her with his good arm. She grimaced and waved back. God only knew what Paul had told his brother about her.

It had been foolish to get involved with Paul. Maybe when the case was closed, but she had her doubts about that. He'd never said he loved her, never promised her anything. It was possible he'd just amused himself at her expense. Uncertainty slid across her mind.

At the quarry, she showed her badge to gain admission to the area then walked over to where the police divers were loading their equipment into a truck. One of the team passed her and she stopped him. 'You're finished?'

He nodded. 'Yeah, this quarry's not that big.'

'What did you find?'

'The usual stuff people dump in a place like this — rusty beer cans, whiskey bottles, old grocery carts, and, of course, that Miata.' He scratched his head. 'Two kids crawled through a hole in the fence to throw stones into the quarry. The Turner car wasn't far from the surface of the water, and a stone smashed the windshield. The boys ran home and confessed what they'd done to their father. He called the police.'

'Could you have missed a body?' Again she had a twinge of grief for Sheila. It was strange, but knowing Paul, Julie felt in a way she also knew his estranged wife.

'No. She's not down there.' He wiped his face with a towel.

'Thanks.' Julie walked over to the edge and stared down into the murky waters.

While she stood there, a van drove into the restricted area and three uniformed policemen climbed out, one holding the leash of a large harnessed dog. The others took shovels from the back of the truck and began to dig in the soft earth around the edges of the quarry. Their fellow officer led the dog around the area. The German Shepherd sniffed the ground but didn't seem to find anything of interest. The leader of the search team told Julie that he'd report their findings to Corbeille.

Driving home, Julie's heart ached. She should have kept her relationship with Paul on a friendly basis. He'd made no move to get in touch with her since she called quits to their brief affair. It looked like he'd been interested in a casual fling, nothing more.

Approaching her front door, she found Jay waiting for her.

'I know you guys had a fight, but you aren't mad at me, are you?' Jay pinned her with an intent stare.

'Of course not. Have you been here long?'

'Just a few minutes. I didn't want to miss you.'

She pushed back the idea of a leisurely soak in her tub. Though she liked Jay, it hurt right now to be with him. He reminded her too much of Paul. Today Jay appeared his old self except for dark smudges under his eyes and the cast on his arm.

Unlocking her front door, she invited him in for a soft drink. Jay followed her back to the kitchen.

He accepted the drink and sat down across the table from her. 'It's good to see you. Are you all right?'

'I guess so.' Seeing his concerned expression, Julie's throat tightened. To divert his attention, she asked, 'How's the arm?'

'Not great, but it'll get better.' Jay shifted in his chair and asked, 'What did you do to make Paul so angry?' Anxiety edged his voice.

'What did Paul say?' She evaded his question, asking one of her own.

A flush crept up Jay's neck, covered his stubbled cheeks. 'Which do you want . . . the original version or the edited one?'

Julie braced herself. Did Paul hate her now? Damn it. She'd never meant to hurt him. Her job just got in the way. If only she could tell him the truth. She took a deep breath. 'I'm a big girl . . . go ahead, give me the unedited version.'

'Paul rambled a lot, but the gist was that you aren't the woman he thought you were. Sheila's deception hurt him. Then he met you, he thought you were different.'

'Is that it?'

'Yeah. I'm sorry, Julie.' Jay reached across the table and touched her hand. 'You fooled me. I thought you cared for him.'

'I do, but there're obstacles. I'd tell you about it if I could.' She bit her lip, not knowing what else to say.

'It's okay.'

She must have looked miserable because Jay began telling funny stories of customers he'd served at his restaurant in New York

City. After a few minutes, she felt a smile tugging at the corners of her mouth.

Jay stood. 'I better go home before he thinks I've jumped ship.'

'Yeah. You wouldn't want him to think you're consorting with the enemy.' That was the last thing she wanted to be — Paul's enemy. Her pain must have been apparent since Jay patted her arm.

'Don't give up on Paul.' He tried to console her. 'If he didn't think a lot of you, he wouldn't be so mad.'

* * *

Paul heard Jay open the back door. Clicking Save on his computer, he stepped into the hall and caught his twin on the stairs. 'Been out for some air?'

'I went over to see Julie.' Jay set his chin in a stubborn line, adding, 'before you chew me out, you're gonna hear what I got to say.'

'Didn't I tell you not to mention that woman around me,' Paul replied. 'As far as I'm concerned, she doesn't exist.'

'Who're you kidding?'

At Jay's skeptical tone, Paul was tempted to wring his brother's neck.

'Is that why you mope around the house and jump when the phone rings?'

'The hell I do.' Paul sputtered and bristled with indignation. Jay was more observant than he'd realized. 'What business is it of yours, anyway?'

'None, I guess.' Flushing to his hairline, Jay added quietly, 'except you're my brother and I hate to see you hurting.' He shook his head. 'You're over here, miserable, and she's just as miserable next door.'

'She doesn't care if I live or die. Boy, did she fool me. For awhile I thought . . . ' He couldn't tell Jay he'd thought Julie cared for him.

'You thought what?' Jay stared at him.

'Nothing. Give me a break.' Paul didn't want to admit he'd hoped she felt the same way he did. In spite of his good intentions not to become involved, he'd fallen hard for Julie.

'I don't know why she'd like such a jerk. But she does.' Jay looked thoughtful. 'There may be a reason she needs space right now. She hasn't said she doesn't want to see you at all. If you don't want to lose her, you better get off dead center and do something. Fast.'

Paul considered Jay's advice for hours. It appeared he had two choices — ignore Julie and lose what they might have together or be her friend. While his brother was upstairs watching the smaller TV in his room, Paul made up his mind. All right. If that's the way she wants it, I'll be her friend . . . until I can convince her she wants more, just like I do. He punched in a telephone number and reached a florist. 'I want a dozen yellow roses delivered tomorrow morning. On the card just put 'Let's be friends.' Sign the card Paul.'

If friendship was all she could handle right now, he'd have to accept it. In time, she might change her mind. Funny that he'd relied on Jay's opinion. Jay. Paul smiled fondly. It was good to have his brother back. Sometimes he almost forgot the lost years.

Now Jay looked happy, except on occasion a brooding expression appeared on his face. No matter how many times he reassured Jay they had to bury the past, the desire to find out the truth about their parents' deaths gnawed at him. What really caused the fire they'd never discovered. Jay and their father had fought for years, but Jay was incapable of murder. Wasn't he?

15

Next morning Julie parked her car then walked across the road to the quarry. Showing her badge to an uniformed officer, she gained admission to the fenced area.

Shovels clanked in the spring sunshine, and the mounds of dirt had increased until little undisturbed ground remained.

'Anything turn up?' She asked a man who walked by.

'No, not yet.' The worker rested his shovel on the ground, wiped his sweaty forehead with a dirty handkerchief.

'How much longer will you be here?'

'Until we get word to stop.' He stretched, picked up the shovel, and returned to his task.

Julie reached in her shoulder bag for the cell phone and punched in Corbeille's number. 'They've been at it since yesterday, yet nothing's turned up. Do you think you should let the Chief know?'

'Yeah, I will. Go home. I'll get back to you.'

Fifteen minutes later, she walked up to her house. A pale pink envelope stuck in the door caught her attention. The card inside informed her that a local florist had left a delivery at the house next door.

The idea that Paul had sent flowers would have pleased her under other circumstances, but she'd made it clear. She'd asked him to be her friend. Feeling a twinge of guilt, Julie reacted angrily. That man just won't take no for an answer. Well, I'll set him straight.

She marched across the lawns to Paul's house. Jay came to the door. 'A florist left some flowers for me?' Aware she was being rude, she stuck the card under his nose.

'They sure did.' He smiled. 'Come on in.' While he went to get her package, she studied a Ferber print on the foyer wall. At a sound behind her, she turned to find Paul holding a large glass vase of flowers.

'Hello, Julie. The florist left these for you.'

'You really are too much. Didn't I make myself clear?' She scowled, prepared to chew him out.

'Hold on a minute.' He led her into the living room. 'Sit down. Please?'

Seated on the sofa, she couldn't help but admire the yellow roses. Her irritability faded as she buried her face in the fragrant blooms, inhaled their sweetness. 'They're beautiful but . . . ' She gazed over at Paul, filled with uncertainty.

'There's a card enclosed.'

Opening the envelope, she read the message in silence.

'Let's be friends. Paul'

A lump formed in her throat, and more than anything she wanted to reach over and kiss him. Maybe she'd misjudged him. Instead she murmured, 'Thanks. I appreciate the thought.'

'I'm sorry I blew up at you.' His husky voice sent a ripple of awareness through her. 'I've missed you.'

She frowned, ready to take flight if he said the wrong word.

'I know, I know. I rushed you too much. If you need some time, we'll just be friends. Why don't you come to dinner tonight?' Her indecision must have been apparent since right away he added, 'Don't worry. Jay will keep us company.'

'All right.' Relieved that they wouldn't be alone, she accepted his invitation. 'Let me take these roses home. I'll see you later.'

That night dinner was relaxed, casual. Jay was full of himself. Everytime she thought he'd run out of jokes, he'd roll his eyes and say, 'If you think that's funny, have ya heard the one about the . . . ' And off he'd go again.

'You should consider show biz.' She teased Jay. 'You're as funny as the comedians on television.' Paul was more quiet though he joined in now and then with a comment of his own.

Once or twice, he glanced at her, a wistful expression on his face, but he didn't say anything. When she stood to leave, he slid out of his chair.

'I'll walk you home.'

'Come on, it's just next door.' Much as she wanted to be with him, she must keep her distance.

'I'll feel better if I escort you to your door. Humor me, please.' He appeared so concerned, she agreed.

On her front porch, she turned toward him and held out her hand. He took it in his and squeezed it. Her skin tingled from his warm touch. She wanted to reach out to him, feel his arms around her again. Instead, she thanked him for a pleasant evening and went inside. Closing the front door, she leaned on it. Tears came to her eyes. The whole evening, she'd yearned to touch him. She wanted much more than the simple handshake she'd offered.

Julie consoled herself with the knowledge the investigation couldn't last forever. Then, maybe Paul and she could be together. She closed her eyes and prayed a silent prayer.

That night in troubled dreams, she searched for Paul in a dark forest. Everytime she caught sight of him ahead of her, she'd hurry to catch up. Wet grass soaked her feet, and the underbrush tore at her clothes and scratched her arms and legs, as she continued, yet when she reached the place she'd last seen him, he was gone. She woke up at first light of morning with a pounding between her temples.

The phone rang while she toyed with a bowl of cold cereal. 'Okay, it's over.' Corbeille's voice sounded stronger today. 'The Chief's called off the search. He says any more digging around that quarry would be a waste of our time and the taxpayers' money.'

'He's agreed to go to the Parole Board?'

'Just as soon as we confirm Forsythe's story,' Corbeille told her. 'I've arranged for us to see him at four o'clock. Meet me at the prison at three forty-five.'

* * *

Waiting for Corbeille that afternoon, Julie checked the time, three fifty. She'd arrived a few minutes earlier and Corbeille still wasn't there. Julie got out of her car and paced up and down while watching for her partner.

A battered red Ford pickup sputtered into the Visitors parking lot and lurched to a stop next to her Honda. The driver jumped out. 'Sorry, I'm late,' a tall, bespectacled man said.

'Corbeille?' He wasn't what she'd expected.

'Yeah. Good to meet you at last.' They shook hands.

She recognized the rough, deep voice that better suited the mental image she'd contrived of Corbeille, a husky brute of a man with a cigar stuck between his teeth. There was nothing intimidating about this pale, skinny man.

'We better go in.' She led him into the prison where the trustee waited.

Forsythe appeared more cheerful than on her previous visit. Perhaps he hoped his time in prison was coming to an end. Julie sat back and let Corbeille conduct the interview. In a firm, no-nonsense voice, her partner explained the Chief's conditions.

'You'll need to give us your information to analyze first. If it leads us to the body and the killer, your sentence could be reduced. It's up to the Parole Board. On the other hand, if all you've got is garbage, you serve the rest of your sentence.'

Forsythe's face fell. 'Is that all?'

'You got it,' Corbeille responded in a firm voice and she nodded in agreement.

'All right.' Forsythe looked around, as if to make sure no one else was listening.

'Go ahead.' Corbeille encouraged him. 'We don't have all day.'

'This guy was serious. He told me he'd been hired to kill a Richmond architect and bury the body.'

'Where is she?' Corbeille's gaze locked on Forsythe.

'His instructions were to bury her in some woods north of the city, but not near the quarry,' the prisoner replied.

Julie prompted Forsythe. 'Go on.'

'It seemed odd to me but his instructions were to use the woods behind an older neighborhood called Pollard Park.'

'That's near Martin's home, isn't it?' Corbeille half-turned his head and whispered to her.

'Yeah,' she said. Doubt blurred her vision for a moment. Julie blinked hard and tried to appear unshaken. Paul wouldn't hurt anyone. Would he? She remembered his rage the night Dorothy called, and when Julie asked if they could be friends.

'Give us the name of the killer and who hired him.' Corbeille proded Forsythe.

'My ex-cell-mate, Ron Barber's your man. He didn't tell me who hired him.' Forsythe smiled, knowingly. Had he heard Corbeille whisper to her?

Julie bit her lip while her fellow officer tried

to get additional information from Forsythe. One thought raced through her mind. If Sheila's body turned up a short distance from Paul's home, the police would immediately focus on him.

'We need more than that. Those woods cover a large area. Think, man.' Corbeille's voice wielded authority. 'What else did he say?'

'Just in those woods.' The convict creased his brow. 'Barber's not a large man and he would have had to carry her body, so it wouldn't be far from the road. Just far enough so no one would see him.'

While a guard returned Forsythe to his cell, Corbeille and Julie walked to their cars outside the penintentiary.

'I'll report to the Chief right away.' Corbeille moped his forehead. In the sunlight, his skin looked flushed. 'As soon as we get an address on this Ron Barber, we'll bring him in to be questioned.'

'You better go home and take it easy.' Staring at her partner, Julie could tell the man didn't feel well. 'This's your first day back at work. I can arrange for a search team to dig in the woods.'

'Thanks. Contact Officer Schwartz.' Corbeille scribbled a name and number on a card and handed it to her. He slumped against his truck for a moment then stood erect. 'Ask him to meet you at the site tomorrow morning with his team. I'll call the Chief. Let me know what time you're to meet Schwartz tomorrow and I'll try to join you.'

'All right. Get some rest.' She waved as his pickup pulled out of the parking lot. He'd warmed toward her since she'd taken his assignment at the prison yesterday. This afternoon they'd worked together to solve a crime. And they'd learned the alleged killer's name. If Barber was their man, he'd be able to tell them who hired him. Dorothy Turner again came to mind. But why would she want to harm her own stepdaughter? It still didn't make sense.

On her way home, Julie parked by the woods Forsythe had mentioned. It reminded her of an area where she liked to play as a child. When Dad found out where she'd been, he had scolded her and said it wasn't a safe place for children.

Tall maples and oaks predominated here, interspersed with pine trees. The undergrowth was thick — grasses mingled with tall weeds and grape vines, broken only by paths that generations of walkers had carved through the forest. The killer had picked well. Sheila's body could be buried anywhere. The hair on the back of Julie's neck prickled.

While she faced the woods, an unseen bird

let out a shrill cry in the treetops. Moments later, a large orange cat slunk out of the undergrowth. The light grew dimmer as day faded into twilight. Still, she had time for a brief walk. Julie locked her car and strolled into the woods.

A few yards into the bramble, the main path divided into three footpaths.

On impulse, she picked the middle one and followed it as it wound and twisted its way through the woods. Within minutes, she'd lost sight of the road, and except for the distant swish of a passing car, could have been miles from civilization, the undergrowth was so dense. Her path rambled on.

Night fell sooner than she'd expected. About to turn back, she noticed lights ahead. Curiosity overcame caution. She'd go just a little further. The trail climbed slightly for a few feet then she stopped and inhaled sharply. Her path ended at someone's back yard.

* * *

Paul had stepped outside to escape Jay's chatter. Near the edge of his back yard, he gazed into the darkening woods. Hearing a twig snap, his nerves tensed.

His anger flared. Someone was spying on

him. Taking the offensive, he dashed into the woods. Something rustled in the brush and he lunged.

A gasp, then he grabbed at a dim figure about to escape. It wiggled through a narrow hole between two trees — and got stuck. Unable to make out who it was, he seized the figure. His hands traced the contours of a slender body from long legs all the way up to high, firm breasts.

'Let me go.' A familiar voice cried out.

'Julie?' He couldn't have been more surprised. Paul dropped his hands, squinted to see her face in the gathering darkness.

'Paul? You almost scared me to death.' Julie slumped against him before stepping back. While she smoothed her tumbled hair and straightened her clothes, she explained. 'These woods have fascinated me since I moved here. I thought I'd walk for a few minutes. Night fell faster than I expected and I got lost.'

'I'm so sorry. I didn't hurt you, did I?'

'No. I just didn't realize it was you. You chased me. I panicked and ran.'

'Let's get out of here.' Paul took her hand, led her back to his yard. 'I've got just what you need right now.'

'You do?' An uneasy expression crossed her face.

'I was referring to a new wine I've found.' He smiled and plucked a leaf out of her hair. 'It's the least I can do after scaring you.'

'All right, but I can't stay long.'

Her voice sounded strained. He'd frightened her, but how could he know she'd choose that evening for a stroll? After all that had happened, his nerves were taut. He'd imagined the police hiding in the woods, keeping him under surveillance, and it was just Julie out for a stroll in the woods. 'Sorry I upset you.'

She laughed and sounded more normal. 'It was my fault. Let's go try that wine. I'm sure we could both use a glass.'

He started to put his arm around her but reconsidered. Holding her hand, he led her back to his house and the wine he'd mentioned. She'd stayed a few minutes then he walked her home, not leaving her until he'd seen her safely inside.

Later in bed, he acknowledged a small warning voice in his mind. Why was she really there? She's never shown any interest in the woods behind their properties before this. Why tonight?

16

Early the next morning Julie slipped out of her house and walked down the hill. She'd been afraid to retrieve her car last night after that encounter with Paul. When he'd walked her home, she breathed a sigh of relief, seeing her closed garage door. If he'd noticed her car wasn't there, she would have had to come up with a good excuse fast. She mustn't give him reason to be suspicious. Damn but she was tired of lying.

Paul's closed curtains and the newspaper on the front lawn indicated he wasn't up yet. Good. He wouldn't see her leave.

As she approached the woods, she found a police van parked a few yards from her Honda. A policeman waited there.

Arms folded, the officer checked the time. Her watch registered seven-fifty, and their appointment was for eight o'clock. This policeman sure was eager to get on with his assignment.

Walking up to Schwartz, she smiled and called out, 'Hope I haven't made you wait.' Julie showed him her identification.

'Not at all. I just got here a few minutes

ago. My wife swears I'll be early for my own funeral.' His bulldog mask of a face flashed a grin then became somber as he got down to business. 'It's the weekend so people are home from work. With any luck, we won't attract many curious bystanders. What have you got for me, Detective?'

'Our informant says the killer was instructed to bury the body in these woods, but he didn't know the exact location.'

Schwartz glanced at the thicket of trees in front of them. 'My God, you're talking about at least thirty acres of forest.'

'Hold on. It may not be as bad as you think,' she reassured him. In an effort to share all she knew, she continued. 'If Barber's file is accurate, he's 5'8', 160 pounds. The missing person report describes the victim, Sheila Turner, as 5'10', weight about 140 pounds.'

'So he'd be about my size,' Schwartz commented.

Julie nodded in agreement. 'It wouldn't have been easy for a man of his height and build to carry the victim. I don't imagine he went far from the path.' A mental picture of the killer with Sheila in his arms flashed before Julie's inner eye, disturbing her.

'Thanks. If what you say is true, we can narrow our search to the area close to the footpaths. I've requested a couple of search dogs, but they haven't shown up yet. It's possible none are available. A K-9 team could save us a lot of time. Well, we'd better get to work. Good to meet you. We'll contact you if and when we find the body.' On that skeptical tone, Schwartz turned away and walked toward the van.

Annoyed by his pessimistic attitude, she got in her car and watched as four policemen in overalls climbed out of the van. Two put up crime scene tape and the others unloaded shovels and a metal detector, carrying them into the woods. She'd better check back later to see how they'd progressed.

* * *

At home, she punched in Corbeille's telephone number. Mrs. Corbeille answered in a hushed voice.

'Dick's had a relapse,' she whispered into the phone. 'I told him he should stay home one more day. Of course, he never listens to me. His fever's so high, his doctor ordered him back to bed.'

'I'm sorry to hear that. Please tell him to take care of himself and not to worry about the case.' Julie sent her fellow officer a message. 'I'll take care of things until he feels better.'

At the end of the call, she squared her shoulders and added Corbeille's responsibilities to her own. God knew how long he'd be bed-confined. Though she was sorry to hear he was sick, it couldn't have come at a worse time. This investigation was heating up, and there was no time out for illness.

At a knock on her back door, Julie's stomach muscles clenched.

'Anybody home?' A familiar voice called.

Opening the door, her gaze locked with Paul's.

'You were out when I called earlier.' His casual words contrasted with the watchful expression on his face.

Guilt gnawed at her, yet there was no way she could tell him how she'd spent her morning. 'Come in. I'll make some coffee.'

'No, thanks.' He followed her into the kitchen. 'I've begun to think I have a rival. Is it an amorous Latino dance instructor?' Though he bantered with her, his tone was dead serious.

'No.' Caught off guard, she spoke from her heart. 'There's only y . . . ' Realizing what she'd almost told him, she stopped.

'Only me? Is that what you started to say?' Paul put his hands on either side of her face, forced her to look at him. She tried to turn away.

'I didn't mean to say that. It just slipped out.'

Paul pulled out a chair at the kitchen table and made her sit down then took a seat beside her. 'Listen to me.' He spoke in a firm yet kind tone. 'You care for me, Julie, even if you won't admit it. I don't think you were pretending the other night. That was real. So what happened?'

'I told you. There was a man where I worked.'

'You were involved?' His blue gaze locked on her face, Paul interrogated her.

'Yes.' She squirmed. His questions made her nervous.

'For how long?' He never took his eyes off her.

'Oh, I guess a few months.' Tears of frustration welled in her eyes. If he'd just go away before she broke down and told him everything. And if she did, would he ever forgive her?

'But you never made love with him?'

'No, I broke off the relationship before we got to that point. He'd changed and I wasn't sure.' She felt her skin flush. 'You were the first,' she muttered. She'd known better but . . .

'And it was special to you. Wasn't it?' His voice became gentle. Paul took her cold hand

and kissed the knuckles.

Julie blinked back a tear that threatened to fall and whispered, 'It was special.'

'Then why all of this?' Paul wrinkled his brow. 'Are you in trouble? Remember, I'm a lawyer if you need legal assistance.'

'It's not like that. I'll be all right. Just . . . can we talk about something else?' Why did he have to be so kind and considerate? He made her feel like a louse even though she had to lie to protect the investigation. She should have never gotten involved with him. If she hadn't followed her heart, none of this would have happened.

'As long as you remember I'm here if you need me,' he replied and planted a kiss on top of her head.

'Thanks. Now,' she dabbed at her eyes with her fingers until he lent her his handkerchief, 'Was there something else you wanted to see me about?'

'Yeah. I'd like to ask a favor. Would you be interested in reading my manuscript?'

'Sure. Bring it over.' She was pleased he'd want her to read his work. Was it a sign he cared? Maybe in the pages of the manuscript she'd gain insight into Paul.

'I'll get it.' He appeared reluctant to leave. 'Don't run away. I'll be right back.'

Paul soon returned, manuscript in hand.

He dropped the story on the table. 'Here it is. Remember, this is fiction.'

Curious about his story, Julie fingered the bundle of paper.

'Maxine has the original,' he said. 'The editor who was interested changed her mind. I'd really appreciate your looking it over and giving me your opinion.'

'I'll be glad to read it.' She didn't object when he kissed the top of her head again before leaving.

Once he'd gone, she still felt his large, warm hands on her face and the slow burning sensation his closeness ignited. It was hard to think clearly after their encounter.

With Paul's manuscript in her arms, she sat down in a rocker on her back porch. She'd start it right now while she had time. Opening the manuscript, she began to read. The story was interesting, but the sunshine and a soft breeze on her cheek combined with the lack of a good night's rest, lulled her.

Her eyelids grew heavy until she lay her head back against the cushioned chair and rested her eyes. The clank of the wrought iron gate at the side of the house came to her as if from a great distance.

'Wake up, Sleeping Beauty.'

Trained to expect the unexpected, Julie automatically jumped and put out her hands to defend herself. Opening her eyes, she was embarrassed to see Paul's face. 'What's going on?'

'From my backyard, I saw you sitting over here. You looked so still, I thought I'd better see if you were all right. I forgot to tell you about Jay.'

He'd been too busy interrogating her. It was no wonder Paul was curious, the way she'd acted. She hoped she'd satisfied him, at least for awhile.

'My brother got a job,' Paul told her. 'Assistant Manager at Lombardis on West Broad Street, and he starts tonight. It doesn't pay a lot, but it's a start.'

'What about a job with a travel agency?'

'This's just temporary until he can take the classes he needs. He also found a new apartment near work.'

She frowned. 'He's moving out?'

Paul chuckled. 'You sound like the worried parent of a teenager. It'll just be thirty minutes from here. We'll see him. Actually, this way's better. It'll give us a chance to spend more time together without a third wheel around.'

As Paul strolled away, anxiety spurted through her. Jay's move made it more difficult. She'd planned to use him as a buffer to avoid time alone with Paul until the investigation ended. Paul was too tempting. It was hard to keep her hands off him, her lips off his. Now what the heck would she do?

No word came from Schwartz so later that day Julie drove by the woods. The patrol car and van were still parked at the curb. Schwartz meandered down the path as she parked the Honda. Seeing her, he came over to her car. She could tell by his grim expression the sergeant was in a foul mood.

'I don't guess you've come to inform us the body's been found somewhere else?' Schwartz sounded out-of-sorts.

'No,' she admitted. 'The con told our informant it's here.'

He frowned. 'Have they located the killer yet?'

'Not yet, but it's just a matter of time until they track him down,' she said. 'He's moved since he got out of jail and didn't notify his parole officer.'

'You need to find him and get him to talk. These woods are too deep.' Schwartz gestured at the thicket of trees and undergrowth. 'Even limiting our team to digging along the paths, it could take us days to locate one body. I've asked for additional help, but so far nothing.'

'I'll be in touch.' Julie waved and drove off. She'd swing by Safeway for a few things. If

Paul saw her return home, the groceries would be a valid excuse for going out so early.

On the way to the store, she considered what to do next. Paul had asked if she'd tried personnel agencies in her job search. Julie hoped he hadn't begun to question her cover story. Maybe she should make a couple of calls, even go on an interview or two. An interview didn't mean she had to accept a position. As she unloaded her groceries, Paul stepped out on his front porch.

'Wait a minute. I'll get those for you.' He lifted the heavy bags in one arm and carried them to her kitchen. With his rumpled denim shirt and blue eyes, he looked most appealing. She fought down the urge to reach out and smooth the lock of hair that fell onto his forehead, straighten his shirt collar. 'How does a dinner of French cuisine and good wine sound?'

'Oh, you've heard of a new restaurant?' Or did he intend to cook the meal himself? The idea of an entire evening alone in his home, with no interruptions, made her pulse beat faster. It might be more than she could handle. When he was near, she yearned.

'Yeah, on River Road. Maxine recommended it.'

'That sounds great,' Julie said, relieved.

'Good. I'll be over at six o'clock.'

Squeezing her shoulder, he let himself out the kitchen door.

Corbeille phoned while she put away her groceries. Her partner sounded excited, despite his raspy congestion. 'The Chief couldn't reach you so he called me. They picked up Barber. He's in an interrogation room at headquarters. Would you go down, just to observe? It won't blow your cover.'

* * *

Elated the end could be in sight, Julie grabbed her car keys and wasted no time driving downtown to Richmond PD. Through an observation window, she watched two detectives interrogating Barber, a scrawny man with a scruffy dark beard. He wore a soiled 'Virginia Is For Lovers' tee-shirt and faded jeans.

His shoulders shook as he sobbed and babbled. Over and over, he moaned, 'I killed her, I killed her. I'm so glad you found me.'

For the record, the older detective asked him to elaborate on what he'd said. Who did he kill and when?

Julie tensed with anticipation. In a matter of moments, it would all be over. Questions filled her mind. How did Barber kidnap

Sheila? Who hired him and why? And where was the body?

The ex-con raised his tear-stained face and cried, 'I admit it. I killed her. I didn't want to kill her. She drove me to it.' He shuddered as if recalling his crime.

'Go ahead,' the older detective patted Barber's shoulder. 'Tell us all about it. You'll feel better.'

Wiping his eyes, Barber nodded. 'She nagged me for years. No matter what I did, it wasn't what she wanted. At last, I couldn't take any more. On the night of March 19, 1995, Mother was snoring in her bed. I couldn't stand the racket she was making so I tiptoed into her room, put a pillow over her face and smothered her.'

17

Her legs shook. Julie gasped and grabbed the observation window sill for support. They'd been so sure Barber was a killer. They'd been right about that. He'd just confessed, to another murder. At that moment she could have killed Forsythe with her bare hands. It was a damn good thing he was behind bars. Frowning, she watched unseen as the two detectives probed Barber's story.

'We had a tip you might know something about Sheila Turner,' The older detective leaned over Barber, coaxed him. 'What can you tell us about her?'

'The broad who vanished here in town?' Barber's sobbing stopped. He wiped his wet face on a corner of his shirt then scratched his head. From his puzzled expression, it was clear he was either the world's greatest actor, or had no information to give them. 'All I know about that is what I heard on the news.' He glanced from the senior detective to his red-headed, junior partner. 'Why the hell would you suspect me of that?'

'Let's just say we had a tip.' The younger detective's tone was harsh, skeptical as if he wasn't convinced Barber was telling them the truth. He ripped a calender off the wall and laid it on the table in front of Barber, his finger pointed to a certain date. 'Where were you on this day?'

A chuckle rose from behind the scruffy, dirty beard then Barber whopped with glee. 'Somebody's been pulling your leg, Detective. Check with the warden at the pen. His records will show I was still visiting him that day.' Laughter shook his scrawny body until a hard glance from the younger detective quieted him.

'All right,' the detective grumbled. 'Maybe you've got an alibi for Ms. Turner, but you've just confessed to killing your own mother. Don't try to wiggle out of that.'

Barber nodded his head. 'The old bitch asked for it. She nagged and nagged until I just snapped and killed her.'

'Get a full written statement,' the older detective ordered an uniformed policeman by the door. 'We'll check on his mother before we charge him.'

A few minutes later, the older detective walked into Julie's room. 'Sorry we brought you down here for nothing, Detective. It looked like Barber was the guy you're after, but that theory's shot to hell now. If his story checks out about being in prison the day Ms.

Turner vanished, he can't be your man.'

'At least you can solve another crime, if he's on the level about his mother,' she snapped. And where did this new development leave her investigation? In limbo, with Paul still the suspect in the case.

The detective seemed to pick up on her frustration because he didn't respond to her rude reply. 'Will you inform your partner?'

'I'm sorry. We really counted on Barber being our man,' she explained. 'Yes, I'll call Corbeille. Let's hope he recovers soon. He's needed on this investigation.'

Once in her car, she pulled out her cell phone and punched in Corbeille's number. His wife answered.

'How is he today?'

'Dick's much better. His fever's gone, and the doctor says if he continues to improve, he can get back to work in a day or two.' Mrs. Corbeille paused then continued, a smile in her voice. 'Of course I may have to tie him down to keep him home until then.'

Corbeille's eager voice came on the line, probably from an extension. 'All right. Tell me what happened. Did Barber confess? Is he the killer?'

'Barber's a killer, if we can believe his story, just not ours.' A loud groan reached her ears through the phone lines and her stomach knotted with anxiety. 'Are you all right?'

'Yeah, I'm just damn disappointed. Guess we should've been suspicious. The information on Barber came too easy. That weasel Forsythe sold us a bill of goods. Wait until I see him.'

'I'll call the Warden and get an appointment to interrogate Forsythe again, as soon as possible.' Here they went again. Would she ever be able to wrap up this case? She'd convinced herself it was almost over.

'Tell me what you find out.' He let out an annoyed sigh. 'One more day and I'm out of here.'

Thank God for that. Since he'd been ill, she'd strained to cover his responsibilities and her own. If he'd been well, Corbeille would have visited the quarry, met with Schwartz, and attended Barber's interrogation.

⋆ ⋆ ⋆

That afternoon, Julie reentered the Visitors Room at the prison. Forsythe seemed to have aged since she'd last seen him. His skin appeared more wrinkled and his body more frail. He wouldn't meet her gaze.

Today she wasn't charmed by his kindly, grandfather act. In a stern, no-nonsense voice, she announced, 'We picked up Mr. Barber today.'

'And you found out,' he said and slumped in his chair.

'Yes. Why did you do it, Mr. Forsythe? Why lie to us?' Miserable at this turn of events, she scolded herself for taking his word. The old convict had convinced Corbeille and her that he was telling the truth.

'Well, he is a killer.' He defended himself.

'But not the right one. Did you think we wouldn't care who Barber killed as long as he admitted to murder?' She could have screamed with frustration. This man must think the police were complete fools.

'No, Detective. But I kinda hoped for a shorter sentence when you found out Barber's a killer. After all, a murder is a murder.'

'The Chief sent you a message. He said to tell you the deal's off.'

The old man's face grimaced with disappointment.

'It looks like you'll have to serve the rest of your sentence,' she reminded him.

With a deep sigh, he responded. 'If I tell ya the name of the real killer, his friends will get me. He's out now. They're still in here with me.'

Disgusted, she raised both eyebrows. This

guy was too much. How could he expect her to believe him after he'd lied earlier. She gave him a cold stare. 'It's possible you could be put in solitary confinement for awhile, or the Warden could have you transferred to another prison. Just give us the real killer.'

Her heart sank as she thought of Paul. By this time today, she'd hoped it would all be over. The case would be finished, and he'd be cleared of the cloud of suspicion that hung over him. Okay, so the investigation still dragged on. It was a bitter pill to swallow. A headache throbbed behind her eyes, and she wondered if this nightmare of a case would ever end.

Forsythe studied his hands for several minutes then he raised his head and nodded. 'Okay, if you can protect me. My life won't be worth a plugged nickel if word gets out I've squealed on another con.'

'Let me call the Chief.'

Julie stepped to the door and motioned to a guard. 'I'll be back as soon as I make a quick telephone call.' Once in the hall, she pulled out her cell phone and punched in the Chief's number, catching him at his desk.

'Is this convict on the level now, Taylor?'

'I can't make any guarantees, Chief, though he appears sincere. I don't think he'd dare pull the same stunt twice.' Or would he?

He'd sucked them in last time with his convincing story. Embarassed Forsythe had managed to trick them, she recalled an old saying of her father's. 'Fool me once, shame on you. Fool me twice, shame on me.'

A moment of silence on the other end of the line, then the Chief agreed. 'Tell him I'll put the wheels in motion to have him moved to another prison as soon as we pick up the real killer. Call me back with the right name this time.'

Back in the room with Forsythe, she nodded. 'All right. It'll be arranged as soon as you carry out your part. Just give me the right man's name. You said he'd been incarcerated here?'

'Yeah.' Another sigh slipped from his lips and he shot a troubled glance her way. 'Mel Peterson's your man. He was in here for passing bad checks. One day in the yard, he bragged about the big job waiting for him when he got out of the joint.'

The old man creased his brow. 'I guess I didn't look too impressed, so he elaborated. He said he'd been hired to kill a local architect and to dispose of her body. He even mentioned he'd been told to bury the broad in the woods behind Pollard Park.'

With his hand over his heart, Forsythe looked her right in the eyes. 'On my dead mother's grave, I swear this's the truth.'

Julie called the Chief with her new information. Forsythe had lied last time, and he'd looked every bit as sincere as today. Not at all convinced with his act, she returned home.

* * *

Fatigued and frustrated by the day's events, Julie's gaze locked on her bedroom phone after she called and updated Corbeille. Seated on the side of her bed, she was sorely tempted to cancel her date with Paul. A slow soak in a hot tub followed by an early-to-bed would be far less stessful. Everytime she was with him, she had to stay on guard. Still, she wanted to see him.

Julie undressed and turned on the hot water. If she hurried, she had time for a bath before Paul arrived. As she lathered her body with her favorite herbal soap, the web of lies and deception she called life gnawed at her.

Today she'd been a police detective on an undercover assignment. Tonight she had to pretend to be a woman with no more on her mind than a dinner date. Soon, she promised herself, no more lies.

She'd dressed in a short floral linen dress and slipped on a pair of sandals by the time

Paul arrived, handsome in a dark suit and blue striped shirt.

'Hey, what's the matter? You look like you've had a bad day. Can I do anything?' Worry creased his brow.

Somehow, he'd sensed she was depressed. What a relief it would be to slip into his arms, lay her head on his chest, and tell him her troubles. Instead, she sent him a bright smile. 'No, I'm fine.'

Light drops of rain began to tap on the roof and through a half-open window, a gentle breeze blew her the scent of wet grass. What a good night to stay home. The idea of a quiet evening, just the two of them, was a real temptation. Her heart fluttered at the thought of Paul's soft words, his persuasive lips, and his caressing hands. Her resolve weakened every time they were together. Before she yielded to temptation, she grabbed her purse and led him out of the house.

'Maxine gives Chez Louise a five star rating,' Paul informed her on the drive down to the river. 'She says the food has a French flair and the manager's from the Deep South with a Parisian accent that wouldn't fool anyone who's been to France.'

Julie's lips twitched. Since they'd met, he'd loosened up, become more relaxed. Though he'd never compete with his wacky brother with his silly stories and antics, Paul had lost a lot of his somber, terse manner. Anyway, there was no need for two Jays. The world wasn't ready for that, and neither was she.

As they stepped into the old mansion converted to a chic restaurant high above the James River, she found a charming dining room furnished with Country French furniture. Pots of purple and pink hyacinths on the tables filled the air with their sweet fragrance, and a view of the river at twilight completed the perfect setting.

From the kitchen, the pleasant aromas of French onion soup and roasted chicken floated into the dining room, promising culinary delights. The hostess seated them at a corner table by the bay windows. The rain had passed and fading streaks of sunlight danced on the waters below.

'This is delightful! Thanks for suggesting it.' Julie's fatigue faded away in the lovely setting. She tasted her wine, a sparkling, fruity Chardonnay. 'What's the latest on your book? Has Maxine had any nibbles since that editor changed her mind?'

'Not yet. She just says 'keep working.' He grinned, boyishly. 'I even hear her in my sleep.'

'I like the story except the ending. It's so sad the way the brothers find one another, then go their separate ways when they can't reconcile their differences.' She stopped to sip her wine. 'Of course, I like happy endings.'

'So do I, but life's not always that way.' Paul's large warm hand covered hers on the table. Her heart skipped a beat.

Julie raised her glass and toasted him. 'Anyway, here's good luck on selling the story.'

'That's enough about my book. What have you been up to today?' His gaze fixed on her face and made her nervous.

'Me? Nothing much. You know — a little gardening, housecleaning, reading the help wanted section. I just can't seem to find the job I want. Maybe I will have to go back to Washington after all.' Her lies weighted her down until it was hard to look right at Paul. She feared he'd see her deception.

'Hold on.' With a frown, he inquired, 'Did you ever try a personnel agency?'

'I've called a few, but they don't seem to have anything for an administrative assistant with my background.' She fiddled with her wine glass. Deceit was part of undercover work, but on this assignment it was much more distasteful since it involved lying to Paul. 'Ah, here comes our dinner.' And not a moment too soon.

While they watched, a waiter rolled a

linen-draped cart up to their table and uncovered their entree-chateaubriand for two. Then he poured them each another glass of Chardonnay.

Before the evening was over, she'd relaxed, smiled and laughed, enjoying Paul's company. Tiny buds of optimism began to unfurl in her heart. Peterson would turn out to be Sheila's killer. He'd confess and the investigation would end. Then a happier future would await Paul and her.

Paul cheered, charmed, and cajoled her into having a good time. He would've shared her burden if she'd let him. Oh, great. Julie could imagine his shocked expression if she told him about her day. A man had admitted to killing his mother and an old convict squealed on a parole to get a reduced sentence. Not only would her cover be blown, it was possible Paul would never speak to her again.

Later, they stood at her front door. 'This has been a lovely evening,' she said. And it had been in spite of Paul's questions.

'It doesn't have to end.' His watchful eyes scrutinized her. 'Why don't you invite me in for a nightcap and we'll take it from there.'

Funny, she'd noticed that same watchful expression on his face several times the last few days. What was he thinking?

'Not tonight, Paul. Remember, you agreed we'd just be friends, at least until I get things straight in my head. All right?'

He shot a piercing gaze her way then responded, his voice fierce. 'No, it's not all right. But this is.' He pulled her into his arms and kissed her hard. Taken by surprise, she leaned into his embrace. His arms tightened and his demanding lips covered hers. His tongue plundered her mouth and swallowed her sigh of pleasure. Breathless, she kissed him back. He tasted sweet like the fruity wine they'd shared at the restaurant.

From her mouth, his lips moved to her jaw then her throat before he reclaimed her mouth with his own. His large hands caressed her back and shoulders, leaving a trail of heat wherever he touched her. His hunger and frustration seemed to match her own. For a few crazy moments, she clung to him like there was no tomorrow and longed for another night like the one they'd shared.

On the brink of tossing caution to the winds, she drew back, pushed against his broad chest. Breathless, she gasped, 'Enough. You're not playing fair.'

A muscle clenched in his jaw and something flickered in his eyes then was gone. In an angry, ragged voice he replied. 'I know you want me. So why the hell do you keep pushing me away? I don't understand you at all.' With a heavy sigh, he walked away.

Julie closed her front door then sank into the nearest chair. Hot frustrated tears rolled down her cheeks. How much longer would he put up with her? She wanted Paul more than anything in the world but, for now, she had to curb her desire and his. If not for her assignment, they'd be making love by now. The sooner her case was solved the better. Then she could explain everything. Dear God, let him care enough to understand.

How long she sat there, she didn't know. At last, she wiped her eyes and started upstairs. Before she reached her room, the phone rang, jarring her already raw nerves. The answering machine picked up before she reached the phone.

'This is Schwartz. Come over to the site.' His voice turned grim as he added, 'We've found her.'

18

Outside, the rain had diminished to a fine mist, leaving the air cool and fresh. Before getting into her car, Julie paused to inhale the fragrance of a neighbor's lilac that drifted to her on the breeze. A quick glance at Paul's house revealed his bedroom lights were still on. She didn't want him to hear her going out again tonight.

Releasing the hand brake, she let her car roll down the steep driveway to the street. It coasted down the hill a ways before she turned on the ignition.

Schwartz's team had set up spotlights to illuminate an area deep inside the woods behind Pollard Park. As she parked the Honda, one of his assistants waited to escort her down the path.

The sergeant stood on a tarp beside the coroner who'd knelt to examine the body. Julie edged closer, close enough to make out long strands of black hair, a denim vest, and a swollen wrist. The coroner carefully turned the head and Julie shuddered. Insects had attacked the face of the corpse and it was unrecognizable. A breeze brought the stench of decomposing flesh.

'Sheila Turner?' In her heart, she knew it was.

The coroner looked briefly in Julie's direction then rose and brushed mud off his overalls. 'This woman meets the Turner woman's general description — tall brunette, mid-thirties, I'd estimate. Whoever it is, the body's been in the ground for awhile. If it hadn't been wrapped in a wool blanket, it would be more decomposed. The body will be moved to the morgue so we can establish her identity.' He stepped aside and two of his assistants placed the corpse in a body bag, zipped it up, then laid it on a stretcher.

'Let me know what you find out.' Julie gave him her telephone number while a coroner's wagon waited at the curb.

On the way home, her thoughts lingered on the deserted woods and gruesome scene. A shudder crept through her body. As she eased her car into the garage, the porch light shone through the darkness like a welcoming beacon. Julie hurried from the car to the house. Once inside her foyer, she wasted no time locking the door. How much longer would it be until Peterson, the killer was apprehended?

While she prepared for bed, a more horrible thought came to Julie. Forsythe swore Peterson was the killer, but the con could have sent them on another wild goose chase. The real killer might be someone else, someone so clever he'd never be caught. Disturbed, Julie slid under her covers. Sleep didn't come for a long time.

* * *

'You're out early.' Julie called to Paul seeing him walk down his front steps next morning. His head jerked then he turned and looked at her in her yard, holding her paper.

'Yeah. Maxine wants to go over a few weak spots in my manuscript.' Speaking to Julie across the lawns bright with morning dew, Paul shifted his weight from one foot to the other and didn't seem to have much to say. 'Well, I'd better not keep the lady waiting.'

Watching him drive away, Julie wished things could be different. Anxiety touched her deep inside. If he'd given up on her, it was her own fault.

An hour later, while she washed her hair, the phone rang. She raised her head from the sink and the shampoo ran into her eyes. 'Damn.' She fumbled for a towel, wrapped it around her head then grabbed the phone, rubbing her sore eyes.

'I've been meaning to call.' Maxine, her

college acquaintance and now Paul's literary agent, took her by surprise. 'There's something I'd like to discuss with you. How about lunch today? I know this is short notice but . . .'

Curiosity got the better of Julie. 'I guess I could. Tell me where to meet you and what time.'

'How about at my office at one o'clock? We're on the tenth floor of NationsBank building on 11th and East Main. Oops. My secretary needs me. Our next client must have showed up. Got to run. See you at one o'clock.' She hung up before Julie could reply.

Julie returned to the bathroom and gazed at herself in the mirror. Why did Maxine want to see her all of a sudden? In college she'd never done anything without a good reason. What was it this time? Her lips curved. Maybe Paul was behind this invitation. He could have told his agent she was unemployed and Maxine called to give her a tip on an available position.

As she blew dry her hair, the phone jangled again. This time Julie let the machine take the call. When Schwartz's husky voice filled the room, she jumped to attention and grabbed the telephone before he could disconnect.

'Taylor? I've tried to reach Corbeille, but his wife said he's at the doctor's office for a checkup so he can return to work tomorrow. I thought you'd like to know about Peterson, the man your convict fingered this time.'

'Right. Did the police track him down yet?' Grasping the telephone tighter, she held her breath and prayed they had.

'Yeah, they did. He'd moved to a boarding house on West Grace Street. The landlady confirmed he was her tenant.'

'That's great. So he's been picked up?'

'I guess you could say that.' The sergeant hesitated before continuing. 'Peterson took a tumble down a flight of stairs at his place of residence last week.'

'Oh, so he's in the hospital?' That shouldn't be a problem. The police could question him there.

'No, he isn't.' Schwartz sounded depressed. 'The coroner's report says he hit his head on the bottom step and broke his neck. The man must have been as drunk as a skunk. Blood tests showed a high level of alcohol in his system at the time of his death. Peterson's in the morgue while they try to locate a relative to come and claim his body.'

Julie was stunned speechless for a second or two, then she licked her dry lips and managed to gasp, 'Dead? You're sure you got the right man?'

'It's Hal Peterson all right. The man Forsythe gave us.'

'Damn. This's just too convenient. Just as we're about to apprehend Sheila's killer, he takes a swan dive down the stairs and kills himself.'

'These things happen,' Schwartz reminded her.

'Maybe he didn't fall. Maybe he was pushed.'

'He was alone as far as we can tell,' the Sergeant informed her. 'We've talked to his landlady and two of the other boarders and nobody saw anything.' Without proof of any wrongdoing, Schwartz seemed ready to accept Peterson's death as an accident. Julie shivered with dread. If Peterson did kill Sheila, he could have become a problem to the person who hired him. Maybe he became greedy and demanded additional funds for services rendered, or his employer feared what he'd say while under the influence of alcohol. Her stomach knotted as a horrible idea slid into her brain. What if Paul were that employer? Repulsed by her disloyalty, she pushed it away.

'We've searched Peterson's room. No clues have turned up so far that link him to the Turner murder, or to who hired him. I'll let you know if we find anything.' Schwartz hung up.

Julie sat on the side of her bed, her hopes in shreds. She could have kicked herself. It had all been too easy. First Forsythe gave them Peterson. All they had to do was locate the man and he'd confess. Wrong. They'd found him all right — stone cold on a slab in the morgue. Someone was a step ahead of them every move they made, someone very clever.

From Paul's description of Dorothy as a snobbish, materialistic socialite, she didn't sound too smart. It didn't take a lot of intelligence to pull out your credit card. No, either she'd misjudged Dorothy's intelligence, or the scheme that began to unfold before her was the product of a mind much more clever than Dorothy's. But whose?

Julie had to admit she wasn't any closer to solving the crime than she'd been earlier. This damn investigation dragged on and on with no end in sight. Discouraged, she dialed Corbeille's number and left him a message.

Disappointment gnawed at her until she felt she had to get out of the house. She slipped on a shirt and jeans then drove a mile to a nearby nursery.

'We have a special right now on miniature rose bushes,' the older lady at the cash register informed her.

'These geranimums are all I want so don't try to sell me anything else.' Julie lashed out at the clerk. Seeing the woman's face flush, she stiffened with embarrassment. Ashamed of her poor behavior, she smiled and tried to make amends. 'I'm sorry. It's not your fault. I had some bad news this morning. These plants are all I need right now, but I'll think about the roses.'

She drove home with a trunk full of small red geranimums to brighten up the front yard and soothe her dashed hopes.

In the kitchen, a glance at the answering machine told her Corbeille hadn't called. In order not to miss him, she picked up her cell phone and carried it outside with her. On her knees, she arranged the flowers along the walk while waiting for his call. . . . and waiting for Paul to come home.

His car pulled into his driveway. A minute or two passed then he loped across the yard and stood over her.

Leaning back, Julie looked in his direction. 'Well, that was a quick appointment. Don't tell me Maxine's already fixed all of your story's problems.' Irritable, she taunted him.

'She couldn't spend much time with me,' Paul said, ignoring her rude remark. 'Another author needed her help in a hurry.'

'I see.' Gazing at him, Julie sensed he'd lost interest in her. She'd never felt so devastated.

'Maxine's volunteered to point out some problem areas in the manuscript at her apartment tonight.'

'Good for you.' She seethed with jealousy, imagining Paul and Maxine alone together in her apartment. There was no reason why Paul's agent shouldn't help him with his manuscript, yet Julie didn't like the idea. In an attempt to appear indifferent, she shrugged and turned back to her plants.

'I wish I knew what the hell's the matter with you.' He stood behind her for a minute then strode across the lawn and entered his own house.

'Fool.' Julie chastised herself. 'You've just driven away the only man you ever wanted.' She yanked the spade out of the soil so fast she knocked dirt into her face. Jumping up from the gardening pad, she made it inside before her tears broke.

Wiping at her tears, she glanced in the bathroom mirror, appalled at the miserable face that stared back at her. Several deep breaths later, she regained her self-control. She showered, put on a short pastel linen suit, and applied her makeup with care.

It was foolish to take out her frustrations on Paul. She'd apologize first chance she got.

There was no reason to be jealous of Maxine. Their appointment was just business. Wasn't it? Though she hated to admit it, she was jealous.

At ten minutes before one p.m., Julie parked her car in the garage under the bank building and rode the elevator to the top floor. Maxine's office was all glass and chrome, sleek and modern, like its owner.

While she waited for the literary agent, Julie gazed through a window wall, admiring a view of the James River. It resembled a silver chain as it twisted and turned in the distance, on its journey east to the Chesapeake Bay. She was on a journey herself, a journey to find the truth. And, at the end of her journey, she hoped to find safe harbor in Paul's arms.

Maxine walked out of her office, stopped by her secretary's desk to sign some documents, then headed in her direction.

'Ready?' As usual, she was dressed to the teeth in a designer outfit, today a two-piece suit in black and gold.

Julie gestured to the window. 'That's quite a view. You must do well as a literary agent.' For a second or two, she envied her classmate for her career. It must be pleasant to deal with people who aren't suspected criminals.

Maxine nodded. 'Very well, thanks. I enjoy

my profession. You meet so many interesting people in this line of work.'

On the way down to street level in the elevator, Maxine suggested, 'Let's take a cab. You can't always find a place to park down by the river.'

Ten minutes later, they sat at a table in the restored Sam Miller's Restaurant in Shockoe Slip.

'I had no idea that all of this was down here.' Julie looked around her. Outside her window in the restored tobacco warehouse, Richmond office workers and tourists rubbed elbows as they moved along the cobblestone streets in front of Italianate style brick and ironfront buildings and by an ornate Renaissance-style fountain. The whole ambience was European, sharply contrasted by the modern skyscrapers on the horizon.

'I haven't been down here for years. All of these shops, restaurants, hotels and galleries. It's amazing how this area has developed,' Julie said.

'Do you miss Alexandria?' Maxine asked. 'It's so close to Washington. Richmond must seem provincial once you've lived in a metroplex like the nation's capital.'

'Not at all. This's a large enough city for me,' Julie responded. 'And all of this urban renewal is remarkable.'

'You've relocated to Richmond, but is that a permanent thing?' Maxine appeared interested, for what reason Julie couldn't fathom. They hadn't seen each other for years, had never been close, even when they belonged to the same sorority in college.

'I guess. So far I haven't found the right job. Thanks to my father's investments, I don't have to rush out and grab the first position that's offered to me. Soon I hope to find something that suits my background as a governmental administrative assistant.'

'Do you still like seafood?' Maxine's bright gaze surveyed the restaurant's other occupants.

'Love it.' Julie read the menu and chose a Warmed Scallop Salad then sipped iced tea while they chatted about old acquaintances from the University. Their lunches came fast. From the business attire of the clientelle, this restaurant catered to people on their lunch hours.

Picking at Crab Newburg and a crisp tossed salad of greens, Maxine commented, 'It's been a long time since we were college students, hasn't it?'

'Sometimes I get the feeling it's been more than four years. And now you're an up-and-coming literary agent.' Thanks to her family. Maxine's wealthy mother had set her up in business after she graduated from college.

'If you say so.' Maxine tilted her head, accepted her praise. 'Of course, I can always manage one more client.' As she ate her salad, Julie felt the other woman's inquisitive glance focus on her face. 'I suppose you wonder why I called?'

'Well, the thought had crossed my mind.' Behind her smile, Julie considered what Maxine was up to now. Her thoughts traveled back to college days. All of her dorm mates had nicknames. One girl had given Julie the name Bookworm because she preferred to study rather than go out with male classmates who called for last minute dates. What had they called Maxine?

Something clicked in her mind while she returned Maxine's bright smile. Devious Dora. And Maxine had turned out to be just that, devious. Several classmates learned by experience that Maxine was one girl you needed to watch. Right now she examined her sculptured fingernails.

'It was good of you to send Paul to me. For a first attempt, his writing shows promise. I have no doubt I can sell his book as soon as we smooth out a few rough spots.'

'He appreciates your help.' Julie struggled to give her the benefit of the doubt. College was ages ago. People did change.

'The pleasure's all mine.' Sipping her white wine, Maxine asked, 'By the way, I don't see an engagement ring on your finger. May I assume Paul and you aren't engaged or anything?'

'No, we aren't.' So that was the reason her classmate had invited her to lunch. Maxine had her eye on Paul. It was hard to say the words but, right now, what else could she say? 'We're just friends, good friends.'

Relief shone on the other woman's sharp features. 'Thats good, because if he's free, I have plans for him.'

'I just bet you do,' Julie said through clenched teeth. Stupid. She should have suspected Maxine was up to no good. She'd grabbed any guy she fancied in college, regardless of which of her sorority sisters he was dating.

Maxine threw her head back and let out a high whinny of a laugh, doubtless picked up from the thoroughbreds her rich mother favored. She examined her Rolex watch. 'Is it two o'clock already? I've got to run.' With a quick glance at the bill, she tossed two twenties on the table for their lunch. 'It was good to see you, Julie.' A gloating smile flashed across her face as she sauntered out the door of the restaurant.

19

Who did Julie think she was anyway? He didn't need her sarcasm. His first inclination had been to avoid her, but he'd wanted to see her, in spite of the way she'd acted earlier. It would have been better if he'd pretended he hadn't seen her and gone on inside his house.

Paul slammed through his foyer, marched into the living room, and threw himself down on the leather sofa. He punched a pillow and placed it under his head.

Whatever happened to that sweet-dispositioned, out-going woman he'd met? They'd had so much fun together. A smile crept across his face as he recalled the day at the beach. She said she wanted to take a few shells home, so he heaped a mountain of shells in front of her while she sat, laughing, on the sand. And there was that disastrous picnic. She'd been a good sport even after the storm hit. They'd just packed up the picnic hamper and finished the evening at his place in front of the fire in his big old kitchen.

Most of all, he remembered and cherished the memory of their night together. Her shy caresses had thrilled him more than the sexual techniques of the women he'd dated in college and law school.

She'd helped him through tough times, encouraged him when he lost his job, and not let him blame himself the day Jay was hurt in that hit-and-run accident.

Now she'd changed into a stranger who wouldn't communicate with him. He sensed she was deeply troubled, yet it was obvious she didn't trust him enough to let him help. He shook his head.

All right. If that's the way she wanted it, he'd back off and leave her alone. He'd waited long enough for her to come around. All that nonsense about being friends wrangled him. The idea of friendship was hard to accept from a woman who'd been his lover. Now he was supposed to content himself with handshakes. She must think he was made of stone.

Everytime they touched, he longed to pull her close, kiss her soft lips, to hold her in his arms, and make love to her like he had once. She hadn't held back, then. That night she was completely his. And she'd admitted he was her first lover.

At last, the day drew to a close, and Paul was glad it was time to keep the appointment with his agent.

In a gated complex of ultra-modern

townhouses not far from downtown, Maxine answered the door on his first knock and led him into her living room.

'Can I get you a drink before we start?'

'How about a glass of water?' Paul admired the sleek lines of the wrought iron and glass table and chairs that filled the adjacent dining room. 'That's an attractive set of furniture. Is it new?'

'Not really. My mother bought it for me when I moved in here. I saw it at the store and told her about it.' She smiled. 'When I see what I want, I have to have it.'

Her comment rang false. It sounded like a remark a spoiled child would make, and didn't fit with his mental image of his literary agent, a grown woman with her own business.

They settled down to work. At first Maxine sat across from him at the table and gave directions like 'turn to that scene on page fifty,' one of his favorite scenes, where the brothers are reunited.

'What's the matter with it?' Paul frowned. That was one of his favorite scenes. He'd thought it was fine the way it was. But she'd offered to help him so he'd listen to her suggestions.

'Nothing except you should draw it out. You're too brief. Here, let me show you.' She got up and stood behind him, pointed out places where he could develop a scene more fully.

After that, she continued to stand behind him, looking over his shoulder while he read aloud several passages. Her ample breast brushed his arm every time he turned a page. The heady Opium perfume she wore and her low-cut red velour blouse and short black skirt made it difficult for him to focus on his work. Though he tried to ignore the warning signs, Paul began to feel aroused. Maxine was hot and sexy and, unless he was mistaken, available. If he didn't know better, he'd think she was coming on to him. And if she was, what did he want to do about it? Julie had shown how little she cared, so he had no reason not to follow his own inclinations this evening or any other time.

An hour later, Maxine stretched, showing her bare midriff. 'That's enough for tonight. How about a drink?'

'Maybe one.' Paul glanced at his watch. 'You have to work tomorrow.' Unemployment both angered and humiliated him. While others he knew went on with their careers, he stayed home. If anyone had told him a year ago he'd be in this predicament, he would have told them they were crazy.

Riffer had gone into private practice since he left the firm and had suggested the two of them form a partnership. At that instant, Paul made up his mind. He'd accept his friend's offer and join him in his law practice. He couldn't wait forever for Sheila to come back so he could rejoin his firm.

He'd also hire another private investigator. The first one had been a waste of time and his funds. Maybe Riffer could recommend someone. One way or another, he had to get out of this limbo.

Paul followed Maxine into the living room and sank into her velour-covered sofa. She opened a small built-in bar then turned and asked, 'What's your pleasure?'

Paul glanced at the well-stocked shelves. 'Scotch, please.'

'Neat, or do you want some ice cubes?'

'Neat, but don't give me too much. I have to drive home.'

They sipped and snacked on a bowl of spicy nuts and chips that she'd placed on the large oak coffee table.

'Paul.' She purred and ran long red fingernails along his shirt sleeve. 'I had lunch with Julie today. She's a sweet girl, isn't she?'

Unsure where the conversation was leading, Paul nodded and waited for her to continue.

'She must feel safer with you as a neighbor. For Julie, I'd imagine it would be like having a big brother next door. Poor girl, she's never found Mr. Right, but she always was shy around boys, didn't date much. It's not that she's a man-hater, but we all thought she was too close to her Daddy. The girls in our dorm used to tease her about being in love with her father.'

From her unkind remarks and the smirk on her face, he realized for the first time Maxine was no friend of Julie's.

'I disagree. She's told me that her mother died when she was very young. Under the circumstances, it's not unusual that she'd be close to her father. He was her only surviving parent.' Maxine's catty remark set Paul's teeth on edge. He'd noticed Julie's expression the times she'd spoken of her father. It was obvious she missed the man but that was normal. He'd lost both of his parents when he was fifteen. The old pain ached like a wound that had healed on the surface but was still there.

'You're right, I'm sure.' Maxine shrugged. 'But let's not waste time on Julie. You're a much more interesting person. Why don't you tell me about yourself?'

'There's not much to tell.' His feelings were jumbled. Flattered that she was interested in him, he was still a little annoyed over her criticism of Julie.

‘That’s not true, I’m sure. You’re a very attractive man.’

Maxine turned toward him, the vee between her ample breasts drew his attention. Paul began to feel uneasy.

‘In fact, at this moment I find you most attractive.’ She slid across the sofa until the sides of her thighs touched his.

‘Thanks. You’re good looking yourself.’ That was the truth. She was a handsome woman with her short helmet of jet black hair and dark eyes, just not his type. His ideal came to mind, light brown eyes, long blonde hair, and skin as soft as a baby’s. He blinked and the image faded away.

‘Do you like me?’ From her keen expression, it seemed important to her that he did.

‘Well, sure.’

In one quick move, Maxine climbed onto his lap, her short skirt hitched up. ‘Why don’t you show me you do?’ She brushed her hot lips against his, her fingernails dug into his shoulders.

Her flesh was feverish and so eager, and he was only human. He kissed her lips and she responded by locking her arms around his neck. Her heady fragrance burned his nostrils until he felt he’d sunk into a perfumed pit, locked in the embrace of a frenzied partner.

Dissatisfied, he drew back. Something wasn't right here.

While he tried to think of a tactful way to get out of a bad situation, she mumbled something he couldn't understand. 'What did you say?'

'Let's go into my bedroom unless you want to screw right here on the f — rug.'

The crude remark killed what remained of his passion and gave him a chance to see the situation as it was, just a casual sexual romp by two people who had no regard for each other. As if on cue, memories of Julie's sweet tenderness drifted into his mind. What the hell was he doing with this woman? He didn't even like her since her snide remarks about Julie.

With one swift move, he lifted her off his lap and deposited her on the floor then got to his feet. 'Sorry, Maxine,' he informed her in a firm voice. 'We both got carried away. This's not the reason I'm here. I came over to work on my book. We're finished now so I'll be on my way.'

Her lip curled with scorn. 'Go ahead, leave,' she said. Her cheeks flushed with spite and rejection. 'I don't know why I've wasted my time. A lot of guys would jump at the chance.'

'Maybe, but I'm old-fashioned. I like to

choose who I make love to, not be tricked into having sex with a woman who just wants to add another trophy to her collection.'

On the drive home, Paul took a deep breath. That had been a narrow escape. Maxine had set a trap, and he'd almost fallen into it. One thing was sure, the episode wouldn't be repeated, even if he had to find another agent.

* * *

Sitting at her kitchen table next morning, Julie rubbed her bleary eyes. She hadn't slept well last night. Paul had been on her mind. When his car pulled into his driveway around midnight, she'd been torn by diverse emotions. Part of her yearned to go next door and apologize for her rude behavior yesterday. Somehow, she didn't imagine he'd send her away. She shook her head. That wouldn't solve anything. At the same time, she burned with anger and jealousy. What had Maxine and he done that evening? The woman had played hard and fast with guys in college. Had she changed? At last Julie fell asleep and dreamed of Paul. In her dreams he left her, though she asked him to stay.

Now, in the early daylight, she slumped in her chair, weary and sad-hearted, and sipped a mug of hot tea. If she could just hold on for a few more days, perhaps then . . . The phone rang and she sensed who it was.

'Julie? I'm coming over.' Paul's voice sounded dead serious. 'I need to ask you something.'

'You sound so grim. Is everything all right?'

'No, it's not. I'll be there in a minute.'

Fear and uncertainty tore through her, waiting for him. Was this personal or did it relate to the case? Though he'd admitted lying to the police about the night Sheila disappeared, Julie still struggled to cling to the hope he was innocent. But what if that lie was just one of many he'd told? Doubt filled her.

Paul knocked on the back door and she let him in.

'Sit down.' She gestured toward the kitchen table.

Shaking his head, he replied, 'Thanks, but this won't take long. I want you to tell me the truth. Do you want me to go away, not try to see you again?' His voice was husky.

'No, please don't.' Her hands gripped the table edge, and she blinked back the tears that welled in her eyes. Regardless of what he'd done, she couldn't bear to lose him.

'It would matter to you?'

'More than you know.' Full of longing, she glanced his way.

Meeting her gaze, a tender, caring expression slid across his face, then he reached over and put his hand under her chin. 'Then, for God's sake, talk to me. Tell me what's keeping us apart.' His voice was unsteady.

'If only I could. Soon I'll be able to tell you everything but I just can't right now.'

'You know I went over Maxine's last night so she could help me with my manuscript. At least, that's the reason she gave for having me visit her at home.'

'And?' A warning gonged in Julie's head.

'Maxine made it quite clear that she likes me. That was flattering since you'd appeared so indifferent. I almost did something stupid. You know what saved me? Before it was too late, I realized I was in the wrong place, holding the wrong woman.' Paul sat down, a miserable expression on his face. 'You're the reason I didn't stay longer. Maxine was attractive and interested, yet all I could think of was you, wanting you.'

Her heart cracked at his words. 'Paul,' she started to speak but the phone rang.

'Don't answer that, please,' he said. 'We need to talk.'

'All right. The answering machine will pick up the message.' Her nerves knotted. It might be police business. How would she explain a call from Corbeille or Schwartz?

A bright girlish voice came on after Julie's recorded message. 'Julie? Just wanted to say thanks again for Paul. He's wonderful. Need I say more? Girl, you don't know what you've missed. Talk soon. Bye now.'

Julie grimaced. 'That doesn't sound like you left early.'

'She's lying.' Paul's lips curled with contempt. 'Maxine was furious when I left. She wants you to believe we . . . You'll have to decide who you believe, Maxine or me.'

'You're right.' Jealousy and disbelief warred with Julie's desire to believe in Paul, set her nerves on edge, gave her a pounding headache. Edwards had suggested she only saw what she wanted in Paul. Maybe her boss hadn't been too far from the truth. Paul could have deceived her. She wanted to believe him, but he'd lied before. Was he lying to her now?

'If you trust me, you'll realize I didn't do what she's implied. I swear I've told you the truth.'

She stared at him but couldn't read his expression. 'I don't know what to think at this moment. Give me a little time.'

'I will, but remember . . . what you decide will affect us both for the rest of our lives.'

20

Paul ached to take Julie in his arms. Instead, he walked out of the house and left her alone, as she requested. If he gave her enough time, she'd realize he'd told the truth.

It was his word against Maxine's. Damn her anyway. Anger seethed inside him and he wished he'd never laid eyes on the deceitful woman. If he'd had any idea what she planned, he'd never have gone to her apartment. She'd fooled him with her business-like manner.

It was obvious his agent had called Julie to get even with him. Maxine needed to realize she couldn't hurt other people and get away with it. Getting in his car, he headed downtown.

While riding the elevator to Maxine's floor, Paul's mind raced ahead to a confrontation.

If he had his way, this would be the last time he saw her. He could find someone else to represent him . . . but there was only one Julie.

Entering Maxine's office, he found her receptionist putting on her makeup at her desk. 'Is Ms. Kent available?'

The woman jumped. It was obvious she was surprised to find him there before office hours, without an appointment. With one smooth motion, she slipped her lipstick and compact in her handbag then flashed a pleasant smile. 'I'll check, Mr. Martin. Please make yourself comfortable. 'If you'd like a cup of coffee, a fresh pot will be ready in a few minutes.'

'No, thanks. Tell your boss this won't take long.' Paul settled back on a chair, leafing through a current news magazine. Though he would've appeared calm and relaxed to anyone who entered the room, deep inside, Paul burned.

If Maxine were a man, he'd invite her outside for a few well-deserved blows. As it was, he couldn't resort to his fists, though he'd make it clear what he thought of her and what he intended to do.

'You can go in now.' The receptionist's knowing smile infuriated him. Had Maxine discussed him with her employee? As he stepped into the agent's office, she gazed out her window at the city ten stories below.

Maxine turned to face him, a scowl on her face. 'You've got a lot of nerve coming here.' She spat the words at him.

'I've got something to say to you.' His finger pointed to her desk chair and he growled, 'sit down and keep your mouth shut. I've never hit a woman in my life. Don't push your luck.'

Maxine paled and slid into her seat. She seemed to watch his every move, as if he were a time bomb, primed to explode.

'In case you wonder why I'm here, I heard the message you left for Julie this morning.'

Anger broke through her fear and she hissed, 'Nobody walks out on me.'

Paul didn't feel the need to point out that he'd done just that the previous night. 'That was a petty, cheap trick you pulled.'

She shrugged.

'You're beyond contempt and I no longer care to be associated with a person of your caliber. You can consider yourself fired. I'll find another agent.'

Her eyes narrowed. 'That may not be as easy as you think,' she replied, her words coated with spite. 'All it will take is a few phone calls to the right people to tell them you're a no-talent, egotistical creep who tried to force his attentions on me, no agency in town will touch you.'

'Don't be a fool,' he rumbled, a tight rein on his temper, hoping their conversation wouldn't be overheard. There was no reason to upset Maxine's receptionist. The last thing he needed right now was for her to believe her boss was in danger and dial 911. The police already viewed him with suspicion. They might take Maxine's word if she said he'd threatened her.

'All that happened last night was you came on to the wrong guy and got your pride hurt.' Paul pulled up a chair beside hers, his gaze locked with hers. 'Unless you're a complete idiot, which I doubt, you realize you're in no position to threaten anyone. So settle down and pay attention. You're going to tell Julie the truth.' Shooting her a long, hard look, he was pleased to see Maxine's bottom lip tremble. She wasn't as self-assured as she pretended.

'I'll think about it,' she sniffed.

'Three hours. If you haven't apologized to Julie by then, I file my charge of sexual harrassment. It's already drawn up. I don't imagine many of your clients will stick around when the word gets out. It'll make you look like a heartless fiend who uses her position to satisfy her sexual appetites.' He was bluffing though she had no way of knowing.

As he left, he heard Maxine's shrill voice on the intercom. He leaned over the receptionist's desk and offered a suggestion. 'If I were you, I'd give her a few minutes before you go in there. She's not herself right now.' Smiling at the woman's puzzled expression, he walked out of the office.

* * *

Julie knelt by her flower bed in the backyard, the cell phone beside her so she wouldn't miss Corbeille's call. The gate clanked and she looked up. Paul stood before her, a worried expression on his face. How she wished she could ease his mind, tell him she believed what he'd said about the previous night. Better still, tell him the truth, the whole truth. But she couldn't, not yet. As soon as her investigation was over, she'd tell him everything. 'I thought you agreed to give me some time.'

'I've been to see Maxine.' Paul seemed to wait for her response.

'That's none of my concern.' Pretending indifference, her voice sounded shaky to her own ears. Julie avoided his gaze and pulled another weed, afraid her eyes would give her away.

'If you'll listen a minute, I'll tell you what happened.'

'Don't. I don't want to hear another word about Maxine,' she whispered. Rising, she glanced at him. If only she could tell him the truth. 'This is getting us nowhere. Please go.'

'I've tried to figure out what's troubling you. Before she made her move on me, Maxine said she thinks you were in love with your father.'

'What a mean thing for her to say. Maxine never knew her own father. Her mother's been married so many times, I don't think Maxine knows the meaning of the word. As much as I loved my father, he was my dad. My affection for him doesn't have anything to do with what I might feel for a man my own age.' Julie pushed a lock of hair off her face then gathered up her gardening tools. She gazed at Paul. 'Please be patient a little longer. As soon as I can, I'll explain.'

He blocked her way, as if he wanted to keep her with him as long as possible. 'Did someone you trusted let you down?' He seemed prepared to explore all possibilities to find the truth.

A deep sigh escaped her lips. 'Please leave me alone.'

'I'm next door. Come over when you're ready.'

Her foot on the bottom step, Julie paused. 'Ready?'

'For us to be together. I'll wait for you.' He left her.

It was the closest he'd ever come to saying he loved her. Touched by his words, Julie tried to blink back the tears that welled in her eyes. She stumbled on the steps but caught herself before she fell. In the kitchen, she sunk into a chair, then the tears broke through and she sobbed.

With her arms wrapped around herself, she rocked back and forth while on her radio on the kitchen counter, Sinatra slid with grace into a love song. The sad lyrics of unrequited love fueled her pain and her spirits sunk even lower.

Misty appeared and put her paws in Julie's lap. Brushing the back of her hand across her wet cheeks, Julie patted the schnauzer's head. 'It's okay,' she mumbled to reassure the dog and herself. With leaden steps, she managed to cross the kitchen and turn off the radio.

She must focus on something else or lose her mind. The investigation . . . that's it, focus on her work. It must go on even if her personal life was hell. With effort, Julie regained control, picked up the cordless phone, and punched in Corbeille's number. When he answered, she inquired, 'Have you heard if the body's been identified yet?'

'Yeah, I was about to call you.'

'Well? Fill me in.' Julie wiped at her wet face then dried her hands on her jeans.

'The fingerprints prove the body's Ms. Turner.'

'I see. So where do we go from here?'

'The coroner has examined the body,' he said.

That was standard procedure yet Corbeille's tone chilled Julie. She bit down on her bottom lip. 'Go on.'

'Do you remember I had a hunch Martin was involved?'

'Sure, but I never found any evidence. My hunch is Peterson did it. We just need to delve into his background.'

'There's evidence now. I was right. Martin's in this up to his eyeballs.' Corbeille sounded smug, sure of himself.

His words hit her hard though she knew it couldn't be true. Paul would never hurt anyone. Would he? The pulse jumped in her throat then she regained control. 'What do you mean?'

'Evidence ties Paul Martin to this crime. The coroner found a folded piece of paper deep in a pocket of Ms. Turner's denim vest. The words could still be made out. It was a certificate of ownership from a coin dealer.'

'So Sheila Turner bought coins. That doesn't prove anything. I don't see — '

'The certificate was Paul Martin's.' Corbeille interrupted her. 'I've looked up the report. He called in the theft of his coins and also reported missing a certificate of ownership, which had been with the coins.' The detective paused then commented, 'Looks like he's our boy after all.'

Julie clutched the phone so hard, it bruised her hand. What would happen now? A sick feeling in the pit of her stomach almost overcame her. It must be a horrible mistake. 'But why would he report the theft of his coins if he killed her? That part doesn't make sense.'

Corbeille was silent for a moment then he spoke. 'He could have staged the whole thing for your benefit. You witnessed his shock when he found the safe empty. And he mentioned the certificate was also gone. That could have been a clever ploy. He could have caught his wife in the act of robbing him and killed her.'

'Wait a minute. He was upset. That wasn't an act.'

'Maybe or maybe he's one hell of a fine actor,' Corbeille replied. 'Hear me out. The coins weren't traceable, but the certificate was. Maybe Martin searched her body after he killed her but missed it. So he lived in dread she'd hidden the paper somewhere. There was always the chance her body and the certificate would be found. The certificate incriminates him.'

'I guess it's possible,' she admitted, not willing to give up yet. 'But it all could have happened differently. How about this scenario — The killer follows Sheila home after she steals the coins. He strangles her and takes the coins, leaving the certificate of ownership in her pocket so when her body's found, it'll incriminate Paul. It's all set up to frame Paul.'

'Richmond PD will never buy that, and you know it.' From his tone, she could tell Corbeille wouldn't change his mind, either. 'We've got our killer. You should be glad. Now you can go back to home base.'

Her first instinct was to run next door and warn Paul. Of course she couldn't.

Wait, there must be some way to help him. Through numbed lips she asked, 'Will they ask him to come in for questioning?'

'That's the other reason I wanted to get in touch with you. A warrant's been issued. We don't anticipate he'll resist arrest but, just in case, stay away from Martin today. A detective and uniformed officer will be over today to pick him up.'

Julie turned off the cell phone and slumped in her chair, her head in her hands. She'd never felt so helpless in her entire life. Paul better have a damn good explanation. While she gazed out her kitchen window, Julie's stomach churned with anxiety. Her longing to be with Paul increased by the minute. Twice she got as far as the door then stopped, her hand on the doorknob. She'd been told to stay away. All she could do was wait. How could she tell Paul he was about to be arrested? She'd have to reveal how she knew.

While she waited, she again reviewed what Paul had told her. Sheila was about to leave when he got home. Her distraught expression disturbed him so much he'd left a message on her machine, asked her to call. He never heard from her again. Later, he'd lied to the police, said he hadn't seen her. Julie hadn't reported what he'd told her, just held on to the information. How would that make her look if it came out?

If the police located a neighbor who'd seen Sheila's car parked in front of Paul's house that evening, he'd look all the more guilty. Her own investigation had turned up no evidence of his guilt. A visit from his ex-wife didn't make him a murderer. If Paul's wife took the coins, he hadn't caught her in the act. Had he? A tiny sliver of doubt edged its way into Julie's mind in spite of her need to believe he was innocent.

The killer might have watched and stalked Sheila, followed her when she left Paul's. Then he'd forced her car off the road or tricked her into stopping. From what Paul had said about Sheila, she wouldn't have been easy to trick, wouldn't have stopped her car for just anyone. She would've stopped for someone she knew, someone she had no reason to fear. A crime statistic came to mind and dread swept through Julie. Many murders were committed by relatives or friends.

Shivering, Julie pulled her cardigan sweater closer while she tried to think of someone who'd help her find the truth. But what if further investigation proved Paul's guilt?

One car door then another slammed outside. She snapped to attention and darted to a front window. A Richmond PD patrol car was parked at the curb. Through her venetian blinds, she glimpsed a tall man in sport coat and slacks, accompanied by a heavyset uniformed officer. They strode up to Paul's front door. He opened the door and the two men disappeared inside. Julie waited, her eyes riveted to the front of Paul's house.

Minutes seemed hours until the door opened again. Paul walked out, his hands behind his back. The two policemen escorted him to the patrol car. Paul glanced in her direction and she jumped, brushed against the venetian blind. She stepped away from the window and hurried downstairs. By the time she opened her front door, they'd put Paul in the back seat of the patrol car. The vehicle traveled down the street.

She'd better let Jay know what had happened. Julie fumbled through her address book until she located the telephone number at his new apartment. He might be there. The restaurant didn't open until five o'clock on weekdays. She punched in his number. The phone rang and rang. At last, he answered.

'The police just picked up Paul.'

'What?' His voice came out higher than usual. 'Maybe they just want to talk to him again.'

'He was wearing handcuffs when they put him in the car.' If only she could confide in Jay. Desperation filled Julie. There wasn't a living soul she could tell she was an undercover cop who'd fallen for her suspect.

'I guess I better go down and see if he's been arrested.' Jay hesitated as if unsure. 'Yes, that's what I'll do. Stay home and I'll let you know what I find out.'

* * *

Paul had been on the telephone that afternoon with the private investigator he'd just hired. The P.I. reported Dorothy spent a lot of time at the mall. That he already knew.

Nevertheless, he asked the man to watch her for a few more days.

He glanced at a photograph of Julie on his desk, as if he needed anything to remind him of her. She drifted into his thoughts a lot these days. Paul frowned, puzzled by her recent behavior. What the hell was the matter and why wouldn't she let him help? He sighed with frustration then picked up his manuscript.

The doorbell's ring broke into his concentration. Walking through the house, he opened the door. Surprised to see two grim-faced strangers on his front porch, he stepped back.

'Mr. Martin?' A man in business attire flashed his badge and identified himself as Richmond PD Detective Mercer.

'Yes, but what's happened?'

'Can we come in?'

'Of course.' He stood back and Mercer and a uniformed police officer brushed past him into the foyer.

'We're here to arrest you on suspicion of the murder of your wife, Sheila Turner,' the detective informed him.

'Murder? Someone's killed Sheila?' Shock engulfed him. He'd begun to think she'd never be found.

'I need to read you your rights. You have

the right to remain silent, the right to . . . '
The detective's voice droned on and on.

Paul stared, speechless.

'We'll take you down to police headquarters now.'

'What? My God, what's going on here?' Shaken by this unexpected turn of events, he tried to pull himself together. The police officers' faces were stern and uncompromising. To them, he was just another suspect to be picked up, taken downtown, and booked. He rallied his courage. 'Will you give me a minute to get ready?'

'All right. Officer McCoy will go with you, if you don't mind.' The officer followed on his heels while he locked doors and slipped on a jacket.

'If you're ready, we'll leave now.' The detective seemed impatient.

'All right.'

'Please put your hands behind you,' Mercer requested.

The gravity of the situation hit Paul. Dread clawed at his stomach and he sucked in a deep breath. 'Do you have to use handcuffs?'

'It's routine in cases like this.' Before he knew what was happening, Mercer snapped the cuffs on his wrists and pointed him toward the door. 'You first, Mr. Martin.'

Paul stepped onto his front porch, praying

no one saw them. A venetian blind in Julie's upstairs window rippled and caught his attention. Was she there? What would she think, seeing him hauled off to the police station like a criminal? In case she or his other neighbors watched, he mustn't appear ashamed or intimidated by the police.

With his head held high, he strode across the lawn and climbed in the back seat of the patrol car.

At police headquarters, Detective Mercer led him to a small, drab windowless room, empty except for a large, scarred wooden table and four chairs. Another detective walked in.

'I'm Ben Oram,' he introduced himself while he unlocked Paul's handcuffs. 'Please have a seat.' His hand gestured to one of the chairs.

'Before I say a word, I want my lawyer.' John Riffer, his friend, would come and straighten things out. The detective brought a phone.

While he waited for Riffer, sadness engulfed Paul. Poor unhappy Sheila. Her life shouldn't have ended in violence. Had Dorothy really hated her enough to kill her?

An hour later, Riffer sat across from him. 'Tell me the truth, Paul,' he urged in a low voice. 'I need to know so I can help you.'

'First and foremost, I didn't kill her,' he said.

Riffer smiled and patted him on the arm. 'I never thought you did, old buddy. Now tell me everything. It'll help me get you out of this predicament.'

'The police interviewed me right after Sheila vanished. I told them I didn't see her the night she vanished,' he said. His uneasy gaze examined the room. They were alone but did the police have the room bugged?

'Right,' Riffer nodded. 'You didn't see her.'

'I lied.' Ashamed of what he'd done, Paul met his friend's startled gaze.

Riffer's mouth dropped open and a frown crossed his face.

'She was about to leave when I got home,' Paul hastened to explain. 'I just saw her for a moment but she seemed upset.'

'You're leveling with me?'

'Yes. Later I left her a message to call me.'

Riffer nodded. 'That's the call the police heard when they listened to her messages on her answering machine.'

'Right. I told them I'd called to check on her since she didn't keep our appointment.'

'You have two options here. You can continue to say you didn't see her that night or tell the truth. I suggest the truth.'

'The police will think if I lied about that, I

could've lied about other things, maybe even about her death.'

'That's a chance you'll have to take. I'll get you out of here as fast as I can. Keep calm and be sure you tell me the truth. I don't want any more surprises. All right?'

They discussed Paul's situation for awhile then Riffer summoned a guard to unlock the door and release him.

A judge gave his permission but it was too late in the day to arrange bail for Paul.

'I'm sorry about this.' Riffer patted him on the shoulder. First thing in the morning, we'll get you out of here.'

He swallowed hard. Julie would worry. 'Please contact my next-door neighbor and my brother. They'll be concerned.'

That night was the longest of his life. Paul tried to sleep on the hard cot but it was hopeless. The jail was like a living creature, a tormented creature, never quiet. Everytime he dozed, a cell door clanked down the dim corridor or a prisoner cried out in his sleep.

Riffer appeared early next morning. Once he'd signed several papers, Paul was allowed to walk out of the jail with Riffer. He sat dazed and tired in the passenger seat while his friend drove him home.

'Get some rest,' Riffer advised him. 'As soon as you wake up, call me. We need to start work on your defense right away.'

Paul called Julie to let her know he was all right.

'Is there anything I can do?' She sounded worried.

'Not right now. I need some sleep. Talk to you later.'

* * *

Jay sat in Paul's living room and read the sports section of the paper while his twin napped. A car parked at the curb outside so he rose and opened the front door before the driver, a man in a business suit, could ring the doorbell and wake Paul.

'Jay, I'm John Riffer, your brother's attorney,' the man told him.

The lawyer's face showed intelligence and concern, genuine concern for Paul.

'Paul says he'll have to stand trial.' Jay whispered, puzzled and disturbed by the whole business. 'How can this happen to Paul? He hasn't done nothing wrong. I'm his brother, and I know he'd never hurt anybody.'

Riffer nodded. 'I couldn't agree with you more. But there's evidence which incriminates him. He'll have to stand trial for murder unless we find evidence, strong evidence, that someone else killed Ms. Turner. Do you have any ideas?'

'No . . . except Paul's mother-in-law has been trying to cause trouble for Paul.'

'Why would she do that?'

'We don't know, but as soon as Sheila was declared missing, Paul told me Dorothy shot off her mouth about his killing Sheila.'

'That's what Paul said but he couldn't give me any reason for this Dorothy's accusations.' Riffer sighed. 'Let Paul sleep awhile. He's had a bad shock, hearing about Sheila then being arrested for her murder.'

'Let me know if I can do anything to help you clear Paul,' Jay asked Riffer. Though he'd managed to appear calm in front of his brother, the experience had unnerved him. For a moment, he remembered how scared he'd been after the fire that killed their parents. Paul must have been afraid, too. They'd been fifteen.

In recent months, he'd realized there wasn't anything teenaged Paul could have done that day to help him. But now they were both adults, and he wouldn't let his brother be punished for someone else's crime.

Following Riffer's departure, Jay sat on the front steps, trying to make sense of what had happened. Julie's door flew open and she stepped out on her porch. Jay stepped onto the lawn and called to her. 'Paul will be all right.' He tried to reassure her.

'He called me a few minutes ago.' Julie sounded anxious. 'Will they really hold him over for trial?'

'Looks like it. He's been charged with Sheila's murder. At least Riffer was able to get him out on bail.' Jay had a sinking feeling in his stomach. 'It doesn't look good for him right now. And I don't know anything we can do.'

Julie stared at him for a moment. 'There may be something,' she replied quietly then went inside.

* * *

Julie laid her plans carefully. First, she made an appointment to see the Richmond Police Chief. He needed to know they'd arrested the wrong man. There was no evidence against Paul except for that paper in Sheila's pocket, and there could be a reasonable explanation for it. Maybe the killer grabbed Sheila after she robbed Paul and missed the certificate in her pocket.

Julie tried to be patient, waiting for what seemed ages outside the Chief's office.

'My secretary told me you wanted to see me on an urgent matter, Detective Taylor. I assume this is about the Turner case?' Curiosity resounded in the senior police officer's voice.

Julie wasted no time letting the Chief know why she was there. 'Based on my investigation of the suspect over the last few weeks, I firmly believe your department has arrested the wrong person.'

His eyebrows shot up. 'That's quite an observation, Taylor. I hope you have proof.'

'From what I've seen, the suspect hasn't engaged in any criminal activity.' Julie stopped, drew a deep breath, and plunged right in. 'And I believe you should investigate Dorothy Turner instead of her son-in-law.'

'Mrs. Turner? The wife of Marcus Turner? Have you lost your mind?' Chief Hood's flat, gray eyes narrowed and his glare pierced Julie.

'No sir. If you'll let me explain.' Why was he so hostile? As Chief of the department, he must want to see justice served. She summarized all that had happened, including Dorothy's harrassment of Paul, her influencing his firm to let him go, and Jay's hit-and-run accident. 'I believe that, for some undetermined reason, Ms. Turner wants Paul Martin blamed for a crime he didn't commit.'

'Are you suggesting Mrs. Turner killed her step-daughter?' The Chief's voice became louder and his face turned beet red.

'No, sir, though I believe she's somehow involved in Sheila Turner's murder. I just haven't determined what part she played,' Julie admitted. 'If you'll let me investigate her, I'll find out.'

A drink of water seemed to calm the Chief. 'No. It's too ridiculous to even consider. From the evidence, Martin did it. He is, after all, his wife's heir. He stands to gain more by her death than anyone else.'

Julie jumped to her feet in protest. 'Excuse me, Chief, but the Turners are second in line behind Martin to inherit.'

He ignored what she'd said. 'As a matter of fact, your visit reminds me I need to call your boss today and thank him for loaning you to us. We appreciate your efforts, but now that Martin's been charged with his wife's murder, your assignment's finished. I'm sure you'll be glad to get back to your own department.' Escorting her to the door, he shook her hand. 'Don't worry, Taylor. He's our man, I'm sure of it.'

'But, but . . . ' She responded to a closed door. His hostile behavior left no doubt in her mind. The Chief's mind was already made up. To him, Paul was guilty, even before he was tried. The Chief had made it clear what he thought of her theories. But she wouldn't quit. She already had Plan B in case he turned her down.

21

Dawn broke in streaks of pink and gray across the eastern horizon while Julie drove up I-95. The last time she'd traveled this road, she hadn't met Paul. What a difference a few weeks had made. She'd fallen in love with a suspected criminal, though she was virtually positive he was innocent. She lifted her chin, determined to find the truth, even if it meant Paul and she could never be together.

Her stomach clenched with anticipation, Julie pressed harder on the gas pedal and sped up the highway. The faster she got there the better. The Richmond Police Chief had turned down her request to investigate Dorothy. It was time to activate Plan B.

Two hours later, she turned off a busy downtown Alexandria street and parked the Honda in the employees garage at her own headquarters. A faint sweet fragrance wafted to her nostrils when she walked past a mini-garden next to the garage. Members of her department had planted several rose bushes and installed a couple of concrete benches, giving their fellow officers a place for quiet reflection. It was a great idea, though she doubted anyone in the department had time to sit there and meditate.

The clock in a historic church steeple downtown struck ten as she hurried across the street and through the revolving doors of Alexandria Police Department. Relief washed over her. Traffic on the highway had bogged down right before she reached Alexandria. Today of all days it was important she be there on time.

As she strode into a small private office, Lieutenant Edwards looked up from papers on his desk.

'It's good to see you.' His hand gestured to a nearby chair then he brought her up-to-date. 'Chief Hood just called to let me know they've closed their investigation.'

'The Chief must be overjoyed to get rid of me.' Julie grimaced. Her pride smarted at the way Hood had treated her. He'd rejected her request, thanked her for her efforts, then sent her on her way. 'He almost pushed me out his office door yesterday. Did he tell you why I wanted to see him?'

'Yeah, to extend your investigation. He assured me it wasn't necessary since they already have their man.'

'The heck they do.' Julie slid her chair closer then put her elbows on Edwards' desk and sent him a long, hard look. She must appear objective and professional, as if this was just another assignment for her. Edwards mustn't find out she'd become involved with the man she investigated. 'They've arrested the wrong person.'

'Are you sure?' Her boss stared at her, surprise on his face.

She nodded. 'There's no doubt in my mind that Dorothy Turner's involved. But when I told the Chief my suspicions and asked if I could investigate her, his face turned so red, I thought he'd have a stroke. Then he turned me down. Here's a copy of my last report to Hood.' Julie slid a large folder onto Edwards' desk. The Chief's rejection still rankled her. She'd racked her brains but couldn't come up with a good reason for his hostility.

'His behavior's understandable.' Edwards smiled. 'Wouldn't you get upset if I wanted to investigate the wife of your best friend?'

'He's Marcus Turner's friend? Why didn't you tell me?' She flushed with annoyance.

'Your assignment was to investigate Martin. It was possible you'd find evidence he'd done away with Sheila Turner. In that event, Hood's friendship with Marcus Turner would have been irrelevant.' Edwards shrugged. 'Let me fill you in — the Chief and Turner were a couple of years ahead of me at the College of

William and Mary. They roomed together through college and have remained friends. Everytime I run into the Chief at law enforcement meetings he mentions Marcus and their golf scores.'

Julie raised her chin and took the offensive. 'Even if the Chief and Mr. Turner are friends, that doesn't change anything. Dorothy Turner could still be involved. Look at the woman. She's hounded Martin, caused him to lose his job, and accused him of foul play in her stepdaughter's disappearance. Nothing links her to Sheila's death so far, but Dorothy's behavior should raise the police's suspicions.'

Edwards raised an eyebrow. 'You sound like you're convinced Martin's innocent.'

'I'm positive.' Well, almost. She still couldn't shake that small, lingering doubt. Paul would benefit from his estranged wife's death, more than anyone else, unless he were found guilty.

'During my investigation, I found no conclusive evidence against Paul Martin. It's unlikely he's the killer.' Too bad Chief Hood of Richmond PD didn't agree with her. That certificate of ownership they'd found on Sheila's body made Paul look guilty.

'From what you've told me, you don't have any real evidence against her.' Edwards flipped through Julie's report. then glanced in her direction. A faint smile appeared on his weather-beaten features. 'I'm not saying I agree, but do you remember what we discussed when you joined the department?'

'Lots, you've been a veritable font of knowledge,' she said. A lump formed in her throat. The past four years hadn't been all bad with Edwards her mentor and friend. She'd arrived at Alexandria PD a green recruit, straight from the police academy, her head full of theory, but not one iota of experience.

'Your first day, I told you not to forget things aren't always what they appear.'

'I remember, but how would that apply to the Turners? Everyone knows they're filthy rich and don't need Sheila's estate.' She wrinkled her brow, hearing her own words. 'Or do they? Maybe they're not as rich as they appear.' she hadn't thought of that.

'I don't know.' Edwards scratched his bald head. 'That's for you to find out.'

'While I'm here, I need to give you my letter of resignation.' She handed him an envelope. The Lieutenant leaned forward to protest one last time but she shook her head. If she couldn't investigate Dorothy as a police officer, she'd do it on her own.

'Please don't try to talk me out of this. My mind's made up. It's time we found out what really happened to Sheila. Maybe I can convince Paul Martin's lawyer to investigate Dorothy Turner, with my assistance. Can I call on you if I need help?' She'd hesitated to ask but figured he could always refuse.

'As head of this department, no. As your friend, I'll do what I can.' He paused then added, in a low tone, 'Don't worry. I won't tell anyone the real reason for your resignation.'

When she tried to thank him, he shrugged. 'If anyone asks, I'll tell them you're burned out and need a change.'

That was the truth. This was to be her last case anyway. Standing in the doorway, she looked back at Edwards. 'Look at it this way. Neither of us wants to see an innocent man sent to prison for life.' Especially Paul. That was her worst nightmare. Her palms turned clammy and her nerves tensed at the thought.

Without him, her life would never be the same. The years ahead would stretch before her like a succession of bleak, empty corridors.

'One last thing,' Edwards cautioned her. 'Watch out for yourself. You seem to think you know Martin, but he may have fooled you. It's possible you just see what he wants.'

During the drive back to Richmond, Julie pushed aside her annoyance at Edwards' last words. He'd been her father's oldest friend and had her best interests at heart. But if Edwards could meet Paul, he'd realize that Paul was too kind-hearted to hurt anyone, including his estranged wife. The same small nagging doubt still tormented Julie, though she tried in vain to ignore it. When it wouldn't go away, she pretended it wasn't there.

At last she could take positive action on her own, unencumbered by her duties as a police officer. First, she'd contact Paul's lawyer. Then she'd go next door and tell Paul she believed in him and would try to help.

Moments after she stepped inside her front door, she had the attorney on the phone. 'Please let me work with you on Paul's case. I have investigative training which could be useful,' she said then added, 'It's my belief that Paul's mother-in-law was involved in his wife's case.'

'I appreciate your offer,' Riffer responded, 'though at this point, Ms. Turner's involvement seems a long shot.' Riffer's tone didn't sound too optimistic.

* * *

Julie sat across from Paul in his living room. Outside, birds twittered in the trees and children could be heard, playing games in a neighboring yard. She recorded those sounds dimly, gazing at Paul.

She longed to reach over and touch him, to reassure herself he was all right, but she didn't. The way she felt about him, It was best she keep her distance. One touch and she wasn't sure she could keep her emotions under control. They must concentrate on his defense right now. So they'd be friends, not lovers, until he was cleared. Then, who knew?

'I'll never forget the expression on her face that night.' Paul's deep voice resounded with sorrow. 'Sheila looked disturbed, even frightened. If I'd just stopped her, forced her to tell me what was wrong, maybe I could've prevented what happened.'

'Hey, don't blame yourself,' Julie said. 'The killer could have stalked her for a long time, just waiting his chance. If he hadn't murdered her that night, he would've found another opportunity.'

'Since the police arrested me, I've told them the truth yet they ask over and over if I'm sure. That one lie I told them sure must have damaged my credibility.'

'Just be sure to tell the truth from now on, no matter what they ask you,' she said, trying to appear supportive. Her doubt lingered. Her heart ached and she couldn't help but remember her boss's parting words about Paul.

At least he was out on bail. 'I asked your attorney to let me help,' Julie informed him. 'He may find something I can do, maybe some research or phone calls.

'You've said Dorothy's attitude toward you changed from cordial to hostile about the same time your relationship with Sheila fell apart. Can you remember what else was going on then?' A gut feeling that Dorothy was somehow linked to her step-daughter's death lingered. But how to prove it?

'I don't know.' Paul rubbed tired looking eyes. 'The police look at me and see prime suspect. After all, I was Sheila's husband.'

'The timing of the crime could cause trouble for you. Her murder would be terrible no matter when it happened, but just before your divorce became final . . . ' Julie didn't need to finish her sentence.

Paul nodded in agreement. 'The day she moved out, my wife made it crystal clear she'd change her will the moment the divorce became final. Until then, I stood to inherit her estate.' Bitterness crept into his voice. 'She couldn't have forced me to touch a penny of her fortune once she'd moved out of our home. If I'm acquitted, it all goes to charities.'

⋆ ⋆ ⋆

At the Henrico County Courthouse, Julie filled out a request form to see Sheila's will. The clerk came right back and Julie carried the will to a nearby desk. The legal document verified what Paul had told her. He was his wife's sole heir except for a few small, personal items left to others. If Paul were deceased, or otherwise unable to inherit, his share went to the Turners.

Laying the document aside, Julie sat in the quiet of the county courthouse and thought of the one time she'd seen Sheila. For a few seconds, Julie again felt the soft mist of rain on her face as she leaned over the shallow, open grave in the woods. Life was so uncertain. You never knew what would happen. A chill raced up her spine then she pushed back her apprehension. This was no time for a case of nerves.

Paul's lawyer examined the copy of the will Julie laid on his desk.

'I've never met Henry Shelton, Sheila's attorney, but he has a prestigious law practice. Let's see what he'll tell me.'

Riffer dialed the other lawyer's number then put his phone on speaker so Julie could hear both sides of the conversation. First Riffer explained he represented Paul Martin. Then he asked, 'Could you please tell me about your last contact with Ms. Turner?'

‘As a lawyer, you know I can’t discuss a client with you, even a deceased client.’ Shelton sounded impressed with himself.

‘I wouldn’t ask you to violate your attorney-client relationship, sir,’ Riffer responded in a polite and respectful tone. ‘But I have a client who’s been accused of a crime I don’t believe he committed. Any information you can share would be most appreciated.’

‘Hold on a minute.’ Shelton left the telephone for a few moments then returned. ‘There’s no harm in telling you this. Ms. Turner called and made an appointment to see me at nine a.m., March 10th.’

‘That would have been the day after she was last seen,’ Riffer replied.

‘That I couldn’t say. All I know is that she told my clerk she needed to make a new will.’

‘Do you have any idea who would have been her new heirs?’ Riffer looked across his desk at Julie as he spoke.

A brief pause then Shelton responded. ‘No, I don’t.’

Riffer thanked the other attorney and ended the call then gave Julie a hard stare. ‘This doesn’t make Paul look good. The prosecutor will say he killed his wife while they were still married to inherit her estate.’

He ran his fingers through his wiry, prematurely gray hair, loosened his paisley tie.

'You're right,' Julie agreed, her heart heavy. Things just got worse and worse. 'Paul swears he had no designs on her fortune, just wanted out of a bad marriage.'

'I know,' Riffer replied sympathetically. 'You think a lot of him, don't you?'

'Do I have a neon sign on my forehead?' Julie sputtered. Was she so transparent? For weeks she'd tried to keep her feelings about Paul to herself, but they wouldn't stay hidden.

'No, though I've noticed the pain on your face whenever we discuss Paul's predictament. You wouldn't be upset if you didn't care about him. That makes two of us. Though I haven't known Paul long, I value his friendship and believe in his honesty and integrity.' Paul's lawyer played with a pencil on his desk, then he stood and strode up and down the room before halting in front of Julie's chair. 'This is probably what the prosecutor will come up with. Knowing Sheila was about to change her will, Paul lured her to his home to get some things she'd left behind, killed her, and hid her body. That way he'd inherit her estate since they were still married at the time of her death. The prosecution will also say Paul knew the police would suspect him since he was Sheila's heir but believed he was too clever to get caught.'

'What about Peterson, the man Forsythe gave us? How does he figure in that theory?' Julie frowned. A dull ache began to pound behind her eyes and she messaged her forehead. This case was enough to drive a sane person mad. It was like a giant jigsaw puzzle with missing pieces.

'I don't know,' Riffer said. 'Peterson's a wild card. The prosecution may suggest Paul hired him to do the job. Sheila threw Paul's plans a curve when she stole his coins. He lost his temper and killed her, instead of having Peterson do it, as planned. Since he'd already hired Peterson, Paul had the ex-con dispose of the body. Acting on Paul's original instructions, Peterson buried her in the woods behind Paul's home.'

The lawyer paced the floor of his office again, lost in thought. He resumed his seat and threw Julie an engimatic glance. 'With your investigative background, I guess you're familiar with Virginia state laws?'

Julie nodded. 'I guess so.' What was on his mind?

'Most states, Virginia included, don't allow convicted felons to benefit from their crimes.'

'So Paul can't inherit Sheila's estate if he's in prison?'

'Right. Under those conditions, he wouldn't get a penny.' A grim expression slid across Riffer's face. He crammed his hands into his pockets. 'You saw her will. It reads Paul inherits unless he's deceased, or is otherwise unable to inherit at the time of her death. If he's convicted and imprisoned for her murder, the Turners get everything.'

'Dorothy must have realized the chance they'd survive Sheila was slim at best. She was thirty-five years old. Her father's in his sixties and Dorothy's fiftyish.' Julie said.

'We'll need proof of Dorothy's scheme,' the lawyer replied in a firm voice, adding, 'if there was one.'

'You think it's possible, don't you?'

The lawyer nodded. 'Now I do. When you first mentioned the possibility, I had my doubts. But the fact is Dorothy would stand to benefit from framing Paul. She could have arranged to have Sheila killed. The trick is to prove it.

'Tell me something, Julie? You mentioned you had investigative experience. Just what did you mean? Were you a private investigator?' Curiosity tinged Riffer's words.

'I worked as a police officer for several years,' she admitted. She deliberated how much she could divulge then added, 'Paul doesn't know this and I'd like to tell him myself.' How would he react? Her stomach lurched.

'That's fine with me.' Riffer's curious gaze lifted and he grinned at her. 'I'm glad you want to help. We'll have to work hard to clear Paul before this goes to trial.'

* * *

'You know, the more I think about it, the less I like the idea of your working with Riffer,' Paul told her that night. 'It could be dangerous. If Dorothy found out, she could come after you. I want your promise you'll stay out of her way. Don't call attention to yourself.'

'Don't worry. She won't know I'm helping Riffer.' Julie yearned for the power to turn back the clock to happier times, like their day at the beach. She forced a smile and changed the subject. 'Did Sheila still have friends in Richmond? At work, perhaps? Or someone she knew when she was growing up?'

'There was a woman at her firm.' Paul wrinkled his brow in thought, then added, 'another architect. Sarah . . . Sarah Allen, I believe. Until last month, Sheila hadn't lived in Richmond for a long time and had lost contact with most of her friends here. Her godmother lives in town, but they didn't see each other often.'

The phone rang and Paul rose to answer it, looking back over his shoulder at her. 'Don't go away. I'll be right back,' he said as he walked into the kitchen.

Tears stung Julie's eyes and the irony of the situation burned deep inside her. Earlier, the investigation had kept them apart. Now the trial hung over their heads. It still wasn't the time to tell Paul the truth.

Loneliness dogged her footsteps later as she walked home. She still wasn't one hundred percent sure of Paul's innocence — but she loved him, even if he was guilty as sin.

22

'A guy at Richmond Police Department owes me a favor.' Riffer told Julie and Paul the next day. 'He'll run a check on Dorothy to see if she has a criminal record.'

'If she does, won't the police be more likely to consider her a possible suspect?' Hope stirred inside Julie.

'They should,' Riffer replied.

'Paul's given me the names of two people who may be able to help us, Beatrice Montague, Sheila's godmother, and Sarah Allen, her friend at work,' Julie said. 'If you don't mind, I'll contact them myself. They might feel more at ease, talking to another woman. I thought I'd start with Beatrice Montague.'

'That sounds like a good idea,' Riffer said. 'At this point, we have no real evidence against Dorothy so we'll take any help we can get. While I'm waiting to hear from my contact at Richmond PD, I'll have a credit check run on the Turners.'

'In the meanwhile,' Paul suggested, 'Why don't I retrace the route Sheila would have taken home from my house that night?'

‘That’s a good idea.’ His determination encouraged Julie, Somehow, they’d prove he was innocent.

‘That’s fine with me.’ Riffer encouraged his client. ‘Talk to the owners of the businesses along the way. Maybe someone saw Sheila that night.’

‘Right. Or her car,’ Paul replied. ‘That white Miata would have been hard to miss.’

‘Julie, Paul told you he’d hired a private investigator to watch Dorothy, didn’t he?’ Riffer seemed to assume he had.

‘No, he didn’t.’ Disappointed, she gazed in Paul’s direction. He hadn’t confided in her. Julie reminded herself that she hadn’t told him everything, either. When the time was right, she had a heck of a lot to explain. ‘What did the P.I. report on Dorothy?’

‘Just that she likes to shop. That’s not news,’ Paul said. ‘This guy’s the second detective I’ve hired. The first got involved with another case and didn’t have time for mine so he referred me to another P.I. with fewer commitments. I’d just hired the second man when I was arrested.’

‘Now that you’re both helping me investigate Dorothy, don’t you think we can dispense with the P.I., Paul?’ Riffer looked concerned. ‘At the rate this man charges, your savings won’t last long.’

'That's a good idea.' Paul agreed with his lawyer.

'Paul's worried Dorothy will lash out at me,' Julie mentioned, 'but I've assured him I'll keep in the background. Dorothy won't even know I'm around.' Paul's concern warmed her heart, made her feel cherished and protected. It was a novel feeling. Since she'd grown up, no one else had been anxious about her well-being and safety, not even her father who'd assumed a trained police officer could take care of herself. In fact, she'd handled a lot worse than Dorothy, though she couldn't tell Paul.

'Did you find out where Dorothy comes from?' Riffer asked.

'No. Maybe Sheila's godmother will know.' Eager to get to her appointment, Julie picked up her shoulder bag and headed for the door. 'Wish me luck. I'll call as soon as I talk to Mrs. Montague.'

Julie parked her car off Monument Avenue, named for the stone monuments of Robert E. Lee and his Confederate generals, then followed a winding moss-edged brick sidewalk flanked by tall hedges of boxwood. The street behind her was a busy thoroughfare, but it was quiet and cool under the old oak trees.

The sidewalk ended at a well-preserved

Georgian mansion. The two-story house, with its dark green trim and ivy growing up the white bricks, appealed to Julie's need for a peaceful life.

A maid answered the door then led her down a carpeted hall to a garden room, bright with sunshine, where a lady knelt to tend her plants. Julie inhaled a spicy floral fragrance. Glancing around the garden room, she located several red geranimums among the array of potted plants and ferns.

'Mrs. Montague?'

The woman pulled herself erect with the aid of her walker. Sheila's godmother appeared to be in her seventies. As she observed the woman's frail physical condition and advanced age, Julie felt let-down. It had probably been a waste of time to come here. She doubted Mrs. Montague would be able to help them.

Then, the gray head raised and a pair of alert hazel eyes sent Julie a keen glance like an elementary school teacher she'd had who missed nothing. Hoping she didn't have a smudge on her nose or a run in her stockings, Julie's gaze locked with the older woman's. The cool, reserved stare turned into a pleasant smile. Beatrice Montague removed her gloves and extended her hand. Her soft little hand gave Julie's a firm shake.

'Miss Taylor? I see my directions were adequate.'

'As a matter of fact, Richmond's my home town, though it's been several years since I lived here. I moved back last month.'

'Oh, I see. Where have you been?' By her tone, it was obvious Beatrice Montague found it puzzling that anyone would want to leave this graceful Southern city with one foot in the past and the other firmly in the present.

'Ah . . . I graduated from the University of Virginia then worked in Alexandria until my father died a few weeks ago.'

'I'm sorry. I'm sure you miss him,' Mrs. Montague's voice softened into sympathy and she patted Julie's arm then gestured to a pair of rattan chairs. Once they were seated, she asked, 'May I offer you some refreshment? Iced tea or some lemonade?'

'Please don't go to any trouble. This won't take long. Like I said on the phone, I'm gathering information for Paul Martin.'

'Such a nice young man. We had a delightful conversation about Richmond and its history when Sheila and he attended my Christmas Open House last year,' the old lady informed her.

Relieved to hear her hostess bore no animosity towards Paul, Julie came right to the point. 'Mrs. Montague, I believe Paul's innocent and I'm working with his lawyer to clear his name.' She braced herself for rejection. Sheila's godmother might believe Paul was responsible for Sheila's murder.

'I liked Paul the one time I saw him, though he wasn't Sheila's usual selection. Most of her young men were weak-chinned wonders who fawned on her, catered to her every whim. My goddaughter always had to have her own way. Even as a child, she was strong-willed and spoiled. Paul didn't strike me as the kind of man who'd let anyone walk over him, even his wife.' Mrs. Montague looked sad and she added, 'Her mother, the younger sister of my dearest friend, was an invalid for years. Her doctors said a heart attack killed Anne, but I always thought she died of a broken heart.'

'Sheila's mother didn't want to divorce her husband?'

'Oh, no. Anne would have taken Marcus back in a minute if Dorothy hadn't followed him here and convinced him to get a divorce so he could marry her. Dorothy told Marcus she was carrying his child. The day they returned from their honeymoon, she informed him she'd had a miscarriage.' Beatrice sighed.

'How did Sheila take to Dorothy?'

'At first she hated her step-mother, later she adjusted. They tolerated each other though they were never friends.'

'Do you think Marcus and Dorothy have been happy?'

'I suppose, until Sheila's grandfather died. Dorothy counted on old Mr. Turner's inheritance. But he hated her almost as much as he adored his grandchild so he left Sheila his fortune.'

'What was Dorothy's reaction? Did she accept the terms of the will?' Julie waited for Beatrice to confirm what Paul had told her.

'Not at all. Dorothy insisted the family lawyer read the will a second time to be sure he hadn't made a mistake then she threw a fit. Marcus had to take her home and call their doctor to sedate her.' Mrs. Montague's mouth twisted with scorn. It was obvious she wasn't Dorothy's biggest fan.

This visit could prove to be worthwhile. Everything Mrs. Montague told her about Dorothy made it seem more feasible that Sheila's stepmother could have been involved in her murder. But Dorothy and Peterson seemed an unlikely pair. How did the spoiled socialite find an ex-con like Peterson?

'It sounds like she counted on the inheritance.' Julie pumped Sheila's god-mother for more information in hopes that

Mrs. Montague would divulge information more concrete than tales of hysterics. Dorothy's obvious disappointment re the will didn't prove she'd committed a crime. They'd been let down by false leads in the past. Would this visit be the turning point?

'I suppose so. They've always lived well. Of course, Marcus is a senior partner with his firm so they may be able to afford Dorothy's extravagant tastes. The last I heard, she wanted Marcus to buy her a small castle in Scotland.'

'Did Dorothy come from a wealthy background?'

'I couldn't say. All I know is they met in Las Vegas. Dorothy won't talk about her family.' Mrs. Montague paused when her maid walked into the sunroom with a plate of cookies. The servant held the plate while Beatrice and Julie helped themselves.

Judging by their warm, cinnamon fragrance, the cookies had just been baked. Julie's stomach growled. It was no wonder since she hadn't taken time for breakfast that morning. Meals didn't seem important with Paul's freedom at stake. Still, she better make an effort to eat. It wouldn't help matters if she became ill.

'Thank you.' Julie selected a sugar cookie, munched for a moment, then smiled in appreciation. 'This is wonderful. Please continue. Everything you've said has helped me to form a clearer picture of Sheila's step-mother.' The more she learned, the more she disliked the woman.

'Dorothy told me once that she'd waited a long time to have what my cousin Marcus gave her, the mansion, the cars, the furs and jewelry,' Mrs. Montague said. 'Perhaps that was her way of admitting her family wasn't well-to-do.'

'How did Marcus feel when his daughter inherited her grandfather's estate?'

'I don't think it bothered him. By the way, Marcus and I are third cousins,' Mrs. Montague said. 'Marcus has never been materialistic like Dorothy. He'd be content with much less except for her. You may find this hard to believe, but one day he confided that Dorothy was furious with Sheila because she refused to share her grandfather's fortune.'

'To your knowledge, were Dorothy and Sheila on good terms when she disappeared?' Julie longed for a tape recorder, though she suspected Mrs. Montague might be less candid if she knew her comments were being documented. Still, she'd make careful notes of the conversation later.

'I doubt it since they hadn't been friends in

the past. Before Sheila inherited, Dorothy ignored her as much as possible. Then my godchild became an heiress and Dorothy turned on the charm. That didn't last long since Sheila made it clear she wouldn't share her new wealth. Dorothy must have been infuriated not to be able to get her hands on the fortune.' The old lady shook her head. 'It's a shame she's such a greedy person.'

'How far do you think she would have gone to get the inheritance?' Julie's nerves tensed, waiting for an answer.

'I don't know.' Sheila's godmother shuddered and some emotion, perhaps fear, flickered across her wrinkled features. The moment passed and she smiled. 'Are you sure you wouldn't like a glass of iced tea?'

'No, thank you. I appreciate your seeing me.'

'I'm glad Sheila's mother's deceased. Her daughter's murder would have destroyed Anne.'

'It was a horrible, senseless act of violence. And it's time the police found the real killer. Paul's been framed for someone else's crime, but his lawyer will prove he's innocent.' Another thought came to mind and Julie beseeched Mrs Montague. 'Please don't mention my visit to anyone. If Dorothy's involved in Sheila's murder, you don't want her to hear we've talked.'

Beatrice nodded. 'I won't say a word. Goodbye, my dear,' She took Julie's hand and gave it a warm squeeze as she stood to go. 'I found the news of Paul's arrest incredible before your visit. Your faith in him has reinforced my belief in his innocence. Let's hope the guilty party is apprehended soon so Paul can be vindicated.'

* * *

Paul stood at his living room window and stared at his front yard. He didn't see the rolling lawn or the tall oaks and maples. His inner eye fixated on the spectre of prison. There were no trees or lawns in prison, just gray concrete. The fact was he could be found guilty of Sheila's murder and spend years in prison. Or worse. He wouldn't let himself think about that.

How did his life get so screwed up? Frustration turned to anger as he considered the reason his freedom was at stake. All his instincts screamed one name, Dorothy.

His hands balled into fists, Paul paced the living room then sat on the leather sofa. Squaring his shoulders, he rallied his courage and vowed not to give up. It wasn't over yet. Riffer was still searching for evidence of

Dorothy's guilt. And he'd do whatever he could to help.

He'd re-tracked Sheila's route home from his house, to no avail. No one in the businesses along the way remembered her.

The will to overcome remained in his heart, though it wasn't as strong as it had been.

To take his mind off his troubles, Paul lay back on the sofa, closed his eyes, and thought of a happier time and Julie in his arms. Mental snapshots of her drifted through his mind. The surprised look on her face the night he rescued her schnauzer, the guilty expression when he caught her snooping in his trash, the softness of her lips the first time he kissed her. Most of all, he remembered and cherished the memory of the night they'd made love. Her shy reserve had blossomed into passion.

His jaw clenched then he sat up. As soon as the charges were dropped, he'd make it up to Julie for all the worry he'd caused her. Her helping Riffer disturbed him. His instincts warned him it could be dangerous for her to get involved.

He read a magazine then dozed. The doorbell jolted him awake. Paul rubbed sleepy eyes then opened the door to Riffer.

'It's good to see you.' Paul shook his

friend's hand, glad to have company.

'I came by to bring you up-to-date.' Riffer slapped him on the shoulder then sat down in an armchair across the room.

'What have you found?' His pulse rate increased.

'Well, we've gathered information that could be useful. For instance, the credit check run on the Turners indicates they're over their heads in debt.'

'I'm not surprised. While Sheila and I were together, I got the distinct impression that Dorothy could spend money faster than any other living creature.'

'Julie called me after her visit with Mrs. Montague,' Riffer informed him. 'It appears that lady has no use for Dorothy. After all, she did steal Marcus from Sheila's mother, Mrs. Montague's best friend.'

'That's not proof Dorothy killed Sheila.' He'd hoped for something concrete. Would this nightmare ever end?

'That's true.' Uncertainty crept into Riffer's voice. For a moment his shoulders sagged then he straightened. 'Don't get discouraged. We're not done by a long shot. I have a friend at Richmond PD who'll run Dorothy's name through the police databases. Let's find out if she has a criminal record. It won't hurt to check.'

* * *

Each time Julie called the architectural firm, the snooty receptionist informed her Ms. Allen was busy and switched her to the office message center. Julie left several messages but the woman didn't return her calls. The last time she called, the architect picked up her phone.

As soon as Julie explained the reason for her calls, the architect crossly informed her, 'I don't want to talk to you. Please don't call me again.'

Julie's temper flared then faded as she hung up the phone. It would be a waste of time to get upset. She must face the facts. Now that she'd resigned from the police force, she was a private citizen with no authority. If the architect didn't want to speak to her, that was her right. She wouldn't give up, though. Maybe a less direct approach would work.

In a well-known florist shop downtown, Julie selected a beautiful, expensive arrangement in a crystal vase.

'Where would you like this delivered, Miss?' The man in the florist shop queried her.

'I'll take it with me. Let me pick out an enclosure card.'

Ten minutes later, she parked her car in the garage under Sheila's office building. The elevator soon transported her to the architectural firm's floor. She walked through the open doors into the reception area.

'Yes?' The receptionist asked in a condescending manner. Her haughty glance raked Julie's faded jeans and hanley shirt.

'I have a delivery for Ms. Allen.'

'Thank you. I'll take them,' the woman replied and reached for the vase of flowers.

Julie stepped back. 'My instructions were to deliver these to Ms. Allen in person.' With a lift of her chin, she dared the receptionist to refuse.

'All right.' The receptionist shrugged then pointed down a hall.

Julie knocked before she opened the office door. A heavy-set woman in a long tailored navy dress looked up from her desk as she entered the room. Pity stirred within Julie at the sight of the unhappy expression on the woman's features.

'Ms. Allen?'

'Yes?' Caught unawares, the architect glanced at the flowers with pleasure. Her flushed round face indicated this wasn't a usual occurrence.

Julie set the arrangement down on the woman's desk. 'There's a card.' Pointing it out, she stood aside.

'Thanks.' Eagerness turned to a frown as the architect read the card. 'Sorry, but I must talk to you. Julie Taylor.'

'Of all of the highhanded tricks, this is the worst.' Then she motioned for Julie to take a seat. 'All right, you've got five minutes.'

Julie pulled up a chair. 'I'm here for Paul Martin's lawyer. It appears Sheila Turner was troubled the night she vanished and he needs to know what was on her mind. May I ask you a few questions?'

The architect shifted in her chair and looked uncomfortable.

'You're grieving for your friend, but do you have any reason to believe the accusations against her husband? Do you think he killed her?' Julie held her breath, waited for her response.

'To be honest, I don't know what to believe,' the architect admitted. She looked out the window then glanced in Julie's direction. 'The police must have proof of Paul's guilt or they wouldn't have arrested him,' she reasoned.

'Perhaps, yet isn't it possible someone planted evidence to make him look guilty?' Julie asked in a firm voice. 'Think back. Did you ever hear Sheila say she was afraid of Paul? Did she tell you he was abusive?'

'No,' the architect said. 'Sheila was upset the marriage failed. From what she told me, Paul was too independent, in spite of his being five years younger.' Her fingers touched the petal of a mauve Stargazer Lily in the vase.

Julie felt the sweet fragrance and bright colors of the flowers fill the drab office until they made it more pleasant.

'Sheila seemed troubled the last time he saw her. Can you tell me what was on her mind?'

'That day she came back from lunch in tears,' the architect recalled. 'It took me awhile to calm her down. Finally, she admitted she'd had a terrible fight with her stepmother.'

'What was the problem?'

'According to Sheila, Dorothy was furious because Sheila's grandfather left her his estate. Before Sheila vanished, Dorothy nagged her about it all of the time. That day, Dorothy told her she'd be sorry she'd refused to share her fortune. Also, the divorce upset Sheila. Personally, I wasn't surprised to hear she'd moved out.'

'Oh, really? Why not?'

'Sheila liked to control people. The little I saw of Paul Martin, he struck me as a man with a mind of his own, a man who wouldn't let himself be led around by the nose.' The archirect got to her feet. 'That's all I can tell you.'

'Would you give a statement, just what you've said?'

'I guess. Do you think he'll be convicted?'

'Not if his lawyer and I can help it.' Julie stood to go. Her finger touched the vase. 'Enjoy the flowers.'

* * *

Later that afternoon, Julie compared notes with Riffer and Paul. So far they couldn't link Dorothy to Sheila's death. 'A bad credit rating doesn't mean the woman's a killer. And the opinions of Beatrice Montague and Sarah Allen are just heresay,' Paul said.

'Right, but they could create reasonable doubt as to your guilt,' Riffer said. 'There's one more avenue we can explore. Peterson, the alleged killer.'

Julie had a sinking feeling inside, but she wouldn't give up. They'd find the truth if they dug deep enough.

The phone rang and the lawyer grabbed it. Seated beside Paul, Julie watched Riffer's expression change from hopeful to irritated. By the time he hung up the phone, he looked downcast.

'Bad news?' She dreaded what he'd tell them.

'No criminal record was found for Dorothy Turner.'

Her heart sank. 'Nothing at all?' Depression pressed down on Julie.

'No.' The one terse word spoke volumes. Riffer stared at his desk calendar. 'The trial's just a few weeks away.'

'Where do we go from here?' Paul's voice was anxious.

Julie wasn't immune to the tension in the room either. Her stomach clenched with nerves. 'There must be something we've overlooked. The times Dorothy called to harrass you, did you record the conversations?' Gazing at Paul, Julie prayed for a miracle.

'No, I wish I had,' he said.

'That's too bad. If we could prove she threatened you, it might help.'

'Wait a minute.' Paul's voice rang with unexpected enthusiasm. 'Before the calls, Dorothy sent me a couple of letters in which she got downright mean. That may not constitute a threat but — '

'You didn't save those letters, by any chance?' Julie cut him off in mid-sentence. Her heart thumped with excitement.

'No, they made me so mad, I tore them up

and stuck them in the compacter.' Paul paused as if reconsidering what he'd just said. 'At least, I destroyed one letter. I don't recall what happened to the other. It might be around the house somewhere.'

'When did the first letter arrive?' Riffer asked.

Paul wrinkled his brow in concentration. 'A few days after Sheila vanished. In that letter, Dorothy all but called me a murderer.'

'This could be the break we've needed.' Riffer stood erect as if energized by Paul's disclosure.

Julie's nerves hummed with anticipation but she just nodded, afraid to expect too much. They'd been let down before this.

At his house, Paul let them in the front door then led the way to the study.

Riffer removed his jacket and rolled up his shirt sleeves. 'All right, Paul. You and Julie take the desk and I'll search the file cabinet.'

Nothing turned up, so Julie pointed to Paul's library. Shelf by shelf, the three of them worked their way through the collection, opened each book and shook it.

'I'd forgotten how many books you have,' Riffer told Paul.

Pushing the hair out of her eyes, Julie sighed. 'Nothing here,' she replied as they finished their task.

'What now?' Riffer looked around.

'Let's try upstairs,' Julie said.

In the master bedroom, they delved through Paul's bureau drawers and night stands then tackled the closets in the bathroom. For their troubles, they found a man's handkerchief crammed in a coat pocket and a stick of gum.

'Let's go.' Riffer rattled his car keys as if impatient. 'This is a waste of time.'

His haste annoyed Julie. This was the best clue they had. They had to search until they found the letter, even if it meant tearing the place apart.

'Maybe not,' Julie responded. There's still one more place we haven't looked. Let's try the kitchen.'

'You wouldn't have left the letter there, would you?' Riffer asked Paul, a dubious expression on his face.

'It's possible. I've spent a lot of time in the kitchen as well as in the study. The mail is delivered late in the afternoon, so I could've read the letter while cooking supper.'

Paul led them through the dining room, bare except for an inexpensive dining set. In the kitchen, they rummaged through the cabinets then searched the floor-to-ceiling bookshelves.

Julie gasped as an envelope fluttered out of

a cookbook and landed on the tile floor. She opened the envelope and read aloud the letter inside.

'Paul,

Sheila would be alive today if it weren't for you. If I have anything to say about it, you'll rot in prison the rest of your life.

Dorothy'

'Let me see that,' Paul examined the envelope. 'That's interesting. This is postmarked March 16th.'

Julie frowned. 'Sheila vanished on March 9th. Weeks later, the police found the body. So there was no way Dorothy could have known her stepdaughter was dead. Unless . . . ' A shiver raced down her spine, as she thought of the woman who'd written those words, and what the date of the letter implied.

Riffer's smile was cold. 'That lady may have just put her head in a noose.'

23

Paul met Julie at his front door. 'Riffer just called. He's on his way over here, and I'm sure you'll want to hear what he has to say.'

Following him into the living room, her stomach knotted with nerves. 'Maybe it'll be good news.'

'Keep your fingers crossed.' Paul grimaced.

She slipped out of her sandals and settled into the sofa, her feet tucked under her. Seated next to Paul, she glanced his way. The dark smudges under his eyes proved he hadn't slept well either. No wonder. In spite of all of their efforts, they'd found no evidence linking Dorothy to Sheila's murder.

'It could be worse, you know.' Julie tried to sound optimistic. 'At least you're out on bail.'

'That's true, thanks to Riffer. If he hadn't convinced the judge I'm a law-abiding citizen and no flight risk, I'd be a guest of the City Jail right now.' Paul gestured at the comfortable room around them. 'These accomodations are more to my liking than bars and cinderblock.'

Close to him, she yearned. Julie promptly reminded herself it was best that she continue to keep Paul at arm's length. A romantic involvement right now would complicate matters.

As if he'd read her thoughts, he sent her a warm glance. In response, a ripple of awareness raced up her body.

'When I'm cleared, we'll think about the future,' he murmured in a low tone.

'All right.' Julie blinked back a tear. The uncertainty of the situation kept her on edge, especially since he was innocent. She'd almost convinced herself that he was. Doubt still plagued her sometimes, though she did her best to ignore it.

Eased back on the sofa, she tried to encourage him. 'That letter Dorothy sent you could be a big help.'

'I sure hope so. It was funny the way it turned up in a cookbook. I must have stuck it in there. The next letter she sent went right in the trash.' A ghost of a smile flickered across his face.

'It could help you.' Julie shivered though the room was warm. Was Dorothy the killer?

'Riffer sure got excited about the letter,' Paul commented.

Julie nodded. 'That's why he's got an appointment with the assistant district attorney scheduled to prosecute you. Added to the bad credit report, the statements from

Beatrice Montague and Sarah Allen, Dorothy's harrassing telephone calls and the car that ran us off the road near the Turner mansion, he's got a lot to tell the D.A. about Dorothy.'

'Don't forget Jay's hit-and-run accident,' Paul said.

'That's one thing we'll never forget.' She certainly wouldn't. They'd come home relaxed after a pleasant day at the beach to find Jay in the hospital. 'Still, we haven't found proof that Dorothy was involved.'

For a moment, Paul let down his guard and admitted he had his doubts. 'I sure hope I can get out of this mess,' he muttered.

He looked so forlorn, Julie wanted to hug him. That wouldn't be a good idea. What he needed right now was a positive response, not coddling. That would be like admitting they might not win. In an attempt to sound like the outcome was a sure thing, she replied, 'When it's all over, we'll celebrate.'

'You sound like you're sure we'll win.'

'We will. If you think of anything else tonight, call me.'

'I still wish you'd move in with me.' Paul kissed her hand.

'I'm safe enough. Besides, we need to concentrate on the case right now.' As she retrieved her hand, her skin tingled all the way up her arm. Paul was too appealing. It took all of her self-control not to ignore the consequences and throw herself in his arms. Not a good idea. To change the subject, she added, 'You know, I have a hunch this will all be over soon.'

His eyes narrowed and he shot her a sharp glance. 'You're not taking any chances, are you?'

'Of course not.' It wouldn't do for him to worry about her safety. 'All I've done is chat with Mrs. Montague and visit Sheila's friend in her office. Neither of those ladies thinks you're guilty.' Julie revelled in his thoughtfulness and concern for her. Her day had been tame compared to some she'd spent undercover, but this wasn't the time for confessions. As soon as he was cleared, she'd tell him everything.

A car pulled up in front of Paul's house. Through the window, Julie recognized the driver. Riffer soon joined them, a new spring to his step.

Greeting them, a grin lit up the lawyer's often somber features. Her heart raced. What would he tell them?

'Want a cup of coffee?' Paul offered.

'Thanks, but I can't stay. Tonight's my son's last soccer game and I promised him I wouldn't miss this one. I thought I'd stop by here on the way home. Are you ready for some good news?'

She heard Paul take a deep breath. 'Sure,' he said.

All she could do was nod her head. Julie waited, half-hopeful and half-afraid to hear what Riffer would say.

'I presented our evidence, everything we've got on Dorothy.'

'What was the Assistant D.A.'s reaction?'

'Well, it's not enough to exonerate you, Paul, but . . . '

'Go on,' Julie urged. Her stare locked on Riffer's face.

'Based on the information I gave the D.A., the police were going to question Dorothy Turner today.'

A wave of relief hit Julie. This could be the break they needed. 'I guess it's too much to hope that she got careless and incriminated herself.'

'That would be great, but by now we know better than to count on anything.' Riffer took off his eyeglasses, blinked like a wise old owl then cleaned the lenses with his pocket hankerchief. 'If Dorothy was involved in Sheila's murder yet managed to set Paul up as the killer, she's no fool. Still, anything's possible. Well, that's all my news. I'll let you know the minute I hear anything new.'

'You do think he has a chance, a good chance?' The spectre of Paul behind bars haunted her. Justice didn't always prevail.

'Of course. And if Dorothy slips up while talking to the police, Paul's chances get even better.' Riffer frowned. 'There's still Peterson. It's strange but he doesn't fit.'

'You're right,' Paul said. 'From his record, he was a petty thief, not a contract killer.'

* * *

Dorothy kept a confident smile on her face and her posture erect. Inside, she quaked with nerves while the detectives interrogated her at Police Headquarters in a room that reeked of stale tobacco and disinfectant.

'This letter you sent to Paul Martin?' The detective slid a xeroxed copy across the scarred table in front of Dorothy. 'As you can see, it's dated March 16th. Let me read it. You write, and I quote, 'Sheila would be alive today if it weren't for you.' 'So on that date, you blamed Mr. Martin for his wife's death. Can you explain what you meant?'

'Oh, I was so upset. Sheila was missing and my heart was broken. What I meant was I'd blame Paul if anything had happened to her. If they hadn't separated, maybe Sheila wouldn't have disappeared.' To convince her interrogator, Dorothy managed to squeeze out a few crocodile tears. It must have worked since the detective's tone softened.

'I see. It must be terrible to lose a daughter. Please let me express my condolences to you and her father.' He stood and looked down on her. 'Well, thank you for coming in today, Mrs. Turner. If we have any other questions, we'll be in touch.'

Her high heels clicked on the faded linoleum floor as Dorothy stalked out of the building. Feeling shaky, she slid onto the soft leather driver's seat of her new beige Cadillac with relief. A sigh of regret escaped her lips. Those letters had been a stupid mistake. Her brother had one rule, never give people anything they can use against you. That included anything in writing. And damn it if one of her letters to Paul hadn't turned up.

Once home, she climbed the stairs to her bedroom, locked the door to ensure privacy, and punched in an out-of-state telephone number. Her brother answered on the first ring and she gave him a brief report. Then she sat back and waited for him to reassure her all would be well.

'I hope you were careful today.' His rough, cross voice lashed out at her. 'You've been quite stupid, those idiotic letters then the hit-and-run. Have you forgotten what I've taught you?'

'I'm sorry,' she stammered, shocked and hurt. Hot tears burned her eyes, blurred her vision.

'Just don't do anything else. My scheme was flawless. If it fails, it will be on your head.'

'I'll be more careful, I promise you.' More than anything else, she'd always craved his approval, his support.

'Let's hope so. There's too much at stake.' He let out a sigh. 'I have to go. A patient is due any minute.'

'Wait.' She clutched the phone, desperate to keep him with her a few more minutes. 'When can we talk again?'

'I'll call you.'

A shudder raced through her body. What would she do if he turned on her? He was all she had.

Taking several deep breaths to calm herself, she descended to the first floor then wandered through the kitchen, a disaster at present with the ongoing renovation. She followed the hall to the back of the house. All was quiet since the workmen had left for the day, and her maid and cook were still out on errands.

Opening the door at the end of the hall, she

stepped into a spacious three-car garage. A dark blue Lincoln TownCar was parked next to the new smaller beige Cadillac. Her fingers traced the dents in the Lincoln's front fender. There was no way she could take the car to a local garage for repairs without a lot of questions about the damages. Though she hated to part with it, she had no choice. The gardener must get rid of the Lincoln.

Her mind flashed back to the day she'd driven through Paul's neighborhood. By chance, she thought she saw him on a bike. Rage took over. She despised Paul for his mere existance. If not for him, Sheila would have come around, been generous. It was all his fault. The Lincoln's front fender hit the bike and Paul's body flew through the air and landed in the gutter. Panicked by what she'd done, Dorothy stomped on the gas pedal and sped away. That evening on the local news, she heard that Jay Arnold of New York City had been hit by a car in Pollard Park. She'd hit Paul's twin brother by mistake. Her only regret was it wasn't Paul.

To cover up her crime, she lied to Marcus, told him a deer ran into the car on her way home from a meeting. As usual, he didn't pay much attention. His head was in the clouds, working out a strategy to defend his newest client, a millionaire accused of tax evasion.

Marcus was a successful tax lawyer with a substantial income. They had a partnership — he earned so she could spend. She'd scraped for a living for years before Marcus appeared in her life so no matter how much money she had, it never seemed enough. Her lips curved and Dorothy reassured herself her brother's scheme would still work. Paul would be tried and convicted. Then she'd have everything she'd always wanted.

* * *

The door bell chimed before eight o'clock as Julie headed for the kitchen and her first cup of coffee. She cocked an eyebrow. Who in the world? She didn't have many visitors and nobody came at this hour of the morning. With Misty at her heels, she opened the front door then took a step back, 'Maxine!'

'I heard about Paul.' The literary agent's usually self-assured voice was hesitant, her smile uncertain. There were circles under her large dark eyes. 'Please, can I come in?'

'I guess so.' Julie stood aside and let the other woman enter. Then she gave her a cool stare.

'You don't know how many times I've wanted to see you. I don't know what got into me, Julie. I'm so ashamed.' A flush rose to Maxine's cheeks.

'You should be.' Angry at Maxine's deceit, Julie scowled at the woman who'd hurt Paul and her. 'You shouldn't have lied.'

'I know. Like I said on the phone the other day, Paul had every right to chew me out. Believe it or not, I like myself even less than you do.' Maxine's voice crackled with emotion and she promised, 'But I'm trying to change.'

'All right.' Julie sighed. Why did Maxine come? She'd already called and apologized. Julie's instincts told her to be on guard, watch what she told Paul's literary agent. 'If you'd like a cup of coffee, come on back to the kitchen. I was headed that way when you came to the door.'

Staying angry with Maxine served no useful purpose, yet she wouldn't be taken in by the agent's apologetic manner.

As they walked into the kitchen, Julie couldn't help admiring the other woman's attractive royal blue silk suit. Her hand smoothed her own shabby but comfortable garments. The cotton of the pink-and-white seersucker robe felt soft against her skin. Compared to the literary agent's polished business attire, she was a mess. But it was just eight a.m.

'I wasn't sure you'd see me.' Maxine perched on the edge of a kitchen chair while Julie poured them each a mug of coffee.

'I don't believe in holding a grudge. Besides, Paul is all that matters to me right now. He's innocent and I'm going to do whatever it takes to see him cleared of this hideous charge.' Julie's nerves tensed, considering his dilemma. Although the police had been scheduled to interview Dorothy the previous day, John Riffer still hadn't called her. Maybe the interview with Dorothy had been unproductive. The woman could be too smart to incriminate herself.

'I know. That's why I'm here, to help you.'

'Thanks, though I can't imagine what you can do.'

'Paul's no killer even if Dorothy Turner's tried to convince the police he is,' Maxine said. 'And speaking of Dorothy, did I ever tell you my mother's Dorothy's friend?'

'You've got to be kidding.' Julie was appalled. How could anyone consider Dorothy a friend?

'Not a friend as you or I would define the word, more like someone to call when you want to show off. Dorothy likes to brag. Sometimes it's a new piece of jewelry, a fur . . . you know.' The agent shrugged. 'This may be of interest to you. A few days ago, she called my mother to crow about her new car. I thought her selection a little out of character since she's always bought Lincolns in the past.'

Julie's ears perked up. In an attempt to sound casual, she asked, 'Dorothy has a new car? That's nice. What color is it?'

'Beige and it's a Catera, one of those new, small Cadillacs. Mother told me Dorothy just stopped driving her Lincoln recently though it's less than a year old.'

'Maybe she wanted a change.' Julie shrugged then sipped her coffee, trying to sound like she couldn't care less. Her senses went on alert. This could be useful information. Again in the investigation, she wished she had a tape recorder handy.

'I guess. She's always said a Lincoln TownCar is her kind of car. Nothing else suits her.' A thoughtful expression crossed Maxine's face. 'Dorothy's a peculiar woman. Mother says the other members of the bridge group talk about themselves, about their childhoods, their families. Dorothy clams up and changes the subject, if anyone asks her about herself.'

'Do you play bridge with Dorothy?'

'On occasion, to fill in when Mother can't attend. The group rotates from home to home.'

Any information on Dorothy was welcome. Julie looked down and toyed with the belt of her robe 'When do they play?'

'Tonight's their meeting for this month,' Maxine said. 'Mother's switched with Dorothy and will host the group since Dorothy's having her kitchen remodeled. The Italian tile she selected for the floor is no longer available and she can't find another pattern she likes.'

Julie gazed at her own kitchen floor. 'That's a project the owner of this house should consider,' she replied and kicked at the tired vinyl with her slipper.

The literary agent carried her mug to the sink. 'Well, I have to go. We expect a new author in the office today.'

Julie accompanied Maxine to the front door. The agent stopped short on the threshold. 'Oh, I almost forgot. Tell Paul I have a peace offering for him. Another editor may be interested in his book. I'll be in touch.'

Julie waited until Maxine's car disappeared down the street, then picked up the phone and called Riffer.

'We need to see Dorothy's Lincoln,' she told him then repeated what she'd learned from Maxine.

'You really think she hit Paul's brother?'

'If she hates Paul as much as she seems to, wouldn't it be a temptation to strike out at him, if she had the chance?'

'Sure,' he agreed. 'She could have lost her cool.'

A plan began to form in Julie's brain.

* * *

Julie called the beauty salon on River Road. Francoise was booked for the next few days, so she reluctantly agreed to be put on a waiting list in case of a cancellation, using her mother's maiden name, Julia Renfrou.

An hour later, she heard from the salon. Francoise had an unexpected cancellation and could do Julie's hair if she came right away. Julie was on her way in less than ten minutes.

'Bon jour. It's good to see you again.' Today the Frenchwoman greeted Julie like she was an old friend. Francoise ran her fingers through Julie's wet hair. Holding up a strand, she asked, 'A trim, perhaps?'

'Whatever you think,' Julie replied. 'I've received so many compliments since you did my hair, I just had to come back.'

'Oui, you were in luck today.' The French woman beamed. 'A client had to cancel out at the last minute due to problems with the staff at her Aruba villa. She's flying down there for a couple of days.'

'I guess you have a lot of important clients.'

'Oh, yes.' Francoise looked pleased. 'Many ladies who live in Windsor Farms, River Road, Robius.' The hairdresser rattled off names of the most affluent neighborhoods around Richmond.

Julie's nerves hummed with excitement. If her hunch was right, Sheila Turner wasn't the only member of the Turner family who used this exclusive salon. 'Robius? I believe a friend of a friend lives out there.'

'Are you referring to Mrs. Turner?' Francoise's smile became warmer, as if she realized she might have underestimated Julie's social standing.

'I believe so. I've never met her though she does live in Robius. Is she your client?'

'She has beautiful hair and I keep it just the way she likes,' the Parisienne declared with pride. When I see her, I'll tell her you asked about her.'

'Oh, I don't know the lady,' Julie hastened to inform the hairdresser. 'It's just that I've heard so much about her.' Enough to think she might be a killer.

According to Maxine, Dorothy's bridge group met that evening so chances were good Dorothy would get her hair done that day. As she left the salon an hour later, Julie made a quick decision. Heading south, Julie parked the Honda on the shoulder of Huguenot Highway one half mile north of the Turners' private road. Then she slid down in the driver's seat and waited.

Just when she'd begun to think her hunch had been wrong, a blonde in a small beige Cadillac drove out of the Turners' road, breezed by Julie's vehicle, and headed north.

Julie had seen pictures of Dorothy on the society pages of the local paper, so she was able to identify Dorothy as the driver.

On her cell phone, she punched in the number for the Turners' residence, asked for Dorothy. The maid who answered, informed her Dorothy wasn't home.

Julie eased her car down the narrow, one-lane road and parked in front of the Tara-style mansion nestled in a thicket of pines. From the back of the Honda, Julie lifted out a large box. With it in her arms, she stepped onto the front porch and rang the doorbell.

A uniformed maid cracked open the door and peered out at her. 'Yes, can I help you?' The sight of a woman in a business suit seemed to reassure her since she opened the door wider.

'Hello,' Julie spoke in a matter-of-fact tone.

'I have the tile samples Ms. Turner wanted to see for her kitchen floor.'

'I'm so sorry,' the servant replied. 'My lady just left for her hairdresser appointment.'

'Oh, dear.' Julie frowned then pretended to examine her appointment book. 'I wrote down twelve noon today on my calendar. I must have misunderstood her. Can I come in and leave a note with these samples?'

Dorothy's servant escorted her to the kitchen where the countertops had been covered in a stone-like composition material. Julie set the box down in a corner out of the way. 'While I'm here, I might as well take some measurements.' She glanced at the kitchen floor. 'Let's see. Mrs. Turner wants the same tile to run from the kitchen to the back door. Right?'

The maid shrugged. 'You'll have to ask her.'

'Oh, don't let me keep you. Go back to your work. I'll just take the measurements then let myself out.' Julie pulled a tape measure from her shoulder bag along with a pad and pen and started to measure the floor.

The servant watched for a few moments, frowning as if she were uncertain what she should do. Then she announced, 'I have to get back to my ironing upstairs,' and left the room.

Julie wasted no time. From the box, she removed a small camera then walked down the hall and opened the far door. As she'd hoped, it led to the garage.

One car was parked there, a dark blue Lincoln Towncar. Turning on the ceiling light, she walked over to the car, knelt beside it. There were dents in the front fender. A chill raced down her spine. Was this the car that hit Paul's brother?

Julie pointed her camera and used up two rolls of film, taking pictures of the front of the Lincoln from different angles. There was a camera shop near Riffer's office that developed film in one hour. Riffer would find these photographs interesting. Hit-and-run was a serious offense.

Satisfied with her work, she stopped to consult her watch. It was later than she'd realized. Better get the heck out of there before Dorothy came home. Julie passed through the kitchen, retrieved her box, and was about to open the front door when a tall, gaunt blonde stepped into the foyer from outside. The cold, calculating expression on the older woman's face halted Julie in her tracks.

* * *

Dorothy had relaxed while Francoise's fingers massaged her scalp and soothed the headache that had haunted her the last few days. She'd slipped into a pleasant lethargic state, halfway between sleep and consciousness. A certain phrase of her hairdresser's caught her attention.

' . . . that friend of your friend,' Francoise was saying.

Opening her eyes, Dorothy stared in the mirror at the Parisian. 'What did you say?'

'Madame? I just commented on your lovely hair. It's more attractive than the young woman's hair I did this morning. Yours is longer, more luxurious. It's interesting, she knows someone who knows you.' The hairdresser shrugged. 'She was a nice young woman, large brown eyes and dark blonde hair.'

Suspicion dawned as slow as a winter sunrise. 'What was her name?' Dorothy forced a smile, trying to appear nonchalant.

'Name? Ah . . . Julie or Julia, I believe. Let me look in my book.' Francoise crossed the room and picked up her appointment book. 'Julia Renfrou. Do you know her?'

'Never heard of her. She didn't happen to mention the name of our mutual friend, did she?' Dorothy tried not to panic. The last few days, disaster loomed around every corner.

'No. I don't believe she did. Why? Is something wrong?'

Dorothy shrugged. 'I shouldn't let myself get upset over little things like this, but I haven't slept well since . . . Sheila's death.'

'That's understandable.' The hairdresser sounded sympathetic while she eased her client back into the chair and messaged the tense muscles in her shoulders.

Dorothy again let herself relax. 'Yes, our poor girl. But soon that horrid brute will be in jail where he belongs and they'll never let him out.' She hoped not. If he was found innocent, she knew who he'd come looking for. Paul was no fool. By now, he must have realized he'd been set up and by whom.

The receptionist stepped into Francoise's cubicle at the back of the shop. 'Excuse me.' Like the rest of the salon's staff, her voice was low and pleasant. 'There's a message for you, Mrs. Turner. Your maid wants you to call home.'

'Hand me my purse,' Dorothy ordered her hairdresser. In a matter of seconds, she'd reached her maid on her cell phone. At the end of the brief call, Dorothy pushed Francoise's hands away. 'I have to go home. Right now!' Her wet hair was half set.

'Madame? What is the matter?' Francoise's eyebrows went up then she patted Dorothy on the shoulder. 'Let me finish setting your hair. You can dry it later.'

The Parisian quickly rolled Dorothy's hair and removed her cape. 'There, Madame. I hope you find everything's all right at your home.'

'Thank you.' She slipped the woman a large tip for her trouble. 'I'll see you next week.' Dorothy strode at a sedate pace out of the salon. Once in the parking lot, she dashed to her Cadillac. Traffic was light on Huguenot Highway and she reached her residence in a few minutes. A small car she didn't recognize was parked in front.

Dorothy jumped from her car and marched onto the front portico of the mansion. As she flung the door open, a younger woman was about to leave. The attractive blonde stood before her. Her large brown eyes seemed to appraise Dorothy.

Dorothy glared at the woman. 'Who the hell are you?'

'I've brought some tile samples for you to examine.' Though the intruder smiled, there was a slight tremor in her voice. 'The word got out you needed new tile for your kitchen and I thought — '

'You thought you'd make a sale?' Dorothy interrupted her before she could finish. 'By trespassing? You pretended to have an appointment with me when you didn't. How do I know you're on the level?'

The woman smiled, apparently unfazed by Dorothy's hostility. 'Please wait a moment. I have just the tile for your kitchen.' She slipped by Dorothy and walked in long, sure strides to her vehicle. But instead of opening the hatch as Dorothy expected, she jumped into the vehicle and gunned the motor.

'Come back here,' Dorothy screamed and ran toward the road. Just as her fingers touched the door handle on the passenger side of the car, the vehicle sped away and disappeared around a bend of the road. The intruder had escaped!

24

Julie spread the photographs across Riffer's desk then stood back and waited for his reaction.

Paul's lawyer pulled a magnifying glass from a drawer and examined each print.

'Good,' he muttered, a broad grin spread across his face. His finger traced the lines of the dents in the front bumper. 'That Lincoln must have hit something, or someone, hard to cause these.'

His keen gaze locked on her face. 'From your past experience, you know the police don't need an eye witness report to identify a car involved in a hit-and-run?'

She nodded. 'That would be the business of the crime scene unit for automobile accidents.' Walking the narrow line between truth and deception, Julie felt apprehensive. Riffer knew she'd worked in law enforcement. How would he react if she told him she'd investigated Paul?

'Right,' he agreed. 'If Dorothy's Lincoln hit Jay, his hair or blood could be on the car. And there's his bike. Was it checked for paint samples?'

Julie swallowed hard. On her request, Corbeille had called the labs about Jay's hit-and-run. A dark blue paint had been found on the bike, but if she divulged that much information to Riffer, she'd have to tell him the rest. 'You'd need to speak to the police about that.'

Julie had always found lying difficult, yet it was ten times worse now because it involved Paul. Still, until he was cleared and she could tell him everything, she couldn't reveal what she'd done to Riffer or anyone else. Paul mustn't hear about her investigation second hand. It would be hard enough to accept from her. She hoped he'd understand the difficult position in which she'd found herself.

Paul's lawyer scribbled a note. He held up one of the prints. 'If she's innocent, why didn't Dorothy have the car repaired?'

'She should have taken it to a repair shop, but she didn't. That's suspicious in itself.' Anger flushed her cheeks as Julie considered the misdirection of justice. Dorothy went her own way, unhindered, while Paul counted the days until he stood trial for a crime he hadn't committed.

The lawyer looked concerned. 'These pictures are great, but don't take any more unnecessary risks,' he said. 'You had a close call today. If Dorothy murdered Sheila, she wouldn't hesitate to kill you, too.'

'Please don't tell Paul what happened,' Julie pleaded. There's no reason to upset him. I promised to stay away from Dorothy.'

'All right, but be careful.' Riffer grimaced, checking his watch. 'I've got to go. It's our anniversary and my wife and I have dinner reservations.'

Julie reached across the desktop and patted his hand. 'You've been great. Paul and I both appreciate everything you've done to help him.'

'He'd do the same for me if I were in his predicament,' Riffer replied quietly. 'We need to get the police out to the Turner mansion for a look at Dorothy's car before she panics and gets rid of it. Why hasn't she disposed of it?'

'Maxine told me the Lincoln's Dorothy's favorite car so she may hate to part with it. Also, she may think that, based on her prominent social position and her husband's friendship with the Chief, the police won't consider her a suspect.' Julie bristled with indignation.

The office door swung open and Paul walked in, unexpected.

'Your car was gone so I assumed you'd be

over here.' Paul sent a curious glance in her direction.

She moved so she blocked his view of Riffer, giving the lawyer time to hide the photographs.

'What's going on?' Paul asked.

'We thought we'd review what we have so far,' she said.

'Go ahead.' Paul pulled up a chair and sat down.

With a quick glance in his direction, she summed up what they had learned. 'First, Dorothy harrassed you, insisted you'd done away with Sheila.'

Riffer nodded. 'She was so outspoken, so adamant in her accusations, the police began to see you as a possible suspect.'

'Right,' Julie agreed. 'And she pressured her husband's firm to let you go.' As she considered the harm Dorothy had done, Julie felt her temper rise.

'Don't forget that incident near her home. A car like hers ran us off the road,' Paul added.

'It sure did. And the car's windows were so deeply tinted we didn't get a glimpse of the driver. At the time, my only concern was to avoid collision with the other vehicle. The worse thing that's happened was Jay's accident. I hope he realizes how lucky he was, he just got a broken arm. He could have been killed.'

'That may be the way we get her . . . the car,' Riffer murmured.

'If we knew it was her car,' Paul commented. 'But we don't, do we?'

To Julie's chagrin, her guilty face gave them away.

'Okay. Fill me in.' Paul leaned back in his chair and folded his arms. .

'Show him the photographs.' Julie said.

Paul looked them over. 'I assume these are Dorothy's car?'

'Yeah.' Riffer squirmed in his desk chair.

'Would you like to tell me how you got these?'

'Well, Julie . . . ' The lawyer's voice faded and he looked in her direction.

Paul turned to her. 'You promised to stay away from Dorothy.' Anger crackled in his voice.

'It seemed a good way to get evidence,' she hastened to explain, feeling both annoyed and apologetic.

Riffer consulted the clock on the wall then rose and picked up his briefcase. 'Sorry, kids. I've got a dinner reservation. Don't be too hard on her, Paul.' He walked them to the door.

'I won't.' Paul took Julie by the arm and

marched her outside.

Once in his car, he ordered, 'Tell me everything.'

She did, at the same time she tried to minimize the potential for danger at Dorothy's home. His expression slowly changed from anger to amazement.

'You put your life on the line . . . for me,' he whispered. Claiming her lips, he took a kiss then another when she didn't object.

She'd missed his kisses more than she realized. Julie put her arms around Paul.

Between kisses, she sighed, happy to be in his arms again. It had been too long. She would've been content to stay in his embrace forever. Instead, she forced herself to face reality. They mustn't delay in dealing with what they'd discussed earlier. Raising her head, she met his tender glance. 'Paul, this may be our only chance to nail Dorothy.'

'I know, just shut up for a minute,' His voice was husky. He kissed her again and again.

The minute stretched into several. With reluctance, she slid out of his arms. 'That was lovely,' she said, 'But now I have to find a pay phone.'

'At a time like this?' Surprise flashed across his face. 'Who in the world do you want to call?'

'The police. We need to leave them an anonymous tip so they'll take a look at Dorothy's car.'

'All right.' Paul sighed as if it was difficult to think of anything except the two of them. Turning on the car engine, he backed the BMW out of the parking slot in front of Riffer's office. 'We'll pick up your car later.'

A few blocks down the road, Paul turned into a strip shopping center. People moved in and out of the Seven-Eleven that dominated a group of stores. Two pay phones stood in front of the convenience store. Paul pulled in a nearby parking slot and turned off the ignition.

Julie scanned the street. No one seemed interested in them. 'Perfect,' she murmured. 'Stay here. I'll be right back.'

One of the phones was free. She inserted coins then dialed a local number. As the phone rang, she pulled out a handkerchief and covered the speaker. Her fingers found a card in her pocket.

Her party answered so Julie read a message she'd scribbled earlier. 'Check out a dark blue Lincoln TownCar with dented front bumper at the Marcus Turner's home on Hidden Trail in Robius in regards to a hit-and-run accident in Pollard Park on April 9th. Ask Dorothy

Turner where she was that day.' Julie hung up the phone and returned to the BMW.

* * *

Paul lounged on the living room sofa at Julie's house while she brought them both soft drinks.

'Don't take any more chances.' He spoke in a firm tone not wanting her to engage Dorothy again. Last time she'd been lucky.

'I won't,' she said.

'By the way, did you ever find out where Dorothy's from?'

'I'm afraid not,' she admitted.

'While you were busy, I did a little research on my own.' He pulled a piece of paper from his pocket. 'Her maiden name was Dotti Peters and she was born near Portland, Oregon.'

'So she's from Oregon, too,' Julie remarked. 'It's a small world, isn't it?' A curious expression crossed her face.

'What is it?' He didn't see anything unusual. 'Lots of people come from Oregon. Like Jay and me and Phillips, to name a few.'

'Don't you see?' Julie's gaze locked with his. 'If Dorothy's from the Portland area, it would've been easier for her to find out about Jay. For instance, she could have a friend or relative who worked in Jay's psychiatric facility.'

'I guess.' Paul shrugged. 'Well, there's nothing else we can do right now. Let me cook dinner for you.' He'd noticed how thin Julie felt in his arms. Hopefully, she hadn't lost weight worrying about him.

'That sounds good.'

'And, after supper, we can watch television, unless there's something else you'd like to do.' Hope brought a smile to his face.

'Oh?' She raised an eyebrow.

Their kisses in the car had brought back memories. If he concentrated hard, he could almost feel her soft skin again and hear her soft murmurs of pleasure while his hands and lips explored every inch of her body.

Lord, how he wanted her. Their kisses weren't enough, just increased his hunger. More and more, he wanted them to be together. Paul frowned when a tiny doubt appeared, like a small dark cloud in an otherwise blue sky. Why kid himself? Julie might want more than he was prepared to give.

'We'll celebrate when you're cleared,' she informed him. 'What would you like to do first?'

'Do you have to ask?' He winked at her and enjoyed the blush that rose on her cheeks.

'Do you think of me sometimes?'
'More than I should,' she admitted.
'Before you fall asleep this evening, remember our night.' He'd never forget.
'Stop.'
Her brown eyes were shiny. 'You're not crying, are you?'
'Of course not. It's just something in my eye.'

* * *

Dorothy cursed under her breath at a soft tap on the door then her maid's round, apologetic face appeared.
'Didn't I tell you not to disturb me when I'm bathing?'
'Sorry, ma'am,' the maid whined. 'There's two men downstairs. I told them you'd retired, but they must see you.'
'Men? What men?' Her heart thumped fast.
'Policemen, ma'am.' The maid's hands bunched up her starched apron, a symbol of her servitude. Dorothy insisted the maid and cook wear uniforms. It reminded them who was the boss.
'What do they want? A donation?' The officers might be there for charity. A gut instinct told her otherwise.
'They didn't say. What shall I tell them?'

'It'll take me a few minutes to dress. Show them into the living room and offer them a beverage.'

As soon as the maid closed the bathroom door, Dorothy jumped out of the tub and wrapped herself in a large bath towel. Were the police wise to her? Panic nipped at her heels while she hurried into the bedroom, slipped into a Mondrian silk top and slacks outfit, then slid her feet into sandals. Though she'd always prided herself on her self control, her fingers trembled as she applied her makeup.

From a prescription bottle, she shook out a couple of Valium and washed them down with a glass of water. In a few minutes, her taut muscles began to relax. She mustn't show the police their visit upset her. That would be a big mistake.

She sailed down the corridor and descended the staircase. The moment she entered the living room, both of the men stood.

'Good evening,' she greeted them with her perfect hostess smile pasted on her face. 'I'm sorry, but I've lost all track of time. Is this the month for the Orphans' Circus Benefit?' Gazing at one man then the other, she got the distinct impression she'd thrown them both a little off balance.

'Perhaps I should introduce myself. I'm Detective Henry Pitt and this,' the man in a sports coat and slacks gestured to the uniformed officer, 'is Sergeant Muldoon. To answer your question, our visit doesn't concern charities. I have a warrant to search your property. There's a vehicle we have reason to believe belongs to you or your husband.'

He reached in his pocket and brought out a folded paper.

'Why in the world would the police want to see our cars?' Dorothy feigned surprise then she shrugged. 'Well, come this way. I'm sorry Marcus isn't here. He's at a William and Mary Alumnus meeting with his friend, your Police Chief. He'll be as mystified by this as I am.'

While she spoke, she led them down the hall toward the back of the mansion.

At the entrance to the garage, she opened the door and fumbled for the switch. The dark space was flooded with light.

The detective stepped into the garage, the uniformed officer right behind him.

Dorothy watched the two men walk around her Catera. 'The Cadillac's mine,' she informed them. 'Marcus drives a Buick.'

'We understood you had another vehicle, a dark Lincoln?' The detective looked perplexed.

'I did until this morning.' Dorothy shook her head. 'Someone stole it while I was away.'

'Did you report it?'

'I tried several times. Unfortunately, your department's lines are always busy. I'll call them again tomorrow morning.' The Valium kept her calm.

'I see.' A skeptical tone crept into the detective's voice. 'Please tell us what happened, ma'am.'

Dorothy led the policemen back to the living room, gestured for them to sit down. 'Please make yourselves comfortable. It was all quite strange. My maid called me at the salon, told me a woman was here to see me about tile for the kitchen. I had no idea what Mildred was talking about.' She paused to examine her long red nails for a moment.

'Since my first tile selection is no longer available, I do need to locate a new one, though I didn't have an appointment to see a salesperson.' Dorothy wrinkled her brow. 'When I parked my Catera, the Lincoln was not in the garage.'

'We'll need the woman's description, ma'am.' The detective brought out a pad and pen.

'I never laid eyes on her. Let me call my maid. Mildred talked to her.' Dorothy stepped into the hall and summoned her employee.

The maid appeared, looking flustered.

'Tell this officer about the intruder,' Dorothy said, prompting her servant and hoping she remembered what to say.

'Yes, madam.' Mildred bit her lip and clutched her apron. 'Well, she was tall with long blond hair.'

'Anything else?' The detective pressed her for details.

'She was quite pleasant,' the maid blurted out then glanced at Dorothy. 'If that's all, madam?'

'Yes, thank you.' At Dorothy's nod, her servant almost ran from the room.

'I'm sorry if we've upset her,' Detective Pitt commented.

'Mildred's a shy little thing. She thinks I blame her for what's happened,' Dorothy said, in an attempt to sound kind. Inside, she seethed. The dumb little peasant should have followed instructions and refused to let the woman in the house. She'd let Mildred go in the blink of an eye if she could. But the maid had helped her that day and Dorothy owed her.

'And do you, ma'am?' The detective seemed curious.

'Not at all, but she's not as careful as she

should be.' Dorothy tried to sound tolerant.

'Thank you for your time, madam.' The detective stood.

The two men headed toward the front door. Dorothy hesitated. Should she tell them about the woman who'd asked for her at the beauty salon? Her instincts for survival told her to keep quiet. From Francoise's description, the woman at the salon could well have been the one who'd escaped from her that day. She couldn't shake the feeling that Paul was behind all of this.

Francoise had given her the woman's name and the telephone number she'd given the salon in case of a cancellation.

The last thing Dorothy wanted was for the police to locate her Lincoln. The second to last thing she wanted was for the police to locate the woman who'd been at the salon and in her home that day.

Her mind made up, she saw the policemen out and closed the front door.

Upstairs in the privacy of her bedroom, Dorothy dialed the number the hairdresser had given her.

'Hello.' A voice that sounded remarkably like Paul's answered. Shocked, Dorothy dropped the phone. The woman was helping Paul.

She placed another call. Her party didn't

answer. Desperate, she dialed another number.

'This is Dr. Phillips' office,' the recording informed her. 'The doctor is on an extended leave of absence, and the office is closed. If you are a current patient, please call back during regular office hours and we will arrange for another doctor to see you.'

'Damn!'

25

Paul leaned against his kitchen counter watching the early news. The doorbell chimed so he strode through the living room and opened the front door. Riffer beamed at him from outside.

'By the look on your face, you've either won the lottery or there's been a break in my case.' Paul led his lawyer into the living room.

'Things are looking better, much better.' Riffer grinned from ear to ear.

'What's happened?' Hope beat its slow drum inside Paul.

'The Assistant DA called me bright and early this morning,' Riffer explained. 'There's been a new development.'

'I'm listening.' Paul gave him his undivided attention.

'The police called on Dorothy Turner last night . . . '

'Well, go on,' Paul urged Riffer. 'What's happened?'

'Dorothy's maid, Mildred, visited Richmond PD yesterday to voice her suspicions about Dorothy's damaged car. A couple of hours later, the police received an anonymous tip that the car had been in a hit-and-run accident Dorothy hadn't reported. Last night, Chief Hood sent a detective and uniformed officer to the Turner mansion with a search warrant. Their timing wasn't the greatest since Dorothy informed them the vehicle was stolen.'

'I can't see why you'd be overjoyed by that.' Paul scowled, the taste of disappointment bitter in his mouth. 'That woman must have a charmed life. No matter how many lies she tells, the police can't nail her.'

'Wait.' Riffer held up his hand. 'Let me finish. I think her luck's run out.' Riffer sounded pleased with this turn of events. 'Dorothy apparently lied when she said her car was stolen. Her maid contacted the police again late last night then led them to the vehicle. Mildred says Dorothy threatened to fire her if she didn't hide the car.'

'Good for Mildred,' Paul responded. 'From what I've heard, Dorothy's mistreated her for years. She may have seen this as a chance to get even.'

'That's true. Anyway, the car's been examined, and yellow chips of paint from Jay's bike turned up on the front bumper. Also, Dorothy has no alibi for the afternoon Jay was hit. We've got her, Paul.'

'That's great. So she's confessed?' Paul

forced himself to stay calm.

'Not yet, but get this.' Riffer leaned forward and Paul could sense his friend's excitement. 'Mildred will testify she overheard Dorothy and Sheila fighting over Sheila's inheritance right before Sheila vanished. Dorothy warned her stepdaughter she'd be sorry, then Sheila ran out of the house. The DA's promised to call me if there are new developments.'

'So now we wait?' Paul braced himself for another letdown. Riffer nodded. He took a seat and reached for a magazine.

Paul stared at Riffer then paced the room, back and forth. His nerves were too tense for him to sit still. Just when he thought he'd explode, Riffer's cell phone rang.

'This may be it.' He gestured for Paul to sit down.

His back ramrod straight, Paul sat on the edge of the sofa and mouthed a silent prayer. Please let it be over.

Riffer finished his call, put the cell phone in his coat pocket then thumped him on the back. 'Good news, Paul. Dorothy's admitted she hit Jay. As soon as her confession's transcribed and she signs it, she'll be taken before a judge for a preliminary hearing.'

'You're sure?' Paul let out a deep breath.

'Would you like to contact your brother or shall I?'

His taut muscles relaxed. He slumped into the sofa for a moment then sat erect. 'I'll call Jay right now.'

At the front door, Riffer stopped and turned around. 'Don't forget. Dorothy's confession is also important to your case. It shows that she's capable of murder.'

Julie came over as soon as Paul called. She stood before him on his front porch, the sunlight glinting on her dark blonde hair. Paul's throat tightened as he held her close, and he wished things might have been different. In spite of his resolution to avoid commitments, he'd been sorely tempted to take a chance with Julie. But he couldn't get involved. It hurt too much to lose those you loved. And if he let down his guard and loved Julie, chances were good he'd lose her too. So he remained silent.

'What is it?' She leaned back and gazed at him.

'Just let me hold you for a minute.' Burying his face in her hair, he inhaled the fragrance of her hyacinth-scented shampoo. She put her arms around his waist and snuggled into his embrace. His muscles tensed in response. Then they separated and she sent him a tender glance.

'What was that all about?' She smoothed her hair.

'Dorothy was the person who hit Jay. She's confessed.'

Jay was shocked then elated by the news. While the three of them talked in the living room, Julie pursed her lips and frowned. What was bothering her? The only possibility that came to mind was she was worried about his upcoming trial. Yes, that was it. For some reason her concern pleased Paul.

Paul put his own personal worries aside and flashed a grin in Jay's direction, tried to look pleased. He was, though the gray cloud of the murder charge haunted him. Was he a fool to hope he'd be exonerated? 'Riffer had to run by his office for awhile. He promised to come back later and fill us in on the details,' he said.

They relaxed and drank glasses of champagne Jay had brought. 'I find it hard to believe she hit me.' Jay's voice sounded a little shaken, off-balance.

'Next, we have to prove she killed Sheila,' Paul remarked.

'Do you think she'll confess?' Julie's fingers traced the rim of her glass.

'Don't count on it.' Paul shook his head. The doorbell chimed and he let Riffer in.

Riffer took the glass Jay offered. 'Would you like to hear what I've found out about

Dorothy?' Eased back in his armchair, Riffer made himself comfortable and sipped his champagne.

'Of course. Where is she, by the way?' Paul imagined they'd all feel better once Dorothy was behind bars.

'About to go before a judge, I'd imagine,' Riffer said.

'In case you're interested, Dorothy did reveal a little about her background in the D.A.'s office. Her parents were dirt poor. They lived outside Portland. Dorothy's father walked out and left his wife with three small children to raise. To take care of the kids, her mother cleaned other people's houses and insisted Dorothy help her after school when she was old enough. As soon as she turned fifteen, Dorothy ran away.'

'Three children? Dorothy and who else?' Paul found it hard to think of Dorothy as a child.

'Two brothers. The younger boy never amounted to much. He was always in trouble with the law, just petty crime. Several years ago he moved to Virginia,' Riffer informed them.

'And the other brother?' Julie seemed curious.

'I don't know,' Riffer responded. 'She wouldn't talk about him, just said he'd be angry. I got the impression she might be afraid of him.'

'Maybe he's a criminal,' Julie mused.

'Who knows.' Riffer stood and placed his glass on a table.

Paul walked him outside and shook his hand. Then Riffer climbed in his Rover, gave a brisk wave and drove away.

Jay called to him as he stepped back inside the house.

'I want to celebrate. You always cook, Bro. Let me take care of dinner tonight.'

'Well, you could order us a pizza,' Paul said, in an attempt to be tactful. His stomach became queasy at the idea of Jay's cooking. 'Don't go to any trouble.'

'Don't worry. I won't.' Jay flashed an impish smile.

Two hours later, Paul pushed back from his dining room table after a feast catered by two cooks from Jay's restaurant.

Jay got to his feet. 'Well, it's getting late so I better go. See ya.'

Though he never seemed to have enough time alone with Julie, Paul hoped Jay hadn't noticed him checking his watch that evening. Following his brother to the door, Paul patted him on the back and congratulated him again. Within a minute, Jay's old jalopy wheezed, sputtered, and disappeared down the darkened street.

Reentering the house, Paul caught Julie fumbling through her shoulder bag. 'Did you lose something?' Maybe that was why she'd seemed withdrawn all evening. She'd misplaced something.

'No, but I've got a terrible sinus headache and I could've sworn my decongestant was in my bag. I'll just run home and get it.' She started to get up from the sofa.

Paul stopped her. 'I'll go if you'll tell me where you left it,' he offered.

'On the kitchen table.' Julie grimaced and rubbed her head.

Paul let himself into Julie's house with her key. The prescription was where she'd said, on the kitchen table.

The telephone rang before he could leave. Julie's answering machine clicked on. A gruff male voice replied.

'This is Chief Hood. Guess I owe you an apology about Ms. Turner. That was good investigative work, Taylor. Our profession could use more sharp young minds like yours.'

Shock fast became cold rage. Damn! She's a cop!

* * *

Tonight was a time for celebrating, yet Julie felt edgy, though she didn't know the reason. Paul walked back into the room and stood by the sofa, staring at her. She forced a smile to her face.

'Here's your medicine.' He dumped the container on the coffee table.

'Thanks.' A cold knot of dread settled in her stomach at his abrupt manner. What had happened? 'What's the matter?'

'You had a phone call while I was at your house.'

'Oh? One of those junk calls?' She tried a light touch to dispel his unexpected brusque mood.

'No.'

'Well then, who was it?'

'The Richmond Chief of Police. He called to apologize.'

Julie sucked in a breath. The moment she'd longed for and dreaded had come at last. She fought down a wave of panic. 'Sit down. It's time we talked.'

'Yeah, I'd say so.' As Paul took a seat on the sofa, a muscle jerked in his jaw.

'You mean a lot to me. Nothing will change that. But I need to tell you the truth.' Shaky and tense, she dug her fingernails into her palms.

'The truth about what, Julie?' There was a

sarcastic tone in his voice that she'd never heard before. Did he doubt her honesty? That hurt though she understood how the situation might appear to him.

'Think back to when we met. Didn't it seem odd the way I turned up next door?'

'Not at the time. Your father had died, then you lost your job so you came back to Richmond.'

'Dad died and I came home, but I didn't lose my job. I was working when we met.'

'Go on,' he demanded.

She took another deep breath. 'Okay, here goes. I was a police detective on an undercover assignment. My boss lent me to Richmond Police Department to conduct an investigation.' His stony gaze stopped her. 'Why do I get the impression you aren't surprised?'

'That could be because of the rest of the Chief's message. He not only congratulated you, he said law enforcement needs more sharp young minds like yours.' Paul's hostility seemed to grow by the minute.

She nodded. She paused then continued, hesitantly. 'My assignment was to get to know you and find out if you were involved in your wife's disappearance.'

'You really are a lying little cheat, aren't you?'

At his angry words, Julie drew back. 'That's unfair.'

'This's crazy.' Standing, Paul shoved his hands in his pockets and glared at her. 'The night we made love. Was that a lie, too?'

'No! That was for real.' Julie got up and held out her hand. He backed away. Her nerves vibrated with frustration while she struggled to keep her voice calm. 'I'll never forget that night. It was very special to me. Still, I had to finish the investigation so I turned cool. Too much was at stake. I couldn't jeopardize my assignment.'

'You lied to me.' His breath came out ragged. Julie tried to touch his arm. He swore at her and shoved her away. 'How do I know you're not lying now? Did you think I'd confess if we made love?'

'Don't be absurd,' she snapped. His accusation wounded her. In a gentler tone, she struggled to make him understand. 'Our making love had nothing to do with the investigation. Believe it or not, I fought my feelings, but I couldn't stay away from you.'

'I don't believe a word you've said.' Rage, controlled until now, exploded across his face and he yelled, 'Get the hell out of my life.'

Pain, so much pain she didn't think she could bear it, seared through her. 'Please don't do this,' she begged. Julie followed Paul to the foyer.

He flung open the door then stood aside. 'Don't make me throw you out,' he snarled.

A sharp sensation attacked Julie in her chest. How did they ever reach this point? This stranger with a hard jaw and cold eyes who stood before her couldn't be Paul. If hearts could break, hers broke with every angry word he spoke.

Wiping at the tears that blurred her vision, she crept past him then darted across the lawn to her own house, where she huddled on the living room sofa, numb and trembling.

She'd known in her heart it was risky to fall in love with Paul, yet she couldn't help herself. Her dreams had been full of a future with him. God only knew what Paul's dreams were. He'd never shared them with her. It had all been an illusion. She'd wanted him, and he just wanted to be left alone.

Reality stung her frayed emotions. Whatever they'd had together was so fragile it lay broken like splinters of glass. She'd been alone when they met. And now she was alone again.

* * *

Currents of betrayal, anger, and disappointment slammed through Paul as he closed the front door and leaned against it. What a fool he'd been not to see through her deception.

She'd taken advantage of his loneliness, moved right into his life and his heart. But no man in his right mind would want a liar like Julie.

Undercover detective — that's what she'd called herself. Just another word for a snoop planted right under his nose.

Sprawled on the sofa, he couldn't relax. His taut nerves wouldn't let him. Through the long, still night, he roamed the house, at one point stepped out on the front porch for a breath of fresh air. In spite of his pain, his glance strayed to her house. Her house was dark. How dare she rest while he was suffering? He remembered how she'd felt in his arms and, in spite of everything, wanted to hold her one last time. Damn! The thought of her lies acted like a bucket of ice water over his head.

He should have known beter. He was her assignment, that's all. His jaw tightened at his stupidity.

Well, he'd learned his lesson. It might take the rest of his life, but he'd forget her.

26

Last night had been the worst she'd ever experienced. Everytime she closed her eyes, Julie saw Paul's angry face and heard his harsh voice ordering her out of his life.

Exhausted, she'd at last fallen into a dreamless sleep. A rustling noise in her room woke her before dawn. Drowsy, she called out, 'Paul? Is that you?'

'It's not Paul, my dear,' a familiar voice replied.

A sudden chill invaded her limbs though the room was warm. Julie pushed up in bed and switched on her nightstand lamp. She blinked with surprise to find Paul and Jay's family friend seated in the armchair by the bedroom door.

'Doctor Phillips?' Grabbing her bed covers, she pulled them up to her chin. 'Has something happened to Paul?'

'Not to my knowledge.' His lips curved into a peculiar smile and her skin prickled. She didn't care if the psychiatrist was the brothers' friend. The gaunt old man made her uneasy.

'Don't tell me I left my front door

unlocked,' she wailed. In her overwrought condition last night, it was quite possible.

Phillips nodded. 'I stepped into the foyer and called your name but you didn't respond. Thinking you might be ill, I came upstairs.'

'Does Paul know you're in Richmond?'

'Not yet. I had another consultation in Washington and stopped by and to see Paul and Jay before returning home. My flight arrived in Richmond late last night, so I thought it best to stay in a motel near the airport and drive over this morning. I'll go over to Paul's as soon as I'm finished with you.'

Though she'd never considered Phillips a threat, a slight ripple of alarm sounded deep inside Julie. 'Why did you want to see me?'

'I'm deeply concerned about Jay and his obsession with his memory loss. Would you tell me if he's discussed it with you?'

'He's mentioned it in my presence. Regaining his memory seems quite important to Jay.'

'Yes, but has he said what he remembers?'

'Just in general. In his dreams about the night their parents died, Jay hears voices, his parents and another person.'

'Hmmm.' Phillips seemed to mull over what she'd said.

For some reason, he put her nerves on

edge, though he was just an odd-mannered elderly man and no danger to her or anyone else. She'd talk to him a few minutes then send him on his way.

Phillips put a finger over his lips, gestured for her to be quiet. He stepped into the hall for a moment then reentered the room, closed the door, and returned to his chair. 'Will you see Paul today?'

'No. We had a fight. I won't be seeing him again.' Even the words hurt her. In time, her pain would subside though right now it stung like a raw wound. She loved a man who hated her.

'I'm sorry to hear that. So you can't tell me anything else about Jay? I had hoped he would have said more.' Phillips' shoulders sagged, whether from disappointment or fatigue, she couldn't determine.

Though she didn't care for Phillips, Julie was moved to pity at his distress. From what she'd gathered, Paul and Jay were the closest thing the man had to family.

In an attempt to help, she shared her impressions of Jay. 'He's determined to regain his memory and clear up the doubt surrounding their parents' deaths.'

An expression she couldn't read crossed Phillips' face and he sent her a piercing glance. 'How interesting.'

'Speaking of Jay, did you hear that Paul's mother-in-law Dorothy Turner was involved in Jay's hit-and-run accident?'

'Why, yes, it was reported on the news,' Phillips said.

'Why would she hit Jay? Paul's the one she's harrassed. Do you suppose she mistook Jay for Paul?'

'It's possible.' Phillips' expression was guarded.

'Even so, why does she want to hurt Paul?'

'That's a good question,' A deep sigh escaped Phillips' narrow lips. 'Perhaps she thought Paul stood between her and her step-daughter's inheritance. I learned many years ago that to understand a person, it's often necessary to examine his or her early years. Take Dorothy for instance. Even as a child, she detested being poor. That's why she ran away from home when she was just fifteen.'

The news release had mentioned Dorothy's confession to a hit-and-run, not a word about her background. There was no way that Phillips could have inside information unless . . . Studying his features, Julie observed, for the first time, a resemblance to Dorothy. Both were tall and raw-boned with sharp facial features and cold hazel eyes.

As she made the connection, currents of

excitement raced up her spine. Julie tossed caution to the winds and asked, 'Is it possible that you're Dorothy's brother?' For weeks, she'd wondered if Paul and Jay's parents' deaths and Sheila's murder could be related. Was Doctor Phillips the missing link?

Solemn-faced, he nodded, his gaze never left her face.

'I get the impression it troubles you that Jay's regaining his memory. That strikes me as odd unless . . . you were there.' Her instincts screamed caution while she interrogated Phillips.

'I compliment your keen powers of observation, my dear.' He bowed slightly.

A small inner voice advised Julie to keep Doctor Phillips talking. He might be able to tell her more. 'Did Jay see you?'

'No. he just heard my voice. I don't guess it matters if I tell you now since you won't have the opportunity to speak to Paul or Jay. I plan to dispose of them before I leave town.' His lips twisted into a sneer, Phillips shook his head in mock regret, adding, 'it's a pity that you got in the way.'

Though she trembled inside, Julie contained her fear. He mustn't realize how much he frightened her. She ignored the threat in his words. 'There's more to this, I'm sure. Please tell me the rest. I love a good mystery and you've whetted my appetite.'

Phillips leaned forward in his chair. When he spoke, his voice became tender. 'It all began a long time ago with their mother, the love of my life until we quarreled over some trivial matter. During that period, she met and married the boys' father. I hung around for years, waiting, hoping she'd reconsider. Her husband lost his job and became an alcoholic two years before they died.

'It was too good an opportunity to miss. At last I was able to talk her into an affair. Things would have been fine if her conscience hadn't nagged her. My heart broke when she called to announce it was over.' His eyes gleamed, recalling the past.

'The night she called off our affair, I lost control. All I could think of was revenge. I forced my way into their home, confronted them both.' Phillips' expression hardened and his voice chilled. 'Her husband tried to throw me out, so I pulled out my gun, forced them into a closet and locked it. Jay must have heard us since he called out then came running. I hid behind the bedroom door and hit him on the head as he ran into the room.

'In retrospect, I realize it would have been better if I'd killed Jay instead of dumping him by the front door after I set the house on fire.

'Later, I talked to the police and mentioned

Jay's troubled relationship with his father. The investigating detective's report concluded that Jay might have been responsible for the fire, but there was no evidence.'

'You saved his life.' What was Phillips' motive? Was it to his advantage to let Jay live? If the psychiatrist had any kindness in his heart, she hadn't seen it.

'In the past few months, Jay's memory has started to come back. Unaware, he holds my life in his hands. Except for Paul, I might've arranged Jay's death in New York City. I couldn't take the chance Paul would discover the truth.'

'You kept Paul and Jay apart.' All those wasted years — only a twisted mind could concoct such a scheme. Their conversation sickened Julie. Her body tensed under the sheet then moved a little closer to the edge of the bed and the half-open nightstand drawer and her revolver.

'I tried. For years it worked, then they got back together. They're more dangerous united. As children, the boys always confided in each other. It follows that Jay will tell Paul what he remembers.' Phillips scowled. 'As you can see, they're a two-headed threat. Alone, Jay would be a less formidable foe but Paul's stronger. If Jay were murdered, Paul would track down his brother's killer, even if it took his last breath.'

Julie nodded as if she understood. 'Maybe if you talked to them, explained their mother hurt you. There must be another solution . . . ' In a calm, sympathetic manner, she discussed Phillips' past crimes and his plans for Paul and Jay while inside her rage burned brighter than fear. Contemplating the pain he'd caused the brothers, it was all Julie could do to lie there and chat with the evil man.

Across the room, she could make out the luminescent hands of her wall clock. He'd just been with her a few minutes yet it seemed hours since she woke up and found him in her room.

'There's no other solution, I can assure you,' he said.

She shuddered with revulsion. The man was a heartless monster. Responsible for the deaths of the Arnolds and Sheila, and planning to kill Paul, Jay and her, Phillips exhibited no sign of remorse. 'Dorothy wanted Sheila's fortune. That's all she cares about,' Julie observed.

'The fortune and her brother,' he corrected her. 'Dorothy will do anything to please me. I convinced her Sheila had to go then paid our younger brother to come to Richmond. Following a brief incarceration, he earned the pay I'd promised him. Later, he got drunk and died from a fall. That's probably for the best.

'It's possible she'll break down and implicate you.' Julie kept her voice even though her stomach clenched with nerves.

'True, but poor Dorothy's the one who'll pay for Sheila's death since I'll disappear when I'm finished here. The authorities will never find me.

'Well, now you know it all.' Rising from his chair, Phillips checked his watch. 'As much as I hate to end this conversation, our time's run out. I'm sure you understand.' His hand slid out of the folds of his overcoat and revealed what he'd hidden during their bizarre conversation. The gleam of his pale eyes reflected on the surface of the revolver he held. He licked his lips and pointed the gun at her.

'You don't want to kill me,' she protested and shrunk back into the bed covers, maintaining eye contact with Phillips. At the same time, the hand she'd dropped off the bed crept into the half-open nightstand drawer . . . and found nothing. Her heart sank as she remembered she'd left the gun in a dresser drawer across the room.

The front door opened and closed. 'Julie?' Paul's voice resounded from downstairs.

'Call him upstairs, my dear,' Phillips

stepped behind the door. 'And be careful what you say.'

'Paul? Come up here.'

Moments later, he stood in the doorway, a worried expression on his face. 'Julie, are you ill? As I picked up my morning paper, I noticed your front door was open.' She didn't answer so he stepped into the room.

Phillips hit him with the revolver handle and Paul crumbled to the floor, unconscious. Julie stifled a cry.

The psychiatrist rolled Paul over so he lay on his back.

'Is he all right?' Her heart was in her throat. Before Paul appeared, she'd managed to keep fear at bay. Now reality cut in and she shuddered. Phillips could kill them both right that minute and have no regrets.

'He's fine.' The psychiatrist shrugged as if he couldn't care less if he'd hurt Paul. With one hand, he held the gun on her while his other hand reached into his trenchcoat pocket and brought out a roll of duct tape, tossed it on the floor. 'Get over here and tie him up.'

Afraid to disobey him, she crept out of bed and knelt on the carpet beside Paul. While she bound his arms and legs with the tape, her mind whirled. Somehow she must change Phillips' mind.

Striving for the calm, non-threatening

tone she'd learned at the Academy, she gave it her best effort. 'You don't really want to hurt us, Doctor. Haven't you told me how much you loved the twins' mother? Just imagine how bad she'd feel if you harmed her boys. Why don't you let me untie Paul and we'll all go downstairs. I'll fix us some breakfast then we'll discuss the problem like mature adults. If we can't come up with a better solution, Paul and I'll help you get away.'

His smile mocked her. 'I'm a psychiatrist, dear, so spare me the mind games. I know what you're up to and it won't work. Be quiet and lie down beside Paul.'

In a matter of moments, she was bound with the tape, also. 'You'll never get away with this,' she muttered, angry with herself for not figuring out who and what he was earlier.

Phillips snickered. 'That's what their parents told me. Don't worry. The smoke will overcome you before the flames reach this room. I'm sorry I can't hang around to watch the fire but it's time I visited Jay. His suicide note will explain he killed you both after you rejected him, Julie.' Phillips' quick steps carried him across the room to the bedroom door which he closed behind him. Seconds later, she heard him on the stairs.

* * *

Julie tugged on her bonds and just made them tighter. She rolled against Paul, nudged him. He opened an eye, winked at her. Thank God. She sighed with relief. He'd just pretended to be unconscious.

'It was Phillips all along.' Julie whispered in case the psychiatrist came back upstairs.

'But why?' Paul struggled to get free.

'Here, let me help you. I'll explain while we get you untied,' she said, pulling on the tape around his wrists. 'He planned Sheila's murder then had you framed with evidence planted on her body.'

'I don't understand. What did we do to him?' Paul asked.

'It was all part of a coverup for your parents' deaths. He killed your parents and tried to blame it on Jay. When Jay's memory began to come back, Phillips was afraid Jay would figure out the third voice he heard that night was his.'

At the mention of his parents, Paul scowled. 'The evil bastard. I hope he rots in hell!'

'I agree. Now let's get out of here.' Julie managed to loosen the tape so Paul could remove it. They both went to work on the tape around his ankles. 'Things were all right until Jay's memory started to return. That scared Phillips out of his mind. He feels that he has to kill you and Jay so you won't expose him.'

'This's taking too long,' Paul told her. 'We need a knife or some scissors to cut through the tape on my ankles.'

'Sorry, I must have tied it tighter than I realized.' She pointed across the room. 'There's scissors on my desk.'

Paul managed to roll behind the desk chair then stretched his arm and knocked the scissors to the floor. Picking them up, he cut through the tape on his ankles.

Julie's nostrils inhaled an acrid odor when she took a deep breath. 'Hurry, Paul.' She directed his attention to a narrow curl of smoke that had entered the room through the heat vent in the ceiling. Grim-faced, he nodded and knelt by her, scissors in hand, and began to cut through the tape binding her.

At the sound of footsteps on the stairs, tension rippled through Julie. Was Phillips returning to finish them in person?

The steps grew closer. Paul hid behind the door. 'Don't be afraid,' he whispered right before the door opened.

Phillips stepped into the room, his gun in his hand.

Paul jumped him from behind then wrestled with the doctor for the gun.

Breathing heavily, the two men cursed and grunted as they rolled about the floor into the hall, then they fell down the stairs and crashed on the first floor. A gunshot rang out.

Still tied up, Julie managed to roll into the hall and peer at the floor below. The smoke was thicker now, and all she could see was a tangle of arms and legs at the bottom of the stairs.

She coughed and tried to take shallow breaths. While elongated fingers of dark gray smoke crept up the stairs toward her, she screamed his name. 'Paul!'

With an effort, Paul shoved Phillips away and got to his feet. The psychiatrist remained in a sprawled position, facedown on the tile floor of the hall.

Paul touched the older man's shoulder then turned him over.

'Is he dead? I heard one shot and thought he'd killed you.' Her heart had stopped at the sound. What if Paul had been killed? Her life, if she'd managed to escape, would have been an empty void without him.

He examined Phillips, felt for a pulse. 'I'm afraid so. There's a gunshot wound in his chest.' Paul ran up the stairs, untied her, and helped her to her feet. 'The gun must have gone off when we rolled downstairs.

'Let's get out of here.' Paul lifted Phillips' body to his shoulder. Coughing, he followed Julie from the house.

Sitting on the curb with Paul, Julie filled her lungs with clean, fresh air. Two neighbors assured them the fire department was on its way.

Smoke billowed from the house as the drapes in the front windows burned. Julie said a silent thankful prayer, then, relieved to be safe, she put her head in her hands and sobbed.

Sirens sounded down the street. In a matter of moments, a firetruck and ambulance arrived. Julie was helped onto a stretcher and an oxygen mask was slipped over her face. She watched the rescue workers place Phillips on a stretcher and verify he was dead. One of the team put a call in to the police, requesting a patrol car and a coroner's wagon for the body.

Rescue workers helped both of them into the ambulance.

'You go ahead. I'll talk to the police when they get here,' Paul said then slipped back out of the rescue vehicle.

Though she hated to leave him behind, Julie lay in the ambulance while the rescue team drove her to the hospital.

In the Emergency Room, she heard the

house had burned to the ground, though the firemen managed to contain the blaze. Paul's house was spared along with the other neighbors' residences.

The ER doctors checked Julie then released her. 'Take it easy the next few days,' one doctor advised her, giving her a sheet of possible side effects. 'If you need medical attention, see your family doctor or come back here.'

Her own clothes were unfit to wear. Julie gratefully slipped into a spare nurse's aide uniform a staff member lent her. Dazed and shaken, she wondered who to call, where to go. Everything she owned had been destroyed in the fire.

A lump formed in the back of her throat at the thought of Misty. She'd left the little dog downstairs last night. No one had mentioned her pet so she assumed Misty was gone too. The appearance of Riffer and Jay with Paul close behind jolted her out of her misery.

Paul nodded at her then an ER doctor took him into another room. In the hall, Julie could hear their conversation.

'Take deep breaths through your mouth, Mr. Martin,' the doctor said while he checked Paul's lungs. 'Any problem breathing?'

'No. I'm a little sore, but that's

understandable after that tumble downstairs. I fell on the other man. His body must have cushioned my fall.' Paul's voice was grim as he added, 'I hope I didn't make the gun go off. No matter what he did, I wouldn't have wanted to be responsible for his death.'

The doctor had x-rays taken and found no breaks or fractures. 'All right, I'm releasing you. Just don't overdo physical exercise the next day or so.'

Paul walked into the hall just as she finished giving her statement to an uniformed officer.

Riffer had waited for Paul. Now he stepped forward. 'I was on my way to see you this morning when I heard about the fire,' he informed Paul. 'Late last night, Dorothy broke down and gave the District Attorney a full confession. It appears she hired a man to kill Sheila though she insists it was her brother's plan. You'll find this hard to believe, but your Doctor Phillips was her brother.'

'I know.' Paul answered, wearily as he wiped soot off his face with his handkerchief. 'He almost killed us.' He turned on his heel and started to walk away with Jay.

'Wait a minute,' Julie called after him. 'Why did you come to see me this morning?' She clung to a faint hope that he'd changed his mind about her.

'What? Oh, I saw a strange car parked in front of your house and Misty was on my front porch when I went out to get my paper. And your door was unlocked when I came to investigate.'

'Thank God she's safe. She must have run out when Phillips opened my front door. I was so worried . . . That's all you came for?' Tears came to her eyes and she sent him an anxious loving glance, hoping against hope he'd forgiven her. Breathless, she waited for the verdict.

'Yeah.' He again turned to go and this time she let him.

'Julie? What's going on?' Riffer patted her shoulder.

She inhaled sharply and struggled to regain her self-control. The pain was deep but endurable. Julie bit her bottom lip. In a husky voice, she answered, 'not much except Paul found out I'd investigated him and he'll never forgive me. Would you find me a hotel?'

'You're welcome to stay with my family,' Riffer offered.

'Thanks, but I . . . her voice broke and she rested her head on his shoulder for a moment. Riffer patted her back.

Raising her head, she managed a watery smile and pointed to the too-large nurse's uniform. 'I don't have a stitch of clothes except this outfit and it's on loan.'

'What a jerk.' Riffer shook his head in disbelief. 'I never thought Paul could be such a fool.'

As they left the hospital, Julie caught a glimpse of Jay's old car wheezing its way down the street. She couldn't see inside the vehicle, yet she knew Paul was with Jay. For a moment in the hospital, she'd hoped, prayed . . . Blinking back her tears, she started toward Riffer's car.

* * *

His twin led Paul to the old jalopy. With every step he took, Paul's thoughts raced. There'd been tears in Julie's eyes when she asked why he'd come to see her. And her voice trembled.

She had no reason to pretend now. He knew the truth. So he must matter to her.

He moved along to the next conclusion. She loved him. He considered how he'd felt earlier. Seeing the fire's blaze, the chilling reality had struck him as hard as a fist. He could've lost Julie. If he hadn't gone in her house, Phillips would have killed Julie then come for him.

If he'd lost her, he would've never recovered.

What did it matter the way they met? So she'd investigated him. So what? It was her job.

At last, Paul made himself face the facts he'd evaded until now. He loved her, terribly, with every fiber of his being.

Jay unlocked the car doors then stood by the car, a curious expression on his face.

'Well, what are you waiting for?' Jay urged him to get in.

'Thanks, but I need to take care of some unfinished business. See you later.' Paul walked toward a cab stand near the hospital. One lone taxi was parked there, waiting. Paul prayed it was available.

Across the parking lot, he saw Julie and Riffer leaving the hospital. Paul hurried to the taxi stand, spoke to the cabbie, then slid into the back seat.

He addressed the taxicab driver. 'If you'll park by the hospital,' he pointed in Julie's direction, 'you may have another fare.' His heart pounded while he prayed in silence. Please don't let it be too late.

⋆ ⋆ ⋆

A taxi pulled up at the curb and a familiar voice called, 'I can give you a lift.'

Shattered dreams of a future with Paul so

filled Julie's thoughts that she hadn't noticed the taxi's approach. 'I don't know if we're going the same way,' she replied. Her grieving spirits lifted, though she cautioned herself he just felt sorry for her. The fire had destroyed all her worldly goods.

'I hope we're going in the same direction.' Paul's smile wavered, as if he wasn't sure she'd accept his offer.

'The whole distance? I'm not into short trips.' He'd never spoken of love. This time, he must tell her how he felt.

'Lady, the meter's running. Do you want a ride or not?' The cabbie complained, unaware more was at stake than a shared taxi ride.

'Please?' Paul opened the door wider. The warmth of his gaze hinted that what he felt for her was much stronger than pity. Before she knew it, her feet moved and she sat beside him.

'Just what do you want to say, Paul?' She held her breath.

'I love you.' He pulled her into his arms and kissed her tenderly. 'All this time, I've loved you. I've lost everyone I've loved, so I was afraid if I loved you, I'd lose you too. But for you, I'll take the chance.'

A wave of emotion — joy, gratitude and love swept through her. Julie had dreamed of happy endings, of a 'forever guy' who'd pledge his undying devotion. Losing Paul, she'd decided love like that just happened in fairy tales. Then he drove up in a taxicab and proved her wrong.

'I love you and I promise I'll never leave you,' she whispered. 'Let's go home, Paul.'

'I'll be glad to drive you two lovebirds home, if you'll just tell me where home is.' The cabbie sounded pleasant now.

Paul gave him directions and sat back, his arm around her.

'We've come a long way, haven't we?' She took his hand. Together at last. It was almost beyond belief.

'We've just started.' Paul kissed her cheek while the cab moved through the busy city traffic, headed home.

THE END

Other titles published by
The House of Ulverscroft:

CLUES TO LOVE

Nancy Madison

Failing to sense the danger that lurks about her, expatriate Kate Stanhope converts her deceased husband's Lake District mansion into an upscale hotel. The first weekend the hotel is open, a Cornish guest is found dead in his room. Detective Chief Inspector Nick Connor soon concludes that Kate was the intended victim. But who would want to kill her? While Nick struggles to find the elusive killer, he falls in love with Kate, in spite of his vow to never love again. Can Nick catch the killer before he finds Kate?

BEHOLDEN

Clare Littleford

Peter is a planning officer at Nottingham City Council. Every day on the bus to work he notices a girl who spends the journey scribbling in a battered notebook. On the day she disappears, instead of getting off at her usual stop, the girl waits and dashes off to the railway station instead, leaving her notebook on the bus. Peter picks it up and starts to read . . . In the ensuing police search, Peter, having read Sophie's diary, knows more about her than anyone else. He also knows that the truth about what finally happened to her is a truth he must keep entirely to himself.

GRANDMOTHER'S FOOTSTEPS

Carol Smith

The cold-blooded butchery of a mother and her daughters triggers a wave of outrage in the media. This is just the latest atrocity in a series, and it appears that someone is stalking and targeting the virtuous and clean-living. It takes the patient persistence of cartographer William Huxley to sense a link the police have missed. Stuck at home as a house husband, William slowly assembles the pieces of the puzzle, aided by a cub reporter and the cleaning lady. When a prominent public figure is hacked to death, events take a sharp curve for the worse — particularly when it becomes clear that William is the next intended victim . . .

A DETECTIVE IN LOVE

H. R. F. Keating

It was six-thirty in the morning when Detective Superintendent Harriet Martens took a 'phone call that would change her life — Britain's number one tennis star and media darling, pretty Bubbles Xingara, has been murdered in the grounds of her big country house. Harriet is now in charge of a case that will have the world's media — already massing for Wimbledon — out in force. But it is not the investigation that is about to explode Harriet's life, it is the burly, young Detective Inspector Anselm Brent. For Harriet Martens — wife and mother, nicknamed the Hard Detective — has fallen madly in love with a fellow officer . . .

DEATH'S OWN DOOR

Andrew Taylor

In the drab 1950s a widower with a distinguished war record is found dead in his summerhouse with a bottle of whisky beside him, and the verdict is suicide. But Inspector Richard Thornhill and his lover, reporter Jill Francis, soon realise there's far more to it than that. The investigation leads to a number of complex characters, including an unmarried mother who lost her virtue and her baby when Victoria was on the throne. Worst of all, to Thornhill's growing horror, the inquiries lead to his wife, Edith, and to another death during a highly-charged summer before the war. But a third death is yet to come . . .